THE HORSEMASTER

THE HORSEMASTER

T. Alan Broughton

E. P. Dutton — New York

The characters and landscapes in this novel are imagined by the author and are only as real as he has succeeded in making them.

For information contact:
Elsevier-Dutton Publishing Co., Inc.,
2 Park Avenue, New York, N.Y. 10016.

Library of Congress Cataloging in Publication Data

Broughton, T. Alan (Thomas Alan)
The Horsemaster.

I. Title.
PS3552. R68138Je   1981   813'.54   81-876
                                        AACR2

ISBN: 0-525-13757-2

Published simultaneously in Canada by Clarke, Irwin & Company Limited, Toronto and Vancouver

Designed by Nicola Mazzella

10 9 8 7 6 5 4 3 2 1

First Edition

For My Mother

THE HORSEMASTER

1

"**T**ell you what, Cassandra. Get it over with, and I'll fill your bin."

Lewis was tired of talking but did not want her to forget he was there. She twisted nervously to bite her flanks and lurched, staggered by her own ripe weight.

Dawn would come soon. He had risen to the clatter of alarm clock and walked down from his cabin through the steep woods, along the stream low and quiet from a late summer drought. With the moon full he hardly needed a flashlight. A raccoon had growled and crackled up the scaly bark of a spruce, and in the lower meadow two deer had lifted their heads from grazing, eyes bright and unblinking. He had been waiting in the barn for two hours.

Cassandra stamped and whinnied softly. In the silence that followed, milk from her gorged udder spattered on the newly spread hay. The light shone on the sweat of her flanks as they shivered and bunched. Lewis had told Howard to be there by four-thirty. He was late, and Lewis glanced at the aisle, expecting him to be standing there at the outer edge of light. The boy, really a young man now that he had turned nineteen, would stride into the barn, shoulders slumped as if trying to deny the lanky frame that perched his face high over everyone.

The mare sagged to her front knees with a grunt, eased down, and rolled onto her side. She had positioned herself perfectly in the stall, with enough room to kick or to move her head freely. Lewis stooped and touched her flank. Her head lifted and swung back, her eyes taking him in with that bewildered look all the mares had toward the end. She was so full-bellied that there could be little comfort for her in that position, but she was also tired by now and giving up completely to the gathering rhythm of clench and release, her breathing irregular and fast.

"Easy now, easy," he coaxed as if she were hauling too sternly against the traces.

The bag of waters burst, clear slime running warm over his hands. The lips were swollen outward, dark skin of the edges only a fringe now on the coral flesh. He slipped a hand along the sac to the bend of fetlocks and pasterns and the soft nose, and then he could see them bound in the smoky caul. The foal was presenting correctly. He kept up his soothing. With each heave the foal was thrust more into view, eyes shut tight, slithering out onto the straw with neck and torso limp as unfired clay. He placed his hands under the head and held one leg, keeping the shoulders uneven, and as always he was surprised by the delicacy of bone as close to the skin as small fingers. The narrowing body came with a rush.

He worked fast, not talking anymore. The mare lay still, her body stretched long as if reaching from hip through neck for some distant fruit. Lewis traced the cord that coiled between the mother and her child. It was not tangled. The foal began to twitch, legs pushing against the caul, and Lewis helped ease it off, watching for signs of breathing. The small barrel of chest was still. He scooped with a finger in each nostril to clean out the thickening mucus, and then he stooped closer, hesitated with his face up to the blunt, wet muzzle. He put his mouth over the nostrils and blew. When he pulled back to breathe, pushing down lightly on the animal's chest, he could taste the musty slime coating his lips. He moved over the nose again to blow in gently. Between breaths he saw Howard's feet at the edge of the stall, but he did not speak, concentrating only on the motions of the foal. As he slipped his mouth forward again, jaws beginning to ache and dizzied by his own deep breathing, the foal's blurred eyes fluttered open. He breathed into the nostrils, watching the blink of those new circles taking in the light. Always he would try to imagine what the creature could see in the unknown lumps of human face, walls, and deeply shadowed rafters.

The foal was taking quick, tentative breaths, and all over the glistening body the cords of veins were pulsing.

"You're late."

"I'm sorry. The clock didn't — "

"Hand me the bucket and rags."

The mare would stand soon and break the cord, and later expel the afterbirth. Howard could help the foal to the teat. Lewis's father had always observed laconically that, unlike a human infant, mewling and flat on its back for too long, a foal would begin to take care of itself quickly, struggling to its feet, staggering toward balance. The colt had already lifted his head from the hay, drew in, and gave a breathy whinny. Cassandra answered, looking back along the stretch of her body. He sponged quickly, leaving part of the hindquarters untouched so that the mare would know her own smell and not think her foal a stranger.

"You do the rest."

Howard followed him down the aisle, and when Lewis reached the sink he turned on the water, thrust his arms under the flow, and shocked his face with cold handfuls. He rinsed his mouth and spat before he turned. Howard was shifting nervously from foot to foot. Lewis held back his anger. That would only confuse Howard and make him less likely to concentrate on his chores.

"I'm sorry."

"Don't go on about it. Maybe if you didn't dream so much you'd wake on time."

"I have to get a new clock."

"Keep an eye on her when she decides to get up. She's not too bright, liable to forget she even has a foal in the same stall. I'm going to tell Coleman everything's okay and then go back up for some sleep."

Howard nodded. No matter how awkward he looked, he could handle horses well.

"Lew," the voice bleated, "I wanted to ask you."

He waited, which did not help Howard.

"Elaine. How come she won't talk to me?"

"How would I know that?" Lewis put a hand on Howard's arm, turning him toward the door. "We'll have a long talk soon."

"I'd like that."

"You worry about those horses for now."

Lewis let go of him and walked out to the ramp. The rising sun dashed so fully into his face that his breath was slapped out of him, and putting a hand to his brow, seeing again in the shade of his fingers the dirt road, white fences, distant turrets of the house, he wondered whether that blurred first vision of the foal fixed some sense of the world forever in its mind. What had he seen first, Lewis Beede, toothless and yearning for a breast? He walked slowly down the ramp. Hard to take that seriously, even if today was his own birthday. How strange to be forty-five and a few hours old and not be able to recall one of the greatest moments of his life.

The old man would be up by now. In the country he always rose before dawn. Usually he would have been at the barn, walking about, talking to the horses, on his way down to the river and back before breakfast, but Lewis had warned him that the foal was due and Coleman did not have to be told to stay away. Lewis's father had tended the horses for the Whites, and for many years now Lewis had held that job as well as being a general caretaker and handyman for the sprawling "farmhouse" and its outbuildings. Although Coleman was much older than Lewis, they had known each other for so long that many things did not need to be openly expressed. *Personal but not intimate* was the way Coleman had described his relationship with Foster Beede, and Lewis had remembered the words, since he wondered if Coleman would say the same about him. Now that it was fall, the old man would be leaving soon for the city. There would be the houses to shut down, the horses to watch over through the long, cold months when the summer people throughout the valley abandoned their retreats, their tax shelters. Occasionally Coleman would telephone or write long letters of instructions, or his daughter, Phoebe, would whirl

4

in for skiing with friends, necessitating a hurried opening of the well-sealed house.

The day would be hot by noon, but with that dry, sharp air of early fall when Lewis could split wood for hours without stopping. The dew on the cropped lawn deepened the green. On the porch steps he turned to look back toward the barn, the rutted drive into the fields, the mountains cut with a fierce clarity out of an unvarying, deep blue. Already their upper slopes were mottled with red and yellow. He was tired but would sleep soon; and again, as often during the past year, his life seemed right at last, an arrival he had earned like coming home from a long trip. Only his dreams troubled him, or sometimes memories over which he had no control, but who ever resolved them? He breathed deeply, put his hands in his back pockets, let the view be all he saw, noting the slim paring of a moon over the peak of Butternut Mountain, the only flaw in a cloudless sky. Why had they always made growing old sound fearful? It was good to be forty-five and to have made up your mind at last about so many things.

"Any problems?"

Lewis turned reluctantly. "Not yet."

Coleman's bent figure, his shock of white hair and white shirt unbuttoned at the collar were meshed in the screen.

"Boy or girl?"

"A stallion, if you want to leave him entire."

The door swung open.

"We'll think about that. Come in."

The hallway and stairs spread back into an elegant rustication of dark, rough wood and stone. He would rather be walking slowly to the cabin, up along the brook in the dappled air.

"I'm pretty tired."

They held the light door, his hand on the wood, Coleman's on the screen, those heavy fingers trembling slightly as they did all the time now.

"I won't keep you long. There are some things I have to tell you."

The old man stared past Lewis into the yard. Maybe this was more than the usual loneliness that often made Lewis the companion for evenings over good whiskey or for afternoons of discussion about the managing of the farm. When his daughter,

Phoebe, and her friends were not visiting, the big house was empty except for Doris, who cooked and cleaned, leaving in her battered pickup truck by nine each night.

He stepped in and the door slapped shut. In the living room some fresh logs had been thrown onto the coals and were beginning to flame. A coffeepot and two cups were on the table by the couch.

"I thought you'd be by soon. She's regular, Cassandra, when she gets about it, although that's the second time she's given us a foal to worry about through the winter."

Lewis took the coffee but shied away from the fireplace since the air, already warming to the sun, was beginning to flow in through doors and windows on the rising breeze. At times like this, Lewis sensed Coleman's age even more than when he watched him at a distance cross the gap in the stone fence into the field beyond the barn, cautious now, steadying each foot firmly on the ground. Lewis preferred to think of Coleman not as nearly eighty but as he had been when Lewis was a boy and would meet him somewhere in the woods, over his shoulder a canvas bag stuffed with dead grouse.

"He looks healthy. Between Howard and me, he'll have a hard time failing."

Coleman stood with his back to the fire and his coffee cup in both hands. "That Howard. When is he going to stop looking so sheepish? I run into that boy when he doesn't expect me and he looks like he's just robbed a bank. Drops what he's doing, can hardly stand up. The other day he was driving the rake and I came up the river path. He didn't see me until he made the turn by the big stone and I thought he was going to slip off the seat backwards. He barely kept the horses from bolting."

Lewis shrugged. "He thinks anyone who comes on him suddenly can see his thought sticking out of his head. Women mostly, I guess. Especially my niece, Elaine. But he's a hard worker."

"Elmore thinks so too."

The more they chatted about Lewis's brother, Elmore, the more he was certain they were only talking around whatever Coleman wanted to discuss. By the time Lewis was reminding Coleman that Elaine would only be graduating from high school next spring, a little young to marry, the old man had stopped listening.

"I'm selling the place." Coleman turned his back to put his cup on the mantel and he leaned there on one hand, looking down into the fire.

"You can't."

"Like hell. That's what Phoebe says too. All you both mean is you don't want me to."

"But you've always owned it. You, your father."

"I'm too old to keep coming here alone every year. Phoebe wants to keep it, but she's never cared for it. I don't want it sitting, rotting down like half the summer places around here, or split up into lots. I want it used, whole. I want to be certain that will happen."

The words were unhesitating and Lewis suspected they had been said often, probably to Phoebe. With a rush of resentment Lewis imagined her thin, self-indulgent face and provocative and lithe body that had already led her through two divorces and now provided her with a line of studs as blankly dandy as the models in fashion ads. She had even twitched her tight-bound butt at him one summer, but he had backed off fast, alarmed by the way he was so easily chafed at the sight of her slim, pyramidal breasts swinging free under her loose shirt as she stooped to talk to him.

"She could get to like it."

"Come on, Lew. She'd love it for a year because she possessed it. Then she'd forget and the weeds would come in, the roofs start leaking. By the time she turned around from whatever new game she was playing, there wouldn't be enough house left to put her dolls in."

Lewis put his coffee cup on the mantel by Coleman's and went to sit in the armchair near the window. He was always amazed at the clear and cool way Coleman could describe his daughter. If he had brought up children, could he ever have seen them that objectively? He suspected not. Even Howard, distant as their relationship was, muddled his reactions too much.

"You've made up your mind."

"What there is of it."

"Nothing will be the same."

7

Coleman eased himself into the opposite chair. "Not for me. I had thought of giving it all to you."

"I don't want it." Lewis jerked away from any ownership that large and settled.

"It would be a curse anyway. You can guess how much it takes to keep it going, pay the taxes. You'd just have to sell."

A truck with loose metal in the back slid to a stop, and Lewis breathed the faint whiff of dust.

"She'll have that pickup till all the bolts fall out and she's perched on naked springs," Coleman murmured, and they listened to Doris thump into the back part of the house, already singing some gospel song that she would never complete, circling back to the beginning again as if the final cadence were saved to hum before she dropped to sleep.

"At least it's a different song each week," Lewis said, but Coleman was continuing.

"Probably won't go up for sale till spring. We'll close the house as usual, and I'll have some things fixed over the winter, get out the quirks I'm used to. I'm going to sell off most of the Percherons this fall, a lot of the equipment too. The next owners won't want work horses, farm stuff. They'll be wanting the place for riding horses, I'd guess, and I'll make it look good for that."

He let him go on. The old man had imagined all the practical steps. But for Lewis the fields would be empty soon of horses, the hum and clatter of disk or binder, and the house would be shuttered and dead beyond the usual winter closure into the heat of summer. The air itself would be blank because of the lack of human presence, those distant sounds that reached his cabin on hot nights when the wind was right, or small figures moving across the landscape when he looked down from his own high meadow. The leathery voice as familiar to Lewis as the rocks and trees and mountains of the land was now calmly describing his own departure.

"I'd like to give you two. I don't know if you can use them or even want them."

"What?" He had not heard.

"The Percherons. Whichever you want."

He nodded, but before Coleman could continue Lewis said, "I'll miss you."

Coleman waved quickly but did not look at Lewis when he spoke. "I'll be back. Maybe rent a cabin from Carbonneau."

But he knew Coleman would rather never come back than stay elsewhere.

"Which horses do you want?"

"Joker and Melissa."

"The geriatric ward. A worn-out stallion and a sterile mare. Where will you keep them?"

"There's the shed up near Foley's place. If you let me keep them here for the winter, I'll have it ready by spring."

"The last of the line, aren't they, those two horses?"

"Yes." But he did not want to talk about his father. "Besides, you can't keep Joker without Melissa. They're inseparable."

Coleman leaned forward slightly in his chair, staring hard at him. "It's not a question to ask a middle-aged man, but what's going to become of you?"

"I'll get older and die." He was annoyed that, even at his age, someone like Coleman could make him feel so young.

"That's too common for you. Where will you work? I'll put in a word with anyone who takes over here. You're the best with horses."

"Not riding horses. Finicky animals owned by finicky bitches. I've got enough saved to get me by for a while, ever since Elmore and I sold off that piece of land down by the road."

"You should have stayed with the acting."

"You wouldn't say that if you'd seen me in New York."

"You were good."

"It's easy to be good in front of relaxed, half-boozed summer people."

"I was whole-boozed."

"You must've been."

Doris passed the doorway on her way up the stairs, a solid bell of striped skirt, white socks rolled over heavy black shoes, voice still tolling her indistinct melody.

"I remember that one summer, anyway. *Arsenic and Old Lace*."

"That could have been a lot of summers. But I know the time you mean. Afterward, down at the Bear, you and Lena made me feel I was the best actor in the world."

Coleman waved impatiently.

"No, I mean it. Even if I knew you were drunk, and I was drunk, and I still knew somewhere that it probably wasn't real, I believed it anyway. I made myself believe and you helped. I couldn't have taken a crack at it without that."

"Had a good little summer theater for a while. We'd get some of the best actors up from New York for the leads." He was staring at the empty doorway. "That was the summer Lena and I had just come back from Italy. I'd not been a very good boy. But she forgave me. For the time being."

Lewis went to the fire to poke a log back that had slid forward, smoldering on the hearthstones. He was impatient to be doing something. What was the use of turning over those layers of old muck? He could hear Coleman rising, and they walked out onto the porch. The sun was high enough to have burned the dampness out of the air and a gauze was on the peaks.

"Always my favorite season," Coleman said, but before Lewis could continue down the steps, the old man grasped him by the arm tightly, his face pushed close. "Lew, I ought to tell you something." Then he snapped his mouth shut, shook his head. "But I won't."

Lewis was just as glad. They could talk to each other for hours on those nights of Bourbon and cribbage, but never did well with subjects too personal. "Tomorrow night?"

Coleman nodded. Lewis was down the stairs now, halfway across the drive.

"I'll tell you something. It's my birthday today."

"Happy birthday, Beede."

Howard was coming down the ramp with a bucket and shovel on his way to bury the afterbirth. When Lewis reached the stall he held still until Cassandra sensed him. She was standing now, her neck sloped, and she looked back at him for a moment only. He touched the hard, high croup. Close to her belly, his small legs still trembling, the colt was nuzzling a teat, his splotched hide rubbed up in swatches where his mother had licked him. When he lost the teat, his grooved tongue sucked on air.

Lewis walked back along the aisle hazy with dust, and paused in the yard near the fence where Howard was digging, shirt soaked with sweat.

"I won't be down again today. Take Melissa and Joker and

mow that field," and as Howard stared, leaning on his shovel, the glistening, bloody pail between them already drawing flies and the slow circling of bees, he gave the boy more to do than was possible, knowing that no matter what he ordered, Howard would probably dream away half of it.

When he came to the road, that black streak of macadam raised above the level of the fields, the one straightaway before it pitched and curved through the passes at either end of the valley, he decided to wait for the distant car to pass. Lewis had lost only one foal in the past eight years. Salute's filly was stillborn. She would not let them lug it away because its seemingly vital motions when they tried to move the carcass made her protective. When they put a blanket over it, Salute remained calm. Later that day, in the field where the dead foal lay stretched on the ground as they dug the hole, Salute passed with complete indifference, not even pausing to sniff.

The car was coming very slowly and Lewis had begun to sweat. The sun bore down straight, any breeze cut off by the high dike of the road. It was a battered VW bus with out-of-state plates, Pennsylvania, he guessed from the muddied colors. The driver perched up in the flatly cut-off window was a pale face with long hair tightly gathered back. Man or woman was always hard to tell from a distance these days, and Lewis began to cross since the car lurched to an even slower pace. Only a tourist would take this section of the road so slowly. The local people exulted in the one hard-surfaced straight line in the county where they could test the willingness of engines they had been hovering over in the summer evenings, and the laden trailer trucks, huge as houses, flattening anything in their paths, would make up for all the curves and hills beyond the valley.

The woman was peering toward the farm so intently that he feared she might swerve off into the field. He had the momentary vision of a long, slim neck and aquiline nose. When she looked at him, her mouth widened as if she were about to speak, but the gears rasped and she was speeding away. He walked on, shaking his head. So many of the people passing through seemed crazy to him. One afternoon he had come down through the woods and crossed the river to find a car with a Quebec license and a woman lying naked in the grass by the dirt road. She was sunbathing as if

11

she assumed no other human beings ever came that way. When she glimpsed him standing there, she grabbed her strewn clothes, cackling at him, the sky, the resisting door of her car, in that French which always sounded vicious to Lewis. He had heard it all his life but never made an effort to learn it.

He crossed the river on the old wooden bridge, unusable now for more than foot traffic. In the next spring flood it would collapse, and then he would have to walk the long way around to Dawson's farm, except when the river was so low that he could leap the stones. As he passed over he looked down into the clear water at the brown, slim backs of trout lazily holding their positions at the bottom of the pool. A few early-fallen leaves clung to the rocks. That same water could be so high and wild that it covered the planks he walked on, tumbling brutally against the far bend where it gnashed back on itself in whitecaps.

The trail up the stream was steep, an old road grown in with spruce and poplar saplings. He stooped and drank from the cold water that a mile above rushed at a slant below his cabin and filled the small pond. When vaguely troubled by a world now farther and farther below him, he liked to think he was drawing up a bridge behind him with every step he took. Today he could not rid himself of a gray taint that could eat into his peace of mind for days.

A woodchuck, lying high on the rim of the cellar hole, whistled and dove. The frogs leaped, startling him and breaking the surface of the pond as he walked around the edge. The whole hillside, now thickly wooded with maple and pine and occasional butternuts, had once been fields divided into parcels, each with house and barn; now only the practiced eye could pick out the raised squares of cellar holes, long filled with fallen leaves and tree limbs, or the slabs of stone that covered old wells. Often in mid-wood, Lewis would find writhen groves of apple trees unable to outgrow the taller maples and spruce, but still bearing enough dwarfed fruit to lure deer that trampled the brush around the trunks.

He stood on the upper bank of the pond. The steeply tilted field swept up to the bare one-room cabin and outhouse before the hovering fringe of trees and steeper ridge. He turned his face to the breeze, looked out across the clear oval of water to the trees falling away, the spread of the valley beyond, hills lifting on the other side, and then, perfectly coned and thrust high over the foreground, Moonstone Mountain. From almost any other direction the mountain sprawled out in ridges and undistinguished humps, but here it assumed a volcanic shape. Today it was a softly benign silhouette, bare peak hazed and bluish. But that same mountain was stark in late fall, a hard chunk of gray in a grayer sky of impending snow, the obdurate bones of some indifference always behind the frail green of summer.

Lewis would not have wanted any other piece of their father's land, did not begrudge Elmore the tracts near the site of the family's farmhouse, gentler fields where their father had for a time made a sufficient living. Elmore had openly said he thought Lewis a fool, since surely that land below was worth more than these woods, the occasional bald spots where a farm had been, the ridge of Butternut Mountain cropping into stones and suitable only for the rookeries of ravens. He could hear them croaking and chortling all year long.

He looked around hastily, then took off his clothes and plunged into the pond. The metallic shock of water risen through stones made him gasp, his heart racing, and he stroked out into the middle to float on his back, staring up into the sky — low puffs of clouds, and higher up a feather or two of motionless white. The sky, the water, his body seemed perfectly balanced, and then he swam hard to shore and walked up the slope to the cabin, carrying his clothes. He would sleep most of the afternoon, thought of getting some fruit or maybe a tomato from the can in the spring where he kept his food cold, but he was not hungry. He sat by the window watching the pond riffle. A thin column of smoke rose straight up from the valley, and the goldfinches twittered by, flashing yellow in their nervous flutter and glide. Talking about his acting with Coleman had reminded him of how Annie would not go to New York that fall. She had said he had a choice — stay in Judson with her or go alone to New York. Silly how important choosing had seemed then. In spite of that separation and many others, they were still together.

He lay down on one of the bunks and covered himself with a sheet. He would have to nail that shelf above him at a better angle since only the other night in turning he had flailed against it and all the books and magazines had dropped on him. But he could not hold back his mind, and as sharply as if the event had not just been recalled but had actually happened that morning, he saw his father standing in the doorway to the barn, the long cinch belt hanging from his still fist, brightly trailing along the patch of sunlit floor like a new-skinned snake. *You'll do what I tell you as long as I'm your father and I'm alive.* Lewis could not see his face clearly, but the flat voice did not waver. He could push past him. Strong as Foster still was, Lewis at seventeen and well into a summer of working for both his father and Coleman, was stronger.

I didn't say I was going to quit the team. I just said I was going to try out for the play this summer and in the fall too. Coleman says —

Says shit. Says nothing. He spat, an arc of brown that stained the boards between them. *Your father says make up your mind.*

He would not push by that lank, hard body, touching flesh to flesh, but there was no way he could say what his father wanted, even if it only meant lying to get through the moment.

I'm going to stay on the team and I'm going to try out for the plays too.

You're going to be quarterback and you're going to win the championship, and no boy of mine is going to mess around with that crowd in the summer or with those pansies that act at school.

I like to act.

The hand moved and the belt shifted along the floor.

You've got a few seconds.

The morning light struck across Foster's head, exaggerating the tight-skinned cheekbones, eyes deep in shadow. The face had become hard since his wife's death and the unrelenting nighttime drinking.

If you touch me with that, I'm leaving here. You can get in the crops yourself. He could hear how lame that sounded. Foster was stubborn enough to do what he could by himself and let the rest rot.

Where will you go?

I'll go live at the Whites'. Coleman said I could if . . .

If what?

If things get worse here.

The belt lashed at him as fast as a glint of reflection, cutting across his ear and neck. But he did not cry out.

That's for talking about family matters with outsiders.

But he's your friend, too. Lewis's voice broke.

He spat quickly over his shoulder. *I work for him. I worked for his old man. Now get on with it. Say it.*

Never.

He did not move under the first few strokes. He tried to watch the quick motions of the arm, then closed his eyes and lifted an elbow to protect them. But the belt goaded, striking indiscriminately on his head, his side, his hip, and anger lifted in him more unendurable than the pain.

The belt coiled around his outstretched arm. He gripped as it cut when his father yanked back, but he did not let go. Neither did Foster until they were standing face to face in the doorway. The horses beyond them were snorting and stamping. He swung once with his free hand. The fist struck hard against his father's forehead, and when the figure staggered aside, Lewis was down the ramp, running, not looking back or pausing until he was into the woods, where he unwrapped the belt from his arm and threw it away. Foster did not come out of the kitchen or speak to him when he returned that evening for his clothes, and even three weeks later when he left the Whites', unable to bear the view of his father's unbending figure doing the harvest on his own, a sight that defeated him more than any whipping, all Foster said was, *The combine needs a new link belt. You'll have to drive up to the Flatts.* Sometimes that summer he had hated Coleman's sympathy almost as much as his father's stony will.

He twisted in the sheet, impatiently pushing back against such long-gone misery. Coleman had brought that all to mind with his nagging about the past. Lewis's eyes stayed closed at last, and he listened to the monotonous fumbling of cluster flies beating to get out. As he began to doze he saw the foal stumbling awkwardly down the ramp, and Howard, his mottled arms wound with the afterbirth, was moving his lips soundlessly. *Watch out, watch out,* his own voice was saying, but no one heard him, and a sharp jerk of his legs against the sheet tore the dream away.

2

When he woke, lying on his side with one arm numbed under the weight of his head, he could not see clearly who was sitting at the table by the window, staring out into the brightly setting sun. The light blurred the dark form, and when one hand idly combed through a strand of hair, the flesh itself seemed as transparent as the slowly released lock. But Annie always wore that perfume.

"Hello," he said quietly, as if she were the one who had been sleeping.

She did not turn. "Happy birthday, Lew."

"You remembered."

"Have I ever forgotten?"

"I can't remember."

He rolled onto his back, keeping his face to her. His arm began to prickle.

"You wouldn't. When is *my* birthday?"

He was trying to remember what else he should be telling her. "June? No, don't tell me."

She waved a hand at the view, then shook a cigarette from the pack in front of her. "Why not? I have to tell you every year."

"That's not true. One year I remembered. I'm sure there was one year."

The smoke curled into the light and haloed her silhouette.

"Are you giving away any of those?"

Her face was in profile as she threw the cigarette to him over the potbellied stove that squatted in the middle of the room. But he could not see her expression or the cigarette. It had landed on his chest. He had stopped smoking for two years, which meant he smoked only her cigarettes.

"I wish you were just getting old, Lew, losing your memory. But you never had one for those things."

"What did you say your name was?"

She laughed that hoarse breath that he loved to hear, most of all when she was closer to him.

"Do matches come with this, or do I just lick it?"

She rasped her cigarette into the tin tray on the table and walked to him so slowly that by the time she had reached the edge of the bunk she had already unbuttoned her blouse and shrugged it off. Her hand took the cigarette from his mouth.

"That can wait. Time for your birthday present."

She bent to pull off the rest of her clothes. As she climbed over him, her face, as it often did in opaque light, seemed unchanged after all the years so that for a moment he imagined the harped jut of hipbones he had known when her body was as angular as her sharply planed face. She lay now in his shadow, and he reached a hand to run back along her cheek and through her hair. Her expression was distantly thoughtful.

"What's up?"

She only shook her head, and he did not ask again. She had her moods and lately he could not keep up with them anyway. He held her close, moving his hips against her own slow motions, and at the end she murmured his name as if it gave them something to hold on to. Lying there while she dozed, he had his cigarette.

When she woke, she stared at him for a moment. "I brought you a bottle of wine." The jug was on the floor under the table and a wide paper bag beside it. "Also some candles and a cake. But it's not homemade."

He groped for a clean shirt in the boxes under the bed, padded to the table, and twisted off the cap. The wine was almost

17

black in the last light thrust at them over the edge of Moonstone.

She took the glass. "I should have brought some steak."

When he returned from the spring he had the slab of beef in his hand, its bloody juices dripping through the bag. "I knew you'd come."

He lit a fire outside and when the coals were right he put the steak on the old stove he had wedged into the stones. He turned the meat often so the juices would work back and forth inside while she cut some tomatoes, and the smell of the fat dripping into the fire, the slow burning of the cheap red wine as he sipped, made him hungry and eager to sit with her at the window, the breeze of nightfall sifting through the screens while they ate and drank and watched lights in the valley slowly blinking on.

"Do you want the lamp?" she said when they had finished eating.

Their chairs were side by side facing out the window. He picked up her cigarette from the dish between them and the ember flared as he breathed in.

"Not yet."

He filled their glasses slowly, keeping a finger over the inner edge so he could tell when the wine neared the top.

"Coleman's selling the place."

She leaned forward. "That bad?"

"What?"

"Money. Jim used to say it would happen to all of them, that money like theirs couldn't keep piling up unless someone in the family was hungry enough to be making it. And he was right. Harper. Iglehart. Sedgwick. None of the families own the big places anymore. Some aren't even owned by anyone."

"I don't think it's money."

He repeated what Coleman had said. Anyway, wasn't Phoebe still wandering here and there, Switzerland, Colorado, the Caribbean, as she pleased? They were quiet as if trying to avoid the thought of Phoebe. Odd how his aversion to Coleman's daughter almost made Annie as jealous as if he were attracted to her. But when she began to talk about those big houses, the places and people they had known all their lives, he wanted to discuss the Whites only, push back against the old man's decision.

"The year the first barn burned was when I saw Lena," he

said. "She had been invited up that summer, just before they married. I was ten, and Dad was on the fire department then. There'd been all those barn burnings and first we'd thought it was for insurance, and then when the Whites' barn burned, we knew it had to be a pyro because they didn't need any extra cash. Turned out to be old Chipper Brandon, remember? — and he hung himself that fall at the state hospital. Dad burned his hand so bad that he couldn't finish the haying, but the Whites hired a man for us that month. I remember thinking Lena was the most beautiful woman I'd ever seen — she stood out in the field with her hair down and helped pass coffee around."

"I was only eight, you know."

"For months you could smell the char after a rain." In the silence that followed he could think of nothing else, so he said, "I don't think I'll see Coleman again after this fall."

"How many years have I heard you say that? He's old enough for you to think that every day you leave him."

"This is different."

They listened to the distant bark of a barred owl, then the answer of its mate. The two would come gradually closer, hunting and calling in tandem up the ridges from the valley.

"What will you do?"

"I won't work for Elmore again. That's no good. Not just for him and me, but the other guys on the job can't handle it, and you know how finally he had to put me off alone, opening up summer houses, splitting wood. I've enough cash for a while."

She drained her glass, poured them both full. "You won't go away?"

"I doubt it."

"But you might."

He had not left for years. Why did she think he would now? He reached for her hand but she had moved away and he could not find it in the dark. The owls were closer and the frogs in the woods and pond had become silent.

"They have such deep voices." She shifted in her chair. "What were you dreaming this afternoon?"

"Why?"

"You kept moaning, turning. Don't you remember?"

He did, vaguely. "The same one. About having a son. I still

19

can't see his face clearly. He's always walking ahead of me, or he'll be in the woods, a branch across his face. I wake up feeling like when I heard you married Jim and I thought you were gone forever."

"Well, I wasn't." Her voice was simple, but she did not seem to be encouraging him to continue. Was it the wine that made him want to? There were more reasons for the dreams that she never needed to know, but there was no harm in describing what he saw and felt. What hurt most about those dreams was the clarity with which he saw the boy's body — his long legs ending in scuffed boots slightly turned in at the toes, the bony hands, red with cold, rubbing together for warmth. Lewis would reach out, holding his own checked jacket to the boy. *Here, take this, go on, I don't need it.*

"Remember that argument I had with Elmore? About how he thinks that when he dies somehow he's going to keep on living because of Elaine and maybe her kids and their kids? I said I don't believe that. When you're dead, you're dead."

The owls called on each side of the clearing and then were silent. She sat back in her chair.

"Go on."

"When I wake up, I'm lonely. That's all. And I know it's nothing that anything else can fill up. Like that summer I was nineteen. When my father disappeared.

She spoke quietly. "When I was seventeen and gave you something that's only for giving once."

Puzzled, he paused again. Was that all the same summer? He was about to go away for his brief attempt at the university. The football scholarship was awarded to him late because someone better had turned it down. He certainly had not forgotten that actual day when he and Annie walked high up Slide Brook on the back side of Moonstone, telling themselves they were only playing hooky — she from the register of the IGA, he from helping his father with the haying. But the bolts to the pitman on the mower had broken and Foster would hardly get back from the Flatts before late afternoon, if not later. Foster's drinking had become habitual and his body was beginning to show the effects. Lewis could not bear to see the usually unflinching eyes go watery, slipping away evasively. The walk was a way to avoid waiting and building up anger at what would surely be a wasted day, an evening sitting on the side porch watching for the truck to rattle off the highway, and then another of those seething, morose conversations in the bare-bulbed kitchen in which Lewis would hear in his own voice the dim memory of his mother's chidings. It would rain the next day. What the hell was Foster going to do when Lewis went to college, with Elmore still in the Army somewhere in Germany? Didn't he know he was just trying to help? Couldn't his father tell him what was wrong? Even as he was doing it, Lewis would be appalled at himself, remembering how before that summer he would never have risked his father's anger and the physical abuse that could follow. But the face would go blank, the eyes turn slowly around the room as if all of its objects were unfamiliar, even flattening on Lewis with no recognition.

"Again, I'm the one who remembers."

"Wait," he murmured. He wanted to think that through. It had not ended in the usual argument with Foster. He and Annie had strolled higher and higher, away from the valley until on the outcroppings of rock above the first falls, they had sat and looked at the high peaks and Northmark with its fire tower. Most of that summer they had not been happy with each other, arguing bitterly over whether he should go or stay until they could go to the university together, she certain that he would find someone else, he saying he would never forget her but not admitting his fantasies at night of compliant women in a new place. By the time they reached the deep, clear pools, the slides and chutes in the smoothed granite, he had forgotten the haying, the weight of his father's silence that had gathered and gathered all that year. She did not hold back at the end as she usually did. Their lovemaking was fumbling and quick as if he had learned nothing with those other girls he went to after one of their arguments.

"That day didn't work the way I wanted anyway. You went away."

"And came back."

"Yes. And went away again."

He turned the empty pack of cigarettes. "And came back to stay. Eventually."

"So far."

The difference had been that when he came home late that afternoon, his father was there, completely sober, the mower repaired. He was sitting on the truck, looking toward the barn where the horses should be harnessed and ready to lead out.

I didn't know you'd get back so soon.

Foster shook his head. *It's no use.*

What?

Sit down.

He slid over on the running board and Lewis sat. More than anything he wanted to talk to his father about Annie, about whether he should leave. But he could not. They had not talked about private things for years, and Foster did not think he needed to go to college anyway.

I tried to sell the place today. Healy's been saying for years he'd take it. I had the papers in front of me. Couldn't do it.

Lewis stood. He was out of breath. *You wouldn't sell. You couldn't. It's not just yours. It's mine too. And Elmore's.*

Sit. Foster waved a hand as if a fly were pesking him. *It's mine if I want to sell, yours if I don't. But anyway, I couldn't. So now what?*

What do you mean?

The mower's fixed. The horses are ready. The hay's up. But I don't give a damn. About anything. To hell with it. The words were dully spoken, frightening in their lack of anger. Lewis watched him get up slowly and walk away to the house. The screen door nudged with a thump on his retreating heel and then slapped shut. All afternoon and evening, not pausing for dinner, barely giving the horses time to drink, Lewis worked with furious deliberation, and the next day it rained and the hay never dried, never was gathered but rotted where it lay.

"I wish I had a cigarette." Her finger nudged the contents of the ashtray. "I thought you were playing it up, using your father's running off as a way of avoiding me. He was always strange, it seemed to us. My dad said Foster was a loner from the start, and especially after your mom died. Some people thought he'd hurt himself, was back in the woods. They had those search parties. And you would go out with them. I didn't see much of you for all those weeks."

He stood and stepped in the dark around the stove and woodbox by habit. At the bottom of a carton under the bunk, deep in the toe of an old moccasin, was the pack of cigarettes, and he tore at the cellophane as he brought them back. He dropped them near her on the table.

"You've had them all along?"

"For emergencies."

She was lighting one and did not answer. The mountains were darker patches against a sky that had begun to glitter with stars, and across the stationary background the blinking lights of an airplane were moving silently.

"You used to think he'd come back. Then one year we figured how old he was."

Now he could not answer, his tongue heavy as stone.

"Look, did you see it?"

He had not, but in the same place her shadowy hand pointed, another star shot down and disappeared.

"I'm going to swim. You want to come?"

"Lord, no." She laughed easily. "I can't stand that pond when it's dark. Something might get me from underneath."

He reached quietly and clamped his hand onto the back of her neck. She jumped.

"Like that?"

He ducked her elbow.

"Don't you want some cake?"

"I'll be back. If I don't get eaten."

He took off his clothes by the door. It was warmer outside than he had expected, the weather probably shifting toward rain. At the edge of the pond he waited until the crickets along the rim began their chirp again, then he dove flatly, rising to the surface, and as he paddled lazily with his hands, he came across cold spots where the springs were bubbling up.

How long the day seemed to him. He had forgotten to tell her about the colt. What made it seem even longer was the way he had spent so much time recalling unhappy events. Odd, since the day itself had been unmarred except for what Coleman had told him, and by now that did not seem very shocking. The cabin was almost merged with the dark hillside, but a match flared and moved slowly, leaving small pricks of candlelight where it paused. The more candles she lit, the more her hand, her bending figure, were revealed. Something moved near the edge of the pond, probably a bullfrog clambering against the steep bank. He thought of her fear of the pond at night, the way even by day she stroked out quickly to the middle and back, not wetting her face, with the wide-eyed motions of someone who had entered water late in her life and never thought of it as a safe place to be.

If only he could have explained to his father then what he knew now, that things often had a way of working out if you let them drift. His legs sank slowly. He was in the middle of the pond where the water went deeper than he could dive. He shivered and stroked quickly to the shore.

When he had dressed, he leaned close to the cake and blew. The candles filled the room with their waxy smoke, but some still burned.

"Do I get my wish anyway?"

3

"What do you want?" Foley rocked so furiously on the porch that his head snapped and the rug nearly slipped off his knees.

His chair was in a swatch of midday sun, still warm although that night the wind had ripped the last leaves from the maples and the grass had begun to wither in the deepening frosts. Lewis had waved as he walked the path from the road, but the old man waited for him to reach the porch.

"You'll get whiplash if you rock too hard." Lewis did not come up the stairs.

"Who's that?" A voice shrilled through the window. It was too dark in there for Lewis to see beyond the bright triangle of sun on the jutting edge of a bureau.

"None of your business," Foley yelled, then muttered, "Always meddling. I never have a conversation but she's got to have a piece of it."

"If that's the mail, I want it handed to me, you hear? If it's addressed to me, don't give it into his hands. I've got my rights."

"It's Lewis Beede, ma'am."

"And he came to see *me*, so go spit in your bedpan."

She rambled on for a while about how he was a mean old man, embarrassing her in front of guests, and then Lewis could not make out the rest. He always spoke loudly enough to include her, and when he began, her voice stopped.

"How you feeling, Foley?"

"Cut it out. Haven't seen you for a month except to wave at when Doris gives you a lift downtown. Come to the point." His feet landed flatly on the porch, the rocker stilled, and he held his head forward, cocked slightly to one side.

Lewis laughed. "Your shed. The old one up on the edge of my property."

"What about it? It's not so old, either. Fifteen years at most. And that was damned sound wood, seasoned. I picked it out myself at Gurney's Mill."

"There's not much roof left, and it's started to lean back into the hill."

"A good ten yards off your line. Can't fall that far."

"I'd like to help keep it up."

Foley snorted. "Bullshit."

Her voice rode in over his and he was silenced, mouth open.

"That's generous, Lewis. Don't let him insult you that way. He's always been cynical and I've told him again and again that if you think of the world that way the world will live up to your expectations."

He was rocking again. "Stay out of this, woman. The man's come with a proposition."

The rocker stilled again, and Lewis went on. "I want to use it till I can build something up nearer my place."

"What for?"

"Horses."

"Whose?"

"Coleman's giving me two of the Percherons."

Foley shook his head. "You're a fool. Percherons are dumb beasts. Bred too much. Not near as sturdy as a Shire or even a Belgian. I've seen them get the founder time and again. Now, your Shire is more trouble-free. The auction's today, isn't it?"

"I'm on my way to watch it."

Foley's face relaxed. "You think someone will buy the place? How much is he asking?"

26

"He hasn't told me."

"Get me something if you can, Lewis," her voice pleaded. "Oh, how I used to love that house. Just get me a little something to remember it by. A paperweight. A letter opener."

Foley spoke mildly. "It's not the house, just the barn stuff, Helen."

"I made a quilt for Lena once. She ordered it, saw one I'd made for the library sale. I wonder if Coleman still has it?"

"I'll ask."

"You can use that shed if you want. Get it in good shape, leave it that way, and you can use it for nothing. For a year. Then we'll see."

"Done." Lewis was surprised how hard the grip was in spite of the frail and bony arm.

Foley spoke so low that Lewis had to lean closer. "It's her mind now. She's pretty sharp some days, like today, but others she forgets who I am, calls me after our son, Jud, or her father, and last week she laughed for an hour, just laughed till she was crying and I had to send for Doc to quiet her down."

"Stop your whispering. What's he saying, Lewis? What's he lying about now?"

"It's business, woman."

"Anything I can get you, drop off on the way back?"

"No. Elaine's been coming by regular. Your brother has some child there, Lewis. I think she ought to be a real nurse. Has a good touch with the old lady."

Lewis stepped down to the yard again. "How's Jud?"

"We don't hear from him much," Foley said vaguely. "I guess they keep him pretty busy, and three hundred miles is just far enough away to make visiting hard."

"What's he say about Jud?"

Foley shucked off the rug, clutched at the unsteady chair, and rose slowly. "Nothing," he yelled to cover up a groan. He held out an arm. "Give me a hand down these stairs. I'm going to get that railing fixed soon, but I don't trust it." As Lewis gripped his elbow, Foley yelled again. "I'm walking down to the road with Lewis."

They moved carefully over the stones of the path.

"Tell the truth, I think Jud's in some kind of trouble. Got

heavy into debt a few years ago, been drinking too much. You can tell by his face. His wife, Martha, runs around some, I've heard." The shade they passed through was cold and the unraked leaves made the footing hard to see. "D'you know, Coleman's even older than I am, but you'd not think it. I told Helen it's not money or living an easier life. Look at Lena. She was much younger than all of us. No, growing old's never easy. I think it's just the body you're given. Doesn't matter too much what you do to it, unless you're talking about drugs and stuff like what I hear the kids do. Coleman was luckier than me, that's all."

They reached the mailbox and Foley wrenched it open, found a few letters and his paper there.

"Bills." He stuffed them in the back pocket of his overalls. "I'll just sit on them for a while." His face was mild when he turned to Lewis. "You say hello to Coleman and tell him I'm sorry. We've something in common, more than just the times I used to take him hunting up on Moonstone or the lake. You never had children, Lewis, so you wouldn't understand how it is to have only one and do everything you can for him, even though you know at the time it's not enough or right, and then in the end have him go strange on you. Someone, I guess it was Dan Jamieson after his son was killed at Iwo Jima, said to me nothing was worse than outliving your children, but I'm not so sure. I wonder if watching them go on living, and living wrong, is worse." He shook his head. "They say Phoebe's a real mess."

A high, thin voice came down from the house, wavering into a melody with unclear words.

"Oh, that Jesus stuff. Doris does that to us. She and Helen sit in there and rock on the bed as if it's the Ark. They sing their holy songs for hours. At least in the summer I can go sit in the outhouse, but by the Jesus even the TV won't cover it in winter."

"Thanks for the shed. I'll let you know how it goes."

"Born again." Foley beat the rolled newspaper in his palm to the rhythm of her song. "Come tell us about the auction."

Lewis walked to the bend of the road, stopped to make sure the old man made it safely up the stairs, then strode on quickly before Foley could turn and see him watching. All the time he was there, Lewis had wanted to say more and had ended by only getting the right to use a shed. But when he tried to think of what else he could have said, he found nothing. On days when he would prefer to be alone, he could not locate words or gestures to fill the space between himself and others. He shrugged, crossed over to the sunny side.

The dirt road ran parallel to the valley, rising and falling sharply with the folds of ridges, crossing the small brooks that cut down toward the river. Houses like Foley's were tucked into the hillside, many of them deserted, some owned by summer people who had shuttered the windows tightly before they left. Lewis could remember almost all the families who had lived year-round on the hill, but now many of the summer people were strangers to him, a whole new crowd since his youth when there were fewer of them and more mingling between them and the townies like himself or Annie. A cautious mingling, though. One summer she had spent time with Alex Perkins, whose white Ford convertible was always filled with tennis rackets, towels, the paraphernalia of what seemed to Lewis a totally idle life. He and Buddy had threatened to beat up Alex, but they had ended by only standing on street corners, glaring at the Ford as it sped by. He had hated the way Annie began to toss her head impatiently at him after a day's hiking and picnicking with Alex and his friends. She would talk haughtily about *the beauties of the mountains*, the challenge of climbing to the top *because it is there*. Lewis, like most of the local inhabitants who had to live with the inconvenience of hills, never bothered with the peaks. Before tangling himself into silence, he would try to defend his own forms of recreation, describing how he felt on a bright fall day when a grouse rose with a startling whir and just as quickly he lifted his gun to fire or not, depending on the immediate assessment of trees and bushes. Alex, he was informed, thought hunting was brutal and a waste besides, since there was more than enough meat in the grocery store. He smiled now to think of his rage, how her posturing had been as exaggerated as his anger. He should have known how borrowed and false those opinions were for her. After all, she and her family were his kind of people, not Alex's. By deer season when all the summer people were gone, she was driving with him in his truck and waiting in it while he walked up the draw in the frozen rain that ticked against the dead leaves.

He hardly ever hunted anymore. In the fall he might walk in

the woods carrying his gun, but often he did not take shells. The etched day was enough, the rapid lift of his own pulse when the bird beat up into sharp light. It was easier to bring the gun than to confess to anyone he met that he was *just walking*. He suspected that Alex Perkins was a very serious hunter now, with all the best equipment, and probably as good a shot as Lewis had ever been.

He leaned on the crumbling wall of the bridge and stared down at the narrow rush of water. He was depressed again, and knew that had nothing to do with what he was thinking. Did Helen and Foley make him sad? They were at a hard moment in their lives. He had always like Helen. She had run a store downtown full of tourist curios — varnished bird feeders, postcards, "hand-carved" knickknacks sold in bulk to her by a company in Brooklyn, and above all the maple sugar figurines she might slip into his palm if she felt generous.

Too many people lately were reminding him that he was childless. Elmore especially. His words had some smugness now that Elaine was nearly grown up. There were things, Elmore would seem to be saying, that you cannot know or understand if you've never had children. Or he would shake his head when some woman with an infant had left his office and say to Lewis with unstated self-approbation, *Christ, I'm glad I don't have to go through all that again*. He had been through it, done well, and Lewis would never have a chance.

Foley did not mean that as a taunt. But the more sensitive Lewis became to it, the more he wanted to blurt, *I am a father*. He could imagine Elmore smiling at first, as he did when he could not judge the other person's tone and feared a joke was being played on him. But beyond those few shocking words, that fact which he could swear by, there was little else to be said — except to describe a failed relationship, a well-severed past. The woman, Monica Kramer, had borne a child. That was a fact. They had lived together for most of the two years he had tried acting in New York. They had decided not to marry and she had given up the baby at birth to an adoption agency. She had not permitted him to know what hospital she was in, entering under a false name, and would not tell him the sex of the child. *At least tell me that*, he would say, but an adamant silence had grown between them. Theirs was a relationship that had diminished as her body swelled through those long months in which she had begun by wanting him to marry her and he had resisted, had ended by refusing him as he pleaded desperately for marriage. He could still recall the moan of an intermittent draft in the nailed-shut dumbwaiter of their brownstone apartment.

At moments like this he did not see Monica, who had blurred to oval eyes, a body slim but somehow fleshy in spite of the outthrust collarbones and sharply triangled knees. Instead he imagined a child. He assumed it was a boy, a vague conjecture, formed from Monica's expression when he questioned her, that had hardened into a certainty. For many years he had ceased to think of the child, but now there were the dreams. He did not know if they were the result of having people like Foley or Elmore say things to him, but it seemed unfair that when his life finally had begun to settle peacefully, the past seeped back up into his mind. But he had noticed that before. It was better to keep moving. Sometimes now he had to admit to himself that perhaps he had been glad Monica had decided to give up the baby. What would they have done with a child? But that attitude, in turn, made him uneasy.

He heard the rattle and popping of tires and crossed the bridge as Doris's truck toiled around the corner and her face began to bear down on him fiercely. She slewed to a stop and rolled down the window.

"Going to the auction?" Her eyes, blue and flecked with a lighter color so that they seemed to have frozen and then cracked in slivers, fixed on him.

He walked around and stepped up into the cab. The seats were punctured with popped coils, but an old chair cushion and grease-stained blanket covered most of the sharp edges. She started off with her usual jerk and slither of back wheels, something Lewis had learned to brace his neck against. She accused a faulty clutch and Gus's inability to fix it, but Lewis and Coleman blamed the coordination of her determined foot.

"I told Gus he'd best come too, but he wouldn't listen. There may be things coming out of that barn worth more than any of us think." She looked at him quickly as if to catch him off guard. "I stopped to share the spirit with Helen. They said you'd been by."

Again the eyes pecked at him. She drove with an unyielding

absence of respect for the variations of landscape so that the downslopes of hills were taken with the dead plummet of a falling stone, the upper reaches were barely mounted by faltering chugs, and Lewis had learned to look anywhere but straight ahead on the wild tilt of curves.

"I was asking for the use of Foley's shed."

"What for?"

"My horses."

She took that in with pursed lips. "Mr. White give them to you?"

"Melissa and Joker."

"Then they're yours. I heard Carbonneau was coming to bid on horses and machinery. I wouldn't want to be up against him when he's set on something."

This time he watched her face, but he might as well have been trying to read Moonstone's rocks for expression, so he said it out loud. "Now, what the hell could Bernie want with that stuff?"

She only shrugged as the road took its final dip and twisted to plunge for the valley. She began singing in that high, frail voice she released through barely parted lips, and even up close, Lewis was never sure what all the words were, was certain she was not either.

She tramped on the brake where the dirt road ended, and the truck shuddered and stopped with its nose well out into the macadam. Luckily no traffic was coming. In the angle of the intersection and back slightly in the field was the blackened rubble of the bar and grill Lewis had owned. The rotted stump of the beech tree that once shaded the parking lot was still a scorched column. Lewis could look at it now with little anger or regret. The high flames had been fueled by exploding propane tanks, the old roof crumbling long before the token presence of the fire truck was there to reflect the heat and glare on its well-polished sides. He had leaned bitterly against the stop sign, baffled by trying to guess who had torched it. But once the anger was gone and he had stopped imagining that he was there in the dark lot to catch the figure who stooped with his rags and can of kerosene by the shed door, there was only relief. Now he did not have to stand around all night listening to his pal Buddy Harlow brag about his guns and holsters or how he shot a chickadee at one hundred yards with his .38 Police Special and nothing was left but bloody fluff, would not have to see the last moaning drunk to the door with the sun almost up and all the dishes to do, the barroom to mop, only a few hours to sleep before Molly or Allison would be letting themselves in to start the coffee and bacon for that whole other group of townsfolk who had gone to bed early, were rising already, and looked forward to making their own kind of exuberant noise as they paused on their way to work. The hole where the building had stood always looked much too small.

She raced the engine before jerking onto the highway. "You weren't half bad at bartending. Least you gave out free coffee for the worst ones. Not like Jake at the Bear, who might as well break up their bodies and send them straight off to the hospital."

How pale her Gus would turn, crouching down on his stool, when, on his infrequent escapes from home, she would stalk in the door, Bible in one hand, the other ready to clutch his arm. Depending on how far gone he was, either she would drag him home while the barroom listened to him bitterly chanting, *Jesus, a man never stands a chance*, or she would have to sit there, firm-lipped, clenching her free hand on her own beer while Gus clamored on about how life in the Navy was supreme — no women, no Bibles, only Japs in airplanes and submarines and your own cozy bunk to die in.

"Thanks. But I wouldn't want to do it again," he said to her profile.

She did not smile often, but when she did, he could not believe the transformation, a face almost girlish and teasing. "Most things I wouldn't want to do over, would you? Otherwise there wouldn't be any point to getting old."

"You're not old, Doris."

If they had been outside she would have spat. "I'm sixty-eight." She frowned. "Or seventy, depending on whether I believe my father or my uncle."

"You still drive a mean truck."

But she was not listening to him. "What do you think, Lewis? When am I going to wear out that old man of mine and get him to listen to the Lord? When he dies, I don't want him going to a different place than me. He's never behaved himself alone."

She set her jaw firmly, looked at Lewis for so long that he

feared she had forgotten she was driving. "If he's not coming with me, I'm not going." She hit the shoulder, swerved back onto the road.

"No gates or angels could stop you, Doris."

"As for you, Lewis, you never should have come back here. And you even had another chance to go after your place burned down. It was insured, wasn't it?"

"I owed it to Coleman for staking me."

She nodded, still not listening but arguing out loud with herself. "Yes, and then if you'd left you wouldn't have gone on mucking up people's lives. Like Annie. None of my business, but what have you got to show for it all? I've always told you we expected you to make it big somewhere else. People who remember you as a youngster might say you wasted your life."

He laughed uneasily. "Doris, I didn't know you cared."

"I was your mother's best friend. Long before I was this cracked."

Although she did not begin singing again, she said nothing more until they saw the cars along the side of the road ahead. She leaned forward and slammed down on the accelerator. "We're late, hang it."

After she parked, she was gone quickly, walking without regard to the traffic that eased through the narrow space. He had no intention of buying anything. Rows of chairs had been set out in the barnyard, and Riley Post stood on a table near the ramp. His voice and breathing were blasted out over the crowd by loudspeakers. Some of the smaller things were up now, and Howard would stoop and lift, grinning awkwardly, or would drag equipment out onto the ramp. The bidding was lively, the sun warm in the pocket of the yard lightly hazed with the dust of motion. The people he did not know would have read the sign posted for two weeks on the highway, or would have seen the advertisement in the *Flatts Daily Observer*. He thought he could distinguish the horsemen, saw a truck from Canada. Lewis squatted down on the slope near the house.

"You'll come by this evening?"

He had not heard Coleman come from the house behind him. The old man was staring at the barn. Now that he was there, Lewis was reluctant, almost sorry he had come.

"Maybe."

"I'll be leaving tomorrow. Phoebe's here with one of her studs, and when they go Doris will close up. Enjoy the show. I'm going out for a drive."

"Want company?"

"No thanks. Thought I'd drive up East Hill and take in the view. They tell me there's been some interest in the house already." He slashed his hand across the view of the barn, turned his back on it. "Don't want to watch it, but can't even avoid hearing it."

If Coleman had stayed, Lewis was sure he would have snapped back at him. After all, the whole damn thing was his idea, wasn't it? Selling the place, having an auction? And it wasn't Lewis's fault that Phoebe was such a bitch. But Coleman walked to the maroon Audi parked by the porch stair, limping slightly. It had to be Phoebe's car, since Coleman usually drove the old Buick he left in the barn all year for his visits.

A VW bus had turned into the driveway as Coleman was trying to drive out, and he waved angrily, yelling that parking was on the road only. It was the same car with Pennsylvania plates, that long face and dark plait of hair, that Lewis had seen a number of times in the past few weeks. She backed out slowly, waited for Coleman to exit, then whined off in low gear, looking for space.

"Lewis, could I see you for a moment?"

He was certain that she would be wearing those tight, faded jeans, the floppy straw hat with its broad ribbon, and he was right, except that as he turned, Phoebe was taking off the hat, shaking out her long, reddish hair. He stood.

"I guess."

Because he never remembered her as friendly, but only those tough lines of anger when they argued about some trifle she had not only asked him to do but also told him how to, he was always surprised when her eyes were shy. She touched a hand quickly on his elbow.

"You're looking well. Could we get away from all this?"

With the front door shut, Riley's unending jabber was muted. They went farther back, into the kitchen.

"Coffee? Or a beer?"

A man was sitting at the table reading a newspaper, one hand idly stirring a spoon in his cup. Square-jawed, wearing a plaid shirt neatly pressed, his eyes still puffed with sleep, he had one of those clean-shaven, perfectly shaped faces that would never offend. Lewis had often suspected that their anonymity was exactly what she needed, that she enjoyed making them into whatever she wanted until they located some last knee jerk of dignity and left her. Or were dismissed.

"Ron, this is Lewis Beede. I've told you about him. Could you be a dear and let us talk alone for a while?"

Ron stood, folding his newspaper, and held out a hand that was much too lax for its size when Lewis took it.

"A beer," Lewis said, riding over Ron's reply, and by the time Phoebe had opened the refrigerator and brought him the bottle, Ron had taken his coffee cup and departed.

"Still at it." Lewis watched her turn the chair and sit astride, leaning her arms on its back.

"Him?"

He nodded. She ran both hands through her hair.

"He's all right. You ought to see him on skis. He can do anything with them. It isn't fair exactly, is it? Some people are only good for things that are good for nothing. They don't get much credit." She laughed. "Oh, don't worry. I give us another week. We've been a month away from snow and can't go back to Chile again just to get things in gear. We have at least a month before there'll be enough snow here or out West. I won't remember his double flips that long."

Lewis drank half the beer without stopping — slow, deep mouthfuls.

"Sit. You make me nervous."

"Say 'please.' "

She laughed again. "Please. People like Ron give me bad habits."

He sat with the table between them.

"Why is he doing this?"

He did not have to ask if she meant her father. "Because he wants to."

She was leaning again, head lying with one cheek on her arm. "Please, Lewis. He must talk to you more than he does to me. I know he doesn't trust me, thinks I'll ruin the place if I have it, and

36

I guess it's too late to persuade him that I can care in my own way as much as he does." This milder voice reminded Lewis of how she had talked as a child, a clear piping as she perched beside him, urging him to let the horses go faster while he drove the baler into the barn. She frowned. "Why is he being so hard on himself? He doesn't have to do this. He seems to want to hurt himself as well as me."

"We haven't talked much about it."

She looked hard at him, then away. "I guess you're telling me the truth. It is bad if he hasn't even talked to you." She stood, went to the counter, and with her back to him drummed with her fingers. "I won't let him do it. I can't." The words began with a stubborn bite but rose, ended weakly, and she turned, her mouth trembling. "He's got to be testing me. I don't have anything but this house. There isn't anyplace else I can go to."

"Seems to me you go lots of places."

"Damn it, Lewis. Don't you know what I mean? That house in Long Island, it's nothing. I was in boarding schools all the time. It's just the place I stayed on vacations. Switzerland? Chile? Snuggling up to some tennis or ski bum or lonely professor on sabbatical? Here isn't a home either, but at least it's a place to start. Fixed."

"You've told him this?"

"He doesn't listen." She sat on the edge of the table. "And I don't talk well to him either, of course. It always comes out crooked."

Lewis drained his beer and turned down the offer of another. "Don't think I can help you."

"You mean you won't," she snapped. "You could if you wanted. You know damn well you're as close to him as a son. The adopted poor boy."

He stared at her, thought of leaving, but her eyes wavered.

"I'm sorry. I really am. I need you, Lewis. That was mean. Sometimes I think I'm just jealous of the way you two are so easy and close, and almost the way he and I used to be." She paused. "I had a dream last night. I was alone in the house and everything had been moved out. Completely bare. Exactly what it must look like without all these things," and she motioned them away with one quick hand. "I was in the living room. There was a horse upstairs. I don't know how it got there. It was walking back and forth slowly. I was frightened when it stopped but could not bear the sound of the hooves when it walked. The windows were shutting one by one all over the house and my father's voice, terrible, as if he was in awful pain, was saying over and over, *Take the key, take the key*, but I had no idea where it was, or what I was supposed to do with it." She stopped and swallowed hard. "I won't have him sell this place. I need it. Do something." The last words were spoken so sharply through her clenched teeth that Lewis's own jaw tensed.

She did not wait for a reply, called out in a different voice, "Oh, Ron?"

"Right."

"Do join us. I've been telling Mr. Beede what a super skier you are."

After a halting attempt at conversation with Ron, Lewis went out the back door, stood with the house between him and the gusting words from the barn, and then walked around to the front again to look down on the auction, more crowded now. Howard was having trouble keeping up.

The sun, pressing on him in warm patches through the branches of the bare maple, and the beer made him drowsy. He sat with his back to the tree. He ought to have spent the afternoon cutting and splitting more of the wood he had dragged to the clearing in four-foot lengths. Once the first few minutes were through and his shoulders, always a little stiff at first, or that wrist he had wrenched badly seven years ago, were limbered up, splitting was something he enjoyed. A mindless, easy rhythm, almost like his own steady breathing before sleep, would set in, and except for a piece with hidden knots, a time would come when the wood fell apart into bright, clean halves. Maybe he would walk into town and see Annie. She would cook him some dinner before he came back for the evening with Coleman. If he did. Seeing Phoebe had soured him on the whole place, and there would be no point in getting into an argument with Coleman when he was about to leave.

Howard held up a placard with a number matching the tag on the last of the machines. Doris had been right. Carbonneau was bidding and willing to pay top price, one hand gesturing for

Riley's attention, the other swiping back over his bald spot with a red handkerchief. Then the horses were for sale and Howard led them out, holding each at the top of the ramp as the bidding started. Cassandra and her colt stepping out unwillingly, jerking and rolling their eyes, were sold together, and Howard tried to put in a bid, holding on and gesturing to Riley, but it did not matter that he was ignored because the bidding went too high and he stood there dejectedly calming the colt. Carbonneau was bidding on the horses too, but the competition was rougher now.

Lewis yawned. He was curious about Bernie, but sorry for Howard, who must have dreamed that he would have the mare and colt. Phoebe was more hurt by all this than he had expected. Maybe he would say something to Coleman after all, if only to see whether he was selling the place to get at his daughter. He closed his eyes. Leading a horse down from the second story would be impossible, not just because of the stairs, but because the animal's panic would be uncontrollable. The winter his mother was slowly dying, he had wakened on the morning of the first big snow to hear one of the horses loose, certain at first that it was trapped in the house. But it was only galloping in circles outside. Foster had gone to stay with their mother at the hospital, and Elmore would not get up, said, *Let them run away. I don't give a damn*. He had paused on the porch steps, turning his face up to the pricking snow, deeper than he had expected and almost over the tops of his boots when he walked into the yard. He could not see the stray horse and guessed it must have gone around the back again. He would close the door to the shed first, then lure the stray back. They did not have a barn that winter. It had burned in the late fall, and although the livestock had been led out safely, everything else had been lost.

From the threshold he was unable to see into the dark, smelling the old hay and fresh manure, warm and fetid air. He stepped inside. The face of a horse on his right was peering at him intently. Gradually the others crowded close, staring at him with large, unblinking eyes. He stepped in farther, turned to see the hindquarters disappearing through the door. The others, with heavy, slow steps, began moving toward the opening. Lewis tried to pull back on the gelding's neck. The horse kept pushing forward, stepped on his boot as he passed, and then was out into the snow. A horse nudged Lewis's back with its nose. He turned, pushed against the shoulder point, but could not keep his footing. He whirled, tried to reach the door and close it, was thrust aside, and fell against a post.

The horses loomed above him — snorting, jostling each other to be out until only the large black was left. The horse turned its face lazily to Lewis as he stood.

Go on, beat it. Get out of here.

The horse did not move, its nostrils widening slightly. Lewis struck at its side twice with his fist as hard as he could, the horse whinnied, and the giant hip brushed him as it bolted for the door. Lewis stumbled into the snow. The horse shied and he chased it toward the shed wall.

Go on. Go on.

The trapped horse reared back, whinnied, and Lewis looked up past the flailing hooves to the huge face, nostrils wide and eyes rolled back. Coming down, the horse struck him with its shoulder, spun him off into the snow. He lay there. The black horse galloped across the field straight into the white as if still pursued. The snow rose from its hooves and they struck with no sound. *She died last night*, his father said when he returned late that afternoon and before he began drinking. For weeks Lewis dreamed of a black horse running in a field of white as soundless as his own inability to weep.

"What do you suppose Bernie wants that stuff for?" the voice was saying, and Lewis opened his eyes. Elmore was standing beside him and staring down to the emptying field.

"I wonder if she would have lived longer," Lewis said drowsily.

"Who?"

"Mother. They do such things now with the heart."

Elmore looked impatiently around as if waiting for someone. *What's done is done*, was one of his favorite expressions, as if he depended on the past to remain sturdily completed, unquestionable.

Lewis stretched and stood. He never could let Elmore off easily. "They said it was the rheumatic fever she had when a child. Damaged her heart in some way. Do you remember how angry Dad would get when she wouldn't take it easy? I'd come home from school sometimes and she'd be stretched out on the couch, pale and breathing hard, and she'd ask me to read some of my lessons out loud, helping me with the hard words, but soon as Dad came in from the barn she'd get into the kitchen, doing something. She didn't like him to see her resting."

To Lewis's surprise Elmore put a hand on his shoulder, almost leaning, looking down to the yard where Carbonneau was talking with Riley and Howard. "Always seemed to me they started off wrong. The child Mother had before they were married. It was only at the end that she talked much about that. At least, around me. She kept saying how she wished the baby had lived, how she'd always wanted a girl."

Lewis looked away. He had never tried to know more about that than the few things Elmore had told him.

"I misunderstood her. I thought she still felt guilty, but later I understood she wasn't confessing. They were both past that stage. She was just grieving for the child, summing up her losses and gains before she died. But I was ashamed. I wouldn't say much or talk with her about it. Later I hated myself for that."

His imagination insisted on bringing the child to life, swiftly aging her. "Strange to think of having a sister, isn't it?"

Elmore gestured impatiently. "She was hardly a person."

"Well, you were tough when Mother died. You made me feel like weeping would be evil."

Elmore's face flushed. "You never were much on crying. Besides, I was only fifteen."

Bernie was strolling slowly up with Riley. Among the stragglers, some of them carrying small objects, Lewis saw the woman from the VW bus, a very boyish, slim-hipped figure in worn jeans. She was standing in the driveway looking around slowly as if she had lost something. Lewis laughed.

"What?"

"Families never lose their grip on you. Here I am forty-five, and when we talk about those things I'm a child again, and I want Mom to have talked to me so I could have a chance to be the better son. Or I want to slug you for being such an ass."

"I don't think I was."

Bernie and Riley were arguing. The woman was staring toward them, hand shielding her eyes from the setting sun.

"Who is that, do you know?"

But Elmore was listening to Riley and trying to look at ease while Bernie grinned and slapped him a few times on the shoulder. Carbonneau was exerting his thrust of friendliness that Lewis always took as a form of aggression.

"You decided to get into the farm machinery business," Lewis said.

Carbonneau pushed his stubby hands under his belt. "They're worth the scrap at the price I paid. But hell, now that they're mine I might as well tell you. It's those communes up in Terryville. They won't use no engines. Fred Baker, he sold them an old combine, top price. They're a damn bunch of fools, but got money from somewhere. They want horses, machinery. I told them I'd get it for them."

"For a price." Riley's voice was husky from all the yelling.

"I shouldn't say they're fools, really. About the horses, anyway. What with the energy problems and all. Besides, Lew here will take a poke at me if I call him a fool, even indirectly." They laughed uneasily, knowing how Lewis and Bernie had taken a poke at each other more than once already. "Those folks would please your dad, wouldn't they?"

Elmore bit, began talking about how Foster, stubborn and ridiculed for not switching to power machinery, had defended the use of horses. Bernie put his hand on Lewis's elbow and steered him aside.

"I understand Joker is yours."

Lewis nodded.

"You going to stud him at all?"

"He's not been used for a while."

"But there's nothing wrong?"

"Just age. Maybe interest."

"Tell you what. I'd like to see if he'll cover Cassandra. We could do it down at Harley's. He's got a trying bar and chute still in pretty good repair."

"I'll think about it."

Lewis was always cautious with any proposition from Bernie. But Carbonneau was probably only looking for the easiest and cheapest way to cover the mare, then get a better price for her. He would have to truck her all the way to the Flatts otherwise. And if old Joker was still randy enough, there would be no purer sire nearby.

"Going to town?" Bernie asked.

Elmore and Riley, both on the town council, were talking earnestly about the new sewage treatment system. The sun was cut in half by the sharp, bare ridge of Moonstone, and the slanted light lifted into relief all the tears and humps in the barnyard grass. What was Howard doing, leaning in the doorway to the barn on one gaunt arm, his mouth open as if he were singing without sound? He shivered. He would go see Annie.

"I'd better walk, thanks. Need to wake up."

Bernie shrugged. "Suit yourself." He began whistling as he walked away, hands deep in his back pockets.

"Elly was hoping you'd come by soon for dinner." Elmore was delivering his usual patter. Eleanor never had approved of Lewis much, although they were friendly enough now. But what was not usual was the sudden turning of Elmore's face, the quiet words. "I wish we could talk more. About many things."

Lewis could hear how blankly his reply, "We will," must have sounded.

He walked on the unpaved shoulder. It would be cold tonight, another frost, although not yet that deep, hard grip of late November that would not unclench until spring. He breathed in slowly. The profiled peaks on each side of the valley were still reddened with sun, and he could smell the woodfire from a house nearby. He tried to concentrate on the road, the setting sun, but could not prevent himself from imagining his mother and father, young and bewildered, frightened by the knowledge of what their bodies had done, because surely they would not have wanted it that way; and for the first time in years he wondered also why they had not simply married, why they had waited until after the birth of the child. Although this town had begun to sprawl and loosen during the past years, he suspected the town of his own childhood, narrow in its views, constantly peering into the private lives of its members, was like the community his parents had grown up in. On an evening like this, everything was much as it must have been when his father would have paused at the barn door, breathing deeply before trudging in for his evening meal, young and in a strange land. Foster Beede, coming as he had from Canada at the age of twenty with his uncle and no parents, must have been closely observed. Was there some hesitation, either his father uncertain of his love, or, more likely, his mother stubbornly refusing to let the child coerce them into marriage? She never let anything force her, even refusing to acknowledge how her flawed heart mastered her. Or was it merely financial, a practical pause while his father established a home? Foster, too, had been stubborn — witness the way he had refused to stop working the farm with horses.

The straightaway ended in the curve of road between out-croppings and twisted through some abandoned fields. He paused. The first star, perhaps a planet, was quavering out of the last darkening blue. What he could not imagine now, and never had been able to, was his parents' impassioned groping in some hayloft, field, or woods. They had never expressed their affection physically in front of him that he could remember, other than that brusque kiss on her forehead that his father might give when he came into the house for dinner. Their affection now seemed as ghostly as his unknown sister. As when trying to imagine infinite numbers, or stars beyond the farthest stars he could see, he was baffled by thinking of all those generations of his blood he had never seen or touched, and all the future ones. Even the most immediate links were invisible; his sister was a word, his own child as remote as the only touch of an infant he had known — that veiled kicking when he put a hand on Monica's belly. Maybe even the things his body touched now were not any better known — Elmore living in ways Lewis knew only peripherally; Coleman, all his life a presence he had dealt with, but a fragmentary one because he saw only the part they shared in the summers. And there was Annie, sometimes as distant as her house from his cabin.

Dizzily spinning back on himself, he glimpsed Lewis Beede, whose skin and bones he had inhabited for forty-five years, the person his person talked to all the time. He lifted his hand. In the last twilight it was only a dark pattern, fingers splayed out like a child's tracing on paper — *hand*, a word, trembling as he held it there. "Lord, Lewis," he muttered as if the hand were a puppet, "get ahold of yourself."

His eyes were shocked by the headlights of a car as he looked back. Instinctively, as if needing to talk to someone, he stuck out his thumb, but the car had already slowed down. The VW bus. The figure inside leaned, the door swung open. She turned her face to him, so dimly lit he could not see her expression. He hesitated and the motor idled unevenly.

Her voice was barely audible above the sputter of the engine. "'I thought you wanted a ride."

He stepped up, sat, and slammed the door, which rebounded open.

"Hold it closed and slip the handle forward. Spring's broken."

He followed directions and it worked. He was puzzled by the voice, as if what little he had seen of her had led him to expect a higher, more nasal tone. In the dashboard glow he watched her slip the shift into gear and turn her eyes up to the rearview mirror. The bus whined out onto the road. She was wearing sandals and he wondered if her feet were cold.

"Just going into town," he said.

She nodded.

"You're from Pennsylvania?"

"Sometimes."

"Your car is."

"My car is."

She spoke a little breathlessly.

"Did you like the auction?"

"Not much."

He glanced into the back, which was almost empty. The car smelled rusted, very used, never much cleaned. "Nothing took your fancy?"

"I didn't go to buy."

"To look?"

She nodded again, this time giving him such a quick glance that he might have missed it if he had not been staring hard at her face. For all the disorder of her car there was something very neat and decisive about her appearance. "To look. Yes."

He laughed. "Is that why you're in Judson?"

She even smiled. "Don't most people come to Judson to look? It's very beautiful here."

"Picturesque?"

"I don't know about that."

"They say so. You've been here before?"

"Not that I know of."

Lewis rarely had trouble talking to strangers, but he could sense her tension more clearly now.

"It's funny." He stared forward. She drove the curves through the fields and dark copses nearer town very slowly. "You live in a place this small and anyone who sticks around more than a day or two catches your attention. A lot of people come through, but they don't stay long. I've seen you a few times already that I can recall, which must mean that I saw you even before I knew I saw you, if you know what I mean."

She turned quickly, mouth open.

"So I guess you've been here a few weeks?"

She shook her head, did not speak.

"Not that you know of."

Ryland's cows were moving along the fence line toward the brightly lit barn door, dark clots humping out of the field.

"Where are you going now?" she said abruptly.

"To a friend's house. You can drop me anywhere in town."

There was only one dirt crossroads ahead before the main intersection, but she might be staying with someone. If he were younger, he would have given her some reason to be edgy. She was attractive, had picked him up, and thinking of how unlikely he was to make even a slight pass at her made him feel older. He laughed.

"What?"

"How old are you?"

"Twenty-four."

"Well, I'm forty-five. Barely. I'm Lewis Beede."

"Miriam Sternberg." She spoke as if flinching.

"Don't be nervous. Look, I'm laughing because ever since I've turned forty-five nothing seems to be the same. I'm trying to decide if I'm really different, or what the hell's going on. Tonight, before you came by, even my own hand seemed to belong to someone else."

When she finally answered he had to lean toward her to hear.

"Who would you want it to belong to?" The face she turned to

46

him, clearer now that they were passing under the first street-lights, was serious. The question seemed very odd to him.

"Who?"

"Yes." Her tone lightened. "Will it away. Choose. Would you give it back to yourself? Your parents? The woman you love? Split it up, a finger for everyone?"

"Oh, come on. I was serious, you know."

"No, I mean it. Always tell the truth to strangers."

They passed Fulton's Garage, where Andy and his brother were bending headless into the open jaw of a racing car. The town's only traffic light hung at the central crossroads ahead, blinking its eternal yellow.

"Letting it all hang out is your generation's idea, not mine," he snapped. But he was immediately chagrined.

"Don't you have any children you could give it to?"

"No."

The bus swerved to the curb and she stamped on the brake. He jammed his hand against the dashboard to catch his balance.

"You don't waste time stopping, do you?"

Her face was expressionless when she turned, but the voice trembled.

"I think this is where you asked to get out."

"This will do fine."

The door swung open freely to the downgrade of the gutter.

"Thanks." He held the door in one hand, leaned in.

She was biting one corner of her lip, staring straight ahead. "Did I say something wrong?"

The head shook, her hand wrenched the gear into place, and he barely had time to slam the door before she spun off. It flapped open, swung shut, and her figure leaned to fasten it as she drove through the intersection. He watched the bus curve uphill and out of sight.

4

Annie lived in the white house where the street ended and the dirt road began its switchbacks to the top of the escarpment and the town graveyard. The house was larger than it seemed from the front, rambling back into a grove of white pines, ending in the shed stuffed with most of Jim Strand's possessions. After he died, Annie had not been able to throw them out, instead had dropped objects hastily into boxes and carted them into the back. Lewis had helped carry them. They leaned and sagged there, the bottom ones rotting where the yearly spring thaw turned the dirt floor into mud.

Lights were on downstairs and a figure was moving in the living room. His motorcycle lolled on its stand in front and Buddy Harlow would be inside, talking, talking. Lewis had not told Annie that he would come, he rarely did, and sometimes the price he paid was having to decide whether he wanted to sit uneasily listening to her chattering with one of her strays or turn and go back to his cabin, giving up her company for the evening. Long ago they had argued that out. He had no final rights to her time, that was her house, and if he wanted to be her lover, wanted to come and go with the casualness that he preferred because he hated saying hours ahead of time what he would or would not do, then he must accept whatever her life was doing when he came. Most of the time she, too, seemed to prefer that randomness, although lately she had been irritated with him when he forgot to show up for something. *You don't own me,* he had growled.

He did not like having to put up with someone's presence when he did not choose it, and Buddy was no exception. She shrugged. *He needs to talk. After all, if you were married to Lucille wouldn't you need to go somewhere?* Later, on those nights after Buddy or Pete Hickey had absorbed most of the six-packs they had brought and staggered off down the block to their own darkened houses, he would lie close to her heavily breathing, slumbering form and know that to change that part of her would be to make her someone he would not love half as much.

He never knocked, just rattled the knob and walked in. Buddy was standing in the middle of the room, his arms flung out, one worn cowboy boot bowed to the pressure of his floppy ankle, the other stiff with the brace it covered. Buddy had been his halfback when Lewis was quarterback of the high school team, but after the accident most of his weight had drooped sadly into his midsection, and they did not talk much about the big games anymore. Of all the men left in town who had gone to school with him — Bernie, Andy Fulton, even his brother, Elmore — Lewis still felt closest to Buddy. They had always lived very different lives but kept some quiet respect for each other underneath it all.

Annie was sitting on the sofa, laughing hard, and they did not pause for Lewis, as if he had been expected.

"So then I says, 'Bernie, we can make a deal. You're tired of having your mailbox knocked over when my plow comes by. Well, I could start to worry about that more.' He looked me right in the eye, said, 'Done,' and let me back in the game. By Jesus, you should've seen his face two hours later when I walked out with a hundred bucks. Hi, Lew." Buddy limped to the mantel, where he had set his beer. "I was just telling Annie here about the poker game last Saturday up to Bernie's house."

As if Lewis had not already figured out the gist by hearing the end, Buddy repeated it, this time probably adding details because Annie laughed again in places. The story contained the underlying pattern of many that Lewis heard, usually at the bar. They could be called "The Tricking of Bernie Carbonneau," most of them probably spurious because otherwise Bernie would be much poorer and more battered and not worth fantasizing about. But Lewis, pouring himself a glass of Bourbon in the kitchen and followed to the doorway by Buddy, found himself laughing, taking a deep drag of the warm, neat whiskey, relaxing at last.

The steel brace on the lower part of Buddy's leg clicked when he walked. *My spurs,* he called it. He would tell anyone about his motorcycle accident, how he wiped out coming back from his job in Mineville at the titanium mines, rolled off into Split Rock chasm, and lost his Harley in thirty feet of water. That incident was true, but some people remembered that the injury to his leg came shortly after, when he was practicing quick draw and the gun went off in his holster.

The story of his poker game had the same ending this time. When Lewis walked past Annie, her hand came up and touched his, and then he sat on the easy chair nearby. Buddy was certain that Carbonneau was going to sell the machinery for scrap, the horses for dog food, and he thought it a shame — someone ought to prevent it. He waved off Lewis's explanations.

"He tell you that? Did he? He tell you that?" His cigarette dashed ashes over his shirtfront. "Christ, you ought to know better than to believe what he says. And I wouldn't go stud any mare of his, I wouldn't."

He finished the beer, Annie brought him another while he protested, promised it would be the last because Lucille and he were off to the dog races in the Flatts that night, and then he started telling about how much his old lady liked to bet on the losing dog, had a regular knack for it, but his heart did not seem to be in that tale, and although he rambled into a description of the last time they had been there, his eyes were going vacant before he stopped. He was hunched down, sitting gingerly on the end of the coffee table and looking down at the half-empty bottle that he held by crooking a finger into its mouth. He drained the beer, his Adam's apple working in great heaves.

"She likes dogs a lot. Hell, over the years we went through a passel of them." He shook his head.

"I know. Most of them shit on my lawn."

He grinned at her, put the bottle down on the table, and started to the door. "Thanks, Annie."

"Come back rich." She stood, stretching high.

"S'long, Lew." He yanked open the door, said, "Je-sus" at the wide-eyed figure of Howard Ryan, an envelope and book held tightly in one hand against his gaunt chest. "It's Edgar Allan Poe," and Buddy ducked around the figure that had turned to stone.

"Come in," she said quietly.

Howard took one step into the room and stopped. "I saw Buddy was here. I wasn't sure if I'd be bothering you. I didn't know you were here, Lew."

Not Howard too, Lewis wanted to say to her, watched curiously as she moved forward, taking his elbow.

"Nonsense. Come on in."

"I would've come by earlier, but because of the auction I couldn't. I wanted Cassandra and the colt." He looked guiltily at Lewis.

"Now where would you keep them?"

Howard shrugged, sat on the edge of the chair that Annie urged on him. "I'm not sure. Dad said I might've tried Foley."

"I've beat you to it."

"Bernie says he's gonna keep those two. Sell the rest. Why does he want Cassandra?"

"Probably," Lewis said flatly, "to sell to me for more than I can afford."

"Why you?"

"Maybe I've got plans. But I haven't told him." Seeing Howard about to speak, he added, "And I'm not about to tell you."

Howard sat still, but his eyes shifted quickly. His hair was combed, his best clothes buttoned and tucked in as if he were on his way to a dance.

"Come back in the kitchen and talk to me while I start fixing dinner. Lewis will want to watch the news anyway."

Howard looked at her gratefully, stood, shied into the coffee table, and followed her into the kitchen. Lewis came behind to refill his tumbler with Bourbon, this time adding ice. Howard was handing her the envelope.

"It doesn't work," he was saying, and Lewis stepped back to

the couch, flicking on the TV as he passed. "I couldn't get the end to say what I wanted."

Bright orange faces burst on and he twisted the dial until the comforting figure of Cronkite appeared. Lewis did not concentrate at first because he still could not quite believe that she had taken in Howard too, poetry and all, and he could hear her say, "Go on, you read it to me," and the sound of her knife chopping at something while Howard's voice broke with seriousness. Cronkite looked reassuring in spite of some grave matter of oil or bombing or whatever it was. Lewis turned up the voice.

Whenever he came to Annie's house in the evening he would turn on the news, but if he was not there, he did not miss it. Afterward he recalled very little, even though at the time he had been moved or angry. He had seen so many things happening there—men bouncing happily on the blank surface of a moon, the numbed faces of wounded children. During all of his country's conflicts he had been at the age to avoid being in the military, and he wondered if that was why the history of his times seemed so remote—it was all voices on the radio, pictures on television. He would rise to punch in the switch during the last commercial, his mind tugged and battered in so many directions, dizzied by the whirl of suffering lives, and then, as the dot of light vanished, her cluttered living room would take shape again in its lumped and familiar chairs and couch. The frying of bacon and liver in a sweet tang of onions would prove to him how hungry he was, and he would wonder if he should think about the things he had seen, do something, at least remember. But it seemed impossible. Perhaps he would find himself bitterly, abstractly fulminating over his heaped plate about the indifference of generals or bureaucrats, or, pouring his beer, he would see again the miraculous image of his own earth rising slowly above the bright, void rim of the moon, and then his life would slowly close over him again. Annie would lean across the table to pass something, her hair wisped loosely over her ears, face preoccupied with the careful motions of her hands, and he would reach as if through a great space to put his hand on her cheek, touching her puzzled expression.

Tonight he could not concentrate. An adviser to a department of something-or-other was talking about inflation in front of mammoth charts so simplified and pictorial that they reminded him of the displays of words on cardboard placards that his teacher had used for vocabulary lessons in second grade. He could not exclude the sound of Howard's voice even though the words were not clear. The tone was intense, and whatever the words were, they were recited much more slowly and evenly than Howard ever spoke. Annie had paused in her chopping. Her back was to him, bent slightly as she leaned on the counter as if she were looking down in fascination at whatever she had been knifing. Howard was out of sight against the wall near the doorway, but from time to time his lanky arm and splayed hand shot out, gestured, then retreated.

His voice stopped. Annie raised her head, held it back for a moment, then she whirled, smiling, her hands clasped together, her voice saying something, and suddenly there was Howard, the same awkward figure Lewis knew, hands stuffing some rumpled papers into his back pockets. Annie pecked him on the cheek. His arms shot out as if he were going to fall, and the pages drifted and scattered over the floor. She was laughing as she helped pick them up, and then she and Howard were out of view, her voice gaily embroidering his.

The face of the man on the screen was kind, and he was answering the interviewer hesitantly, as if he did not want to be sitting in that chair. It seemed to be his own home, and when the camera backed off slightly, a woman appeared beside him, sitting on the arm of the chair and watching as he talked.

"You say there was no warning?"

"None. After the noise and tumbling, I called out, no one answered, I heard my brother Arnold moan and then there were hours of silence except for some sifting and settling, and I didn't dare to move."

The camera cut away; the announcer, in front of a very glassy building, was explaining that this was the spot where forty years ago the tenement had collapsed and everyone had died except for Joseph and this was the anniversary of the passage of some important building codes. But Lewis could not stop thinking of the man's face, and he was glad when once again the camera returned to the room and Joseph was saying, "No, I don't think of the past. You have to go on. Strange, though. You think you've been through so much that you're ready for anything, but trouble's never the same."

Lewis looked away from the commercial, and the next segment did not interest him. Cronkite liked it, though, half smiling as he told Lewis that was the way it was, and Lewis leaned forward to snuff out the voices. Howard was standing in the doorway, clutching his envelope again.

"What about tomorrow, Lew?"

"What about it?"

"I'd like to help clean up. Or get the horses into the vans and all. I haven't found a job yet."

Lewis stood and stretched. "Then I'll see you there."

Annie opened the door and walked out onto the porch with Howard. When she returned, Lewis followed her into the kitchen.

"What was all that about?"

"If you're going to make fun, I'm not about to talk."

"Who's making fun? I just asked what the Walt Whitman bit was about."

The plate spun slightly when she put it down. He slipped into the chair that filled the small space between the refrigerator and the counter. Since he was curious, he gave up that tone.

"Is he any good?"

She sat too. There it was, one of his favorite dinners: liver fried crisp with bacon and onions, a big baked potato, and in the middle of the table a bowl of salad with her own Russian dressing. As he pressed his fork into the liver, so tender he did not have to use a knife, he looked at her gratefully. "That's damned good."

"Flip had it in special today."

They did not talk for a while. He cracked open the refrigerator to retrieve a beer and passed on half the contents to her.

"So? What do you think?"

"Of what?"

"Howard."

"How would I know if it's good poetry or bad? I like it, though. It's funny, some of it, but once in a while he'll read something that's just the way I've been thinking of it myself, or did a long time ago."

"What are they about?"

"Things he thinks about or sees. Sometimes even you."

Lewis grinned, mushed the melted butter around in the spread, soft potato. "Lewis Beede in a poem. Immortalized."

"Sure. Lewis Beede the midwife. Lewis Beede the hauler of horse dung. Lewis Beede taking a crap in the stall the afternoon Mrs. Whitworth came by to see the pretty horses."

He stopped chewing. "Who the hell gets the good parts in his poems?"

She smiled. "Howard Ryan. And Annie Strand."

"Double billing?"

"Now, don't make fun. I think Howard is in love."

"With you?"

"Sometimes with me. Often Elaine. Mostly women in general."

His fork rang against the knife when he put it down. "It's bad enough I've got to have him mooning around in the morning, dragged out because he's been up all night fondling himself, but now I've got to know he's plastering you all over the inside of his sticky head?"

She slid the rest of the liver onto his plate. "You never wrote me poetry."

"At his age I didn't need to. I didn't have to imagine it."

"Maybe all he needs is something real."

He used his knife and chewed slowly. "This piece has gristle."

She fetched another beer, pushed his half toward him. "Just spit it out."

"Don't you think he's a little young for you?" Even as she was speaking he had been thinking of that woman in the bus, her lithe body. What if she had stopped, pulled over, leaned to him eagerly? Unbuttoning her shirt. Tight cones of breasts. Her hands fumbling at him. *Teach me, teach me.*

"I can't believe it." She was looking at him, head to one side. "You really *are* jealous."

His face flared. "Hell, no. Unless you think I should be."

"I'm going to call you on this one, Lew. You're jealous because I pay attention to him, I take him seriously. Yes, and even like him."

He put his hands up. "Okay, okay. I'm sorry. His poems are beautiful. He sings like a dying swan. Truth is beauty and roses flower even in a dung heap. I believe."

She glared as if this could lead to one of their spats, and since Lewis had long ago come to see that what they argued about rarely had much to do with what was annoying them, he wondered what this was all about. But she laughed.

"Lewis, you've bred horses too much. Nobody's talking in your world. As soon as you turn your back, they've climbed onto each other and started humping, humping, humping."

He tried to be insulted, but he imagined his friends — Buddy quietly pumping the torn seats of the town snowplow, Howard fluffed into his scattering pillow.

"Let's try it." He stood and came over to her side of the table.

"Lew, for heaven's sake."

"It's humping time, it's humping time," and suddenly he was all over her, making mock thrusts while she giggled and wrestled. Her chair began to tilt. Lewis was too unbalanced to do anything about it, so that they were staring wide-eyed at each other, and then they were on the kitchen floor, tangled, sprawled, and laughing harder. Annie stopped so abruptly that he did too, even halting his hand that was thrust through the gap in her blouse. He saw the toed-in shoes, long legs, Howard's face looking down with shocked curiosity.

"I forgot my math book," he blurted out of the blaze of his face, holding the book up as if it were a dead cat and striding so quickly out of the room that he beat his shoulder on the wall. The door slammed.

She was staring at the ceiling, out of breath. "Oh, Lord. Now look what we've done."

"He'll get over it." Lewis started to withdraw his hand.

She shook her head. "I think the heroine just turned into a witch."

He kissed her on the neck. "Pretty witch." His hand moved back again.

"Are you staying the night?" she said in his ear.

"Might be back. Told Coleman I'd be over."

"Let's go upstairs."

He stood and helped her up. "I wonder if I'll ever act my age."

Her hand rose to his cheek. "Dear Lewis, there are some things I hope you'll never change."

He followed her up the narrow stairs.

"You lovely old fool," she said and turned out the light.

By the time he reached the driveway to the farm it was almost nine o'clock. The bright half-moon made the tin barn roof glow dully, and the field of stiff, dead hay almost looked like drifted snow, but the air had turned warm. The lights in the big house were blazing on every floor, and even as he passed the barn Lewis could hear voices pulsing, interrupting each other, and finally, as he stood on the porch, clearly angry. Phoebe. Coleman. Then both at once.

"I wouldn't if I were you." A voice came out of the dark angle of the porch. The heavy rocker cracked as someone moved. "Terrible time they're having. A real out-and-out. I've already been banished. Caught in the middle for a while. I can tell you, they gave me a mangling." Ron's hand moved into the light and lifted a glass.

"What's up?"

"Not a question of that, old boy. Everything's up. Like a bomb. Pieces still floating down. I say, she does this often, Phoebe? These tiffs with the old man? I mean, I thought I'd seen her mad, but this is something else. Remarkable."

During a lull Coleman began again in a controlled monotone, Phoebe swooped in at a high decibel level, and Coleman's voice began to rise toward hers.

"You see? End-of-the-world sort of stuff. Opera without a score. You simply don't talk to your father that way and vice versa without ripping up a lot of concrete."

"They're used to it."

"It's the end for me, I know that. A bit odd to sit and listen to one's own funeral service."

Lewis tried to see the man's face more clearly but only his waving hand, the upthrust toes of his shoes were caught fully by the light from the window.

"How so?"

"She'll have it in for me, won't she? There's her dad raving on the heath and disowning her and accusing her of every kind of filial lapse, and she's screaming back with every witch twitch she's ever learned, and it's simply got to be a standoff. Again. So it'll be a bad time in the outposts, old man. I'll have my balls flayed and served up for breakfast. And I'd forget the peaceful cribbage if I were you. But maybe Mr. White operates differently."

Lewis's distaste from the moment he had heard Ron's voice gathered strongly now, as if the figure hunched so laxly, obviously drunk, gave off a stench.

"Enjoy your breakfast," Lewis murmured and started to move away.

The man laughed smoothly. "Oh, I say. I didn't deserve that. Listen, why don't you slip around the back? Dotty Doris is there with the whiskey bottles. Pick up one and join me. We could have a good chat. Make our own sweet music."

"I'm going to check on things in the barn."

"What do you mean?" Coleman's voice came clearly through the open window where he stood now with his back turned. "You've never cared for anyone but your own self. Your mother . . . " and Phoebe shrilled with the precision of a high-speed drill, "Don't bring her into this. I tell you this is between us."

Lewis stumbled off the porch in his haste to be away from such clarity and into the known darkness of the barn, warm with animals hunched in their stalls, thickly fetid with the ripe, familiar smell of dung and urine and dusty hay. At the entrance to the barn Lewis had to swallow back against the tightness of his throat. By tomorrow only his own two horses would be there, and soon nothing. Never in his lifetime had this building been empty.

How often he had retreated to the horses—Shires, and Percherons, and even once some Clydesdales. The Whites had the money to care for them and keep up the breeds when all the country around and, as far as Lewis could tell, all the world were exchanging horses for engines and heavy machines that pressed the soil down harder and harder until the earth was demanding, like some addict, bigger and bigger machines. Foster, too, stubbornly adhered to the use of real horsepower on his small spread of fields, but his loyalty to horses was seen as fanaticism, and he railed against the tolerance shown to the Whites. They were rich, he would say, could afford to be eccentric, and the horse for them was a game. But Lewis came to see that was not entirely true; Coleman's love of the Percherons, that breed he finally settled on, was as deep as Foster's had been, although Coleman lived at a greater distance from them.

Often when he was young, Lewis had thought his father was closer to horses than to the people around him. He rarely spoke to his sons with the subdued affection that he could express as he harnessed his pair, stepping with impunity around their gentled hooves and drooping necks. He had chosen Lewis to pass on his lore to, day by day teaching him how to move and talk around them, how to persuade an untrained horse to accept the bits and bridles of a lifelong drudgery. Lewis had never seen his father "break" horses. He simply, firmly, with unwavering hands and voice, talked them into it all. Foster's choice of Lewis as apprentice had been as clear and rational and cruelly stated as so many of his decisions were; once he saw what he thought was right, Foster Beede could not deliver that vision with tact or kindness. At dinner one night he said, *I don't want you around the horses anymore, Elmore. You've no knack for it. It's Lewis has the touch.* Elmore flushed, stared hard at the slow pendulum of the clock on the mantel, and later that night they both heard their mother's berating voice. *You could have said it differently. Not like that.* The door slammed, the old Dodge spun its wheels and roiled off into the dark toward town.

He could tell by the attentive silences followed by shifting that the horses had sensed him entering, and he spoke in a low voice, touching a croup as he passed, until at the farther end of the light he came to Joker's stall. The old stallion's tail switched quickly, and in the dim interior his face turned back. Lewis moved slowly forward as if he were blind, feeling his way along the taut hide recently curried, from croup to coupling, loin to back and barrel, until with his hand on Joker's throatlatch he was staring at the unblinking, slightly rolled eye. Neck drooping, Joker was at ease, and he nickered as if he were muttering in his sleep. Lewis talked to those listless ears, not even thinking of what he was saying. It did not matter as much as the tone of voice, and Lewis was used to talking out loud to the animals while his mind went elsewhere. He had found that mode of conversation was useful not only with horses.

The other clear descendants in that barn of horses Foster helped to breed had been sold or had died, replaced by horses that Lewis thought were more worthy of showing than working. His father had been insistent. *Someday,* he had told Lewis, *they'll want real horseflesh again, to pull and drag, to turn and shear the earth and do all the things a damned puny man can't do on his own, and then they won't have any need for mincing, lazy-bred, high-strung nags that won't hardly lift a hoof unless there's a ribbon in sight.* Foster Beede's evangelical conception of the farm prevailed while he was there. No disagreeing with him was possible anyway. How often Coleman had told Lewis what Coleman's father had told him — how the first thing Foster did when he took on the job of caring for the Whites' horses was to look the old man in the face and say, *You can call these your horses to anyone you like, but between you and me, they're mine, and what I say goes. Or else I do.*

The old stallion nuzzled vaguely at Lewis's shirtfront. Running his hand along the crest, Lewis found a mat or two, would tell Howard tomorrow that he was tall enough to have reached there with the combs, and then he traced his way back along the horse to the aisle and sat on a crate. He had chosen Howard from a number of local boys who had applied to work with him. He was a natural at it, but had much more to learn. Howard had agreed to continue helping Lewis for a while without pay. *For the experience,* he had said. An occasional bat fluttered in the high lofts or swooped in from the distant doorway. There were fewer of them now. Most had hibernated.

Even if Lewis had a knack with horses, the talent was pale compared to his father's. As a young boy, Lewis had regarded with awe Foster's rapport with them, partly because he sensed a superstitious respect in the other men. He was seven when he saw his father lead into a barn a willful gelding someone had broken badly. In his fierce, low voice, Foster told everyone to leave, then closed the doors. The men stood around in the heat of the yard, glancing at each other, talking in low voices. Lewis was afraid. The horse had almost killed one of the hands that morning, kicking out with sheer malice as the man stooped to tighten a nut on the rake. Why weren't the men doing something, rushing the doors to drag his father out before it was too late? Suddenly in that dry and dusty silence, across the scorched ramp and yard where even a thistle could not grow in that summer's heat, they heard the sound of Foster's voice, not clear words, but a bagpipe's drone of incantation. On it went, and on, a sound Lewis would never forget, had heard echoed only in the stage voice of a performing hypnotist. Two hours later, Foster Beede came out, pale, drenched as if he had been plowing all day, but the horse that followed him, droop-necked, soaked from nose to croup in a lather of sweat, was even more exhausted. *Never again caused trouble,* Coleman liked to remember. *Broke his spirit in half, your father did.* Magic, the men called it. But Lewis's mother shrugged across the table. *Your father can talk a person to death if he wants to,* and since his father laughed, he and Elmore did too, but in admiration.

You take a toad and stab it, careful not to break any bones, Foster had said to them both one night as they sat on the porch, too hot to sleep. *And you put the body of the toad in an ant heap, and after a bit, when it's all reduced to bone and the moon is full, you take the bones and drop them in the river, and the one that floats upstream is your magic bone. You can stop any horse you want with that.* Hardly daring to breathe, the brothers had sat hunched on the stairs, and Lewis could clearly imagine the water of the dark, still pool by the bend in the clay banks, the shimmer of moon. The bone moved like the upturned belly of a fish, but against the slow downward drift; and who would ever have the courage to bend, hand out over the deep water, and grip the quivering power? In their room that night Elmore had said in hushed and frightened voice, *He was just pulling our legs. You know that,* and after a pause, *Wasn't he?* Both of them knew how the men shook their heads knowingly when Foster stepped down from the combine or disk to walk away, sometimes for a long interval, and the horses never moved forward.

Lewis stood, stretched, ambled down the aisle toward the door. He did not believe in all that now, those tales of jading and drawing substances, the witchcraft of a trade that mostly took skill and some intuitive sense. He had that. Howard did too, for all his gawkiness. He leaned in the doorway, shivered to cool air settling in the fields. Some lights blinked from the second story of the house as figures passed the windows. If he really intended to see Coleman, he had better go.

But there was a magic for Lewis. Not the kind men whispered of, but a sense of wonder that had never left him. Was it his earliest clear memory? He could feel hands under his armpits, hard forks of flesh lifting him up and up above the gnarled ground into an air of molten sunlight, past the great mound of animal, and then, blinded by light, he was taken even higher by other hands. In the gap of passage, before the second hands took hold, he seemed to float up. Then he was on the back of the animal, staring forward at the ragged crest, the sharp tents of ears, and the blazing world began to pass around him, green and gold and heaving with the effortless strides. All the magic of that world was gathered in the creature that deigned to bear him.

"Too late for our game, but come sit for a while." Coleman's voice came out of the porch, even darker now that most of the lights in the living room were turned off.

Lewis pulled the empty chair out from the wall and brought it closer to Coleman's leg stretched into an oblong of fallen light.

"Help yourself." The man leaned toward him with the bottle, an empty glass. "If you want ice, you'll have to brave Doris. She's fallen asleep at the kitchen table and I don't have the guts to wake her. She and her God are hard on me when Phoebe and I get to yelling. Did you talk to that brainless stud?"

Lewis swallowed, breathed out slowly. "Not brainless. Just a little numbed." He was uncertain why the sound of Coleman's voice irritated him and did not trust what that might make him do.

"Money says he'll be on the bus tomorrow."

They could hear her voice high over them. The words did not reach them but the tone was clearly angry. Coleman's free hand came down hard on the arm of his rocker. "Damn it. How long do you have to wait for your child to grow up?"

"Seems to me what she's doing isn't very playful."

"Who said anything about play? And you stay out of this. No, get into it. Hell, maybe if I hadn't been so old when she was born, I'd have brought her up better."

Lewis hoped his silence would help move the conversation to something more trivial.

"Why the hell can't I give up? I ought to throw her out on her bum, cut off her allowance, disown the bitch. Comes a certain point, and your child is just a person, someone you tolerate or don't, like anyone else. But damned if I don't want something from her, and I don't know what it is, and she must feel the same, because here we are still going at each other."

"She wants this place."

The hand waved. "I know that. But this place is only a thing. A piece of goods. And anyway, she can't have it."

"She acts like it's more than a thing."

Coleman leaned forward. "She's been talking to you. Are you taking sides?"

Lewis laughed sharply. "You kidding? I wouldn't wander around between you two. That territory's mined."

"Then what is it? How come she cares all of a sudden about this place?"

"She says she hasn't any other."

Coleman snorted. "She wouldn't if she had this either. She'd find that out in two weeks. That woman has no place because she carries a big blank around with her. She turns any place into no place."

"And what kind of place will this be after it's sold? What makes you think she'll do worse by it than anyone else? Come to think of it, isn't selling it off pretty selfish too?"

The figure drew back slightly. "Explain."

"You're tired of it all. You sell it. Well, what about her, what about the horses, the land itself? Me?"

"Oh, ho. I thought it was odd to hear you defend Miss Phoebe. Who's being selfish now?"

Because the blood mounted hotly into his neck, Lewis kept silent.

"Sorry, Lew. That wasn't fair. After I've had one of my bouts with her, I get mean. You know I'm worried about what will happen to you. I've always felt as much like a father to you as a friend. And I love this piece of land, this house — "

"Bullshit." To steady himself he poured more whiskey, but it slopped over. "Aren't you turning out to be like all the others? Summer folk. Buy the best pieces of land, put up houses that five families in this town could live in but not one will ever step foot into except to dust or fix the pipes or cook, and you come up when the weather's good, bitch when it rains too much for the tennis, then sell it off to another rich bugger when you get tired of it."

He was breathless, surprised by the venom of his own words.

When he spoke, the old man's voice was strangely calm. "Most of what you say's true, Lewis. We both know that. I'm not going to try to argue about how the Whites have not been that way. But maybe it all adds up to the same thing." He paused, and the hand that crossed into the patch of dim light gestured loosely. "You know, you sounded just like your father."

Shut up, Lewis, shut up, he was saying to himself, staring hard at the distant barn light as if to hold on to it. But he could not.

"Could be I'm beginning to see how he was right in many ways, how for the sake of your own pride or some independence you should never forget certain differences."

"Damn it, Lew. We've never denied we were different. But that doesn't mean we couldn't understand each other, help each other out. What your father was doing came out of something else. More like hate. For everyone, almost everything. You understood that better than I did."

He laughed bitterly. "Understood. I don't know what I really understood or what I had to make up to get by, or what I might have come to understand if he hadn't run away, if you hadn't come between us."

The dull shock told Lewis he had done something he would not want to remember.

"I'm sorry, Coleman. I don't know why I said that. It's not the truth, at least in the sense of your doing that on purpose. If you came between us, I put you there, needed you there."

"Thank you. Lord, what a night it's been." He did not speak for a while, his glass held in two hands and head bowed as if seeing something in the drink itself. "Do you recall, Lewis, how it was when Phoebe was a child — Lena and Phoebe and myself, when we'd be here all the summer long? Of course I'd come and go. Busy in those days. Convinced I was making money in some important way, better way. She came late for us, you know, a hard birth for Lena, full of worry because of her age, and then she was so perfect, a whole and lovely child when she was born. Do you know, from the beginning Phoebe and I were always very close, closer than she was to her mother. We went to England once together when I had business. Just Phoebe and myself because Lena hated to travel, hardly even liked driving to here. She was nine then. We stayed in London and had rooms adjoining, and every night we'd leave the door open between us so she could hear me walking around, and if she dreamed, I would be there to hear her call. She had such awful nightmares, even when she was young." He paused. "I can't remember when it was we started yelling at each other. Or why. It came to be a habit." He looked up. The face was not turned directly to Lewis but stared beyond him into the yard.

"I'm dying, Lewis." He paused again, not as though expecting a response, but gathering his thoughts. "I had not intended to tell you that, but it's been growing in me how that wouldn't be fair."

"What do you mean?" Lewis was shrinking away into a clear, cold wish that the man were not saying these things.

"How? Hodgkin's. That's simple. There was that operation last winter, and some treatments, and they didn't lie to me. It didn't work. The worst is coming soon." The face did turn now, but both the voice and expression were calm. "Pray it'll be quick, Lewis. I'm seventy-eight, and ready to go, if anyone can be, but I hate pain. I'm not the least bit brave."

"She knows?"

Coleman shook his head. "She will in due time. I told her the doctors said the treatments were working."

"She ought to be told."

"I don't want any phony truces."

Lewis swallowed hard against a new swell of anger. He was angry at Coleman for his unreasonable pride, almost as if for a moment Lewis had become Phoebe, could feel the demand such silence represented, an unbending need to be loved freely but so unremittingly asked that no free gesture was possible, angry that Coleman would have told him about his illness so that now he had to look at him as disappearing irrevocably. Finally there was an anger that took in everything he could touch or recall in that world around them — the hunched figure of the man, the half-dark house, those unknowing animals asleep or shifting in their stalls, his parents' lost child, his own, the chill air settling toward the bedrock of winter, anger at the spirit that held all that and always tore back the ordered surface of the day.

"God damn it." Lewis threw down his drink. He walked through the shattered glass onto the lawn and stood there until he heard Coleman's footsteps on the porch, the screen door slapping shut.

5

Buddy lifted his can of beer, leaning back in the rickety chair. "I know your father wanted you to take that buck. When Jim got it, I thought Foster was going to blast you."

"Instead he took Jim hunting next season again."

"That was like your dad."

Lewis laughed abruptly and shoved a stick of wood into the stove. "You mean because he wanted to let me know how inept I was? He wouldn't take *me*."

"He was kinda pissed."

The pewter sky pressed down on the cabin. All day Moonstone had faded more and more grayly. Buddy leaned forward, fumbled in the wide pockets of his stiff jacket, and extracted another beer. "Sure you won't?"

"No thanks."

"I wouldn't have another if I didn't know the day was over for me." He glanced at his gun where it stood against the wall. "Shit, I can't see how I missed him. I swear, Lew, ten points at least. If I'd fired right off instead of trying to sidle around that goddamn thorn bush, I'd at least have clipped him and had a good trail to follow."

He pulled back the ring with a hiss, took a mouthful, and held it for a moment before swallowing. "Beer is the best stuff the human race ever invented."

Lewis expected to see friends from town on the weekends of hunting season. Buddy always stopped by late in the afternoon after a day of tracking. Lewis's land had some of the best hunting, mostly because of the old apple groves, and since it was back from the road and steep in places, only the best hunters came, and always local. They would chat politely for a while, a quiet way of thanking Lewis. But it was not asking permission. They all agreed that no one owned some aspects of the land, and when the summer people posted it, their houses suffered.

"You gotta admit it surprised the hell out of all of us to find Jim Strand was that good with a gun."

"I guess we didn't think anyone could learn to hunt in Arkansas." Once Buddy started remembering something he was bound to wring out all the details, so Lewis considered having a beer after all.

"We should've known when he brought along that gun. It must have been handed down by his dad to him."

Jim Strand, his sister, and his mother had moved back to Judson after his father had died. Jim had been their age, but born and brought up in Arkansas because Mrs. Strand had moved there when she married Carl. Jim had come into tenth grade tall and shy, with an accent hard for them even to mock, and his limbs were so elbowed and gangling that it was not his punches that won him the first few fights but the random flailing of limbs that kept any blows from landing. When Foster had offered that fall to take Lewis and some of his friends hunting, he had done so expecting Lewis would show them all how well he had been taught.

"Ever tried that place on Moonstone again?" Buddy circled the contents of his can to check how much was left.

"Dad and Elmore and I did." He paused. "And Dad and I took that big buck out."

Buddy nodded. "It won. You beat out Jim that year."

"What the hell, Buddy. That's what we said. Dad shot it."

Buddy let the front legs of his chair come down hard on the floor. "I'll be damned."

"That's what I meant about him being angry. He took out Jim the next fall to look him over, get an idea how good he really was. Made Jim feel he was doing it because he thought he was the best shot around. I even think he taught him a few things to make sure he was, and Jim never knew the difference, always liked my dad. The year after that he told Elmore to stay home and he took me out and we walked those woods until we found the tracks of the biggest buck you could imagine."

"I recall old Vince had to jack up the bar on the hanger to keep the carcass from dragging on the ground."

"I'll take one of those beers."

Buddy grinned, reached down, and pulled out two more. He opened both and handed one to Lewis. "Sometimes I think I don't nail my buck anymore because the cans get to clunking in my pocket."

Lewis swallowed two big mouthfuls, then held back against the belch. The beer was still cold. "I woke early, and when I went out to piss, that buck was moving along beyond the birch grove, upwind. I thought, shit, I'll show the old man something. He wasn't awake yet. I got my gun, hardly had to walk back more than ninety feet. Had a shot clear as day. I was too eager. I missed."

"Doesn't sound like you."

How could he make Buddy understand those two years of living with Foster's disgust that *a weak sister, mama's boy, son-of-that-fuckhead Carl Strand* could beat him out. It was just a good tall tale for Buddy.

"If you think you'd seen Dad angry, you missed what it could really be like. When he was that angry, he didn't speak or hit you or anything. We went off tracking, walked around up there for seven hours. It was about dark when we saw him again. He didn't say a word. He reached over, took my gun, and dropped that buck with one shot. 'You shot him,' he said when he handed it back to me."

"Wouldn't some folks have been surprised to hear that?"

"You can still see the record. Jake's got those old plaques hanging up down at the Bear."

Lewis looked up and saw Buddy staring at him and he could tell he did not have to warn him he would still prefer nobody else knew, did not have to describe for him how he could, in the middle of a long evening over too much Bourbon, look up to the wall in that barroom and be baffled by a twist of sorrow and anger. Sometimes he wished he had found the courage to tell Jim Strand before he died.

They both heard the crack and echo of a distant shot, and Buddy said quietly, "Sonnabitch. I bet old Howley got my buck."

He walked stiffly to the window, his brace rattling, and leaned on the table as he looked out.

"Sounded pretty low on the ridge, though." Lewis was used to judging the origin of sounds that ricocheted in odd ways around his valley.

"Look at that." Buddy was smiling when he returned. "Snow at last. By Jesus, there'll be an hour of good tracking before dark. I'm going to get me my buck." Already he had his gun, was buttoning his jacket. "S'long, Lew. Obliged for the heat."

"Don't get lost."

Although Lewis knew that area as well as any human being could since he had tramped it for nearly forty years, he had no doubt that Buddy and some of the other people in town knew it just as well. He stood at the window and watched him limp slowly down the bank, along the side of the pond, rifle crooked carefully on his arm, face down, looking for tracks. Often Lewis would glance up from the table in the early morning or evening and see a deer amble cautiously onto the rim of the pond, then down for a drink, especially in spring when the grass in the clearing would grow earlier than in the forest.

The snow did not even tick when blown against the window, fading the scenery into a grainy blur. Starting that fine, it would continue, in an hour or so falling so thickly that after he walked to the outhouse and back, Lewis would shake off clouds of it, surprised again how something so insubstantial could cover him in such a short time. There would be no real twilight, only the afternoon glow snuffed into darkness.

He opened the door and stood there. The air was steely damp. The touch of the snow brought out every last odor of the season: the must of long-fallen leaves, the rotting boards of the cabin, even some faint hard fragrance he associated with wet stone. The snow, which had no odor of its own, heightened any that was there, pressing it out before the long, harsh freeze would kill all smells except that tang of ice or the sweet smoke of his own maple logs. He breathed in and out slowly, letting the room fill with cold, fresh air. He closed his eyes, listened to the hiss of wind, the swirl of the brook. The first snow, almost more than spring, made him feel things were starting all over again, fresh and new.

When he opened his eyes he saw a figure far off at the edge of the clearing where the trail came out of the woods. The human shape, muffled in parka and boots, was so blurred by the snow and dimming light that Lewis could not even be certain if it had a gun. The figure stepped forward, paused, then plunged back into the woods.

Lewis shivered and swung the door shut. He loaded on more wood. The person must have wanted to use the last light hunting rather than waste it on talking with him. He turned up the wick, lit a lantern, and hung it from the hook on the rafter. He would split wood tomorrow. The snow would stop, probably cold, clear air would fall on them from the north, and he could work in the still dazzle of clean snow. Annie might have come up that afternoon, but instead had gone off to the Flatts for some appointment he could not clearly recall. He could walk down now, carrying his snowshoes in case he needed them the next day. But there were evenings and nights when he coveted his solitude, and he would sit as he did now at the table facing out the window, his back to the hot, drying iron of the stove, at peace in a way he never could be in anyone else's presence. He wondered how some of the people he saw could stand being so closely surrounded by others — wife, children, relatives, even neighbors whose houses pushed up close, the sounds of their lives filling the narrow spaces between. He yawned, made sleepy by the close, warm air, and let his head sink onto his arm.

He woke with a start, his forehead numbed where it had been lying hard on the bone of his wrist. The window reflected his wide-eyed face in the vague motion of descending snow. He was certain a loud noise had waked him — a shot? or merely a log tumbling against the side of the stove? His feet were cold and the fire was almost out. He had begun to turn when a sharp rap came on the door as if someone had smashed a small, hard object against it, the same sound a rat's head would make when his father swung it against the stall door, making sure the trap or poison had done its work. Again. But this time more insistent, repeated rapidly. A voice.

He opened the door, the snow bit his face, driven parallel by the new, harsh wind, and a whitened figure stumbled around him. He closed the door quickly. She was so covered with snow that it slid off in chunks, melting and spreading out on the boards.

"Who is it?"

She threw back the hood, began to unbutton the parka, and he recognized the tightly swept-back hair and thin face of the woman who had given him a ride.

"What are you doing here?"

She was shivering. In spite of her parka, the high leather boots, her clothes were soaking. She had dropped her coat and it sagged like a slowly deflating balloon.

"I'm lost."

Her arms were held stiffly at her sides but slightly out, as if she might have to catch her balance, and all the time she stared at him almost without blinking.

"How the hell could you have wandered so far from the road? I don't remember your name."

"Miriam. I wasn't lost before the dark came. Then I was. For a while."

He laughed. "And now you're not really lost, just a little lost?"

She opened her mouth, snapped it shut. He had started moving toward her parka to put it near the stove when her voice stopped him by its abruptness.

"I'm not lost at all. I know exactly where I am. I came here directly the way I was told, and I had planned to come in earlier, but when I reached the place where I could see your cabin, I couldn't go on. I tried to go back. That was when I got lost. I chickened out."

For a moment he was certain she was crazy. Her face was so set, yet she was breathing as if she had been running hard. What would he do if this strange young woman cracked on him?

"I'm your daughter." Her fists opened with a jerk.

"My what?"

"Your daughter."

"I don't have a daughter."

Her laugh was more like a shiver. "They told me it's never the way you imagine. I'm supposed to say, 'Here I am, Dad, your long-lost child,' and you're supposed to say, 'Oh, my beloved little girl,' or something like that, and we all fall together in a heap of happy tears. Right?"

With the mention of tears she looked watery-eyed but not happy.

"Long-lost child?"

"Stop it. Don't keep repeating it like that. Don't make me feel this is a dream or something I made up."

"I have to sit down." Lewis walked to the table.

She moved close to the stove, suddenly much calmer, and took a deep breath. "Sorry. I should be worrying about you. Please don't have a heart attack. Do you mind?" and she opened the stove door, slipped two pieces of wood onto the coals.

His heart *was* pounding heavily. She slapped the door shut with her foot, then sat gingerly on the edge of the woodbox, as close to the stove as possible.

"I had a child."

"I *am* that child." She continued to stare. Even that far away she pressed on him.

"Prove it." He spoke as if driving in a stake hard.

"Documents, you mean? Birth certificates, adoption records? They're in my car. I'll show them to you when you want. *If* you want. That's the point. I'm here to give you a choice, although an hour or so ago I changed my mind and almost went back to where I was earlier in the fall, deciding to forget the whole thing and drive away. I've left Judson and come back three times already. After all, we've both gone all this way without each other." She looked down at her feet. "But I got lost. The dark came sooner than I thought."

He could find nothing to say.

"Do you understand? I'm saying I am your daughter, put up for adoption, who wanted to find you, find her mother. I have at

73

least half of that wish. But it isn't all for me to decide. I can try to walk away if you want it that way."

She snapped off the rubber band that held her ponytail and shook her head, letting her hair fall around her face and shoulders. The ends were wet and straggled together.

"I don't know what to believe," Lewis said slowly. Her face was turned down slightly. Looking hard at her, he could see nothing of himself or Monica, and certainly no emotion was aroused in him other than confusion and a growing irritation. "You might be someone who found out about my past and want to hurt me in some way."

She smiled slightly. "So far you're batting one thousand. You're running straight through every reaction they said you would."

"Sorry to be so predictable."

"Don't worry. I've had years to get used to all this, to imagine it in a hundred different ways. Haven't you ever?"

"What?"

"Imagined finding me, meeting me." But she did not wait for an answer. "You can't believe the sense of power I had this fall when I first picked you out and began following you around. I would sit somewhere when I knew some of your routines, like when you would go to the P.O., and I'd watch. I'd say, 'That's my father, Dad, Daddy, Pop,' making up a thousand ways to come at you, imagining every kind of reaction. For a while it was so exciting that I realized I could get fixed on it. I could have bought a house here, stayed, gotten to know you, and never told."

He was beginning to calm. "Please tell me something to make me certain."

"Are you always this cool? Well, you got there much faster than they said you would. That was supposed to take days."

"Who are *they*?" He was troubled to think she might have been asking questions around town. Did other people know about all this before he did?

"Counselors trained to help people like me know what to expect, how to go about this. In spite of all that, I've done a lot of it wrong, and I guess I'm lucky you didn't just shut down and boot me out. They say that happens, and it's worse than if you never tried to find your parents. My lawyer who traced you down was worried I might get in legal trouble. He knows I'm not careful. Or discreet."

Lawyers, agencies, counselors — the terms bore in on him more and more coldly.

"You could sue, you know."

"For what?"

She was appraising him carefully as if he really might sue. "There are laws that make it very hard for someone like myself to see records. The way the lawyer obtained my papers wasn't entirely legal. Luckily, he's the kind of lawyer who gets angry about things like that. I almost think he wants to be sued, wants to test those laws." Her voice was getting tighter as she spoke, and he jumped slightly when she threw up her hands and shook her head violently. "Jesus, it makes me mad. Why should they protect the parents that way? What protection did I have when I was hours old and you gave me up? What rights did I have?" She ran her hands back through her hair and breathed deeply. "Sorry."

"I'm not the suing kind."

"Is my mother?"

"I wouldn't know."

"By which I guess you mean you haven't seen her recently."

"How old are you?"

"I told you. Twenty-four."

"It's been about that long."

She shook her head again. "You really are something, aren't you? Just cut it off and walk away."

"You didn't prove who you are yet."

She sighed. "How's this. I was born in New York City, Columbia-Presbyterian hospital. My mother's name was falsely given at first on the hospital records, but she was forced to give her true name on the adoption papers. And you were John Doe. That must have been the price for such an easy way out. Her name was Monica Kramer."

He stood, and turning his back on her, he leaned with his elbows on the high windowsill by the door. His head was only a dark outline on the glass through which he could look onto the blurred mounds of white. The name so simply and clearly uttered had driven down into him, and he had to turn away. In all those years he had never heard that name spoken except by his own mind.

"I wish I had memories. I wish I were some mad genius who could claim to recall the womb, like Salvador Dali does. Do you know I even tried hypnosis? Some kook in the commune where I was living said he was hypnotized into remembering the taste of his mother's milk. I had this crazy idea that I would see her face, maybe yours. What bullshit."

If he glanced to one side he could see her dim reflection in the lower pane of glass. He breathed deeply, opened his palm flat on the bare skin of his arm. "My child would not have seen me in its head. I never saw it, knew nothing except that it was born, was given away. When Monica came back from the hospital she would not tell me more than that."

Her voice was more shrill. "It? What do you mean *it*? Me. I'm a person."

"All right. You."

"That's better." She pulled her hair back again from her face. "You know, because you were John Doe I had you pegged as someone very important whose identity had to be kept quiet. Like Frank Sinatra or John Kennedy."

"Disappointed?" He still did not turn.

"Not yet. Even unadopted kids imagine they had different, famous parents, and not the real, dull ones they have. It used to drive me crazy when my friends would talk as if they wished they were adopted. But anyway, I figured I was lucky to find you at all. At first we wondered if you were just a fly-by-night. If you hadn't been her only companion then, you would have been impossible to trace down. And you haven't moved as much as she has."

He could hardly listen to her, but when the silence came, it seemed to last longer than he could bear. The fire flapped against logs and stove, the snow billowed at the window, and suddenly into that absolute space he recalled for the thousandth time, but this time as though his present flattened palm were there, the lurch of an unborn foot against the taut belly's skin as he and Monica lay in the dark room with the knowledge that this was all he would ever know of that being formed by their own groping and stubborn cells.

He turned. She was staring at the floor, her mouth open slightly, breath held. He thought he would reach out to her, but he could not, as if seeing her so clearly again filled him with disbelief. Every kind of question swarmed at him. She was groping in her pocket for a handkerchief.

"Excuse me." She sneezed in three short bursts like a cat, then blew her nose.

Lewis went to his bunk and began pulling out boxes, burrowing into the piles of old clothes. The smell of his own sweat, of mildew, of woodsmoke and dust rose, and he paused, his arms deep into them.

"What are you doing?"

"You'll need some dry clothes."

He heard her walking over, standing behind him.

"That would be nice."

"They won't fit."

"Dry will do fine."

"And nothing's very clean."

She did not answer, and so he turned slowly to see her standing above him. He looked back into the box and leaned on his hands. She knelt beside him.

"What is it?"

He shook his head.

"Tell me."

He sat back on his heels. What he disliked most of all was the panic. If he could only bolt. He had no idea what to do and was ashamed to think she could see that. She frowned slightly, her lips severely pursed.

"You believe me, don't you? Tell me that."

"I think I do. But I'm too confused."

Having admitted that, he found that he could take the simplest and more practical motions. They selected clothes and he turned his back to tinker with the stove, finding her soon in front of him, a long-haired clown in search of a rope or string to hold up the impossible hoop of pants. They draped her own clothes over the rafters, discussed which bunk would be best for her, began to sort some food, which finally gave him an excuse to pluck the bottle from the shelf and pour himself a tumbler of whiskey. He offered her some. She looked at the empty glass, then nodded dubiously.

"I don't drink much. I wish to hell I could reach my car, though. I left my stuff there."

"Stuff?"

"I only smoke a little, nothing worse."

"I have a lot to get used to, don't I?"

"Slowly."

He took a full mouthful, let the heat gather on his tongue, swallowed. "It's a pretty fast pace so far."

But only later, after he had snuffed the lantern, groped quickly out of his clothes, and pulled the blankets around him, did he realize how tense he had been all evening in spite of the whiskey he downed by the glassful. All the time he had felt as if he were someone else watching himself, and suddenly the cabin was very small.

The fire cast flecks of light on ceiling and floor. She lay still in the bunk that butted against his at right angles, their feet almost touching. In the familiar darkness, the muscles in his shoulders and back began to ease.

"Don't worry if you hear me at night. I'll have to put more wood on the fire. Annie tells me I'm actually asleep when I do it."

She did not answer for a moment, then said, "Is Annie the woman who has the white house at the end of the street?"

"Yes."

"Why aren't you married?"

"She was."

"But she isn't now? Never mind. Don't answer that yet. Will you tell me when you can? Are you the kind of person who needs questions?"

"As long as I don't have to answer all of them."

"I am. I never tell anyone anything, but if they ask, I can't stop. I think it's because I don't really believe that anyone cares about me, and when they do, I want to take advantage of it. Of course, sometimes I find out they really didn't care at all. Did you build this palce?"

He laughed. "You're hard to keep up with."

"I'm sorry. Sometimes I'm surprised my mouth can keep up with my mind. It's like jumping stones across a river. You fall in if you don't keep moving. I can't hold back anymore now. I did all evening, you know."

"I built it. Only the first time I did, it was very different. My father and I built that one, mostly me, although he helped lug the stuff up on the sledge in winter with the horses. We had to put huge pads on their feet to keep them from going through the snow. That cabin was for our hunting. For Dad and me and my brother, Elmore, or sometimes Dad only. He really preferred to hunt alone. After he left and we knew we couldn't keep the farmhouse, and I was going to go off to be an actor, I built it into a permanent place to live. I had this idea that I'd be so good I would leave New York every summer and come back here to stay, like the summer people I'd seen all my life."

"You did come back to stay."

"With a vengeance."

He waited in the brief silence. Talking began to seem easier, even pleasant, and he remembered how sometimes he and Elmore would ramble on late into the night when they were young, Elmore's voice coming muffled from the mattress of the upper bunk.

"Can you tell me about my mother? About you and my mother? Or is that too hard?"

"I never have."

"To anyone?"

"To no one."

"Not your brother? Not Annie?"

"No one."

"That must be lonely."

"I'm used to it."

"Did you know her for long? Have you heard from her since? No. Start where you want. I'll be quiet."

He closed his eyes. *Once upon a time there was a young man who thought he would be great.* But he held back for a moment longer. If he could not keep it simple, honest to whatever he might remember, he would quit.

"I'd been to New York before. But always with other people. I went down with my American history class from high school. Once my uncle took Elmore and me and we went to see a baseball game. The Yankees won, of course. That was during the war.

79

Uncle Cecil got very drunk one night and Elmore and I snuck out of the hotel and wandered around. It was dark because of blackouts, and we thought we were being brave and adventurous. We stole into a movie and watched Japs getting blown to bits and then went back to the hotel. I remember even thinking, 'Well, this is a snap. Big city, phooey. I can handle it.' "

Lewis put his hands behind his head and glanced toward her. The pale oval of her face was turned to him. He rolled back and watched the wavering stripes of light on the ceiling.

"When you're twenty, you think you can do anything. At least I did. Maybe other people helped me believe that. Anyway, I had two suitcases, a little money from the sale of our house from a man named Coleman White who my father had worked for. He promised to send more when I let him know I needed it. I guess it was about three months before I wrote him. Called, actually. I was flat broke. He understood right away how hard that call was, and from then on the money came regularly, every two weeks. No questions asked. Which was just as well. I had a job for a while, didn't pay well, a small apartment, and eventually some help from your mother. She had her own money. I had school expenses, too."

"School?"

He swallowed. Was it so hard, then, to remember and say all that? He was not getting it right. He was imposing a tone, a direction that was not true to the confusion and ignorance, even the seriousness. But he could not stop. Even as he spoke, surprised that his voice kept going, he felt as if a great wind were pushing him forward, arms and legs flapping loosely in undetermined space.

"Nothing was as easy as I had expected. Anyone could have told me that, if I would have listened. You don't just leap onto Broadway strutting and gesturing and saying, 'Here I am, take me while you can.' I stood in line with all the others, I blew my chances like ninety-nine percent of them did too. I learned soon that any part worth having went to actors coming over from agencies. I saw the impossible happen, though, just enough to let me believe, and the time I was most impressed was when I stood in line with a woman and we talked as we moved up. She told me about this school she'd been to, and how all the people getting jobs had been there at one time or another, and I said, hell, I didn't need that kind of book learning, I wanted experience, and then I saw her come out and she said, 'I got it,' I went in, was turned down after reading three sentences, and she hadn't walked even two blocks before I caught up to her and asked her again for the address to the school. And her apartment."

"She was Monica Kramer?"

"No. She gave me the address, but not to her apartment. Christ, I was lonely."

He paused. He should tell her that the last loneliness was worse — after he and Monica separated, when he spent those bitter months back in this cabin feeling nothing but his abject failure and retreat, before those days of coming and going from Judson, driving to any city, working when he could for a month or two. He had forgotten until now those late afternoons in their nearly empty apartment in New York, a winter sun that never reached his windows visible in the last yellow rectangles high on a neighboring apartment building.

"That all changed for me when I met Monica."

"How?"

"I was less lonely. Not lonely at all for a while."

"I mean, how did you meet?"

"You're sure you want to know all this?"

"I do."

"I worked as an all-night bellman. The only thing good about the job was I could usually get two meals, one when I came on at eleven and another after I quit at seven in the morning. I got on well with the cook, who liked to hunt and had been up around here a few times. But the pay was bum, and I was supposed to make that up in tips. Sometimes I'd do all right. I learned to stand around the room after I'd handed over the key, to stare and look mean and make people want to pay something to get rid of me."

"You're not telling me about Monica Kramer."

He turned on his side, laughed. "Yes I am. I carried her suitcases up to her room. She arrived late, one or two in the morning. It was January, a big snowstorm, trains delayed. She had come from Chicago."

"What for?"

"To visit."

"Friends?"

"To get away from Chicago, or some suburb of Chicago. She never named it. Refused to, I should say."

"Winnetka."

"What else do you know?"

"Not much. She was an only child. Her parents both died ten years or so after I was born. There are no known surviving relatives."

"She hardly ever spoke of her parents. Mostly she talked about the boredom of the place she lived and how she wanted to, but couldn't, leave."

"Wait. Begin at the beginning. You carried her bags."

"I carried her bags. I had a small couch by the phone behind a pillar where my station was. The couch was too small to sleep on comfortably, they made sure of that. But you could doze. So I was only half-asleep when I came to the front desk. She was very awake, very angry."

"At what?"

"Trains. Weather. Cabdrivers. Ready to be angry at anything. So when I took us to the wrong floor and we had to go back and wait for the elevator to come up to us again, she began to transfer a little onto me. Then they'd given me the wrong key at the front desk. That wasn't my fault, but it might as well have been. I fetched the new key, and when I came back she was sitting on the suitcases with her shoes off. She wouldn't speak to me. I let us in, lugged in the suitcases, made sure the heat was on, the lights working."

"She tipped you?"

"More than she should have. 'Look,' she said, 'do me a favor. Just look over the register and tell me if this guy is checked in.' I can't remember the name. She was nervous. I was supposed to call her."

"Was she beautiful?"

Lewis stopped, already in his mind downstairs at Mrs. Maynard's switchboard checking through her list. "Beautiful?" He tried, pressing his eyelids tightly shut, to recall those first images of her, but they were too layered with other blurred scenes—Monica at the railway station in her spring dress, returned from Illinois forever, she said; Monica stepping out of the shower in their narrow bathroom in a cloud of steam, laughing as he held on, her warm, wet body soaking his bathrobe. "Yes. She had large bones, big cheekbones. I was always surprised when I stood close to her how small she really was."

"Did you stand close to her soon?" There was no mockery in the voice.

"Not that night, if that's what you mean, although much sooner than either of us probably expected. But wait. You're going even faster than we did."

"I'm sorry. The name on the list."

"Not there. I called her back. She said, 'Oh, damn,' and hung up. Half an hour later my phone rang and she was asking for a drink. I said the bar was closed. She'd been traveling often enough to know what a good night bellman can do for you. 'Oh, come on,' she said. 'How much?' I was charging ten bucks for a bottle. So she asked how much a drink and I told her a buck, and she said she'd start there."

"Steep prices."

"I told you the wages were poor. You had to make it up. Besides, I didn't get all of it. Some of it went back to the bar. It was something Ricky and I had worked out."

"Did she drink it all?"

"She was into her third when she bought the bottle, but I don't think she finished it. I brought it up, and some ice, and she was in her bathrobe, her hair down. She put a bed between us. I didn't have any intentions, but she wasn't taking chances. I did ask if she wanted company, told her I didn't want to go back to sleep. To tell the truth, I wasn't too eager to stay. She had seemed pretty mean to me. I wasn't feeling much like holding someone's hand, which is usually what happened into the third drink or so. I had enough troubles of my own then."

"Other women, I suppose."

"More that I didn't have money. But mostly I couldn't face talking to anyone about what I was doing because by then I knew I was no good."

"At acting?"

He grunted, surprised how hard it was to admit even now. "I knew she'd want more than one drink. I didn't want to have to keep coming up. She looked dubious, so I said, 'Look, you can

83

keep the bottle, I'll be on duty at eleven tomorrow night. Pay me what you owe me then.' She ignored that, said, 'You won't make a pass at me?' I really hadn't considered it until she said that, but I said no, and she told me to sit down."

"I bet you did make a pass."

He laughed. Her inferences about his ways with women both pleased and embarrassed him. "No. I watched her lap up half the bottle at least. It made her a little nervous at first that I wouldn't have a drink too, but she got used to that soon. I hated the feeling of having to walk around at five-thirty, empty in the gut, old booze burning holes there. She was a good talker, had me telling about myself too. I was afraid she'd be a sad case of some sort, like some of the others."

They were silent. Everything began to slow down in his mind, a reluctance dragging at his words before he could say them. When the logs settled with a thump, her feet started, then eased back against the end of his bunk.

"But she was unhappy, wasn't she? She must have been to want to drink like that. Who was the man?"

"Someone she was having an affair with. He was married and lived where she did and was well enough known so that they couldn't meet in Chicago. But she already had suspected he wouldn't show, and she knew that meant he never would again, that his wife and kids had won. Half of her wanted to celebrate the end of it."

"And all you did was talk that night?"

"I liked her more and more. She was spunky. She decided to do some things in New York anyway. Stay a few days. Have fun. I ended up telling her about myself. She was interested. Had always liked acting herself, although she'd spent more time with music. Voice lessons. I asked her to sing. She laughed, said maybe someday when I knew her well enough to forgive the ear damage. The phone rang. Front desk was mad as hell at me, Mrs. Maynard said. She was a nice old lady, and I always told her where I was going if I thought it would take time. So I had to go."

"You did that sort of thing often?"

He waved a hand in air as if she could see it. "That's one of the big differences between the night bellman and being on during the day. In the day you're just carrying bags around, hustling up meals and newspapers. At night you're keeping people afloat."

"That wasn't much of a first night." She sighed. "I can see we're going to have to talk a lot if I'm going to understand."

He leaned up slightly on his elbows. Suddenly he recalled the incredible surprise of Monica's slim, small body when three nights later he sat on the same side of the bed with her and she did not turn aside his wandering hands.

He lay back, closed his eyes. "Understand? Who ever does? Anyway, I apologized that night."

"Why?"

"For not making a pass. I felt bad about it. Said even if she had made me promise not to, it wasn't right, given the way I felt. She laughed, said, 'Some other time.' And that was it."

He rose, went to the stove, and shoved in two more logs. He was very tired, his tongue heavy as iron, and a dead taste in his mouth.

"Then what?"

He tucked his blankets around himself and said slowly, "To be continued."

"Sleep now?" she murmured and in her voice there was relief, so he wondered: Had she long ago wanted to stop but been trapped into listening? Lord, how he had run on, and what was the point of it? Worse than that, there had to be something very wrong with your life if you could come so close to describing to your daughter the first time you laid her mother.

"Sleep."

"Good night." Her pale head lifted for a moment. "Are you Father, or Dad, or Pop, or what?"

Everything sounded peculiar. "We'll think about it."

After a brief silence he heard her turn sharply. "Did you ever try to find me?"

"No."

"I was afraid you'd say that."

At first his mind would not let go. But it must have done so with the abruptness of a fist unclenching because when he woke, as he almost always did to the increased chill of the air as if his body were the stove's thermostat, and moved quietly to the wood-pile, then lifted the door slowly off its latch, he sensed how deeply beyond dreams his sleep had gone, so far away that he had to look quickly toward the other bunk to be certain she was there. His waking thoughts began again slowly from where he had left them, so practical and ordinary that he was certain the evening had not been a dream. Did she mean to stay, live there, move in? There was not enough room. It was all very well to discover you had a daughter, and if she wanted to visit from time to time, of course she would be welcome. He would try to find that out soon. Her intentions. Surely she did not expect his whole way of life to change. But on the other hand, she seemed in the past weeks to have had nothing else to do but hang around Judson, watching him, deciding whether to speak to him. What was her life attached to? She had spoken of a commune. But she must have a home, her other parents, a job.

He was wide awake now and pulled a chair quietly over to the stove, away from the cold rim of air near the walls. He was ashamed of his thoughts, of his slight anxiety when he glanced at the lumped and sleeping form. What could she really do to him after all? And why couldn't he be simply generous, accept the fact that something would have to change now? But as he stared at the fluttering grate the clear, cold thought that had been working its way up made him nod his head as if someone else in the room had said it. Nothing *had* to change. It might be better for both of them if they went on about their own lives. They had not needed each other up to now. Why should they hereafter?

You're hard when you're angry, Monica would say, *cold as rocks. Why don't you just let it out?* But she, too, would be sitting clenched in her chair, arms hugging herself as if someone had just struck her in the gut.

He hated the way that when she was angry at him, or at something else in her life that she would focus on him, her accent would take on an exaggerated veneer — that brittle, tight-jawed spitting of syllables he associated with so many of the women he would see in the summer in Judson. It did not seem to matter if they were from Chicago or New York or Washington, the accent was something they had to be imitating from a source Lewis never saw in its original, probably passed on from mother to daughter, from ex-debutante to debutante. *Bitch lingo,* he and Buddy called it, and had learned to mock it as they crouched over a beer at the Bear, listening to the two women they had been caddying for only a few minutes ago talk about birdies and putts as if their faces were cased in amber.

What difference does it make? she had said. *I was born with money, you weren't. It brought me different clothes, different houses, but we'll both have to die. And after a certain point you look for the good people, no matter what they're wearing.*

What he regarded as her sentimental conception of the power of love always raised a cold fury in him. Besides, he had discovered it was always the wealthy who pleaded most easily the plight of common man. That night he had known their argument was not about anything they were discussing, but neither of them could really find its source, so they merely disgorged all the old remnants, each of them growing more venomous as they wobbled further and further away from what they needed to say. She, however, always became more precise in her use of words — clear, sharp jabs of phrases that stung him because he only stumbled into greater silence, his voice catching in his throat, rage tightening his shoulders.

Look. It doesn't matter what you're saying. That has nothing to do with it.

Oh? I thought you were accusing me of being wealthy?

I was saying there are certain things you won't ever understand, can't because you never had to suffer lack of something. You think you can just understand everyone and pity them and hand out a few bucks and it will all be okay.

Dear me. You never told me, Lewis. Was there a potato blight in Judson?

He leaned tightly to the tabletop as if his elbows could dig into the Formica. *That's not fair.*

Her face flushed. She would not cry he knew; she did not do that anymore since he had made it a point always to walk out when she did. *That slop won't work,* he had said.

Fair? Then what's fair about throwing my father's bank account in my face whenever we argue about anything? Why when I prove something to you, when you can't show me I'm wrong, do you always have to tell me I can't understand no matter what because I was born with money? Is that fair?

When she stood, which she did suddenly now, turning away

to the sink to lean there, her back to him, he could see for a moment the lift in her belly under the smock, the way that even with her back to him the alteration in her shape was visible, and his throat would clench even more tightly. He would want to rise, run his hands gently along the bare contours of her shifted body, to be bewildered as he was almost every night by the desire he had for her so painfully heightened by her obdurate refusal to marry him. But also he wanted to put his fisted hands under the table, to lift and throw it over, smash through this irrelevant drama they kept acting out. He stood.

Don't walk away like that.

I need a glass of water. She twisted the faucet.

He strode past the table and spun her around. Her face was held back from him, expressionless.

What is it you want? he was shouting. *What do I have to do?*

Why don't you start by not shouting. Then you might stop bruising my arm.

She was doing it again, those eyes half-opened, her face taking on a languid air as if he were a servant who had not quite done her bidding correctly. He leaned closer.

Marry me, he said through his teeth.

She laughed slightly, but she was very pale. *Really, Lewis, don't you think that's a rather ridiculous proposal? Me with my belly up to my chin, you holding a shotgun to my face?*

When he struck her it was not a punch with the full force of his body because it came so quickly, as if someone had cut a tether holding his straining arm and it had inadvertently swung across her face, and later he tried to tell himself he never could have struck her at all if there had been any time for thought to intervene. She staggered back against the wall and crouched down, her face in her hands for a moment, and when she looked up her lip was bleeding. He could not move.

Well? Her voice was hoarse, almost a whisper. *Why don't you finish it? You could kill two birds with one fist.*

But he was not listening, could not understand the odd, cock-eyed grin she gave him as one side of her face began to swell. Instead he was in a remote space where his own pulse ticked monotonously, his breathing rose and fell too evenly. Later, lying awake as he did all that night, he would understand that he knew now he could kill — maybe not her, although if that moment had been otherwise the blow might have done it, or if the fist had been a gun. The fact was simpler and more frighteningly impersonal. All his life he had never believed he was capable of killing a human being. But he could do it. As easily as anyone else.

Her hand was at her cheek again, one finger wiping the line of blood.

Marry me, he said slowly and watched her face over her crouched knees harden.

Interesting. My parents have hated each other for years now. But he never would have done that to her.

My father could have, he said dully.

Of course. But that's breeding, isn't it?

The fresh logs blazed up from the coals. Miriam moaned, uttered an indistinct phrase, and was still again. Lewis stood, turned to the window, waiting for his eyes to lose the orange impression of the grate's slits, and now he was weary but uncertain whether he would find his way back to sleep. Why did memory have to hold so clearly those worst of details when he could not recall what happened next but knew they had been reconciled, and in fact something followed the next day that now filled him with a vague but completely pervasive sense of her body, her voice, all the intense tenderness for which he really had loved her. But there it was, unfocused, elusive, spreading away from him even as he tried to have it back. He could see the snow now, still fluttering against the window. He turned, pausing at Miriam's bunk on the way to his.

She was curled tightly, only the top of her head and a long strand of dark hair out of the covers. How in the world would he ever explain this to Annie, who knew nothing of a child born, only the vague confession that there had been a woman? He had always described his relationship with Monica as if they had indulged in a brief and casual affair. But in that space between himself and his sleeping daughter, as he hovered over her, he saw clearly the gray fall streets of the city, the puzzled face of the cabbie who kept turning to him, not even objecting anymore after the second hospital. They drove to every one he could think of, until at Mount Sinai he had made a dash for the maternity ward, certain she had to be there, kept hidden from him, and the nurses ran after him yelling, *But, sir, this is not visiting hours.* Beyond the door in a ward room were rows of beds, the women suckling their babies, all the sleepy faces unrecognizable.

He reached out slowly and touched the strand of her hair.

6

"**S**he's in heat."

Lewis stood squinting in his long johns at the cabin door, blinded by the bright sun on snow. He shivered as the cold air tumbled over him. Bernie Carbonneau had unbuckled his snowshoes, was grinning out of the wool cap pulled tightly over his ears and low on his forehead.

"Goddamn cold out here." He was stepping in.

Lewis gave way, heard Miriam mutter, "What?" as she waked. He closed the door. Bernie's grin hung while he took in the spread of her dried clothes, the small pile of borrowed articles beside her bunk, and finally the disheveled head and blinking eyes that were staring back at him.

"Who's he?" she said.

"Sorry, Lew, I didn't know."

"Know what?"

Bernie shrugged. "Anyway, Cassandra's in heat."

"So?"

Bernie dug his hands into his back pockets. "Last week you said to let you know."

Lewis stooped to slip some wood onto the coals.

"Why the hell you want to get that mare pregnant this time of year, I don't know."

"Why waste time?"

It was Lewis's turn to shrug. He had no desire to blunder around in the murk of Bernie's motivations. "You got a teaser?"

"Borrowed Spike's pony."

"She'll accept that?"

"Already has. That's how I'm damned sure."

Miriam leaned up on one elbow, her shoulders bare.

"Bernie Carbonneau, ma'am. I'm counting on Lewis here to get my mare pregnant."

Stooping with the poker in his hand, Lewis glanced at her, wishing she were not there. But she was looking at Bernie hard, gauging something before she said in her clear, firm tones, those eyes set unblinking on Bernie's waiting face, "I'm Miriam Sternberg. A friend."

"Pleased to meet you. Sorry to wake you, and I guess I shouldn't have just popped up like this, but I didn't want to miss with my mare."

"When did she come into heat?"

"Yesterday. I figure that means if we give it a try today, we still got day after tomorrow for another go."

Lewis stood. "I'll be down in an hour or so. You call up Howard, tell him to get her ready."

Bernie clapped his hands once. "Yessir. Oh, Cassandra, there'll be a hot time in the old barn today." He looked at Miriam to see if she would laugh. Undaunted, he clomped to the door. Lewis was already there, hand on the knob.

"It's been a while for Joker. No guarantees."

"Same deal you said before? If she takes, I pay; if she don't, it's a free fuck? Sorry, ma'am."

Lewis stepped into his boots and moved out with Bernie, pulling the door closed behind him. The cloudless sky was glazed a deep blue, the nearby hemlocks drooped under the weight of snow, and when a slight breeze shook their tops, a fine white pollen drifted out.

"Big snowfall for this time of year." Bernie's voice was strained by the effort of bowing his rotund body as he strapped the snowshoes. From his stoop, he peered up. "Listen, Lew. Mum's the word. I didn't even see her."

Lewis frowned down at him. "I couldn't care less if you did."

Bernie was up, shaking his head, grinning. "Lewis Beede, I have to hand it to you. At my age, I gotta pay for anything that young."

Lewis considered one quick punch. He would have Bernie at his mercy in those wide duck feet, but as if he knew that only too well, Bernie moved off deftly over the drifts, and when he was at the stream bed he looked back, waved, said, "In an hour," and a few sharp words in French, and then he was off across the open field, slightly hunched, moving with the sure, slow lope of a wolf.

Lewis staggered through the drifts to the outhouse. He would have to shovel the path, but now, his anger still smarting him, he did not mind the cold shock of snow folding into the tops of his boots. Someday before long he and Bernie would have it out again, probably down at the bar on one of those nights when they both reached a sodden state somewhere before dawn. When that happened their punches were mostly ineffectual and the booze provided sufficient local anesthesia. Why he and Bernie had been at each other since they were schoolmates, Lewis could not say for sure. There were times when they were very close. After each one of those scuffles brought on by a few years of increased chafing at each other, he would be certain that they had resolved that enmity forever. *Shit-a-goddamn, Lewis,* Bernie would say, *your left hook gets better every year.*

The last square-off, about two years ago, had been half-hearted because Lewis had apologized even before Bernie started to swing. He had not meant to remind Bernie of that time he had gone over to the Carbonneaus' for dinner, back when they were both in junior high. Bernie had been as hot a prospect for the varsity football team as Lewis was, but there was no conflict since Bernie was a center, and that was exactly the way it worked out — Bernie hunched over the ball, shoving it back with firm accuracy into Lewis's waiting hands. Lewis had never been to Bernie's house before. The Carbonneaus were Catholic, one of those four or five families in town with children filing forever through the school system. *Getting a license from their Pope to propagate and take a free ride on our taxes,* Foster would say. Bernie

93

invited him shyly and the whole family was very polite when he came. Philippe Carbonneau, Bernie's father, kept filling Lewis's plate, frowning at the younger kids when they acted up. But Marcel, Bernie's oldest brother, came home from the sawmill drunk, pushed one of his sisters away from the table so he could have her place, and kept calling Lewis a skinhead. His first fight with Bernie came the next day at practice after he had spent the morning recess mocking the dinner loudly to his friends. The coach had put an end to that one, making them run ten laps in full uniform. They were too stiff and tired the next day even to think of fighting.

When Lewis returned from the outhouse, she was half-dressed in her newly dried clothes, her back bare as she started to slip the jersey over her head. He tried to look away, but she turned toward him unselfconsciously, her face rising out of the shirt, her breasts naked, then pressing sharply against the shrunken cloth. He tried not to think of Bernie's leer.

"Sorry if I've complicated things. But who is he?"

He explained as best he could.

"I wouldn't want to wake up to see him first thing in the morning. I felt like yelling 'Rumpelstiltskin, Rumpelstiltskin.' " She was watching him carefully as he tied his boot. "Can I come?"

"Why?"

"To watch. I've never seen it before. I mean horses."

He fumbled the bow and had to start again. "There's nothing much to it."

She laughed. "There never is."

Now he was blushing.

"I won't if it bothers you."

"Hell, why not? Ever used snowshoes?"

She shook her head. So he went out with her after she had combed her hair and wound it up under her wool cap, and he stooped to adjust the bindings and buckle her in, then rested one bare hand on the toe of her shoe. Her foot seemed very small in his grip. She was looking away into the sun when he glanced up, uncertain what he wanted to say.

From inside the cabin as he fetched his old wooden skis, he could hear her trying the snowshoes, scraping the frames together. She would have to widen her stance.

In the restaurant where they stopped for some breakfast, she leaned to him and asked, "Am I going to be your friend for a while, or do we admit I'm your daughter?"

He did not answer as Bella set down the sloshed cups of coffee, her eyes shifting quickly from Miriam to Lewis. "You want bacon with the special, or sausage?" She tucked at the fringes of her beehive hair.

"Bacon." As she moved slowly away from their table he said to Miriam, "Both," and Bella turned.

"You gotta choose." When Lewis and Miriam laughed, she snapped, "What's so funny?" and Lewis waved at her. "Bacon, bacon's fine."

"I don't explain anything to Bernie. Besides, it's not anyone's business."

"They'll make it theirs. What if Monica Kramer had appeared on your doorstep?"

When she asked those sudden questions, her eyes would fix hard on him, her voice slightly raised. He wanted to tell her to talk more quietly.

"That would never happen."

Partly to keep her from asking more questions, he tried to describe in a low voice that afternoon when he returned from his class and the apartment no longer held her belongings. The note was brief, neither self-justifying nor accusing, simple statements of fact except for where she would be going. Within two weeks he had quit the school and returned to the cabin. He had never been back to New York, in spite of traveling to almost every other part of the country in his subsequent wanderings.

By the time he jabbed into the eggs, the yolks were congealed, but he was hungry.

"The difference being," she said with an edge, "that both of you could walk away from each other forever, but you left me with a need to know. That's a blank I had to fill."

Much to his relief they ate for a while in silence. He should have told her not to come along. He needed time to think this all out. Maybe he ought to ask her to go for a few days. He shoved his plate away and groped for the check. He was certain everyone else in the room was staring at him and he began to sweat. He did not even want to say hello to the people he knew, as if he were in one of those dreams where he would look down and discover he had come downtown without his clothes on.

But he was beginning to discover that her silence did not mean that a topic had been dropped.

"Maybe I'm just angling for an invitation. But I could go away again."

"Where to?"

"Philadelphia, mostly. A college friend. She has an apartment, lives with one of her teachers. They had an extra room and even gave me a key. She works all day, though, so I don't get to see much of them."

"And you? You don't work."

She stared at him. "How did you mean that?"

He shrugged. "No offense. Most of us do, that's all."

"Some people get nasty when they say that, or mean it bitterly. No. I don't need to, for a while. But I'll want to soon. When I was in the commune there was always something to do. Now I seem to be floating. Just looking at you, looking for my mother. But I don't think I'll be able to go on with my life until I've settled this."

Even though her words made him more curious, he rose as if a fire alarm had sounded, catching his chair as it started to tumble. Her voice seemed to penetrate the wadding of casual morning conversations around them.

"We haven't solved anything, have we?" she said as they walked out. "But you don't mind if I stay for a while? If I bring my things up to the cabin?"

The snow was sliding off the roofs of the town as if each house were a hunched animal waking and shifting about. He strode toward her bus.

"If you want," he muttered.

"Do you want?" Her breathless voice shook near his shoulder as she jogged to keep up.

"Let's talk about it later."

"You're stubborn, aren't you?"

"They'll be waiting."

The road to the barn had not been plowed, the big house was shuttered tightly, but Bernie's truck had slewed its way up to the ramp. Howard was waiting, his hands in his jacket pockets.

"Sure you want to come?" Lewis asked as she pushed open her door.

"Wouldn't miss it for anything." She walked ahead of him, and when she passed Howard she said, "Hi, I'm Miriam," in a determined voice.

Lewis took Howard by the elbow so that he had to turn and tramp beside him.

"You got the mare ready?"

"Who's Miriam?"

"Later, Howard."

At the far end of the barn was the open space they always used for breeding in bad weather, round so that no one could get trapped in a corner or up against a wall if things did not go well. Bernie was holding the mare's halter, stroking her nose. Lewis, starting from Cassandra's face so she could see and smell him, worked his hand along her body until he was at the neatly bound tail, the ooze and unmistakable odor of her heat.

"I couldn't bring the pony along. Don't have a big enough truck."

Lewis nodded. Cassandra had never been a difficult mare to breed. He was more concerned about Joker, retired from stud for two years now. The old horse was still potent, that he knew by the semen spilled on the hooves or the floor of his stall. But whether he would still be interested enough to mount would have to be seen. Miriam was standing well back against the wall by the window. Bernie waved and grinned but she did not respond. The pail of warm, soapy water and the sponge were waiting nearby.

"Stay on the right side of her head," he said to Bernie, and then he wheeled, walked back along the rows of empty stalls. "Bring the bucket." He could hear Howard coming along behind him. "Has he been edgy?"

"He knows. We walked her by a few times."

In all the long barn only two stalls had horses now. Melissa's rump came into view, and then Joker's, his tail twitching. The wall between their stalls was low and she was nuzzling him as Lewis walked in, speaking softly. Once past the stallion's croup, Lewis could see that the penis already hung down stiffly, twitching. Joker blew heavily as Lewis backed him out, keeping a close hold.

"Keep his head down now," and Howard took the halter

while he moved back along the animal, soothing, talking. He stroked the belly until Joker was used to his hand, then gently ran it along the soft, filmy skin of the unsheathed penis, took the sponge, began gently washing it down. The horse did not shy. When Lewis came around again to take the halter, Joker snorted, neighed, moved readily with him down the aisle. The mare sidled as they approached and Lewis watched carefully to be certain Bernie was in control and to see if Cassandra showed any signs of kicking. She neighed, but held still as Joker moved close enough to smell her.

"He'll do, he'll do," Lewis was saying, and bringing Joker at right angles to the mare's left side, he held him down until he was certain the stallion was ready, and then he gave him the rope. Joker lifted his head, sensed his freedom to move, bunched the huge muscles of shoulder and thigh, and then he was rearing up, high over the mare, high over Lewis. When Joker came down, his front legs were over the mare's back, his broad underline pushing against her. Slowly he worked his way back, hind legs staggering under his own unbalanced weight, and Cassandra did not shy away, her own neck down, legs slightly splayed. He was in position, curved supply from his nose that burrowed in her crest, down the long bow of back to croup and legs, his forelegs spread out around her heaving sides. Stepping in close, with one quick motion Lewis guided the stiff flesh as it thrust past his opened hand, and he stood away as Joker tightened in. Both horses moved with a slow rhythm. Even the expression of their long faces was sleepy, turned inward, their lips drooping. Then Joker's tail lifted, he heaved against her, she staggered slightly but held, and his tail was pumping and flagging.

"Done," Lewis murmured. "You old beauty."

But looking past Joker's twitching rump he saw Miriam, and she was laughing, her hand over her mouth. When she saw him glaring at her, she stopped and said in a clear, loud voice, "They look so silly." Both horses sidled to the strange voice, Lewis stared at Howard as if it were up to him to do something, and then he had to concentrate because he could tell by the backing of hind feet that Joker would dismount soon.

"Hold her tight, now."

He had seen a stallion badly kicked while dismounting, and

he moved in close to grasp Joker's halter and guide him off safely. But Cassandra only danced sideways slightly as if relieved to be rid of the weight.

Lewis stroked the long nose, looked at the drooping eyes. How often he had helped the stallion in his younger days service sometimes forty-five mares in a season, and Lewis would come to the end of the week dreaming that his hands were still soaked in slime and sperm, and that the buckets he plunged his arms into were filled and overflowing not with water but with a golden honey of pure heat.

He would not look at Miriam. Obviously the girl had no sense at all. Even if she had never been around horses, she should have noticed this was a tricky business. Well, he would know better next time, and he was not interested in educating her. Howard held Joker while Lewis washed him down. He was turning the stallion back to his stall when he saw Annie standing in the aisle, hands in the back pockets of her jeans.

"Walk him up and down the aisle a bit first," he said to Howard and the boy moved off with Joker.

He could tell by her blank expression, the slight bend forward of her neck, that something was wrong.

"Where were you yesterday?"

"Yesterday?"

Bernie was moving the mare in slow circles around the room, but walking on the inside, his face toward them.

"I guess you forgot."

Then he remembered he had been supposed to borrow Elmore's car, drive to the Flatts, and pick her up at the dentist's.

"I forgot."

She laughed in a very unamused way.

"I don't know what's going on up here." He fingered his head. "Not even a trace until you appeared now."

She was staring at him levelly. "Maybe you've been too busy."

"Busy, busy, busy," Bernie clucked.

"No."

"They tell me you have company."

"Who?"

"That's what you know and I'd like to know."

"I mean who says?"

"Friends."

As Miriam moved forward, he could see them both in line, Annie still facing him, not aware of Miriam yet. He wished he could stop everything right there.

"This is Miriam Sternberg. Annie Strand."

Annie turned with a jerk. Miriam's hand was taken for the briefest of wrings. "I've seen you hanging around. I thought you were from the commune." Annie's tone was flat, as unfriendly as any Lewis had heard her use.

"I used to be. But not any nearby."

"Look, Annie. I'm going to explain. But not now." He tried to roll his eyes toward Bernie, but she was too angry to be able to catch small gestures.

"Later is just fine with me."

Howard hulked in the doorway, mouth open.

Miriam smiled slightly. "You're making a mistake."

The mare was not moving and everything was still.

"I made a big one a long time ago." Annie swiveled. "Howard, have you got your car?"

He nodded.

"Take me home." She seized him by the arm. "When you do come by, Lew, knock first, okay?"

He did not answer. She turned Howard with such a jerk that his head snapped.

Miriam lifted her hand. "Look, I'll just catch them and . . . "

"No." What the hell was Annie doing? Was he some kind of Gus being dragged around now by a Doris? And who did this girl think she was, muddling it all up? Couldn't she ever keep quiet? "Let her go," he growled. "I'll catch her later."

Joker neighed and kicked the stall.

"And get that damned mare out of here before Joker breaks loose and jumps her again."

"Sure, sure, sure." Bernie and Cassandra moved quickly down the aisle, the mare shying at Joker's stall.

Lewis began collecting buckets, sponges, the unused hobbles and nose twitch.

"Anything I can do?"

He stood up but stared at the wall beyond her. "Yes. Sit still in one place and quit talking."

They did not speak until they were back in the bus again.

"What can I do?"

"Nothing." He put his feet closer to the heater. He was already sorry that he had snapped at her. "Maybe in a few days this will seem very funny. Unless she takes it out on poor Howard."

She was beginning to pull out when the high wail of a horn slashed down on them. A trailer truck swung by throwing a cloud of snow and shaking them in its wind.

"They don't waste time," she said.

"Not here. Damned good straightaway."

She drove into town and he did not have to tell her where to take him.

"Shall I wait for you?" She stopped at the traffic light.

"No. Where are you going?"

"Back to the cabin, if you don't mind."

"What if I did?"

She was biting the corner of her lip. "I'd go anyway."

"Then help yourself. I'll be along."

"When?"

"I'm not sure. Whenever she cools down enough."

"What if *she* doesn't want me to stay up there?"

"No one's telling me what to do. That's my cabin."

The Ryans' car was pulling away from Annie's house at the far end of the street. At least he would not have to contend with Howard.

"Weird, isn't it," she said quietly. "What those horses were doing was so funny and simple. We seem to make it all so complicated."

He took a deep breath and then grinned. "Sometimes that's half the fun of it."

7

Lewis moved the spoon because it was catching the sun so brightly, glinting between them. He put his hand flat on the manila envelope she had placed beside him on the table.

"I'd rather have you tell me than read it to myself."

Miriam was looking out the window toward the pond, her face still sleepy and hair disheveled. She breathed the steam from a teacup she held in both hands.

"I'm not very good at telling stories. What I wrote out is only a start."

He spooned some sugar from the can into his cup. "Yesterday it was hard for me to make Annie believe. She said if you were my daughter, I would know more about you by now. But then she said, no, it was like me not to ask you much."

"I wish I could tell you everything, wish it could be as simple as pouring my life over you." She sipped from the cup, then held it again a few inches from her face.

Her tone of frustration expressed exactly how he had felt the day before, watching Annie's dazed face as she listened to him try to describe his own past, stumbling around as if he had been dropped onto a wide gray plain where the facts of his life with Monica had petrified and he lifted their awkward shapes, lugging them, piling them in front of her until he began to see some expression of understanding again in her eyes, her questions. But she had kept some quiet reserve. What had surprised him most of all was the way he had ended by defending Miriam, expressing reasons for what she had done. By the time he returned to the cabin, he was relieved to see her there, looked at her as if they had gone through something together.

Miriam glanced at him. "Did Annie forgive you?"

"There's nothing much to forgive."

"Is that what you say, or what she says?"

He drank some coffee, already lukewarm. "I think she was relieved at first. Then confused. When I told her you were my daughter I took away the woman she was angry about, but I put another woman between us out of the past."

"Wasn't she jealous? I would be." She put her cup down, leaned her head on one hand so that she was staring at him. "I was living with someone once. He used to tell me about all his women in the past. He thought he was complimenting me, saying, 'Look how many women I've had and could have still, but I've given up all that for you.' But for me it was as if I had so many women to be jealous about and they were almost worse than the one who finally did slip between us. At least I could have a try at beating her out."

"You lost?"

"I'm not sure whether she won or I let go, or pushed off. It was about a year ago. He liked talking about her on the nights he spent with me, and I suspect he did the same to her. That made me compete at first. Then it was just boring, like listening to someone you live with telling the same story over and over when different guests come to the house."

The icicles that had formed along the eaves were melting fast, beating a complicated tattoo on the snowbank under the window.

"Did she forgive me?" She still stared at him intently.

"For what?"

"For coming back. For interrupting your lives. For changing everything."

He leaned forward, staring at the unfrozen black center of

the pond. He balked at that. *Everything* was too extreme, and besides he had not made up his mind about anything yet. Annie had reached the quiet mood that took her when she was trying to listen far inside herself, and he had not hesitated when she asked him gently after dinner to leave, to let her be alone to think. For him to push now would be only to meet curiously vacant gestures of affection, as if he were a child being patiently, absentmindedly tended to.

Above all he resented the idea that he or anyone needed forgiving. He did not answer. There were too many simple, practical questions, and yet he could not seem to ask them directly even though he had rehearsed them during a restless night. Would she stay up here with him? For how long? How could he support her? Did he need to? Did she even *want* to be here with him, and wasn't there something wrong about that? Even if she was his daughter. Having another person so closely shut up with him in that small cabin already annoyed him. It seemed to him that he had not been alone for days and days.

She pushed the envelope toward him. "Please. It's not a bad place to start. Remember I'm older than when I wrote it. I don't think I'd say those things in the same way now, but the facts are true. When I wrote it out I thought that if I found you or my mother, I'd send you this rather than come face to face with you. I had been told that was easier, a quiet way in. It would give you the opportunity to say no without my being there."

"Your lawyer's advice? Maybe you should have."

She pulled both hands back through her hair from the temples, then lowered her chin onto the arms she crossed on the tabletop.

"If I didn't want you to say no, why should I give you that much chance? It might look like I didn't really care. Anyway, it was my therapist's advice, and actually when it was all written, I realized he was using it for his purposes. It was a confusing time for me. I'd hired a lawyer, he had begun to find some facts, and suddenly it was all becoming very possible. And my adoptive parents had just died."

She said that without pausing but swallowed before she went on.

"Died?"

"They were in a crash. Their own plane. Arnie had a pilot's license and they owned land in the Virgin Islands. His father had bought it when it cost almost nothing and Arnie had decided to start developing it, thinking that soon, once a hotel was up, some houses, a golf course, maybe he and Myra would sell the family business and move there. A sort of retirement without really retiring."

"Have you ever been there?"

"A few times. It's beautiful, and mine now. Luckily the building had only just begun. I could get the lawyers to cancel the contracts. And anyway, it was tied up in court for a while. Arnie had a sister and that side of the family didn't like the fact that everything was left to me. They didn't mind losing money, savings accounts. But not property, land, things they said belonged to 'the family.' Strange. Arnie and Myra spent all my childhood making me feel that being adopted didn't make any difference. I don't know if I would have openly started looking for you as long as they were alive. They would have been very hurt. But when they died, everyone reminded me how I wasn't really part of the family. At first I wanted to wreck everything. Sell all the property, destroy the business, live up to their worst dreams."

Lewis was already so confused that he could not think of what to say. But she had paused only to breathe deeply, sit back in her chair.

"They disappeared. No word from any airports except for the stopover they had made in Savannah. There had been a very thick, unexpected fog the day they were to land on St. Croix. A few days later the wreckage was spotted on the side of a remote hill on a nearby island. No one had heard a thing."

"Sorry."

She blinked, shook her head. "Anyway, it was hard at first. It helped to become obsessed with the idea of finding you. I'd read newspaper articles about other adopted children who'd grown up and set out to find their parents. I'd even corresponded with one woman for a while until I was afraid Myra or Arnie would some-how find out. So when I really started to take the first practical steps, hiring an investigative lawyer, trudging about to various offices on my own, I began to be paralyzed, guilty, as if I were doing something dirty to Myra and Arnie. That's when I ran away with a friend, joined the commune. I almost turned it all over to them, the business, property, my trust fund. But I couldn't, finally. I'm much too selfish." She glanced at the envelope and breathed deeply. "Still, I wish I'd had the guts to start it all when they were alive. Maybe they would have understood. There was no way to make them understand once they were dead. Crazy logic."

"Surely they would have understood, though."

"You can't say. You didn't know them. My analyst would say that, and I would tell him the same thing. Emotional logic can't be reasoned with."

"But you didn't stop."

"I couldn't untangle all those feelings. I still haven't. I just rolled them up in a ball and walked away from them. I accepted a kind of ruthlessness in me. There was no way I was going to stop my life from moving, no matter how good people had been to me. That same way of thinking let me barge into your life."

He was going to say, *Yes, you did,* but he thought maybe it was not necessary. After all, she had said it. He stood and went to feed the stove. His right leg was very stiff. Trudging up that night, he had slipped off the trail, caught one ski tip on a sapling, and thrown himself into the bank.

"All right. I'll read it."

She stood, stretching high on her toes, her slim arms reaching toward the low crossbeam. "Can I use your skis? I've never tried cross-country. I don't want to sit here while you read."

"If you're careful. I don't want to have to carry you out."

"I've skied a little. Once Myra and Arnie took me to Stowe. They tried to give me lessons, but I was in a sulk because I was in high school and they'd taken me away from the big basketball game that weekend. When I wasn't in my room crying, I was sitting in the lounge pretending I was a captive princess."

"Did your prince come?"

She took his arm in both hands and leaned her head on his shoulder. When he released himself he intended to shy away, but found instead he was holding her against him a little stiffly.

"He was working his way through college. On the ski patrol. He tried to put me on skis once or twice, but neither of us were much interested in that. Myra and Arnie couldn't understand why I was sulking as much when we left as when we came. Arnie got mad halfway down the interstate. Said I ought to make up my mind since I couldn't have it both ways." She lifted her head. "I told him I didn't care what he said. I was going to have it both ways, forever."

Lewis laughed, and she sat on the bunk to put on her boots.

"When you're out there and you come to a tree, don't try to go around it both ways."

"Thanks for the advice."

She pulled the frosted door tight behind her. He could hear her dropping the skis onto the snow, struggling with the old bindings. The envelope was stuffed, and when he turned it upside down, the pages came into his hand, but also a number of variously shaped photographs fluttered onto the tabletop. He shuffled them together and pulled a chair away from the table to sit facing the stove. Already he could see her inching along by the corner of the cabin, poles splayed out on each side. He did not want to be distracted.

He looked at the photographs first. A few were in color, gaudy in their excessive greens and blues, but most of them were black-and-white. The lack of chronological order made her life seem totally disjunct. A thin face with a forced smile and overly bobbed curls glared out of a halo of light in a high school picture; a baby, surely too fleshy to be her, with a bulbed nose and no hair, was balanced on her belly, head and legs arched up, and a mysteriously disconnected hand was spread in one corner as if it had rolled out the infant. One picture was labeled — a skinny-legged girl with an orthodontic device around her mouth was standing beside a bicycle and two adults were on each side of her. The girl was labeled *Miriam*. The man, who had one hand tightly on a handlebar, his other on the back of his balding head as if he had just slapped a fly, was *Arnie*. The woman, *Myra*, taller than all of them, her face slightly back and hands hung at her side, looked as if she were about to swoon or melt into the stairs of the building entitled *Poconee Inn*. Each one of them was so caught up in an internal motion that Lewis held the photo to one side expecting to see that it was a clever triple exposure. Then he looked more closely at the man and woman, thinking how he would never know them except in her memory. The most recent photograph was a small brownish shot of her head and shoulders, passport size, probably taken in one of those machine booths, and he suspected it had been made especially for the letter itself. The expression gave that away, a starkly pleading helplessness in an overly serious face as if she had looked hungrily into the camera, seeing himself and Monica beyond the flashing mirror of the machine. He put the rest aside. He would wait, look at them with her when she could explain them, describe where Poconee Inn was, why Arnie was beating his own head.

There were five typed pages, carefully corrected, although the typist struck unevenly and the right-hand margin never found a consistent point of arrival. He held it and looked up to the ceiling where the stovepipe was smeared with irregular streaks of coal tar. He was not sure why he hesitated. The photographs had piqued his curiosity. But they pained him too. He had missed forever all that irrecoverable time. That sudden rush of blood he heard in his own ears as he closed his eyes might be simply a flood sweeping them all along even now, and they were missing something, missing something, all the time. Quickly he looked into his lap, held up the first page.

Dear Mother, dear Father,
I have written and rewritten this so many times that I almost gave up. I am trying again. I think I am doing all right and then I reread it and I am sick. There is so much more I want to say, and I want to say it so much better. So I rip it up. You would think I would know how to do this by now. Ever since Myra and Arnie told me I was adopted I have invented our meetings, my words to you. I have met you on the streets of cities I have never been to, I have imagined you standing hand in hand on my doorstep when I opened the front door to go to school, I have seen you waiting in our dark living room when I came down to check on strange noises that were only the wind, I have seen you in a crowd on television, caught accidentally by the sweep of the camera – two faces exactly like mine. Once after we read about Orpheus and Euridice I made up a play for my literature class about a girl who went to hell to bring her parents back, playing her guitar as she climbed up the longest stairs imaginable. Of course she looked back. Did you? Do you? That's why I'm writing. I hope I can bring

you back. If I ever find out where you are. As for the play, I never turned it in. I was scared they might do it at school and then Myra and Arnie would know what I was thinking. That seems a little silly now since they probably did anyway. But I was seventeen and thought that secrets were secrets. Maybe I'll never turn this in either.

I have already learned in trying to write this that I should not even begin to write down everything I can remember about me or my home. That's not the point. The point is to try to make you understand that I want to meet you. If you let me do that, then I can tell you more, and find out about you and if we can love each other. In my other attempts, I tried to make myself sound so wonderful that you would not be able to say no or pack up and change your social security numbers and move to different states. But I can't. That ends up sounding phony. You can see by the picture I'm sending that I am not any more beautiful or unusual than anyone else. I don't think I'm ugly, but I am plain. Same goes for inside. I can be pretty mean some days, and especially seem to be able to hold a grudge for a long time. All my boyfriends have said that, and Arnie called me Bulldog Sulker. All I can say is that if you let us meet, I would try very hard. I expect it to be difficult for you too. I'm not seventeen anymore.

Lewis heard a small cry, shrill as a hawk, and when he turned to the window, she was heaped in front of the apple trees, a tangle of skis, legs, poles, and elbows. But she rolled back, straightened her skies, tried to stand, grabbed a branch, and was up, floured with snow. She was unhurt, but he pulled the chair around to sit at the table. Maybe he had better keep an eye on her. She looked over at the window as if ashamed, grinned, shrugged, then waved to turn him away, and to make her feel at ease he put a hand on his brow, looked back down to the paper spread in front of him. But he cheated, glanced through his fingers quickly to see her snowplowing unsteadily to the far level of the field and the butternut tree. She missed it.

Arnie and Myra Sternberg adopted me only two months after you had given me up. I gather I was lucky that way. Memory had not really begun for me, so I had no sense of a gap that some adopted kids have who are four or five before they are taken. It was, as far as I'm concerned, exactly as if you, Mother, held me up from your bed and

Myra or Arnie took me and said, "Thank you," and walked away. The Sternbergs died. I wish you could have said "Thank you" to them.

Because as far as I can tell they did at least as well, probably better, than most parents. If anything, they made problems for themselves and me by loving me too much. Arnie was one of those fathers who should have been a mother, if you know what I mean. He fussed around me a lot, liked doing anything just to be with me, even helped cut out dolls' clothes, and when I was a teenager he'd talk with me about the other kids at school, didn't mind my girlish bitch, bitch, bitch. On the other hand, I learned how to throw one hell of a curve ball. Arnie had considered a contract with a Phillies farm club when he was in college. He got fat and bald and didn't take care of his body after he was forty, but even two years ago he'd bring our gloves along when he came to visit me and we'd have a catch. I never did get the knack of a screwball, although he tried hard.

Myra was fine, not cuddly, but since Arnie made up for that, I didn't miss it. She was the aristocrat, or her family claimed they were related to Rothschilds, somewhere so far back in Europe that it didn't mean anything financially. Anyway, she worried a lot, got upset if I showed odd behavior, and once we had a long period of silence between us because she'd become very angry at something I'd said when I was doing my teenage thing and blaming them for all the insufficiencies I felt were keeping me from being as perfect as everyone else. She had said, "Well, maybe it's not our fault at all, you know, maybe it's just your chromosomes." Odd thing is, in retrospect, I see how any parent has a right to say that, and she was right when she insisted later that what actually had happened was she felt so much like a mother she'd forgotten I was adopted. She was sorry as soon as she said it, came as near to crying in front of me as I've ever seen her, but you can imagine how I played that up. It did hurt, but not as much as I hurt her back by pretending I didn't know her for a while. She was very emotional, but in control, or keeping control. Arnie was emotional, but never in control. I've seen him cry often, even red-eyed after a movie. I never saw Myra weep. Oddly enough, although I know I feel closer to Arnie, I think I'm more like Myra in that way. Arnie's bathos was innocent, but I've known other men who use that kind of behavior as a display, a way to get what they want from you. Maybe that worked a little too often on me until I found out few people are as truly childlike as Arnie.

Thunk. A bright splotch of snow struck the window, and as he looked, a second snowball hit the corner and softly exploded. The two centers began to melt, slipped down, and she was standing a few yards away, up to her knees in snow, grinning expectantly. She waved, stooped, shoveled snow up toward him with both hands in a cloud. When it cleared she had turned to dive and roll past the skis that were plunged upright. She stood, even her face frosted with white patches.

He could not stop watching her. She seemed so thoroughly absorbed in her play, an almost serious expression on her face as if the adult in her were saying, "So this is what it's like to have all this snow to play in." He was tempted to slip outside, heave a snowball at her before she could know he was there. He had not thrown a snowball for years. But she was lying down flat on her back, her arms and legs making scissoring motions as if she were signaling to something far off in the sky. She stood carefully, looked back at her imprint. She was dissatisfied and started making another angel. He was content to watch her, but could not help wondering if he would have been as good a father as Arnie, teaching her baseball, even playing with her dolls.

He tried to begin reading again, but the words did not hold his attention. For a moment he could not keep himself from thinking how his own father had never played with him. He had seen Foster playful only once or twice, and that was not even with him or Elmore. One day he had been sent home early from school because Miss Hickey caught him with Donny's copy of January from a Petty Girl Calendar. He had dreaded arriving to explanations, scoldings, the boredom of being sent to his room. The late spring day was clear and the ground had dried out. In the dust he could smell the mingling of last fall's old leaves and the new green rising under that mold and decay. Something was moving in the small paddock beyond the white pine saplings. The motions were wheeling and quick, and the sounds were of hooves and a voice laughing or grunting. Full of the sun but obscured by the thick screen of young trees, the scene was a glint and whirl of light. Lewis walked into the trees, stood there quietly before he reached the rail fence. His father was playing with the colts. Sometimes he mimicked them, stooping like an ape, hands touching the earth, or he rushed them, let them shy and then canter back. They would swing their necks at him as if he were a colt himself, and he would sprawl in mock defeat while they gathered suspiciously to nuzzle his shirt and pants. He would rise with a shout, they would curvet away to begin their prance and chase again. Lewis had ached, wanting to leap that fence and join them. But he had known that if he did, the whole thing would stop, just as his mother had said happened if you found elves dancing in the woods and tried to step into their magic circle.

Lewis looked down again.

How was I brought up? What do I believe in? Are these your questions I feel or a way of reminding myself how little direction I have now, am still waiting for? Neither Myra nor Arnie were committed to Judaism. Arnie had been brought up strictly, suffered all the usual rites and initiations, but had shrugged from under all that as quickly as he could. Myra recalled Orthodox great-grandparents, but one of her aunts had even married a Gentile in a very Episcopalian wedding in Scarsdale, so she was no scourge to bring Arnie back to the synagogue. We went, though, from time to time. For Arnie the Day of Atonement was a way of quieting for a while the berating voices of parents and relatives who gathered like harpies in his head on crucial holidays.

Then there was my grandfather. His father. Through him I learned what being a Jew was all about and almost joined him. He visited us from time to time. Loving and gentle and my constant companion when he was with us, he was his son's religious conscience, and at his worst he seemed to expect Myra, on a Saturday when she would treat it like any other day of her suburban week, to turn to a pillar of salt. I loved the man, came to see that for all his religious inflexibility, he had that soft, perfectly absorbent core like his son. He would take me sometimes to synagogue, and I even enjoyed those long services with him in which he bent and fluttered over me, explaining quietly, then plunging totally back into the service himself. A whole separate part of the refrigerator had to be kept for him so that our laxly non-Kosher food would not contaminate his. He died suddenly in Philadelphia, on Broad Street as he was chasing his hat that had blown off on a windy morning, and he was not identified for three days. I wept for at least that long. But without him, Judaism made no sense. I studied it when I was trying to go to college, hoping the mind would prove to me that my dreams of Grandfather, who sometimes came to stand, his head tilted and slowly shaking back and forth as if to say, "Miriam, Miriam, I had such hopes for you," were right. No deal. It was my grandfather I loved, not that sense of cosmic history.

I used to think I believed in love. Or Love. You know, Make Love, Not War, and all that sort of thing. I've gotten a little confused about all that. If only I could leap right over the pile of mucky memories like most of my friends do — the ways in which whatever men I've lived with have betrayed or I've betrayed, or the ways that friends turn hard on one side, move to other cities, stop writing. Hooks and barbs and dragging anchors seem to be around us in spite of our smiles and opening hands, and every time I try to leap out into that place I sense where all creatures sit in light and feast happily together, the tether at my neck yanks hard, I gag, I think, "If love fails me so much in the smallest touches, how can it work big?" My friends say I'm too logical. Forget that. Drift out. Give up Western Inhibitions. Have a drag on this, a sniff of that. Listen to this koan. Shave your head and let the rays pour down. Open your thighs and let D. H. Lawrence into your soul. Here, carry this placard against war, nukes, anti-abortionists, gay haters. I tried, and you see how cynical I can make myself sound? But it's only because I wish, I wish.

I wish I could believe that I am a free floating but cosmically connected cell, that it makes no difference whether I know you or even will, that these concrete details of fact and history are not as important as that undifferentiated white light we all see in us. But I am hopelessly bound to the concrete. Brueghel is my favorite painter and I wish I could see all the world so "thingy." I wish I could have been born with that sort of certainty my friends have, the figures of their parents as clear as the wall of a swimming pool to flip-turn and push off against. I wish I could stop writing this letter to you that I may never send, and which, if I do, may have so pushed you away by now that I will never be given the chance to argue my needs in person.

So I will stop. Turn off this voice. Father, Mother, one dark night you gave, you received. That moment was enough to make me. This letter is my moment, my shot in the dark. Take me back.

Lewis stood abruptly, staring down at the page where it lay in the wedge of sunlight. She had never sent this letter. What if she had not been able to trace him? Or had not come? If she had driven away that night after giving him a lift and never returned? He saw his hand splayed out on the page. The fingers were trembling uncontrollably. He raised his head, eyes unfocused to the dim shapes in bright light, her form on skis again in staggering motion. He put his hand forward and laid it flatly on the windowpane. Looking beyond the fingertips to the nearly melted stumps of icicles on the eaves, to the sweep of snow roiled where she had played, to the pond and its black hole of slightly rippled water, out over the bare gray trees to the valley, the ridge of Moonstone, its hazy white peak, the sudden blue sky, he breathed deeply.

She yelled. She was drifting with increasing speed down the slope. Her skis were so straight, her knees bent in such perfect form that from the waist down she seemed to know exactly what she was doing. But her shoulders jerked, her arms and the loosely tethered poles flung widely around in the air. She was descending into the pond.

She crossed the last hump as if she had been traversing moguls for years, and swooped down the wind-scoured bank. Her skis went out onto the snow of the partially frozen pond, she slowed, began to sink, and with her arms still waving as if she were signaling a distant observer on Moonstone, she plunged into the water.

He was out the door, racing down the bank, sinking into drifts, wrenching his knee, and finally he slid to the water's edge. She had turned to him, her head above water, cap askew and eyes wide with surprise.

"I can't stay up," she shrieked.

"A pole, a pole." He was up to his knees in the water so cold that he could hardly speak through the shocked intake of breath.

Her arm struggled up, her head back now, face barely out of water. She flung her hand toward him. The pole surfaced but stayed behind her. He waded in to his waist. The edges of broken ice cut at him. "Again, again." As her mouth went under, eyes still wide, the pole flipped in a lazy arc from behind her, he had it, was dragging, his feet slipping on the mucky bottom as if a tide were pulling them both down. But she came, face up again, her arm in his grasp, and he hauled until she was beside him, then pushed

114

her toward the bank, and she was clawing out of the water, a creature made awkward by slats and poles skewed at angles. She lay on her stomach in the snow, panting. He loosened the bindings, threw the skis to one side, pulled the loops of the poles over her hands, not caring that the mittens came off too. Her arm around his neck, he hauled her up, she stumbled against him, he almost fell back with her into the water, and then he was making her scramble with him up the bank, into the cabin.

Still he did not speak. She stood but was not even shivering, her face pasty white, lips blue. He tore at her lead-wet clothes, pulled them off. She seemed unable to understand what he was doing, did not move to help him haul the dungarees down over her hips. When she was naked she began to moan and he rubbed her roughly with a towel, then ripped the blanket from his bed, rolled her in it tightly, lifted and placed her on the bunk. When he had stripped off his boots and wet pants, he lay beside her, back curved to his belly, pulling the other blanket tight around them, holding her closely with his arms and legs. She began to shiver.

Her hair was wet on his face. He breathed hotly on her neck as if he could blow fire into her.

"My God, that water's cold," she said.

He began talking quietly to the back of her head, smoothing her cheek with one hand.

"It doesn't take long when it's that cold. Sometimes it's the shock. I saw an ice fisherman go in when the ice was too thin. He was almost close enough to the shore to wade out, but he couldn't move, as if someone had run a thousand volts through him. He was so numbed before we could get across the ice that he couldn't even lift an arm to take the plank we pushed at him. It was heart failure that killed him."

She was breathing steadily now. "I guess I'm not too good on skis."

His hand moved back along her neck. She felt warmer.

"Trouble is, you were doing too well. If you'd fallen, it would have saved you the trouble of a dunking."

"I don't know how to stop." She was shivering less. "Thank you."

"Feeling better?"

She nodded. For a while they lay there listening to the steady

115

dripping beyond the window. Now that the event was over, he could not rid himself of his shock at touching her suffering and naked body.

"Did you read it?" she said almost sleepily.

"Yes."

"And?"

"I'm glad you did not give up on me."

"I couldn't."

"You may yet."

She laughed. "Not if you keep saving me."

He started to edge away, tucking the blanket around her as he left.

"Don't go. It's like one of my best dreams when I used to lie at night and think of finding you. But better."

"You'll need some tea, something warm inside."

He stood in front of the bunk, brushing one hand over her forehead, embarrassed now.

"I have a question."

"What's that?"

"If I find my mother, will you come with me?"

He looked into her eyes, then out the side window to the big rock with the spruce growing in its cleft.

"No."

But even as he was shaking his head she was saying, "We'll see."

8

"**L**ewis? Are you there?"

He was in the stall shoveling muck into the channel where the hose was running. When he stood up straight, the muscles in the small of his back loosened slowly, so he leaned on the shovel, waiting for Phoebe to come into view. Above her bulky down parka, her pale face was unusually chiseled, a cameo in the oval of her hair.

"I didn't mean for Doris to have to open the place up by herself. I thought she'd hire more than Howard to help."

Lewis arched his back to shake out the last kink. "She said she wanted to do it alone."

She touched Joker's flank and he shifted slightly.

"You'll want me to move them out soon," he said.

"Maybe you won't need to."

He had not seen her since Coleman's death, and he resented the way she could speak as if nothing at all had happened. But her long-fingered hands trembled so much when she opened them that she had to curl them into fists again.

"I guess you won," he said flatly.

"Nobody won. You know that. Can't we talk a minute?"

He leaned the shovel against the wall and walked, listening to her footsteps follow him. In the tackle room the coils of the space heater were rattling. He pulled out a stool for himself and handed her the chair with broken spokes along its back. She sat on its edge, folding her hands tightly in her lap.

"It's so damned cold up here." When she smiled quickly she reminded him of the kind of horse she liked, a high-bred filly in blinders on its way to the gate. "I was in Florida for a while after the funeral. I went to see his sister in St. Petersburg. Have you been there?"

"Spent some time in St. Augustine, working. Key West. Never the other coast."

But she was not listening. Set in the stiff down jacket, her face swiveled disconnected from the rest of her body when she moved her head. "She's younger than Dad was. A stepsister, but they were very close for a while. She couldn't come to the funeral. Bad heart. All she could talk about was Mother. Did I know Mother had held Dad back from some wonderful deal once because she wouldn't move to Chicago? Did I know Mother had never really wanted children, that those miscarriages were something her mind produced? Did I know that Christian Science could help me overcome my this or that? I left in two days, went to Miami." She looked hard at him as if deciding whether to stay or leave, biting the corner of her mouth.

"I would have liked to go to the funeral. I wish it had been up here."

"Out of the question, or course. All his associates were in New York. You got the announcement I sent, didn't you? The newspaper clipping."

He picked up the cinch strap that had fallen off its hook and began winding it around his hand in a tight coil. "They always do that." He laughed harshly through his nose.

"What? Who?"

"Oh, like some animal. Is it elephants? Go somewhere else to die and be buried. You summer people, I mean. One August you are there, doing what you always do, and then we hear or read that you died and that's all. But it's more like vanished, for us. The end is always offstage."

"I suppose it is odd. But they'll probably have a service this summer downtown."

"Yes, yes. The other ritual. Members of the club put down their mashies and putters for an hour to say bye-bye to Coleman. I'll come downtown and help park cars." When he came to the end of the strap he yanked it tight, then let it unravel.

"You're in a great humor tonight, Mr. Beede." But her voice did not have the snap he would have expected, so he looked at her curiously. She was still perched on the edge of her chair like a small bird holding on in a wind. "Look, I know you loved him, Lewis."

He did not like her to use that word or even to attempt to describe their relationship. "You don't know the half of it," he muttered. Above all he did not want to admit to her how shocked and bitter, then lonely he had felt when he had learned of Coleman's death. The old man had not written to him after he had left Judson, then there was only that impersonally printed announcement from the Whites' secretary and the Xerox copy of an obituary from the newspaper stuffed in with it, and worst of all, he had learned of Coleman's death casually. Buying a loaf of bread at the IGA, he had been making small talk in line with Bess Moore when she said, *Too bad about Coleman White, but I guess he was pretty old anyway,* and he had nodded, held back the panic that made him fumble his change, a cold sweat breaking out on the palms of his hands. The obituary revealed more facts to him about Coleman's life and accomplishments than he had ever known, and in doing so, made the man seem like a stranger. Above all, he had been completely unable to express his feelings to Miriam. She had been puzzled, kept asking, *But who was he, anyway?*

"Tell me, then."

"There's nothing to tell. I knew him longer than you did, but in a different way."

"I'm not sure. I was his daughter. Other people have told me he was like a father to you."

He stood quickly, snapped the buckle over the hook so that the belt hung straight down the wall. "What is it you want, Phoebe? I don't feel much like talking." When he sat again, he was very tired.

"Could we start with a truce? I didn't come to argue. Will you miss him? Tell me you'll miss him." Her voice was pleading.

"That goes without saying."

"But we can say it to each other, can't we? Since my mother died, you and I have been closer to him than anyone else. No matter how badly he and I treated each other."

"I'll have to take your word for that. He must have had many friends at home."

She was shaking her head vehemently. "Lewis, sometimes I think you're an awful fool. Surely you could tell that someone like him had very few close friends, and that he never let anyone come as close as he let you. I used to be very jealous sometimes."

Those words should have made him feel better, but they only weighed him down further as if they carried some obligation that he had failed to carry out, and now never could.

She laughed so sharply that Lewis winced. "Speaking of fools, let me tell you what I did. In Florida. I hired a boat for the weekend and had it take me way out for marlin. I waited until dark and finished a bottle of Jack Daniel's I'd been working on all afternoon, told the captain to get lost when he tried to make me, and about midnight climbed overboard."

Lewis did not stop looking at her, but her eyes shied off.

"I had meant to sink, and to hell with it all. But I started yelling. I've always had awful nightmares about sharks. About being alive and watching while they eat my intestines. They pulled me in and went right back to Miami and tossed me and my stuff on the dock as if they'd thrown me up." She pulled down the zipper so quickly that white coils of a heavy sweater burst out of the pod of her jacket. "Really, for a moment before I started yelling, I thought dying was so silly. I mean *my* dying. The last silly act of a silly person. 'Dear daffy Phoebe drowned today. Now wasn't that a silly thing to do?' So I started yelling. Damn it. Now I'm hot."

She slipped off the jacket, pushed up the sleeves along her stick-thin arms. Even as his mind was repulsed by what she had described, he was trying again to understand why those skinny limbs, pale flesh, never failed to attract him, and always with a quick, unavoidable stroke.

"You knew he was dying, didn't you?"

He nodded.

"So did I. He thought it was his little secret. But I knew." Her voice took on that hardness he was more used to. "I wasn't about to let him know I knew. We have the same doctor. After his operation last year and then the treatments, I went for a checkup. I knew perfectly well Dad wouldn't tell my anything, that he'd find a way of using that between us. I pretended I knew. I pulled a long face and said to Dr. Tillotson, 'How long do you think he can go on?' He said he wasn't sure, maybe a year, two. Once he'd put his foot in that far I leveled with him, told him I wanted all the facts, made him promise to let me deal with it and not let Dad know I knew."

"But why?"

She was pulling nervously at the turtleneck of her sweater. "I wanted to know if he'd ever give in, tell me on his own, start treating me as if . . ." but she waved her hand, shrugged.

"He didn't?"

She shook her head. "He was in intensive care at the end. I hate hospitals, even though they were all very nice there. He was tubed and wired, and over his mouth and nose was a plastic mask so when he spoke his voice was changed. They'd only let me stay a few minutes at a time. When I came in the first time he looked at me as if to say, 'So there, surprised you, didn't I?' I didn't pay any attention to that. After a while he fell asleep. It was hard for him at the end, because he didn't want to give up. Stubborn. When I got home, I knew what we'd been doing. He was going to die, really die. By going through that business of saying we knew or didn't know, or knew that other person did or didn't know, we'd made it all into a game. Like what we'd done for years."

The barn door had shifted back on its rollers, then closed. Howard appeared in the doorway.

"Hello, Miss White." He looked at their feet as if he had interrupted something he should not see.

"*Phoebe*, for Chrissake," she snapped, and with a hard set to his face that Lewis would not have expected, Howard looked at her directly, face reddening, and said, "Phoebe."

"You want to finish mucking those stalls?" Lewis said, and Howard moved off without another word. "You've gotten to him fast."

She only half smiled. "He's growing up."

The sharp, quick strokes of his shovel grated over the concrete.

"I waited two days. They said it could go on for weeks. But when I went back he was in a coma. I stayed in a room with cots for families, and they were supposed to call me if he woke. He never did. I'd go in and put my hand in his and it was always limp, did not know I was there. I didn't care if we never spoke again. We were never any good at that anyway. I just needed that hand to clench on me in any way it wanted, anger, or affection, or surprise."

She was staring at Lewis with her voice quite steady, and then she breathed deeply, relaxed her shoulders so that she slumped, and she scrabbled in a pocket of her discarded parka until she found a pack of cigarettes.

"The farm is mine. I took it off the market right away."

"What will you do with it?"

"I didn't win, I didn't win. But I couldn't sell this place. Surely that isn't what he really wanted. I'm calling off the game, that's all. He defaulted."

Lewis stood, went to the doorway, and leaned with his back to her. Down the aisle Howard was stooping to pick up the hose and turn the nozzle, increasing the pressure.

"What will you do with it?"

"First I'm going to open it up, stay here when I want, bring some friends maybe."

"What about horses?"

"Probably." Her voice was much closer to him. "Will you stay on, help?"

"No. I'll have Joker and Melissa out soon as I can."

"I'll need you."

"No."

"Why?"

Still he had not turned. "Maybe I don't like your kind of horses."

"Maybe it won't be what you think. Maybe it will be draft horses again. Like Dad was doing, or Grampa."

He wanted to be away from her immediately, but even the idea of walking tired him. "No. I can't."

"Think about it for a while. We have a lot in common."

Howard was disconnecting the hose. For a moment she

122

seemed so close to him that he was certain her breath was on his neck, then something rustled and when he turned she was lifting her parka. The cigarette in her mouth was still unlit, and as if she saw he was looking at it, she said, "I'm trying to quit. Friend of mine suggested this. Keep it in your mouth unlit until you can't stand the taste of it." She spat it out, her lips down. "So far it doesn't work well." She held the parka out to him. "Would you? The damn thing's so big I can't find the armholes."

He held it for her and she backed in, the length of her body brushing against him. She turned quickly.

"I hear you have a daughter. Surprise, surprise."

Within a day or two after he had told Doris, everyone in town knew. The fact that no one seemed very surprised told Lewis a great deal about the way the town regarded him.

"I hope we can meet soon. They say she's unusual. Did you know she'd be coming?"

The words *You stay away from her* snapped across his mind but luckily he heard how ridiculous they sounded.

"No."

"A surprise for you, too." Then she dropped that gayer tone and quite seriously she said, "Father Beede. It puts you in a whole new light, Lewis."

So suddenly that he could not step away, she threw her arms around his neck, gave him a wiry hug, and backed out into the aisle.

"Come on, Howard. Doris and I need some muscle."

She did not look back to see if Howard was following her, but he was.

Lewis walked down the ramp to the paddock where Joker and Melissa were standing head to tail grooming each other. When he opened the gate, Joker came to him. He would not need to grasp the halter, the horse would follow him and Melissa would trudge behind, but he did anyway, if only to hold on to the slow, strong ripple of the horse's walk. He would have liked to be indignant at Phoebe for Coleman's sake, but for too long he had seen how whatever they did to each other, even now what Phoebe might be doing by not selling the place and using it as she wished, was their complicated way of treating each other. Depressing how all relationships had to be so tangled — Doris and Gus battering each other across the open pages of Scripture, Foley and Helen yelling through doors and windows, even Elmore lately, pushing at his wife, Eleanor, as if she were everything that troubled him. Near the top of the ramp he heard Melissa's hoof scrape and slip on ice, and both he and Joker turned to see her catch her footing and plod on. He could still feel the sharp bone of Phoebe's arm on the back of his neck.

He could not foresee those moments when the mention of his daughter by anyone other than Annie would seem like a vicious invasion of his privacy. When Elmore found out, he had trudged immediately to the cabin, breathless from the effort of the unaccustomed exercise of the climb, more insulted and angry than Lewis had seen him for years. *You could at least have told us before it was all over town,* he had blurted. *Elly was deeply hurt.* Fortunately Miriam had left for three days to visit friends in Boston and was not there when Elmore arrived. Lewis had made a contrite visit to Eleanor. He was duly forgiven with the proviso that they all be introduced as soon as possible. Then he had been angry at himself for apologizing. What right did they have to make him feel guilty? All that was his business.

Yet there were times when he needed having Annie to share it with. She had come to the cabin very soon after he had told her about Miriam, and he recognized a firm kindness in the way she treated his daughter that had to come out of a clear decision on her part. But he also watched that determination relax and disappear into relief as she found someone in Miriam she could like to be with, even if Lewis still often caught her watching the younger woman with puzzled intensity. It was Lewis who felt a little anxious, since the two women began to spend more time together and Annie kept a room available in her house for Miriam whenever she wanted *to get away from the old grouch,* she had said once when Lewis was showing his impatience at some conversation he had thought was trivial. But what were they discussing when he was not there? Sometimes Miriam seemed to smile slightly at him afterward as if she knew more about him than Lewis would want her to.

Joker, sniffing at the cleaned floor, plodded into his stall toward the trough of oats, and Melissa, pausing a moment to be certain her companion would not back out, trudged into her own. They had been inseparable for years:Melissa, born defective so that she never came into heat; Joker, the champion stud, who had adopted Melissa from the beginning, defending her against any aggression from other horses in the pasture. The great hollow chewing began and he walked in beside Joker talking, soothing his palm along the animal's hide. The muscles of the horse's jaws bunched and he blinked lazily. With his palms spread flat against the solid neck, Lewis could feel the pulse, the constant flow beneath the hide. In the aisle he pulled a stool close to the wall and leaned back, closing his eyes.

The horses were not young anymore, and before long he might have to put them away. Joker first, probably. Foster had taught him that, too. He and his father had led the old horse up the tilting meadow toward the edge of the woods. It was spring and the ground was spongy. The slope glistened with a fine layer of water that would run off for at least another week as the snow melted back in the woods and until the warm winds gusting from the south dried everything. The hole was easy to dig for the first foot, then Lewis worked with pick to break through frosted earth until he was four feet down. His father spread the bottom with quicklime.

Ajax was nearly blind, his legs so arthritic that he staggered over the uneven ground. *I won't give him up to the knackers,* Foster said that week. *No horse as good as this one will go down to the hammer.* He carried the pistol tucked in his belt. *Stand him on the uphill side.* Lewis heard the pin drawn back as he led the horse around the hole so that Ajax stood beside it, head drooping. *Don't look away,* Foster said, and Lewis made his eyes stay fixed on the horse's head, his father's hands.

For a moment Foster put one hand flatly on the depression behind the horse's ear as Ajax sniffed vaguely, eyelids lowered. He stood back, raised the gun, and fired in one smooth, precise motion. The hind legs buckled, the lips drew back over the mottled teeth, head thrown up and eyes wide, and Ajax rolled heavily sideways into the pit, legs convulsing in the air. Foster leaned down, fired again behind the other ear. Bright blood spattered his arms and some chips of bone and flesh were flung against the earth. They tucked the legs down, did not need to break them to make the body fit. Both of them took shovels and covered the horse, letting the earth rise high. For years Lewis would pass that mound on his way to hunt, noticing how it gradually sank until there was a slight declivity lush with grass and wildflowers, and later the saplings encroached from the woods.

Foster sat with him afterward. He leaned their shovels against the granite boulder nearby and carefully rolled the cigarette he allowed himself three times a day. Lewis said nothing, knowing his father would begin talking, and he treasured one of those brief moments when the man stopped his clenched forward motion. What Lewis kept seeing were the fragments of bone and blood in a kaleidoscopic pattern against the black earth. *I had a horse once,* Foster said, *when I was your age, in Canada. But he was blind from birth. Diseased, though, not inherited, so we could use him for stud, and he sired some of the best. I brought him up from a colt, led him in and out each day, kept watch on him, and helped him cover those mares. Jesus, how he'd know by smell where he was and what to do, and I even had him trained to the plow. Got too worked up one morning when a damned fool who had some mares to cover led one by too close before we'd got him out of the van and he busted a leg. Well, he had to be killed. My uncle sold him off for tallow. I couldn't sleep and I kept seeing that blind horse led into the knacker's shed where sure as hell he must have smelled the death all around him, his head held up in that room, no more light there than had ever been for him, and then the hammer coming down on his brain from nowhere.* He finished his cigarette in silence, and in the same silence they walked down the meadow together. But Foster placed his hand on Lewis's shoulder and they walked that way until they reached the road.

Lewis stretched when he stood, and his feet were numb with cold as he walked the aisle slowly. He turned off the space heater in the tack room and stepped out the door into the late-afternoon darkness. Every window of the house was lit up and smoke hung in the still, cold air. He wished he could move the horses. Foley's shed had been in worse repair than he had expected, and lugging the new beams and two-by-fours up the meadow had taken time. Buddy had come by on his snowmobile one afternoon and with the delighted pride of a child had dragged the last stack of lumber up the slope on a sledge in ten minutes. Then he had given Miriam a ride around the field, whooping while she hugged on to him, her eyes wide. *Goddamn, goddamn, don't she take the corners, though?* Buddy had yelled over the revving motor when he let her off, and together Lewis and Miriam had pounded nails while Buddy took three more spins around the field, standing as if he were water-skiing, and then with a whipping of his arm he had jumped the hole in the fence and ridden off toward the beaver swamp where his traps were set. Lewis had been pleased to find that Miriam could pound a nail accurately with full, methodical strokes. *The commune was good for something,* she had said.

"Will you ride with me, or are you eager to get frostbite?" Doris pulled up beside him at the gateway.

Lewis walked around to the other side and climbed in. Wound up in a shapeless woolen coat, a knitted cap pulled down to her upturned collar, Doris looked as solid as a mound of fired clay. The only flesh showing was a small section of face and the brief circumference of legs between her white socks and the wet hem of her coat. The truck jerked, spun, and bucked onto the highway.

"Four-wheel drive ain't worth shit, far's I'm concerned. But Gus swears by it." With no change of tone she said, "She'll eat him up."

"Who's eating who?"

"Phoebe. Howard. She's a spider, that woman, when it comes to men. But I say this is starting too young."

"Howard probably doesn't."

"He wouldn't know what he's getting into."

Lewis tried to see if her eyes gave any hint of what her attitude really was. "Howard has been hoping to get into anything for some time now, Doris, and Lord knows what he's tried instead."

She glanced quickly at him. Her words came out of the flaps of her collar. "Howard is no different than any boy his age. But Phoebe is lots different than any woman her age."

"How so?"

"Worse."

Lewis laughed.

"Men. Well, I had to leave the house. Cleaned it up anyway, top to bottom. Don't know if I can bear to come back in the morning and cook. I made all the beds like she said. Now I suppose I'll have to go back tomorrow and change the sheets all over again."

"Come on, now. Howard may be eager, but even Howard has his limitations."

"He'll find out what they are tonight."

Lewis was always surprised when he saw a tall tale forming in front of him as clearly as he might watch clouds lifting into the anvil shape of a storm.

"They'd already messed up two rooms by the time I'd left."

"I don't believe it." He was uneasy imagining Howard and Phoebe tumbling from one bed to the next in that empty house.

She shot a glance at him. "Think old Doris doesn't know what that thump-thump of uneven bed legs that gets faster is, and all the moany-groany and silence?"

"If it was Howard, he spread his wings and flew after two times."

She swerved, slammed on the brake so that they skidded past the standing figure waggling its arms. Howard caught up to them and hopped in beside Lewis. Doris stared beadily at his profile, then drew back her foot from the clutch so savagely that the truck grunted and nearly died.

"Doris was telling me you were real helpful this afternoon, Howard."

The boy's eyes jerked around the cab nervously.

"Lew, I gotta talk with you, please."

Doris snorted. "Talking won't help, boy. I'd pray, if I was you."

"She's crazy." Howard was muttering barely loud enough for Lewis to make it out over the rattle of the truck, so he was certain Doris had not heard but uncertain whether it was intended for her or Phoebe.

"A drink, Howard?"

"Damn it, Lewis Beede." Doris's hand beat down on the horn so that it bleated. "The boy's in bad hands. Howard Ryan, your daddy ought to get his fists on your backside."

"Now?" Howard said to Lewis.

"Soon as he can," Doris yelled and for the first time her mouth was clear of the collar.

The truck was already well into town. Lewis said, "This'll do," as they passed the Black Bear Bar and Grill. She stopped as if she wanted to throw them through the glass and onto the hood. Howard was out by the time Lewis had turned to her.

"Join us?"

Doris turned her face, voice low. "Help the kid, will you? His father's as good as they come. I'll take the drink some other time."

He put a hand on her muffled arm. "I'm coming along to see you soon."

She nodded. "Gus and I aren't doing much but arguing."

"Four Roses?"

"We'll use less wood in the stove that night if you do."

While Lewis clambered down she was already shifting and he barely had time to let go of the door. The jerk of the truck slammed it neatly. Howard was waiting on the sidewalk where the stuffed bear reared behind him, lips perpetually curled at something on the far side of the road.

"Listen," Howard began, but Lewis shook his head, turned the boy with him.

"I can't take this without a drink."

The bumper pool was in use, the lights low, only a few figures hunched on their stools. Jake Roy was half sitting on the ledge by the cash register, foot up on the bar. Lewis steered Howard past Wilbur and Don, who were too caught up in their game to say hello, and into the booth by the silent pinball machine. A record was spinning in the far corner, a woman's voice mourning the empty nights. Howard sat, his face still turned to Lewis.

"Bourbon, beer, what?"

"You paying?"

"Damnit, Howard. If you were a few years older, I'd say you'd taken me. Bourbon?"

Howard grinned quickly. "Thanks."

Jenny was standing in the doorway to her kitchen when Lewis passed. She smiled. "The corned beef is good tonight. I made a fresh apple pie."

Any other night Lewis would have stayed, but he had promised to eat at Elmore's, would be late already. Jenny was the best cook he had ever known, better than Annie. He liked those weary eyes, the slim body with its slight gathering at the gut, the way she would leave her kitchen late at night to sit at the bar, a constant cigarette in her hand, sharing her own bottle of Scotch if she liked the person next to her. Even when his own bar competed with theirs, Jenny had never held it against him. He only paused to tell her no, and why, and she scolded him for not coming much anymore, holding his arm lightly, and then he was at the bar, watching Jake measure out their booze. What Jenny lacked in stinginess was compensated for in Jake, who had a way of eyeing the heaped dinner plates that passed his counter as if watching someone burn good money. But the kitchen was hers.

"They caught Leo," he said laconically as he shoved the drinks across the bar.

"For what?" To lay hands on Leo Jaques at any time of day or night would be to apprehend him in some crime.

"Broke into Shady Rest Motel up to the Flatts. That one they close down every fall. Found him dead drunk in a cabin with two bottles of Jack Daniel's down his gut. He'd took a crap in the lobby, busted the safe."

"Geesum," someone down the bar said.

"No money. Pissed him off so he got drunk. Damn near poisoned himself."

Lewis was backing off, drinks in his hands, glad someone else had taken up the slack. The other voice said, "By Jesus, it's not the stealing or the breaking in they ought to get him for but the crapping, the pig," and someone else began talking about how they always do that, folks who break into empty places.

Howard had the glass to his mouth before Lewis could sit. Everyone in Judson learned to drink young, mostly from sitting in bars with their parents in midwinter because at home there was nothing but the TV that they had watched all day anyway, or the sound of the furnace going on and off. But Lewis had thought maybe Howard was different because his father hardly ever hung around.

"I think she's trying to seduce me."

He might have laughed, but Howard's expression, caught somewhere between fear and eagerness, snagged him, and with a twinge of jealousy he dimly remembered what it was like to be that old and suddenly understanding that it was possible, not just something that other, real people did.

"What gives you that idea?"

"After Doris and me and Phoebe moved the beds out from the wall so's Doris and me could get the mattresses turned and the sheets on, and Doris had gone to work on the furniture downstairs, she asked me to stay."

"Well?"

"She wanted me to help move the beds back, but she said she mostly needed someone to talk to for a while. Said she was nervous."

"When isn't she?"

Howard leaned forward. "I've never seen a person so nervous in all my life. Her hands shake even when she's got them in her pockets. She asked me to come to her room. Her bedroom." He grinned quickly. "She made me sit on the edge of her bed and she walked around and talked and smoked and asked me questions. About girl friends and things like that." He paused.

"That's it?"

The head shook. "It wasn't the first time. She'd done the same thing yesterday when she got in and I'd come over to help with the storm windows. After a while she sat down at the chair by her mirror and looked into it but I could see she was looking at me, too." Howard, shamefaced suddenly, stared at his hands. "I'm no damned good talking about things. I don't know what to say. She kept smoking, asking me for matches. When she walked over I thought she wanted a match, so I was trying to find one and she was right there and grabbed my face and kissed me." Again, he stopped dead. His glass was empty.

Lewis pushed his over. "You need it." Howard held it. "That's all?"

"No. She went to the other side of the room. She took off her clothes. Right there. She says, 'I'm going to take a bath and I'll be right out.' She didn't mind I was staring. I couldn't keep my eyes off her. I've never see a *real* woman with all her clothes off."

The look on Howard's face when he stared at Lewis was like the slightly cocked and listening expression of a dog who has heard a distant, high whistle. Lewis had to laugh, but nervously. Howard slugged down another mouthful.

"I ran."

"You what?"

"I took off."

"Just ran off on a naked woman?"

But the face that Howard leaned to him was pained and his hands swept both glasses dangerously close to the edge of the table. "You've got to help me, Lew. What was I supposed to do? She would've come out, I know, and expected me to do something, but I don't know what. Do I take my clothes off then? Do I wait? Was I wrong? Maybe she's just crazy and she didn't want it at all. And am I supposed to do all those things they do in magazines and movies?"

Lewis held still a moment. "What things?"

"We went into the Flatts last June, a bunch of us. We went to the new porn store and saw the films. There were all sorts of things those people do to each other, and afterward Jim and me decided we didn't think we could. I mean, how can you want to, Lew? Is that what she wants, you think?"

The face was close to tears. So Lewis put one hand on the boy's arm, retrieved the glass of Bourbon with the other, and offered it.

"I wouldn't worry about all that, Howard. I think you've got two options. You can go back soon, maybe tomorrow . . ."

"Not tonight?"

". . . and see what it is she wants. If that's what you want. Or you can stay away. Bag it."

"I know what I want," Howard said firmly.

But Lewis shook his head, and a pulse of bitterness pushed out his words. "It's never that simple. You never get just what you want. I don't think you'd find anything in that bed you couldn't handle. But there's a person back there who sure as hell will muck around with more than your body."

Howard stared at Lewis, mouth slightly open as if he would speak, then snapped his jaw tight.

"You're jealous," he muttered. "I shouldn't have told you. I knew Jim would be jealous, but I didn't think you would."

"Not jealous. Not Phoebe. But you're sure determined."

"I shouldn't have run off." Howard almost howled.

"Here, now." Lewis stood. "I'll show you how generous I am. One for the road. To screw up your courage."

The face turned up. "I should go back? You think I can handle it?"

"Just go easy. If she doesn't give you the time of day when you get back there, don't be surprised."

He made Jake empty the glass first because he knew how the man liked nothing better than giving a short shot on watered ice.

"Now, drink up," he said, still standing. "I'm due at brother Elmore's."

Howard stood. He downed it in three great bobs of his Adam's apple, wiped his mouth with the back of his hand, and then they walked together past Don and Wilbur. They were at the glaring stage now. That might end sometime around eleven in a punch thrown, some broken glassware.

Under the reared bear, Howard put a hand on his shoulder. "Thanks, Lew. I won't forget this."

When he was at the crossroads Lewis looked back to see Howard on the other side of the road, his thumb out to an approaching car. The lights flared red, he was in, and the car spun off through the snowy cut. As he walked slowly to Elmore's house, Lewis was oppressed by the thought that being Howard's age made anything possible. But it did not take long for that simple act to become more tangled than the wildest positions that arms and legs could assume. Age did not diminish the opportunities, but the fear of consequences did.

9

"**S**orry I'm late." Lewis stamped his boots and struggled with buttons. The heat blew fiercely at him up the hallway grate, and Eleanor held out her hand for his jacket.

"Elmore just got back from the office. He's in the shower. A drink?"

Through the doorway he could see Elaine in the den. She was dressed in her peppermint-striped hospital smock, her face lit by the TV. She waved. "Hi, Uncle Lewis." Lewis waved back, followed Eleanor down the hall to the kitchen and smells that reminded him how hungry he was.

"Help yourself." She stirred a pot, dipped in her finger, and tasted.

Lewis filled his glass with ice and a heavy dose of Bourbon. She was sprinkling from some bottles of herbs, bending slightly over the pot. When she was younger, Eleanor had been a little too thin, her face bony and gaunt, but that hollowed shaping gave her room to gather flesh and lately it was as if she had bloomed into her true body at last. Elegance was what she had, although Lewis always thought some warmth was lacking.

"Jon's waiting. I have to run now." Elaine stood at the door, groping into her coat. She had Elmore's build, stocky, blunt-featured. "I'm sorry, Uncle Lew. My evening on."

Her mother turned. "When Jonathan brings you home, remind him it's a school night and he's not to come in, and that doesn't mean I want to listen to the sound of his motor running for an hour while you sit out there."

Elaine turned to Lewis, ignoring her mother. "When am I going to meet my cousin?"

"Anytime you come up."

She smiled. "I will." She moved quickly to Lewis, reaching up to peck his cheek, but her self-consciousness made Lewis want to draw back. She paused at the doorway, shoving her hands into fluffy gloves.

"They say she's kind of a hippie."

"You'll have to judge."

"Anyway, I think it's exciting. I've never had a first cousin before."

The door slammed. Eleanor did not turn from the stove. "Forgive her. She's full of Florence Nightingale these days."

While she turned the pages of her cookbook, then traced a few lines with her finger, he tried to find the right words in the jumble of false starts. He had hoped to find Eleanor alone for a while, and now that he had that opportunity, he could not speak. What to say always seemed so clear until he was in the presence of anyone he imagined consulting. Lately Annie was too close to the situation. When he talked to her, he found something about Miriam clarified, but Annie would be suddenly cool and watchful as if she had spoken mainly to see his reaction. He needed another woman, even if she had no suggestions. He suspected all he wanted to do was find a way of fingering the knots that Miriam's presence had tied around him.

If she was in Judson he moved reluctantly when he started back to the cabin. Often he could not recall whether she was there or whether she had gone away again for a few days. She could not seem to make up her mind and never completely unpacked her knapsack. Sometimes only a note would be on the table — "Gone to Philadelphia for the weekend. Be back soon," or "Call me if you want, 215 – 864 – 4250." He never called, partly because by the time he began to wonder if he should, there would be a knock on the door, or he would meet her in the woods awkwardly clambering up in her new showshoes. He had no sooner begun to settle into his old routine than she would return, had no sooner begun to think he could arrange some kind of life with her constant presence than she would leave.

As he trudged up the hill to his cabin, his mind did not enjoy the old sense of solitude surrounding him again, but was tensely fixed on whether she would be there or not. Standing at the edge of the woods, smelling smoke from the stove already lit, he would have to push hard to swing his snowshoes out into the clearing that no longer seemed entirely familiar, in spite of the same trees crusted with old snow, the unchanged, frozen oval of the pond. But it was equally baffling how in the middle of a casual conversation with someone downtown, he would want to gabble about how his daughter had come home, was living with him now on the hill, had they seen her? wasn't she something? and he would break into a sweat afterward thinking how foolish he could have been. Surely they already gossiped about him enough.

He looked hard at the loose heel strap on Eleanor's shoe, shook the ice in his glass, breathed deeply, and found himself saying, "I guess Jonathan has nudged out poor Howard?"

"Sometimes I think it's poor Jonathan. She's pretty demanding. But, yes. For the time being, Jonathan seems to have won. He has his own car, after all."

A brief silence followed and then Lewis, his heart racing, muttered, "I've been thinking, Eleanor," but she had twisted away from the stove.

"Lew, Lew. What's got into him? What's wrong? I can't bear it."

Her eyes in their deep sockets were brimming, and her hand, still holding a small bottle, tipped sideways, scattering green flakes on the floor.

"Rosemary," she murmured, then looked beyond him quickly.

"Lewis? You there?"

"Hello," he called back too loudly.

His brother was squinting in the doorway as if he had come out of the dark, his recently dried hair tufted.

"Damned hot water ran out. That daughter of mine is going to run a shower someday until the reservoir goes dry."

"At least she's clean." Lewis filled his brother's glass with ice, trying to see what Eleanor was doing in the closet. Elmore pushed aside the Bourbon to reach the Scotch.

"What were you two up to, looking so guilty?"

"Spilling herbs," Lewis said.

Eleanor had reappeared and was sweeping the flakes into the dustpan.

"Exciting." Elmore looked tired, his dark-jowled face moving that slow way he had when something was on his mind.

"Dinner will be twenty minutes yet. Why don't you two sit, start a fire?"

Lewis filled his half-empty glass, paused to look hard at Eleanor's back, then followed Elmore. His brother stooped to the fireplace where the logs were piled ready on paper and kindling. As usual all the brass shone, the windows glinted beyond the carefully valanced drapes. Lewis sank into the gay print of an easy chair where cockatoos perched in an endlessly repeated jungle.

Elmore continued to stoop in front of the fire, staring at the flames that were fluttering up the paper. Lewis tried to think of something they could discuss. When Elmore began talking, his voice was so low that Lewis had to lean forward in the chair to catch all the words.

"She lives in the Flatts, Lew. I met her at Pike Cement last year. She's a secretary there. We'd get to talking when I went by to order or pay up on contracts. She could remember all the scores of those games when I was in school, used to follow the Judson Panthers even though she went to Flatts Central. I started taking her out to lunch once in a while, then she cooked for me at her apartment. She's been married twice. She's waiting on her next divorce." His face turned quickly to Lewis as if checking to see if he was listening. He reached to the mantle, pulled himself up, and sat nearby on the sofa. Lewis shifted, waiting with a quiet, sunken feeling.

"Eleanor doesn't know, probably won't ever know. The woman at Pike and I called it off yesterday. I don't love her, she doesn't love me, we put out a little bit, and that's that. I guess I can tell you, Lew, because it means so little." Elmore was staring at the glass in his hand as if searching for more words. "But that's what makes it so bad this time. How come it means so little?" He drank, pulled his glass away, an expression on his mouth as if the words in there were bitter. "It's not the first time, although the only one Eleanor knows of was ten years ago, and once we got through that, I think she hasn't worried anymore. But it used to all mean something. Or don't you know, Lewis? You with your unmarried life, that easy moving around."

As he put his glass down, Lewis shifted away slightly so their knees did not touch. "But you really didn't care for her anyway."

"She was swell. We even had this past we could share, in a way. She'd dated people I'd known, and vice versa. It finally got so we had talked ourselves into believing we had known each other. But all the time it was make-believe, just the motions. Putting your hand in the right place, saying the right things. I'm telling you about her because she's the easiest way to tell you about the part I can't express or understand. That's everywhere for me now. When I put my key in the lock to the office door I feel like I'm pulling rocks down over my head. When the phone rings and it's Benson Hospital Supply or maybe Dillinger Tools and they want a bid on a new building, I feel like a paper weight is on my tongue. I don't even really get pissed when the hot water runs out."

The smile was such a poor attempt that for the first time Lewis's chest tightened in panic. His brother had never spoken to him like this, and what he confessed to was not what Lewis would have imagined. He tried to hold in place that established image of stolid, plodding, big brother Elmore.

"I'm sorry," Lewis muttered, then saw how Elmore's lips twitched slightly as they would when he was holding back a laugh, and that made Lewis angry. His words were inept, but why did he always revert to being little brother, helpless before Elmore's superior experience? And he had his own problems, didn't he, that no one would listen to? He stared back, but Elmore's laugh never came, the eyes went dull again.

"I wasn't laughing at you. I know there's nothing more you can do than say that. I was thinking of something totally irrelevant. How Buddy Harlow drove his snowmobile right through the back door and into Chase's kitchen yesterday, he was that mad about Chase beating him at poker."

When Elmore's face went blank again, Lewis was framing a question about Buddy to lead them out into their usual territory of anecdote and gossip. But Elmore leaned forward, spilling Scotch over the rim of his glass, and said in an intense whisper, "Do you think I'm going a little crazy, Lewis? I'll be trying to concentrate on understanding what the hell is wrong, or telling something important to Eleanor as I was to you just now, and wham, my mind leaps off into something completely different that makes no sense for me to be thinking of. I can't get it in sight. Anything." He gripped Lewis's knee. "I was lying in her bed. In the middle of making love. It was almost over. And I started laughing, couldn't stop. Laughed so hard I lost it and had to quit. I'd remembered that time Dad and I had to chase a chicken with no head because Dad had lopped it, and we chased it clear across the field. It ran right onto the road and got hit by the milk truck and Dad was going to make old Estes pay but when Estes couldn't find the chicken's head, he refused." He was not laughing now, sat back quickly again. "Of course she thought I was laughing at her."

"Almost ready." Eleanor's voice came brightly from the kitchen.

"Have you talked to anyone about all this?"

Elmore shook his head. "Eleanor surely suspects something."

"She seems to."

"What did she say to you?"

"You came in. Listen, Elmore, I was trying to talk to her. I probably ought to with you."

"It's not talking that will help. You and I, Lewis, we can't go off to the Flatts and pay some young state doctor to tell us what went wrong when we were kids. Elaine's into all that. She says I'm having male menopause. She picks up that stuff working at the hospital."

"You've talked to her?" Lewis sat back again. Jesus, what a circus act. No use trying. Elmore kept his eyes tensely on the kitchen doorway.

"Not really. She caught me one afternoon sitting in the car with the motor running outside the stands at the football field. I was staring through the fence at the snow. She stood for a long time, I guess, and watched me before she came and got in. Said I didn't move for ten minutes so she got worried that I was dying of carbon monoxide. I told her some lies about how I was thinking of the good old days and football. I wasn't. I was looking at the snow. Looking at how flat it laid out across the field and how if you stared at it long enough without closing your eyes it began to look like water and moved." He swallowed.

"Ready." She was standing in the doorway.

Lewis glanced at her quickly, but if she had seen or heard anything, she did not show. She was the same poised and somewhat distant Eleanor, insisting that Lewis eat well, implying that the irregularities of his life made it essential for him to take advantage of what comforts he could snatch. He waited for them to question him about Miriam, but they were concentrating so hard on finding impersonal topics that she was only mentioned once, and Elmore jerked the conversation into another direction as if to imply that was none of their business and they should not pry into it. Lewis drank so much of the wine that they had to open another bottle. After dinner, they urged him to stay and did not seem to want to be alone with each other. But he could not bear the silence that surrounded their frantic conversation.

Finally, as if she sensed that the only way to keep him there was to be more stringent, she interrupted Elmore and said primly, "I don't think it's right she should be there."

Lewis could tell by the way Elmore glared at her that she was expressing something they had already discussed.

"That's up to Lewis, don't you think?"

"What is? What's on your mind, Elly?"

"Miriam's a grown woman. Even if she is your daughter, you didn't know her all those years and now suddenly she's living with you in a one-room cabin. It's not right."

"Oh, c'mon." Lewis waved sharply. Now all he wanted to say was, *None of your damn business.*

"Just think for a moment what it looks like. What they might say in town. You ought to have her come stay with us."

"Or Annie maybe," but Elmore looked even more uneasy after blurting.

"That wouldn't help much." She always regarded Annie as someone who contributed to Lewis's unstable life, as if he would have married, settled down, been very different without her.

"I don't give a damn what they say. Never have."

"No, you haven't." Was it the wine? Lewis had rarely seen her neck flush red like that. "But that's your problem. Don't you think it's a little selfish to impose your attitude on her? What if she wants to go on living in Judson? Respectably, I mean."

He laughed sharply. "Look. I know the difference between a daughter and just any woman. How sick do you think I am?"

"I didn't say that. I assume you do know the difference. But you can't assume everyone else does."

"Come on, you two." Elmore had kept drumming his fingers on the arm of the sofa and now he slapped down his opened hand. "She does have a point, Lew."

"I can't go around worrying about how depraved other people's imaginations are. Let them have a good time thinking we're up there screwing if they want." He said it as baldly as possible because he knew it would offend Eleanor, and he was right. What he had not counted on was the way it shocked him to say it so overtly. So he muttered, "Sorry," and after a pause in which she retreated to the kitchen to bring back a bottle of cherry liqueur, Elmore found a new topic for them to discuss, and they all took it eagerly.

"Talk to him, please," Eleanor said quietly when Elmore went looking for a pair of gloves that he said were too big for him and he would throw away if Lewis did not take them. But he could not find them. Lewis waved from the front walk and, buttoning his coat, trudged in the squeak of old snow, only then feeling how drunk and tired he was. Annie's house was as far as he could make it that night.

He paused on the sidewalk. When he thought of Miriam probably asleep in the cabin, he regretted not slowly pushing the door open, cracking the ice seals where the warm air had leaked around the seams, hearing her drowsy voice say, *That you?* before she rolled back into sleep, and the next day she would not even recall his arrival. How good it would be to turn on the lamp, have one more drink. She would sit up blinking, lean her back against the wall, tucking the blankets tightly around her so only her bare arms and shoulders were exposed. He would draw his chair up close to her bunk after stoking the firebox, would offer a drink, and they would talk for a while. He could tell her about Elmore and Eleanor and she would laugh with him about how silly it had been, his trying to talk about his own confusions, blocked by theirs. And there weren't really any confusions for him, were there? He would see that clearly, watching her sleepy face become unnumbed. He would put his hand on her bare shoulder, stoop to kiss her good night. It was all simple. She was his daughter. When he felt that clearly, all their problems together seemed like mere inconveniences.

He beat his cold hand once against his thigh, and began walking again. Why when he was away from Miriam could he feel so certain and clear, and then, standing beside her, or waking slowly to see her stooping to her clothes in the dim light of dawn, he would clench, the words and gestures held deep inside him? She would make breakfast for him, moving now in the tight space of the cabin with complete assurance as if she had been there for years, and he would not be able to say anything, cutting his responses to the bare necessities of communication. He would resent the ease with which she took the frying pan from its hook or casually moved his boots away from the doorway. Sometimes if she touched him in passing, he would pull back inside as if the pressure of her body were slowly filling the meager space around them. But most of all he could not bear her endless questions. How could he remember all those things? Why should he? No, there were no photographs of his mother. Well, she looked like most women did then. No, his father was not always mean. Just mostly. He could barely control his turning, seething inner self, and when she did not even sense that, he only twisted tighter until he would start tying on his boots to go or would take down a book and hold it open to an unseen page, frowning and muttering if she continued. As soon as she had gone or he had tramped off on some errand he knew was unnecessary, he would be torn with a pain as if someone had struck an ax into his breastbone. Why couldn't he simply answer her, show her the affection he knew was really there?

He stamped along the sidewalk, turned, passed the path to Annie's house and turned again, walking a repetitive sweep to keep his feet warm. Very clearly he imagined a man sitting in Elmore's car, staring out across the football field, but it was himself. Miriam's face appeared by the closed window, blurred by the frost of his breath. She was worried. She was pleading with him to open the door, let her come in. Then he remembered Elaine when she had been a child and he would take the book she handed to him, adjusting his own posture to provide a secure lap for her, and as he read, her head would sink back against his shoulder. Her eyes would stare past the book, her breath as even as if she were asleep, her whole body absorbed in what he was saying and she would fit into his curve as if they were molded to each other. Now he clutched his arms to himself tightly, shivering. He wanted that to have been Miriam so badly that he could not forgive her.

Annie was wide awake, sitting in a living room thick with the smoke of cigarettes, probably a pack at least, Lewis guessed by the overflowing ashtray. The TV was on but she was not watching it, riffling the pages of a magazine on the table in front of her. She would not let him take his jacket off, zipped herself into her yellow parka.

"I want some fresh air," and he found himself beside her on the path, walking out with her arm tight around his. She turned them along the road up Monument Hill. The slopes were white silhouettes flecked with dark pines, but the moon, flatly bright on hard-packed snow, widened the sky and diminished the mountains. For a while they did not speak and she kept them moving fast. They walked this way together in all seasons when either of them felt the house pulling tight.

They passed the stone gateway, but kept on toward the flattened top and statue of a single soldier leaning moodily on his rifle. In the moonlight only his slumped posture was evident, a sentinel sleeping at his post.

"What are we going to do, Lew? Or what are you going to do, I guess I should say?"

"About what?"

They stopped under the figure. There was no wind, and when their footsteps were not grinding on the snow, a silence hung over the landscape so thick that it made his ears ring.

"Miriam. What does she want?"

"Ask her. You're together enough."

Once when he had come by, Annie and Miriam had been leaning over the kitchen table, the coffee cold in their cups, talking so intensely that Annie had said as if brushing away an annoyance, *We're talking, Lew, couldn't you come back in an hour or so?* and he had bought a few beers at the Bear.

"She's honest with me and I like her. But she hasn't decided anything. And you haven't either."

"We need to?"

"Soon." She folded her arms, walking toward the railing of the outlook.

He followed. "I can't see what there is to decide. You make it sound like we have choices."

"She changes things for us. Sometimes I think we're never alone anymore. Even when she's not here."

They stood where the hill dropped away to the roofs of the houses below, streetlamps in the webs of trees and far off a car coming along the distant highway in a valley filled with gauzy moonlight.

"I'm not sure there's much to be done."

She clasped her gloved hands on the rail. "You always drift along through these things, just let go and see where they take you. It makes me nervous, angry. I want to grab hold, shift them, get something in place."

"How can you when there's nothing clear to snatch?" He was impatient with the old argument.

"But that's always true, isn't it? With you, nothing's ever clear until it's over and then you're only grabbing what has resolved itself anyway. What's the use of that?"

"What the hell would you like me to do, then?"

Her face turned, a white disk with eyes. "Christ, Lewis, some of it's simple. You could find out if she's going to stay on, make some decision about that. She could tell you something about what she's going to do with her life."

He shrugged. He had forgotten his gloves and so he kept his hands deep in his pockets, but the tips of his fingers were numbing. "No one ever knows that."

"You never do."

She turned, moved toward the other end of the parapet. Again he walked with her. The voice was so quiet he had to lean close.

"Maybe I'm getting tired. After Jim died, after that year of waiting and watching him go down through all that pain, I only

144

wanted to be free and alive and alone, whenever I wanted. I was happy we could be together again without having to sneak around. What a sense of power that gave me — you going in and out the front door, me tromping up through the woods whenever I wanted and not worrying would anyone see me, would someone tell Jim." Far to the right, halfway down the hill, a maple cracked with the cold, a sharp chock as if it had been struck once with an ax. "And remember those years of quiet cheating, and our struggles to quit, then starting again? How awful I felt when I told him near the end because I couldn't bear the thought of him dying and my having to feel guilty always, since he was the only one to confess to. And he said he knew."

Lewis waited to see where she was going, thinking of that day in late fall when he had met Jim on the edge of the woods near Foley's, both of them hunting grouse. Jim had suddenly cocked and lifted his gun. Lewis ducked, the gun blasted near his shoulder, and he had looked up at Jim, who laughed once and held out a hand to help him up, saying, *You fool, I could have killed you long ago*, and they went looking for the dead bird. Later that year, gaunt with pain, Jim Strand had risen on his bed to clutch one rail, his voice slowed but clear. *We've too much in common for me to hate you, Lewis Beede. But I sure come close sometimes.* When he walked out into the hospital lot, Lewis had not been able to hold back that taint of his father's presence, the flat voice saying, *You let that boy beat you. I don't care if we cheat or not, as long as folks think you beat him back.* When Annie was married, Lewis would come and go from Judson, but even if he always returned to find her equally incapable of forgetting, there was no victory in that.

"I know," he said when her silence continued.

"No." She spoke simply. "You know very little about Jim and me. Only what you can imagine."

"What are you getting at?"

"Sometimes I wake in the middle of the night and get out of bed and I can't remember for a moment whether that door is the closet or the front door or the way downstairs or if I'll bump into the stove. Am I at home or in the cabin? It's like camping out. Now I hardly ever come to the cabin, and sometimes that seems worse because when you're not with me, I miss you, and when you are, often you aren't really here."

She did not turn. He wanted to push all that away. Didn't he have enough to think about? He stared toward the town where the distant light of the intersection was blinking — on, off, on, off.

"So what do we do?"

"I'm getting cold." She shivered and started to walk. He paused, listening to her receding footsteps, but caught up with her quickly. "I can't answer that question any better than you can. But there it is and I'm tired of walking around it. I'm looking for an answer, though. Hard." She put her hand lightly on his arm. "Lewis, how I loved being alone for a while. I even thought I was going to tell you to quit seeing me for a year or so. Just lying there in my own bed, the house all around me, the rooms clean and empty and waiting for whatever I wanted to do with them, felt so damned good."

"Not now?"

"Things change."

They held still at the gate to the graveyard. Something scraped across the snow like a leaf in a breeze, but there was no air stirring. A dark object shifted near one of the stones, then held still as a shadow.

"A rabbit," Lewis said quietly.

It moved the long stretch of its hind legs and the ears perked up before it gathered into a ball again. She put both arms so tightly around his chest that he could not breathe, pressing her warm face to his neck.

10

Miriam was sick, propped up in her bunk with a box of tissues beside her. Her normally chiseled face was puffed, eyelids droopy. But she had not stopped watching him all morning. There seemed to be no place where her gaze could not scan him.

"You're sure there's nothing I can do? Something I can get you in town?"

Although her words were clear, her voice was hoarse and muffled. "No. It's just a cold."

But Lewis, imagining fully the stuffed and pounding weight of her head, the heat and chills of fever, could not bear the thought of simply lying there like that. He hated it when his body attacked him, would struggle and refuse merely to lie down. She had folded up immediately, staring at the wall, breathing unevenly during those first hours when it was at its worst. Finally impatient with his helpless flutterings, she had turned her head sharply. *It's perfectly natural to be sick sometimes. You make me feel it's wrong.* He had gone outside to split wood. Only trying to help. But he could not stand the idea of catching it himself, and he had waked the next morning breathing carefully, swallowing to be certain he had not succumbed.

"Do you feel guilty sometimes?"

He put down the catalog he had been thumbing through for the tenth time. Her question came out of a long silence.

"About what?"

"That you never came looking for me. Never tried."

"Why should I?" He kept his eyes on the rows of gunstocks.

"I'm not accusing you. I'd like to understand better. I wanted to find you so much, ever since I can remember knowing you and a real mother existed, that I can't imagine being able to put it completely out of my mind. It doesn't seem natural."

He shrugged. "I'm probably a freak."

"That's not what I meant and you know it. You see what I mean? You get so defensive when I ask you about all that. You must feel guilty."

"Would it make you feel better if I said I was?"

Her laugh turned into a cough. "You mean, would it shut me up? No. I'd probably want to know how it felt to feel guilty and not do anything about it."

"Oh, for Christ's sake."

He slammed his open hand down on the table and the coffee cup rattled in its saucer. When he turned, they glared at each other for a moment, and then she closed her eyes wearily.

"I'm sorry. Didn't sleep at all last night. Probably the fever, but I kept being half-awake and not knowing where I was and then thinking you'd been towing the cabin somewhere on a long rope until you decided to cut it and the cabin was starting to skid down the hill."

She kept her eyes closed, breathing slowly, and he thought she had dropped off to sleep, but then her lips moved and she said, "Look, I'll try not to nag at you. But promise you'll tell me when things cross your mind, when you remember anything? I feel like we have so much to do, to make up for all those years, but you never talk to me about anything except the weather or your horses or the shed unless I ask you."

Her tongue licked at her lips. In the silence, her eyes opened languidly to search him out, and then she was asleep and he wished he had gone downtown earlier since now he did not want to disturb her by leaving. He turned to the section on fly rods.

But it was almost as annoying when she stopped asking

questions. He could see them in her eyes, even a number of times at dinner he would notice how thoughtful her face had become, her lips would start to move, and then she would stare at him and shake her head and ask for another beer. The questions he imagined she was framing were worse than any she had asked so far. Why the hell should he feel guilty? Of course he didn't. Ridiculous. He had been an adult then, not an infant. A man had to go on about his life, make the best of it. You couldn't go mooning around torturing yourself for the mistakes you had made here and there. Besides. Besides. And with a jerk he would barely keep the ax from flying down the slope as it glanced off the log he had aimed at inattentively.

"Well, I wish you'd wear something," he finally snapped. "A nightgown. Pyjamas."

The argument had begun soon after she recovered from her cold. Partly because she had been ill, she had been with him for three full weeks. He walked into the cabin, his pack loaded with groceries, to find her standing naked in the galvanized tub that she had moved into the middle of the floor and filled with steaming water. All the way up the trail he had been completely removed from his surroundings, arguing with Coleman as if he were striding beside him, so that when he first saw her standing sideways in the tub, her arms held high as she squeezed the sponge onto her upturned face, her sharp breasts, the concave stretch of her lean belly ending in the mound of dark hair — he saw only a strange and beautiful woman. She faced him, soap glistening on her bare flesh and her eyes blinking through the water. She smiled and kept rubbing at her uplifted arm, and he had to make himself look away, his heart pounding.

"Sorry." He lurched back toward the door.

"Don't open it again, please," she said gaily, then sneezed.

He leaned the pack against the wall, stood with his back to her and looked out the window at the snow squall.

"I didn't feel up to walking all the way to Annie's and back. Hope I don't make too big a mess, but I really couldn't bear the smell of my own body anymore."

He did not answer. He wanted to say, *You knew I was coming back, you could have done it earlier*, but instead he stood there stiffly.

"Oh, come on. I am your daughter after all."

"You are," he said, pulling out each word like a nail, "also a grown woman and should act like one."

That was when he suggested nightclothes. Her whole attitude to nudity, like so many things they had stumbled across, differed hopelessly from his. Ever since she had arrived he had been removing his clothes after the lantern was turned out, never taking all of them off, keeping his trousers close to his bunk and groping into them under the covers at dawn. He bathed at Annie's, even felt a little odd sometimes shaving in front of Miriam, and he had made a sliding bolt for the inside of the outhouse door. When he was alone, he could sleep naked, or walk around with no clothes on when he first woke in the morning. Sometimes even with Annie he preferred to turn out the light before he lay down beside her.

Her splashing stopped.

"So much for the bath." Her voice chipped out the words. "I guess you've forgotten you took all my clothes off once."

"That was different. Even if you were my daughter, you wouldn't behave like this."

"Even if?"

"I mean if you'd been brought up in my home."

"Home? Where is your home, Lewis Beede?"

"Here. Maybe you'd better not forget that."

"How can I? You certainly keep reminding me it's yours."

He was unable to turn, arguing at a strange disadvantage like trying to catch someone while blindfolded.

"Anyway, I wasn't brought up in your cabin. Myra and Arnie were never ashamed of their bodies or made me feel ashamed of mine, and we all went skinny-dipping together lots."

"I'm happy for you. I prefer some privacy."

Her feet padded on the floorboards, coming down angrily on heels.

"Damn, you're a repressed character. Sometimes I just want to shake you and loosen up all the nuts and bolts. You must be in pain all clenched up like that."

He heard her dragging the tub to the doorway, but he did not help. She kept her back turned to him the rest of the day as she read in a chair by the stove. But the worst part was the dreams that night in which he kept walking into rooms or running around corners to find her naked, bending to pick up her dropped clothes, reaching high for them on a shelf beyond her hands, and yet her face did not show surprise or regret, but smiled as if wanting him to come closer. Sometimes he would step forward and she would become Phoebe, laughing and pointing at him. For days he could not bear to look at Miriam because her body insisted on revealing its hidden shapes under the contours of her clothes.

For a week he had been telling her she needed to put in one more scoop of coffee grounds. She had finally said, "It's not good for you to have that much caffeine," and then she listed all the deforming things it did to his body. The next morning he had taken the coffeepot out of the drainer as soon as he rose and filled the basket with coffee. She only tasted her cup and pushed it away. "That's vile," she said slowly. He did not answer, but the next morning he forgot to make the coffee and when he poured his cupful he shoved it at her, sloshing stains onto the table.

"Damn stuff is clear as water. I could read through it if I had to."

Her motion was so fast that he could only flinch in response. She swung her hand out and sent the cup and saucer flying and they smashed against the stove. "Damn it, damn it," she wailed, dropped her head onto her folded arms, and sobbed. He leaned forward. He could not bear the sound and placed a hand on her shoulder, but she shrugged violently, choked out some words he could not understand. He had to do something, so he rose and began picking up the shards.

When he came back from the outhouse she was packing her knapsack.

"Where're you going?"

Her back was curved to him, the sack sloppily stuffed.

She stood. "I think we need a vacation. It's not working."

He wanted to tell her to stay. But the stubborn set to her mouth angered him. "Suit yourself."

"I am."

She was gone for three days. At first he was relieved. He walked around the cabin or out on snowshoes along the ridge as if he had been away for a long time. He did not go down to Annie's that first night. After all, there was no need to get away. He woke the next day from dreams he could not remember, but which pressed at him so that he paused as he repaired the sink, wrench in hand, certain he was supposed to be doing something else — picking up Annie? going to Elmore's for dinner? — and then he sensed that whatever he had dreamed was terrible. By the second day he realized he had bought too much food before she left and some of it was beginning to spoil. He was angry at her. What a waste. She could have made up her mind earlier to go away, let him plan for it. That night he was restless, overstoked the fire, ate too much hamburger, decided to go down to Annie's, and buckled himself into his snowshoes, then imagined being at her house, not really wanting to talk to her either, and stood the snowshoes back up against the side of the cabin. That night he woke still not recalling the details of a dream that had made him cry out, but he was unable to prevent himself from thinking of her anymore, and longed to hear her turn, a knee or elbow bumping against the wall.

She came back the next evening, standing hesitantly in the doorway. "Shall we try again?"

He nodded and, not looking directly at her face, said, "I was going to come looking for you."

"Thank you," she said simply, and for a while they hardly argued at all, even laughing about the flannel nightgown she had bought.

The mistake he made the next day was asking her where she had gone.

"I stayed at Phoebe's."

He stood so suddenly from pulling on the wrench that he hit his head on the lip of the sink and had to hold tightly onto one faucet.

"I'll bet that stings."

"How long have you known Phoebe?"

"We had some drinks together one night. She drove me to the Flatts that day I had to get a new muffler."

"You stayed at the Whites'?"

She laughed. "How ominous. You sound like the voice of doom. It's a lovely house. Phoebe's kind of a nut, but we get on well."

"What next." He shook his head.

"She told me a lot about you. And her father."

He could not bear the thought of them talking about him together.

"She likes you a great deal, you know, although she told me about how mostly you argue with each other. But that helped. It seems I'm not the only one."

"She's sick."

When Miriam finally answered, her voice was quiet. "About some things."

"Men, for instance."

"Sex, you mean."

"Damned right I do."

"I don't know too many people who have no problems with sex."

"Is that so?" It disgusted him to think of her in that same house with that slut, probably watching Howard gangle around like a fledgling satyr. "I don't want you seeing any more of her."

"Look. When I said we had a lot to make up for, I didn't mean you had to treat me like a kid."

A figure flashed by the window and knocked on the door. Elaine. Lewis wished he could tell her they were busy. He moved nervously in and out of the cabin as his niece did her best to "get better acquainted," which she self-consciously announced as her purpose for visiting.

"More than anything I wish I could be out of high school, away from Judson."

Elaine sat on the edge of the bench, her socked feet forward and hands pressed between her legs. Stooping under the sink, Lewis groped for the pail's handle.

"Then leave. That's easy." Miriam shrugged.

"Is it? I wouldn't know what to do. I've hardly ever been out of Judson. Besides, I really want to go to nursing school at the university. I have to graduate to do that."

"Sounds like you don't want to leave." Miriam sat at the table, carefully scrabbling the shreds into her cigarette paper. Lewis suspected her gesture was deliberate. When the match scraped, he turned with the pail in his hand to see her light up. "Have some?" She extended it to Elaine.

"Oh, no thanks. Really. I've tried it and I don't like it."

She glanced at Lewis. He could not tell if she looked embarrassed because she was lying or if she was hoping he would not tell her parents. But he was annoyed at Miriam's truculence. Elaine sipped from her mug of tea and the bittersweet smell of hemp filled the room. Since he refused it too, Miriam always smoked alone. As far as he could see, it had very little effect on her.

"Uncle Lewis tried for years to teach me how to hunt, but I was never any good. I always hit targets but I can't help missing when it's alive. Has he been teaching you?"

"I've never seen him with a gun." She turned her eyes on him flatly.

"Have you given up hunting, Uncle Lewis? It's true he hasn't brought us any venison for years."

"Elmore and I might take it up again. Next year."

A wind whirled snow against the window, clattering the nearby branches.

"I heard you lived in a commune once. What was that like?"

"I'm going to get some water." Lewis reached for the door. The section of pipe he had been trying to repair had frozen that morning when the fire died, and it had not yet thawed because of the steady draft of cold wind.

Miriam's level voice was speaking with as few words as possible, and he cut it off by closing the door. Elaine's snowshoes, brightly varnished, leaned against the cabin wall. He walked in the drifted track toward the brook, which was only a seam in the banks of snow. He stooped to the nearest pool, let his knees sink into the powder, and stared at the water, black and sinuous. When the wind gusted snow onto the surface, the white skift vanished. Above the silent pool the water was churning through rocks. Even on the coldest days and nights when everything was turned to stone, he could hear some motion if he knelt there, as if listening to the pulse of a deeply sleeping creature.

The cold worked into his knees and still he did not move. The water was clear but so darkened by the narrowness of the opening that he could barely see one or two brown stones on the bottom. He wished he could quit worrying about what he should do. His mind could not seem to get anything clear. Whenever he paused to think, he was aware of a smothering grayness. Why the hell couldn't they leave him alone for a while — Annie, Miriam, even Elmore. Now Elaine. But everyone kept at him. Miriam's ques-

154

tions were the worst of all. In spite of the quick push of resistance whenever she asked one, he wanted to be able to answer, and sometimes, long after they had moved on to some other topic, the question would return and he would find himself halfway down the mountain muttering to himself, hands gesturing to an imaginary listener as he slogged along in his snowshoes. But his attempts to answer only shattered what he thought were fixed and solid memories. Had he really experienced that, or was it what he had hoped he would do, or an image like some dream invented from many lesser events? Had he totally misunderstood what he was doing? He could see himself in the living room of their apartment in New York. Monica was asleep on the couch where she had curled up to wait for him, *Even if I have to stay up all night*, she had said. The room was blurred with dawn, so she must have dozed at last. He was looking at his own figure, his mind as separate from his body as a camera. Yet it was not possible for him to have seen himself leaning angrily with one arm against the unsteady wall, the cramped pose of her laden body an accusation more stinging than any words that followed. If he had not been able to see himself like that, what had memory done, and could it be counted on? Again and again he would sheer off, saying to Miriam, *Look, I just don't remember*, and she would say, *You mean you'd rather not.* Those words annoyed him at first, then he understood he would prefer her to think that. It was far worse to have to admit his past life was thinning, dissolving, finally as insubstantial as a fog.

He plunged the bucket full and cold water sloshed across his hand. When he opened the door Elaine was saying, "Mother doesn't think so. She says we ought to finish college at least, find out where we're going. I don't know. Jonathan says he doesn't see why we can't do that together."

"But why get married?"

"You mean live together anyway?" Elaine tossed her hair back.

"That's a possibility."

"I could. But Jonathan couldn't. He's very strict. And our parents would be upset." She looked so thoughtful that Lewis was pained. She was taking Miriam seriously and did not know her well enough to see how uninterested her cousin was. Miriam took a deep breath, let the smoke out slowly through her nose.

"Well," and with a puppetlike lifting of her arm, Elaine peered at her watch. "I really have to go. Won't you come soon for dinner? Mom asked."

"Thank you." The voice was noncommittal.

Elaine stooped to find her boots under the table, pulled them on, and lashed them tightly while Lewis put the bucket on top of the stove. The snow on its sides melted and hissed. When she was beside him, Elaine reached to peck him on the cheek. She took his hand firmly and did not let it go as she moved to the door.

"Will you help me into my snowshoes? There's one stiff buckle." At the door she turned quickly. "Please do come, Miriam. It's been nice to see you again," and she did not wait for a reply, pulling him along, shutting the door behind them.

She slid her boots into the harnesses. He could see which buckle was going to give her trouble and he knelt, her hand resting on his back as she pushed her foot in.

"Uncle Lewis, what's troubling my daddy?"

He pulled hard, his fingers stiff and pained by the cold.

"I'm not sure."

"Please tell me."

"I wish I knew."

He stood. Her eyes were steady on him.

"Will you tell me when you know? He won't talk to me."

He nodded. His heart beat heavily as she began to walk away, swinging her short legs in wide arcs. She stopped after a few paces and turned her face to him.

"She's hard to talk to, Uncle. Or is it just me?"

"We're tired today."

Before she twisted away, the smile she gave him was like her mother's, lips barely moving, all of it held in the eyes. She settled into a choppy rhythm as she went down the slope, and he wanted to call out to her, say something. He waved when she glanced back from the edge of the woods.

Miriam had not moved. "I guess I was hard on her."

He took their empty cups to the sink while she rose and stood by the stove, hands held flatly above it. Her face was flushed over the cheekbones, her forehead very pale in contrast.

"I can't handle all your family too."

"My family?" He noticed the confusion in her glance.

"I can't seem to accept them yet. All those years I concentrated so hard on *mother* and *father* I forgot that would mean uncles and aunts and cousins and everything else that a family is."

"They won't wait on your convenience. They're out there, real and alive and curious. And easily hurt."

She stared at the door. "How can you take a family seriously when all their first names begin with *El*? And she's something of a flutterbrain, isn't she?"

His throat tightened. "At times. But she certainly meant well. I sort of helped to bring her up, you know. Anyway, that's the difference between family and acquaintances, isn't it? You don't get to decide whether to take them or not. They're there. So you learn to love them."

She folded her arms, gave that small, all-knowing laugh she resorted to sometimes when he struck a nerve. "Learn to love? Oh, c'mon. You can't take love to school and tell it what to do." She walked to the window, her back taut and straight.

"I wish to hell you wouldn't smoke that stuff around other people. If you want to stink up the cabin, that's one thing."

"I've smoked the last of it and I don't imagine I'll find any in Judson. So you don't have to worry. But you ought to try it, especially when you get so uptight."

"If you'd been my son and I'd caught you younger, I'd have thrashed you."

"But not a daughter?"

"No."

"Why not?"

"It wouldn't seem right."

She sat very stiffly at the table. "I'm sorry I couldn't be a son. I hear that's what you really wanted."

"Says who?"

"Annie."

"You seem to talk about everything. Well, I don't have that dream anymore."

"I cured you."

She breathed deeply, and then her voice was firm and quiet as if she were talking with forced patience to a child. "Haven't we

157

wandered off the course again? You don't have to agree with my opinion of Elaine. In fact, it's because she's my cousin and not just some acquaintance of yours that I get to make up my mind."

"Fine. But maybe you don't have to tell me."

She whirled. Her pale face was burning all over now. "Damn it. Why not? Why can't I tell you anything, everything?"

"Why don't you start thinking more about the people around you? You seem to want a lot, and to be getting pretty much what you want."

She tilted at him, one hand on her chest. "I have? Twenty-four years of waiting and hoping to find you and having to make up my mind whether or not to, all on my own, and having to accept the fact that my parents were so in love with the convenience of their own lives that they could not face each other or accept me? I didn't have to be a bastard. The least you could have done was be a married couple so poor you had to give me up. And you can say I've gotten what I wanted? Fuck it, did I come all this way to hear you accuse me like that?"

His muscles tightened in his arms as if to strike her. He stepped back. "Don't you think we'd better turn this off?"

"Damn you, damn you." She turned back to the window and leaned on the table. "Is she pushing you — Annie? Do I get in her hair?"

"No one pushes me. It's between you and me."

"Bullshit." Her voice calmed suddenly. "Look. I think she's wonderful. I don't want to foul up anything. But what the hell, you two have had long enough to make up your minds what you want to do, and if you haven't yet, it's not my problem. So I couldn't be much in the way."

"We won't get anywhere talking about Annie and me."

"But it's the whole thing, isn't it? The way you live. Do you ever make up your mind about anything? Do you think the rest of the world, no matter how lovable you are, can bear just to float along down the river on your raft? Can't you see Annie, me, even yourself although you don't know it, waiting for something, some signal?" Her face relaxed. "I'm sure I'm not the first one to say this to you, am I? I can imagine my mother waiting and waiting to hear you say one thing that would be clear enough for her to act on."

"She had no trouble acting."

"Yes, but I've begun to see how it had to be on her own. The kind of step out of space into space you have to make sometimes."

"You seem to know a lot about the things you've never seen."

She shook her head, looked at her hands. "Parents disown their children after years of living with them, why not a few months? But at least I will have said something that you should hear." Her expression hardened again. "I'll go on. I can see all this because I see you and Annie. Why the hell don't you give her a break?"

"Explain."

"What do you think she is? Sweet, patient, little woman waiting around for you all the time?"

"Oh, oh. The feminists are coming."

"Don't hide behind words you don't know anything about."

"You do, of course."

"Judson's got a long way to go, Daddy."

"You talk as though I never made up my mind about anything, as if I were a bum wandering off all over the landscape. You forget I decided to come back, live, work here."

She shook her head slowly. "'You're only thinking about geography now."

"I think," he said quietly, "that I need a drink."

The Bourbon was in the closet over the sink. He poured a tumbler, not bothering to dip snow into the glass as he usually did. The cabin seemed much too small, the sun unreeling too slowly across an endless afternoon.

"Everything's so changed I don't know what to think anymore."

"I don't take it back. Anything I said, even if it's muddled."

"I didn't ask you to." He drank again. "I'm going to town, eat at the Bear, walk the long way down through the woods."

He drained the glass, and for the next few minutes while changing his shirt, putting on boots, collecting his money, he did not look directly at her still figure.

He took the old wood road that slanted along the hill's contours, hardly descending at all until it reached the bald spot at the end of the ridge. He kept the road open by pruning back limbs in summer so that it was a trail wide enough to snowshoe or ski without having to stoop and be whipped by twigs. The deer tracks were so fresh that he knew they had been walking in the deep snow as he had left the cabin, and he came to the place where they must have sensed him entering the woods. The roughened holes of their startled, wide leaps turned abruptly downhill and the clear path ahead was untouched except by the scattered marks of squirrels or voles.

He stopped. The sun cut stark shadows around every object and the bare limbs of maples and birches tangled across the blue sky. In spite of the bright day, nothing was melting; cold air still gripped tightly. It would be one of those nights when he could walk out of the cabin door to an air cutting into his lungs as if he were breathing crystal fragments of bright and layered stars. Now his breath blurred the woods ahead. High up the ridge a wind made the trees rattle. He walked on.

A flock of chickadees chittered and dipped through the trees, paying no attention to him. He concentrated as hard as he could on the smallest motions of the woods around him, but could not hold on, recalling how the same winter sun had filled the rooms of the house flatly after they had returned from his mother's funeral. Better to watch the chickadee jerk and swivel its head when it gripped the limb of the sapling. But the harder he pushed his mind toward the trees and birds and glazed rocks, the more strange they became, objects so separate from him that they seemed totally dead. The chickadee's black eyes were only mechanical beads.

He walked blindly down the hill toward town.

11

Jenny leaned at Lewis through the smoke. "Let me know when you're ready for that steak." She slipped off toward the kitchen before he could answer.

Lewis was two hours into his evening and pleasantly numbed. He knew almost all the voices. Nearby he could hear Hickey's high whine and Sally Holt was angry about something, as usual.

"Starting early, Lew?"

He turned to the side where a hand was resting on his shoulder. Buddy nodded as Jake set down a beer and shot of whiskey. The whiskey went in a gulp, the beer followed more gradually. Buddy sat on the stool beside Lewis.

"I hear," Lewis said slowly, "that you've been parking your snowmobile in odd places lately."

"By the Jesus, you should've seen the old bugger's face when I come into the kitchen. His old lady run in with her teeth still out because she thought the new gas stove had blown." He was laughing, stopped abruptly to tilt back his beer. "We'll see what the judge does to me. But I feel the better for it, even if it costs."

Lewis put a hand on his shoulder. More than once he and Buddy had waked in the light of early morning, Harlow's truck parked in a field halfway home and empty bottles under their feet.

"Neither of you turn fast or I'm squashed. I'll take you up on that drink now, Lewis."

Buddy tried to twist his head only. "Evening, Doris."

"Whiskey was your offer, wasn't it?" she asked when Jake stopped in front of them, and Lewis said, "Four Roses."

They squeezed so tightly together that Lewis did not have to raise his voice. "What brings you here?"

She put her hand around the glass Jake set down and did not lift it for a moment. "Gus took sick again. One of those asthma bouts he gets, only this time they wanted him to have oxygen so they put him in the tent over to the hospital."

"Too bad."

"Oh, he doesn't mind. He's used to it. Kind of likes lolling around while all those young women bring him juice with a glass straw and all. Paid vacation. His miner's insurance covers it."

"How long?"

"Two, three days. I'm the one gets the worst of it. Hate cooking for myself. Don't like to visit him up there. Hospitals give me the creeps. Never spent time in one. Hope I just drop down somewhere." She lifted the glass, took a mouthful, held it with eyes closed, then swallowed.

"That's better. And what are you here for?"

"Celebrating the shortest day of the year."

"Says who?"

"The calendar."

"By now, it's the longest night."

"It wasn't when I started."

She shrugged, glanced at his glass. "Looks like you're planning to run some of that darkness over into the next day."

"I'll see."

"If you can by then."

Knowing they could go on talking like that depressed him. Suddenly he did not want to be there, but leaving seemed worse. Doris was swirling her ice with one finger.

"I got to thinking about your mother the other day, about that time she and I went for a year to work in Poughkeepsie. Before she was married."

Lewis glared at his drink.

"Your mother, I said, I was thinking about."

"I heard you the first time."

"Well, look out. Lewis Beede's feeling mean."

Lewis shrugged.

"Okay. I won't tell you about me and your mother. I'll just drink this nice drink you gave me and watch you sit there. Nothing I like better than watching you sit there."

When a hand touched his other shoulder, Lewis swiveled too quickly, almost putting his face into Elmore's.

"Jenny's got your steak cooking and we have a table. Hello, Doris."

She squinted. "You two don't look alike at all. Which one was found in a basket?"

Lewis stood and picked up his glass. His back had stiffened from sitting so long. With hardly a hitch in her voice, Doris was saying, "Turn all the way around here, Buddy Harlow, and tell my why you weren't in church last Sunday," and Buddy rotated, a shy grin already on his face.

Eleanor smiled at him, but Elaine was talking intently to the thin-faced boy next to her whose hair began in a lush, dark cascade and straggled out into ratty wisps around his shoulders. The dining room was even smokier, and the tables were over-crowded, the waitresses squeezing past backs of chairs, trays held high.

"You know Jonathan Dinsey, don't you?"

The boy put a hand out, had to use it to grab the glass of water he nearly upset, and settled for a wide, red-faced grin. Lewis sat between Eleanor and Elmore, and as he pulled his chair up, Elly's hand fluttered onto his arm; she leaned and kissed him lightly on the cheek.

She looked tired, but smiled brightly. "We're celebrating. Elaine and Jonathan are engaged. They've decided to get married this summer."

They were peering into their place mats, but by the way Jonathan's arm was flexing he must have been crushing her hand under the table.

"Congratulations." But he thought they looked sappy sitting and grinning, so he added, "How will you make your first million dollars, Jonathan?"

He leaned forward earnestly. "I've been doing very well with our band, Mr. Beede. Well enough to save up something. But I intend this spring to go back to helping my dad in the store and he says he wants to be retiring soon." He sat back quickly, his face perspiring.

An arm came down by Lewis. The steak was broiled to perfection and large enough so that there was little room for anything else around it.

"You don't eat here much anymore," Jenny said. "Now that you've signed on a daughter as well, I don't stand a chance, do I?"

"I don't either."

She did not seem to hear him. "Does she cook well?"

"Well enough."

She was gone before he could properly thank her for the steak. Jonathan was frowning at the peas he pushed with his fork against the wall of his knife. Elmore, cutting the half chicken on his plate, started to say something to Lewis, but he did not want to talk with his brother so he leaned out over the steak.

"Going to be married in a church?"

Elaine began describing their plans. He hardly had to say a word to keep it going. Finally when Eleanor and the children were arguing about the number of guests to be invited, Elmore said quietly, "Is this one of your nights, brother? On a bender?"

"Maybe."

"For a reason?"

"Who needs reasons?"

Elmore nodded. "This doesn't help much," and he lifted his glass. "The confusion lingers on, you might say." He kept his voice low. "Lew, I've stopped wanting to talk to anyone. Even saying something about the weather sounds like a lie to me. It's as though a split second before my voice gets out of my mouth I can hear it in my own ear and I want to stomp it down, throw stones over it. Sometimes I think of Dad and I remember how moody he was and I wonder if this happened to him, too. Then I wonder if what I'm doing is what happened near the end, before he killed himself."

"He didn't kill himself."

Elmore laughed once as if he had been jabbed in the gut.

Eleanor turned, puzzled, but Jonathan was listing points on his fingers and she had to listen to him.

"Call it what you want, then. He killed himself to all of us, to this place. He walked out over the mountains, kept moving. That's a form of suicide. You say, 'Not this life, thanks,' and move on."

"Sounds good to me."

Elmore glanced at him. "Hell, I thought we were having a serious conversation."

"I'm sick of serious conversations."

"Come on, you two." Elly put a hand on Lewis's arm. "Let up."

Lewis spoke to his plate in a firm, clear voice. "One of the damned things about living in a small town is you can't get away from everyone else's problems, much less your own."

But when no one else answered, Lewis found it very easy to forget what they had been talking about. He was beginning to lose to the whiskey, and every part of him had to move deliberately now. He cut the rest of the steak slowly, one small bite at a time, chewed the meat to a pulp, swallowed, and lifted his glass, and each motion was numbered and diagrammed. His mind was so blank that only those physical gestures were present to it. He was not hungry, and yet he ate until the plate was empty, then put his knife and fork carefully on the mat.

He looked around. Everywhere he saw faces grimacing, lips pursing and stretching, mouths taking food, releasing words, hands flung up in emphasis or lying flatly abandoned on chair arms, bodies in a chaotic weave and bob like polyps in a water of contradictory currents. All of them were taking in food and blowing out the gas in their heads. He thought he would be sick. He closed his eyes. Now their voices were a tight matting of sound that might smother him. He breathed deeply, slowly.

Lewis opened his eyes. He would go into the next room and have another drink. Eleanor was staring at him. "Well, folks, I think I'll mosey on into the bar."

"Suit yourself." Elmore was moving a toothpick around in his mouth with his tongue.

Lewis lifted his glass, tipped it at Elaine. "Congratulations again. Have a long and happy." He did not wait to hear her answer, but stood and concentrated on moving between the tables.

"Damn it." The woman who had turned abruptly to walk into him was Phoebe, rubbing her nose where she had bumped it on his collarbone. She was looking her very best, hair gathered in a ponytail, the silk blouse deeply unbuttoned. "You're drinking again, Mr. Beede."

She wagged a finger, but he grabbed it so quickly that she blinked, they heard the knuckle crack, she winced, and then he let go. The chock of pool balls made their own random beat against the rhythm of the jukebox that had begun its night-long howling.

"I wanted to talk to you, Lewis. I'm going to have an enormous party in a month or so. Won't you come? You and Annie and Miriam? A costume ball, a sort of Northern Mardi Gras. People will be coming from all over the world." She said it lightly, but with that brittle self-mockery that often prevented Lewis from being certain whether he should believe her or not. She put her head to one side. "You certainly are talkative tonight."

"I don't think we can make it to the party."

"Shame. Other engagements?"

Now he saw she had been serious. "I'm not much on parties with people from all over the world. I can't speak for the others. Ask them."

Phoebe put her hand flatly on his chest. "Let's be nice to each other for two minutes, Lewis. I'm going away for a week or two, skiing out West, see some friends, and I'm serious about the blast. I've sent out invitations everywhere. It's going to be the biggest party that house has ever seen."

"He was right, wasn't he?"

"Who?"

"Coleman. He said you'd use it like a toy."

She blinked. "Did he really? I'm so glad you told me that. But I was on my way to the john and since I don't have an infinitely expandable bladder, I'll continue." She started to move around him, but paused and looked up. "That was mean, Lewis. But I'm going to tell you what else I had on my mind to say, even if it was nice. I like Miriam. Very much. I think you're lucky. Don't blow it this time around."

She walked into the narrow corridor that led to the back area.

He watched those lean hips, the lanky and determined stride, her long hair spreading like a fan down her back, and lurched after her. She had a hand on the doorknob but turned quickly, face startled. He gripped her arm, she winced, tried to shake loose.

"That hurts."

"You stay away from her."

Her eyes were half-closed. "You think she'll pollute me?"

He wished the hand were strong enough to crush her thin bone. "You're a crazy whoring bitch and you muck up everything you touch. I know your type and I've watched you for years."

"Really?" Her nostrils were pinched in a pale face. He could smell the rot of full trash bins, the sharp disinfectant beyond the bathroom door. "I bet you have. I bet you've sat thinking in the barn for years, stuck with the hard-on I give you. Here." Her free hand grabbed his and crushed it against her crotch. "Is that what you've wanted, Lewis?"

He drew back both hands with a jerk.

"You bastard," she spat and before he could move again she slammed the door and slipped the bolt.

Jake did not even ask, but filled a fresh glass and brought it to him. Lewis eased onto a stool. His hand was trembling when he reached for the glass and he had to grip it against the cold surface. He could still feel the sinewy arm, the rough denim of her pants. What shook him was the clear image of what he could have done if she had not closed the door — his own body falling forward, pressing her to the wall, his face hard against hers.

"How's it going, Lew?" The hand that struck down on his shoulder drove his face forward as he was lifting his glass, wetting his nose in the Bourbon. "Sorry. Have you seen Phoebe? Can't find her."

Lewis breathed out slowly. "Phoebe's pissing."

Howard slouched onto the stool. He had a long-stemmed glass in one hand containing a creamy green liquid. Lewis took a deep drink of his Bourbon.

"What kind of toad spit is that, Howard Ryan?"

Howard looked at his drink, took a sip, then placed it on the counter. "A grasshopper. You never had one?"

"Since when — "

"You can have a sip, if you want."

"I don't drink toothpaste."

"C'mon, Lew. Give me a break."

Lewis decided to do just that. It was Howard, after all, and the first person he had felt like talking to all evening. "You all right?"

"Maybe."

"I'll buy you a real drink, if you want."

"I wanted to try it. Try anything. I never could afford to before." He flicked his eyes at Lewis, then down at the large, bony hands that made the glass seem so hopelessly delicate. "She can afford to."

"So you're trying everything."

Howard began speaking in a rush as if he might be snatched away. "Sometimes we have this drink in the morning called Bloody Mary and we sit in the kitchen or make a fire in the living room, and lots of times we'll take a bath or shower together after that and go back to bed and even sleep some again, and then she'll cook me something for lunch or we'll drive all the way to the Flatts just to buy a sandwich in the deli. Sometimes she'll wake up and push me and tell me to get lost, and I'll dress and walk around or come here for breakfast, but I've never been so happy and unhappy all at once in my life. What am I going to do?"

Slowly Lewis shook his head. "You're on your own now."

He was staring at his hands again. "I know. My folks won't let me in the house. When I'm not with her I sleep at Buddy's on the couch, and Lucille, she preaches at me in the mornings, but then we watch the soaps together and have some coffee, and I wait till I have the guts to call Phoebe or come back. Sometimes I just go out to the barn. Melissa and Joker, I talk to them a lot."

"I'm not sure I want my horses to know all those things. Is she taking you on her western tour?"

"She hasn't made up her mind yet. I've never been away from here. It would be something." His glance was that sudden, knowledgeable slant which always took Lewis by surprise.

"I shouldn't worry about you at all."

Howard was blushing again, trying not to laugh, but the slight swagger of his shoulders did make Lewis worry. The gesture was not convincing and he suddenly saw Howard as a young boy again, more vulnerable than ever.

"When in all this do you go to school, buster?"

"I was already a year behind, Lew. I can finish up evenings sometime if I want."

"Listen, Howard Ryan." But Lewis could not go on. What was the point? He could not untangle his own life at forty-five. "Drink your toad spit."

Looking over his shoulder, Howard leaned furtively to Lewis. "She never mentions me, does she?"

"Who?"

"Elaine."

"Secrets, secrets," Phoebe's voice was saying.

"Want to sit?" Howard stood, but Phoebe had taken his hand, was pulling him away as if his arm were a rope.

"We've got a game against Don and Wilbur. I've got ten bucks on it. Night, night, Lewis."

He did not look at her but waved a hand beside his head.

He was not certain how much later Annie put an arm around him and leaned onto the counter. He held his glass to her and she drank as if it were water.

"Easy, easy."

"I'm way behind you."

When Jake turned, Lewis ordered a drink for her and watched him reach for the glass, the bottle, scoop up ice, fill the glass, bring it to her. He decided time was very peculiar. He took an ice cube from his own glass and bit into it.

"How long've you been here, Lew?"

"Two hundred years."

"Where's Miriam tonight?"

"You've got all the questions stacked up, don't you?"

"Sorry. Thought they were simple. Let's start again."

He leaned his elbows on the bar and stared ahead at Jake's feet moving in intricate patterns over the wet floor. Her hand was loosely on his thigh.

"I had a letter from Jim's mother in Tallahassee today."

"Thought she was dead."

"She's eighty-one now, and still sharp, clear. Even her handwriting."

"Why does she write you?"

169

"We always liked each other. She says she's thinking of getting married. Wants my permission."

"You know the guy?"

"They met in the old folks' home where she stays now."

"Too old to marry."

"He's only seventy-two."

"What will you say?"

"It's not my business. But I know she doesn't write her own daughter anymore. Angry at her for being put into the home. Maybe I should go see her sometime."

"Everyone goes to Florida, sometime or other."

Her hand moved on his leg. He had never been able to imagine well what it would be like to be very old. But sometimes when he held the razor to his cheek, about to stroke, he would see with sudden objectivity the worn flesh of his face, the eyes in their darkening net of lines, and he would think that was a mask, not him — the one who lived inside was still as young and unknowing and frail as an adolescent.

"Penny for your thoughts."

"Not worth that much. Is marriage what you want?" He turned his face to her.

"I couldn't tell them what to do."

"I mean for us."

"I never said that."

"That's not what I asked. I said is it what you want?"

"What difference would it make?"

"I don't know. I was asking you."

"To marry you?"

"No. Asking you what you think."

"I'll think about it, then."

"Take your time."

She smiled. "Another thirty years?"

"If I ever ask you again, I won't be joking. And I won't be drunk."

"Which you are now."

"One of the above."

He had crossed into that territory where keeping the lights and figures outside him from moving and rolling would soon be an effort of the will.

"Annie?" Phoebe was calling across the room.

Annie looked at her but did not answer. She could never yell like that. The voice was saying, "Come on. We'll take on the guys. If Lewis will give you permission."

"What does she mean by that? Don't go away, Lew."

"I will probably stay until I drop. And what she means is, 'Fuck you, Lewis.' " He was speaking to the counter and suspected she did not hear.

He had swallowed enough booze so that small amounts would keep him where he wanted to be. He could hear the clacking of balls, and Wilbur or Don laughing. They would strut, joke, pretend this was a lark, but Phoebe and Annie were sharp enough to begin to take the game, and then the men would have to settle down, concentrate, start blaming each other for inaccurate shots since, if they lost, neither Wilbur nor Don would want to be beaten by women. A gravelly voice from the jukebox was insisting she was treated *unkind, I got mean things, I got mean things on my mind,* repeating, repeating in a harshening tone that made that meanness credible — *I hate to leave you, baby, but you treat me so unkind.* "Oh, good, good," Phoebe squealed. Annie would have made a shot, her expressionless face flushing. She would not like that kind of dithering going on, but would want to keep the game clear and focused and silent. She liked to win.

Again he watched Jake's feet moving around the floor, managed almost to see them as independent of the man's body — black with pocks, laces with leather pompons that flicked and bobbed as the feet shifted. He always forgot how fancy they were, wondered how many Jake would wear out from the walking, and they must be wet most of the time — water, spilled beer soaking in the sides. It was better to let his eyes blur, let everything weave like those shoes, like the milling dots that sometimes filled his eyes if he stood too quickly, because all the room was washed with random motion. He jerked his head away from the counter that seemed to be rising at him as his elbow slipped off into space. *I got ramblin', I got ramblin' on my mind.* The voice was pure steel now, no complaining left in it. He looked around, but no one was watching him. Christ. Nodding off. Was he that tired?

"I would've shot the bastards if I hadn't been so drunk," the voice on the stool beside him was saying to someone else. "But I'd conked out on the best booze I'd ever had in my life and they had to come along and wake me up." Leo the jailbird, probably out on bail, was full of beer and outrage. "And as for those turds on the floor, I didn't drop them. I ain't saying who it was 'cause I'm no tattler like that bugger is who turned me in. Just you wait till he comes back to town. I figure he's got to've called in after he left me there, squealed. Or even set it up ahead of time. How else they gonna know to go to an empty motel looking for a break-in? Huh?" His voice rose in a rasp of bitterness, brute, outwailing the jukebox.

Leo kept craning his neck one way and then the other as if everyone must be listening, and Lewis tried to be certain he did not catch his eye. He did not like Leo's squint-eyed angers.

"Why they want to put me up for that rap? Them rich buggers, what do they care? Come here a few months each year. Like all them damned out-of-staters. Soak up our bucks. So I busted a window. Drunk their booze. Big deal." His hand with finger extended rose in a furious gesture at some imagined figure in midair over the bar. The voice of the man he was talking to growled something in reply. "Damn straight," Leo said, "here, this un's on me. Hey, Jake," and when the man came Leo ordered with the swagger of a tycoon. Lewis was concentrating on Jake, trying not to hear Leo anymore, but the voice cut through everything, and now it was suddenly maudlin, on the verge of a broken sob. "Sometimes I wish I was fuckin' dead." Lewis jumped when the fist hit the side of the counter flat and hard. "But by geesum, when I go I'll take a bunch with me, the buggers."

He was going to have to move, Lewis decided, when a voice whooped, "By Gawd, here's Jud Foley come home," and someone else yelled. "Here, Jud, shake on this, boy."

At the door a crowd of heads bobbed around, moved toward the bar, and Jud Foley, hair coiffed tight, his wide-striped suit rumpled but tie in place, was grinning, already reaching for the beer Jake held out to him. Lewis looked away quickly, did not want to have to yell hello across the space as if he cared. And true to his expectations, he heard Jud say in that high-pitched, pressured voice, "Drinks on me, Jake. One all round for everybody." Well, Foley and Helen would be glad to see him. If he ever got up the hill. Lewis had made that mistake once. Having seen Jud on one of his triumphal entries at the bar, he had said to Foley two days later, *It must have been good to get a glimpse of your boy,* and met Foley's puzzled gaze, the words *You mean Jud? Haven't seen him for three months now.*

The shot glass was dropped in front of him, filled past the line. Jake was generous when the rounds were on someone. Lewis looked up. Obligatory eye contact with Jud. "Hey there, Lew Beede," and a smile, shot lifted, nod of head, then what the hell, why water it, so down the hatch all at once. Tilting his head took Jud out of his vision, so when he brought his eyes back down, he could concentrate on the pure burn of the alcohol, the flush up his nose, slowly down his chest into the gut. That would ruin the careful adjustments of the past hour, put him over the edge into a new circle. Blood began to carry the news to his whole body. Mayday, mayday. That's what you get for cadging a free one.

"I'm going home now, baby."

Had he nodded off again? He let the four eyes of her face pull together into two. She looked tired.

"D'you win?"

"Split. Won two, lost two."

"Bet Phoebe blew it."

She had her arm around his waist, put her head down on his shoulder for a while. "I'm tired. Didn't really want to play those games. Came to have a few drinks with my old man. But I can't take the noise anymore. You're staying on, I can see."

"Probably till I can't see," and he found himself laughing, stopping as abruptly as he began.

"I drink too fast when I'm playing." She had not lifted her head, so her voice was clear although she spoke softly. "You coming along later?"

"If I get anywhere, it probably won't be up the hill."

"I'll leave the back door open. Someone busted into Sally's the other night. I don't like leaving the front door open now."

"Back door's good enough for me."

Her doubled face pulled back, became one, her arm let go, she was spinning backward but he caught himself on the bar, and she waved, smiling, and walked away. An amazing feat, walking, he decided, and also was certain that no one in the room had a body as beautiful — tight in its old jeans, the blue shirt with frayed collar, all swaying away, gone. He would have to find his way to her. Later. Good fresh air on the way back. Look for stars. Orion, Big Dipper. Used to know how to find the Dragon, Draco. In the summer, was it? None of them looked like the pictures. Just stars. You make the connections. Lines in the sky that aren't really there. Probably snowing anyway. Navigate by instinct. Homing in.

His elbow slipped again. Steady. He tongued the liquid in the glass he held up. The taste displeased him. Something different needed. He waited till Jake turned his way, crooked his finger at him. The man came over, face impassive.

"Brandy."

"Plain?"

"Just brandy. None of that fruit crap cough syrup."

Jake had a snifter for him huge enough to cover his face. He set it down, leaned on both hands in front of Lewis.

Lewis lifted it, looked at Jake through the warping glass. "Only time I see you smile, Jake Roy."

Jake was not smiling.

"You ought to smile more often. People wouldn't only love you for your money then. People would love you for your beautiful soul. They'd say, 'Jake Roy, he has the most beautiful soul in Judson.' "

"If you can't wipe your ass with it, who needs it?"

Lewis lowered his glass, sipped, was glad he had changed to brandy. "Goddamn, that's good," but Jake was already gone.

So were more people than Lewis had noticed leaving. He could see clearly to the pool table, just Don and Wilbur in their perpetual stoopings. Don teetered slightly when he tried to lean on his cue. There were gaps at the bar now too. A tight knot still at the end talking with Jud, who had let his tie droop down from the unbuttoned collar. Serious talk. Business. How to invest. Tips from the local boy who made good. Listen carefully. Free drinks, kiss ass, slap on the back, and *Christ, we missed you, Jud.* They would be telling each other what Jud said for the next week. *I know this guy works over to Syracuse, see, says the market's gotta go up.* As if they had pennies to invest in more than beer anyway. He could not help recalling how after he returned from New York, no one paid any attention. That was acting, after all, and a baffling vocation for a man as far as they could understand. Not business. No drinks on the house when Lewis limped home.

He let his eyes look high onto the wall straight ahead, above the rack of mugs with names on them. The varnished plaques were hard to read at that distance but he did not have to. He knew exactly which one had his name. Wouldn't they get a swift kick in the ass if he were to tell them about that? Right now. But hell. Who was left who recalled all that anyway? Jim was the only one who would really care.

Mean drunk. That's what he was. Good. He squatted on his stool, his whole body tightening up. Dwarf body. Take a punch at the first guy who touches. Which someone did, hand on his shoulder, and he was too surprised to swing. Bernie. Drunk too. Tell by the fixed, stupid grin, jerk of eyes.

"Did a damn good job, that Joker. Gonna help me when it comes?"

"I might."

"Been drinking at the Flatts. Went up to see the bare boob dancing. Stopped for one at every bar on the way back. Drink, that is. Jesus, you should've seen the tits on one of them broads." He held his hands three feet in front of his chest. "And straight out. No sag."

"Good, Bernie. Good for you. Bernie's been measuring tits tonight, Jake."

Jake was mopping the counter, eyeing them both.

Bernie took his hand back. "C'mon, Lew. Don't go sarcastical. What you drinking?"

"Brandy."

"Well, hoo-ey. One for both of us, Mr. Roy, sir. And torch the crepes while you're at it."

Don't think of that, don't think of that. Lewis chained his mind tight. But no good. The word was a very unfortunate reference to fire. *Very unfortunate indeed,* he heard his mind's voice saying over. Although he could control what his head put into words, he could not control the images, even the smell, which had come first. He had lifted his head in the dark bedroom, the air, usually thick with stale cigarette and beer fumes since his room was over the bar, cut sharply by the bittersweet odor of kerosene. Even as his groggy mind gathered and he sat up, the burst of light showed in the

175

stairwell, the hall, then steadied down, and from the window when he tore the curtains aside, he could see the squat figure running low, can in hand, face not clear, but stance vaguely known. Even as he tried to get down the stairs, had to turn back, lungs seared, breaking the stuck window with the chair, pausing, then dropping onto the rain-soaked ground, he was trying to recall where such a figure had run like that before, arms, legs cantling out like a backing crab.

No one was feeding the jukebox anymore. A low grunt, deep breathing came from behind Lewis. He jerked his head around and in the spinning center of his vision were Don and Wilbur bent low over the pool table from opposite sides, arm-wrestling. The low-slung light cast a cone of yellow on their bowed heads, tensed shoulders, and splashed in a circle on the bright green baize of the table. They were staring down at their elbows, and the corded tendons of their flushed necks bunched out. Lewis could feel his own gut knotting, pulse lifting as if he were watching two boxers slug out the final moments in a round.

"Go Don, go Wilbur," Bernie hooted and Lewis swung around again to the face with its grin that faded into puzzlement. "Something eating you, Lew?"

"Yes."

"What?"

"You."

Bernie shrugged, lifted his brandy, and waved his hand as if the sight of Lewis's face were a swarm of gnats. "Oh hell. Is that all?" But his expression deadened.

"That's not enough?"

"Listen. Is there anyone in this town who doesn't hold things against me I can't do anything about? I start from that every time I sit down on a barstool, then I work out from there. Sometimes I'm lucky and I get to forget I'm Bernie Carbonneau."

Lewis had been here before, and usually he would turn his back, talk to Jake, walk out so that he would not have to be the last customer, trapped with the sound of Bernie's monologue. But this time the words quilled him. He tried to focus on Don and Wilbur, still locked over the table like two rams.

"You don't think it's fucking hard? The same things someone else might do and get some respect for, I get sneered at. So I've made a little money, pulled off some pretty smart deals. I'm good at that, I know. But I've never really cheated anyone. I've only done what every damn businessman does. Your brother, Elmore, lands a big contract and all you hear is how great he is, how good he is for the town. I pull off a deal, I make some loot and pay my taxes, and so what?"

He was breathing as if he had been running, the sound magnified as he cupped the big snifter over his face. Then he began muttering in that language Lewis could not understand. But it sounded even more mean and angry than if the words had been intelligible. The muscles on Don's face grimaced, the sweat in his eyes making him blink, but neither man was even grunting now.

"All right." Lewis swung around so hard that he nearly gyrated too far, caught his balance with a clutch at the counter's edge. "Tell me something."

Bernie had his head far back, was draining the snifter, but his eyes slid sideways to look at Lewis, and he brought the glass down slowly.

"What, Mr. Beede?"

"Who torched my place?"

The snifter was on the counter now and Bernie's face went blank as a plaster cast. "What place?"

"My bar."

Bernie's head moved slowly, eyes half-lidded as he stared back. "Who cares?"

When Lewis flung his hand onto the counter, a hard thwack that sounded like a shot, Bernie flinched to one side as if ducking a punch. "I care," Lewis yelled. "Tell me."

"I don't answer to commands. You aren't still calling the signals, skinhead."

Lewis saw the rest of the room with clarity now, the two or three other hunched figures at the bar with heads crooked to them, Jake's hands stilled, holding a glass in a towel, and the two wrestlers paralyzed.

"I bet you know. You know every goddamn thing that can be found by turning over the shit in other people's outhouses."

"Shove it," Bernie said as if spitting, and when his fist came flat on, a hard direct chop, Lewis had time only to move his head slightly so that it took him above his ear, glancing, and he could hear his head thump and the sound of Bernie's knuckles cracking before the ear went numb. In reflex he was off the stool, had swung once and missed, and then, because they had moved too close, they each clasped the other's shirtfront, staring, waiting for one to let go and throw a punch. But that was when Jake leaped the counter, had them by the shoulders, pushing toward the door.

"Do your goddamn fighting out there, you bums."

He flung them against the door so the latch shattered and they were out into the shock of cold air, stumbling slightly as their feet hit the snow. They steadied, wide-stanced, holding on exactly as they had been inside. From the corner of his eyes Lewis could see the men bunched in the doorway, saying nothing.

But he should not have let his attention wander because Bernie broke the clinch and rammed a fist into Lewis's gut so he had to hold off the punches while he caught his breath, taking the blows on his arms, shoulders, one that got through and grazed his cheek, and then he moved in, threw a few tentatively at the air to the side of Bernie's quickly moving head. His vision cleared, the pumping of his heart settled down, and legs firmed under him. Bernie was still good. He had expected that. As they circled, moved in for flurries of punches that thumped and caused hot blasts of pain, his mind was only remotely connected to everything, was quietly trying to recall when the last good fight had been.

He found himself sitting down hard on the concrete front steps, staring at the tips of his shoes. But it only took one shake of his head and he was up again, Bernie bobbing to the left this time, which was unfortunate for him because Lewis had been so inaccurate with his punch that it went that far off target and now it was Bernie's turn to sit down with a look of surprise on his face, hands flat in the snow.

When he was up they pitched into each other. There was a new figure on the circumference when they whirled, but Lewis could not make it out, and suddenly they were in one of those clinches that neither one was going to break from because he would be too unprotected and that was when the bucket of cold water came down over their heads and Jenny's voice above them was saying, "Goddamn it, you two pugs bust it up," and they did, breathing with shocked, wide-eyed faces. They stared, hands at their sides. Lewis was waiting to see if Bernie would throw another, unwilling to start again himself.

"All right," Bernie said in short catches. "Fact time, Beede. I know who."

"Who?"

"Why the hell do you care after all this time? And why should I tell?"

"Why should I believe you?"

"Leo."

"Why?"

There was blood on Bernie's cheek, and Lewis wondered dully if it was his or Bernie's. The heavy wadding of liquor was beginning to surround him again, even numbing the pain of cold on his soaked head and back. Bernie laughed, would have kept laughing, but he did not have the breath to continue and it choked off.

"Oh, you goddamn fool. You people never see, do you, never understand? The way you can insult a guy. Just by how you stare at his shirt or say hello."

Lewis waited. The figure standing in the light under the sign was Miriam, perfectly still, her gloved hands at her sides. He could not see her face clearly.

"It wasn't you, anyway, that Leo wanted. It was your father."

"Leo was only a kid when Dad left."

"But Leo's father wasn't. Don't you recall that summer Foster bought the upper pasture from Stringholt?"

"No."

"Well, Leo does. Ask Leo. Your dad cut out Leo's and it wasn't money. His was as good as Foster's. But his religion wasn't. Leo's got a good memory for things like that. So do I. Trouble is, I wouldn't have waited. I would've burned out your daddy. But I can't hold on like Leo."

It still was not clear. But as if a weight had followed down on him long after the falling water, Lewis did not care. He already imagined himself waking up sometime the next day, head pounding, his bed, whatever bed it would be, careened, and all the things he had not begun to deal with circling his topsy-turvy mind. She stood there, immobile as the signpost, as if to remind him.

"Want more?" Bernie said quietly.

Lewis stepped forward slowly. Bernie raised his fists, ready to go on. But Lewis stuck out a single hand, the knuckles aching and stiff as he opened it.

"Enough for now."

Bernie looked warily at him. Lewis held it there, almost hoping the man would not take it. But Bernie's hand came out, then the other one added to the grip, and he was saying, "Well, what the hell, why not, what the hell," while a grin broke grudgingly over his face. "Come on," and he chopped one of the freed hands on Lewis's shoulder, "that'll hold us for a while, no? Buy you one for the road."

Inside, the heat slackening his muscles, Lewis said, "No thanks. I've got just enough zip to get me to bed now," and Bernie did not object, so Lewis walked around the deadlocked figures of Don and Wilbur, and plucked his coat off the hook. As he passed Jake, the man nodded and said, "I'd wash that cut good, if I was you, and then buy me a new door latch," and that was the first time Lewis was certain whose blood it was.

She was waiting for him on the sidewalk, and when he came close enough to see her face he could tell she was not about to treat him with much sympathy.

"I guess I got here a little late."

"No, just about in time."

The stuffed bear was stiffly rearing. Her hand rested on the crook of his arm, and she was very adept at keeping up with the unsteady pattern of his walk.

"Going to Annie's," he said dully.

"I know. I waited for you there." When they turned up the side street she said, "Why were you all upset about your bar? I thought you didn't care about all that?"

He started to smile but his mouth hurt. "I don't know. Seemed important at the time. I really don't give a shit."

"That's what you say." They walked on slowly. "Do you do that often on Saturday nights?"

"Only on very special occasions."

"What's this one?"

"Longest night of the year."

"But that happens once a year."

"Sometimes I sit it out."

He steered them around the back. Before he opened the door he remembered he had not looked at the stars, so he craned up, almost tipping over.

"What now?"

"The stars, Miriam. Look at the stars." He had his arm around her waist.

"They're always there." Her strained voice showed she was looking up too.

"Yes, but we're not." He looked down at the pale disk of her upturned face, the dark glistening of eyes. His voice was hoarse when he looked back up again and lifted his free hand to point. "Big Dipper, Little Dipper, North Star."

12

In the beginning he was certain it was a dream and told himself so. He was too old to be in that small bunk with Elmore stirring above him, and had long ago moved away from the house with tall windows. He floated out of the bed. The whole room breathed with Elmore, slowly in and out, and Lewis tried to look back from the window to the upper bunk but some figure cast a shadow in the way even though he waved his hands with slow, swimming motions. All the horses were out, their hooves a muffled pounding in the snow. He opened his mouth to call to Elmore, but nothing came out, and even when he tried to clap his hands together something kept them from touching.

When he heard the voice, he turned to the window. His father's mouth was not saying words, only pulses of noise. Foster stood in the drifted roadway, the barn door open behind him, and out of that dark hole the last horse was leaping, legs tucked high. Again Lewis tried to cry out. The horse grazed Foster's shoulder, landed heavily in the snow, galloped to join the other horses circling the house. His father spun, as light and empty as if he were only those flapping clothes. He was drunk and had let the horses loose, spooking them so that they chased each other wildly around and around the house. Lewis put his hands over his ears to stop the noise Foster's head was making.

His mother was coming slowly down the ramp. Her feet were bare under the hem of her nightgown. Lewis tried to beat against the window, but some layer kept his fists from reaching the glass. Foster did not see her. A hood dipped low over her face and in her arms a naked child was either asleep or dead, limbs hung limply, head lolling from side to side. Foster's arms flailed, his mother kept walking, the snow puffed under her footsteps, and the horses veered, bearing down on them in a bunched cloud of snow and hooves and lowered heads. Foster rose in front of them, his ragged clothes the flapping wings of a crow. His mother was not there. The child lay naked in the snow, was becoming snow, a white dust rising under the horses' hooves, blurring them, filling the air so densely that soon Lewis could not see anything but the blank window. He pushed with both flattened hands as hard as he could, his muscles aching, feet slipping back on the cold floor. The whole frame gave way and he was tumbling into white air that was thick as water. He cried out, *Horses,* but the voice was Coleman White's and it came from behind him.

"Horses." He woke sweating. A hard clear daylight hit him. His gut ached. Before he could decide why he was yelling in Annie's bedroom, he had to plunge out of the tangled sheets and stagger to the bathroom, where he vomited with a rush into the bowl, then stooped as his gut heaved and heaved in knottings he could not stop. When it ended, he washed his face with handfuls of water and groped back to the bed past Annie, who was in the hallway, dressed, her arms crossed. He lay on his belly, closed his eyes, thought he heard her in the room, then the door closed and he was sleeping again in a darkness unmarred by even the slightest dream.

He woke hollowed out, his eyes aching at the light and head a single large nerve of unvarying pain. He did not try to sit up but concentrated on holding the room still. The chest was hunched low under the windowsill, and the closet door was open like a loose flap of wall. Annie moved in the chair by the door.

"Want to try this?"

He heard the tablets being ripped from the package. She

came at him, her arm extended through a break in the blast of white light from the window. He took the glass, drank its contents, lay back again.

"Wiped out," he muttered.

"Damn fool."

He closed his eyes. "What's the time?"

But she must have gone. His gut cringed, numbly objecting to the liquid that came down him in a wave. He could have beaten at the wall with his fists in a childish tantrum. Now he would lie there for hours waiting for his body to forgive him. The time would be a total waste, a long struggle out of self-created pain. He always thrashed against the idiocy of this one abuse that seemed impossible to avoid. He tried to concentrate, recall why he had done it this time. Nothing, no confusion, was worth this. Yet within a month or so, he would probably do it again. He groaned out loud.

Lewis told himself often that he could never really become an alcoholic. To have his body working well, quietly pumping along in good health, was too pleasing to him. But he could do this, had done it so often that when he woke he would have to search himself to know whether he had been retreating from something or just having a good time. Sometimes an exuberance would push him on and on into the night until he would find his arm around the shoulder of a stranger in the bar, or worse, someone he had always detested who would suddenly seem the epitome of all human friendship. Then he would know he had gone too far, would stumble out into the night already cursing the day to come when he would lie like this, shattered, waiting for peace. Bernie and himself and Buddy. From center, to quarterback, to halfback. Perfect hand-offs. At times like this he could imagine the three of them hunched over their stools, canes hooked on the rim of the bar, three old veterans of some war. Endless war.

Or was the peace that came afterward partly why he did it? After the pain and nausea a euphoric state would fold over him like the times when he had been truly sick, tumbled into the bewildering wasteland of some childhood disease—mumps, measles, whooping cough, he had suffered them all. And when the sudden high fevers broke and subsided, his mother's hand would be there touching his head, placing another mustard plaster on his quieted chest, and for a moment he would be a bird gliding on a swift, warm current, hardly moving. He would ride the wind of his own breathing, high and free. She did not seem to have time to be that openly affectionate when he was well.

When he woke fully, he could remember periods of shifting, rolling, even once staggering to the bathroom again, but all as if he had never really lifted out of sleep. He breathed very deeply a few times and opened his eyes, surprised to see that the window was dark, the hall light casting a yellow square on the wall. A shadow moved through it.

"Want some soup?"

"Yes."

"Here?"

"I'll join you." He lifted his head. "Been sleeping, I guess."

"I guess so."

"Where's Miriam?"

"Waiting to eat."

Annie stood by the bed and he put a hand on the back of her thigh. She did not pull away, and then he said, "Well, here goes." He swung his legs over the side of the bed, sat up. The room spun, then held still. He rubbed his face with his hands.

"There."

He looked up, could see her more clearly now that the light was behind him.

"Sorry," he said flatly.

"You look it."

He put a hand on her thigh again, rubbed it slowly. He was hungry.

"What were you trying to settle, Mr. Beede?"

"My life, I guess."

She laughed genuinely. "You might settle that more quickly by hitting your head with the bottle itself rather than the contents."

He stood and put his hand behind her neck, leaned for a moment.

"You're an awful woman."

"Your soup's getting cold and you stink."

She drew back slightly. Stubborn as usual, but right. Nothing was resolved.

185

"I'll take a shower first."

When he joined them at the kitchen table, they were sitting opposite each other, spooning their soup, talking quietly, and Annie stood to ladle out a bowl for him. Miriam was watching him. He was clean, a little wobbly, but the physical relief was still with him.

"So what did you do today?" Lewis dipped his spoon, took a mouthful.

It was a thick soup of potatoes and vegetables and mingled spices, and even if it was hot on his tongue, he took more, certain he had never tasted anything so good. Miriam looked at him with that slight toss of the head as if she had hair in her eyes, but which he had come to see was a sign of some determination.

"I went for a long drive. South through the gorge, over to Moose Head Pond. I watched the ice fishermen for a while, walked around to some of the shacks."

"Just looking?"

"I've never seen ice fishing. They were nice guys. Some of them gave me a sip from their bottles."

There were times when he was glad she was so grown up that he would not have to feel responsible for what she did. Those men could be rough, mostly workers from the titanium mine. They would be drunk as they sat on their stools with the stoves warming the tight little huts, their refuges from wives and children and even tighter shacks or trailers. But something carried her through those things unscathed. He imagined her stepping inside, asking those clear, practical questions about lines, and what was that hinged stick for? and the men would be pleased, flattered, her bearing too direct and firm to tempt them much.

"I drove the bus right out onto the lake because one guy's car wouldn't start. He had jump cables." She paused. "Then I drove around some more. I stopped near Mineville and watched six deer cross the road."

Annie was looking at him flatly. "Your face is a mess."

The mirror had shown that. He had forgotten the cut, wondered why the whole side of his face was numb, but the reflection showed a thin line down one cheekbone that was puffed and bruised. The cut was not deep but stung when he washed it, and the bruise would last for days.

"Beauty is only skin deep."

Miriam did not look up when she spoke. "Obviously you can be ugly under the skin. What did Carbonneau do to you to make you want to shoot it out?"

"Sometimes Bernie and I don't know how to rub each other any way but wrong."

He did not attempt to explain further. But she said she thought there were reasons, asked him what were his opinions about Catholics, about people of French Canadian descent, did he consider himself prejudiced? Did he judge people by the color of their skins too? Annie watched carefully, and the questions came fast enough so he did not have to answer most of them. He tried to change the subject by telling them about the fire.

"Something my father did to Leo's father, Bernie says. Hell, if it really was Leo it wouldn't take anything that definite. I could've just shortchanged him one night."

"How did his nose get blue?" Miriam was finished eating, idly turned her knife on the tabletop.

"Frostbite." Lewis wondered how she knew which one was Leo, but she had learned everyone's name quickly. "Drank too much, passed out in a snowbank. He lost two fingers, almost lost the tip of his nose. Dead flesh, and he can't get it really cold again or it will have to go."

"Now what are you going to do about Leo?" Annie was taking away their plates, put them in the sink and began to fill the coffeepot.

"Who cares?"

"You did last night. You know you won't just forget it."

"I'll think about that later."

"My father's motto," Miriam said.

"Remember" — Annie punctuated her words by putting the coffeepot down hard on the burner — "Leo is a different creature than Bernie and Buddy and all you arrested developments. Leo really doesn't give a damn about anything. When they made Leo Jaques they left out the conscience."

But Miriam was shaking her head. "I still don't understand why Bernie."

Annie came back to the table. "These guys give him a rough

time. Jim did too. Said he never trusted him. I suppose there's always got to be one in a town."

"One what?" The kitchen began to be stuffy. Lewis wished he had stayed in the bedroom.

"One person that everyone can dump on and who is willing to survive by letting that happen."

"That's too damn easy. I like Bernie. He was the best center . . ."

"Football." Miriam sounded disgusted.

His head was starting to ache again. For a while they listened to the coffeepot hiss and then begin to perk.

"Had enough to eat?" Annie said.

"Too much."

"Are you a hair-of-the-dog type?" Miriam asked.

"If I were I'd worry about becoming an alcoholic."

"And you're certainly not." Miriam's eyebrows rose.

"Did you say 'becoming'?" Annie snorted.

He looked at them both uneasily. As if they had finished with him for a while, the two women began talking quietly to each other about some store in the Flatts they had seen, and how the lady who owned it had gone into business late, on her own. He stirred cream into his coffee, unhappily remembering that he and Elmore had nearly argued last night and he had probably done worse things he would recall later. Maybe Miriam would understand better if he tried to tell her about that time when he and Buddy and Bernie were seniors in high school. But the women did not stop talking, and he was too tired. What did she know about football anyway that gave her the right to sneer like that?

The last game he and Bernie and Buddy played was the championship, and it was theirs. It literally belonged to the three of them. No one denied that they were the core of the team, and the precision of Lewis's ball handling and passing, the brute blocking by Bernie, those churning runs by Buddy when tacklers bounced away from him had filled the stands all season. The day afterward they were restless. First Buddy had driven over in his father's truck and Lewis had said, *Take me out of here,* even though he knew he should be helping his father all day. They cruised around for a while, the heater on full blast because it was the first harshly cold day of fall, almost all the leaves fallen and sun not strong enough anymore to soften the air. For a while they had been satisfied with talking to the girls who sidled up to the open windows when they parked in the grocery store lot. But Lewis and Annie were having one of their spats and it depressed him to see how easily he could have had someone else. They did not interest him as much.

They found Bernie standing on the corner by the intersection, his back to them, hands deep in the pockets of his jacket. His shoulders slumped and he was staring up the road at nothing. Buddy stopped the truck. Bernie grinned, paused, then climbed in.

I can't figure what to do next. He took the cigarette Buddy offered as they drove slowly out of town. *I sure to hell don't see much reason in finishing school, and, Christ, what's there to do around here?*

Get laid, Buddy said as he always did, partly, Lewis suspected, because he never had, even though he tried to talk as if it were a frequent occurrence. Lewis had never called him on it, but his descriptions of laying this girl or that seemed more like what he had hoped it would be than what Lewis had learned it really was.

They drove slowly up the road to the big hotel, shut down since September and the end of the summer season. When Buddy parked at the gate where the dirt road went off into the reserve, they all climbed out and began walking aimlessly.

It was Bernie who said, *Well, what the fuck are we doing now?*

They had been talking about the game, and Lewis had tossed a long pass with a pinecone to Buddy as he ran ahead.

Let's go on to the lake, take one of them boats and paddle up, Buddy said.

At the other end of the lake were elegant camps of the richest members. In the boat they horsed around, scaring Bernie because he could not swim, but it was too cold on the water and the harsh wind sawed at them after they rounded the point. They dragged the boat onto a dock, walked slowly up the spread of grass to the wide porch of the living quarters. Off to the side were a kitchen and dining cabin, wood house, and a separate cabin for the guide who would come along to cook, make fires, and row down for the mail each day. They had all been to these places, but only as helpers to one of the guides. Lewis had come once with the Whites and they had treated him almost as if he were part of the family, but he had bunked with Orin Phelps, their guide.

Buddy cupped his hands to the glass and peered in. *I wouldn't mind a fireplace like that in my own house.*

Bernie hung back as if there might be someone there.

Lookit, Bernie. Buddy turned slightly. *They got some of them old Indian snowshoes over the mantel.*

Bernie shook his head. *We shouldn't be here. They'd think we were busting in.*

Buddy always liked getting a rise out of Bernie. *We are.* He chopped quickly at the glass, reached in, unlatched the window, and was halfway through with a whoop before Bernie said, *You dumb fucker.*

Buddy swung the door open. *Welcome, gents and Bernie.*

Lewis hesitated too, but it was done, so he walked in. He turned to hear scuffling, laughs, Buddy holding Bernie's arms tight in a bear hug while he said, *No Jews or priestly Canucks allowed in this club.* They usually said that to Bernie when they passed the gate on the road because it was a club policy.

But the silence of the room subdued them, and soon they were walking around shyly as if the host had only gone upstairs. Bernie had a way of touching something, picking it up, and replacing it gently as if he had great reverence for the smallest bric-a-brac. Then Buddy disappeared and they heard drawers opening and he came out in a wool coat made from a blanket of many colors and he was waving an old pistol in his hand.

Long live Pancho Villa. His voice echoed, but they all jumped when the pistol went off into the air and splintered a rafter.

Buddy's eyes were wide. *The buggers left it loaded.* He grinned and fired at the moose head on the opposite wall. Its nose disintegrated into wires and stuffing.

Cut it out, Bernie yelled, but he was laughing too.

As if they could not bear the silence pressing back at them, they began throwing, turning over, wrecking whatever they could touch. Buddy took a crap in the drained toilet and Bernie threw knives at the deer heads. Even as he was prying open a locked drawer with a poker, Lewis wondered what the hell he was doing — he had never stolen or broken into anything.

They were throwing around the contents of the drawer, mostly papers and photographs, when Bernie held up a picture he was about to draw on obscenely. It was Coleman's face.

Hold it, Lewis said.

Bernie looked puzzled, then he recognized it too.

Buddy shrugged. *Must have been a few years ago.* But he put the photo face down carefully on the desktop.

It was not the Whites' camp, probably the Chases' or Igleharts'. But they were all friends of the Whites, and Lewis kept telling himself Coleman would never know. They pushed off in the boat and rowed down the lake. Bernie was the only one who said anything. *Why the hell did we do that?* All the rest of the way they watched for other boats, and as soon as they reached the truck they sped down the back road. Lewis had never been able to pass the gate again without a sense of violation and dread. But that was not what he would tell Miriam. The point was him and Bernie and Buddy. Together. No matter how often they scrapped.

Miriam and Annie stopped talking. A car went slowly past the house, used the driveway to turn around, and then drove off.

"Listen," Miriam said so abruptly that he was startled. "The reason I spent the afternoon driving around was so I could think."

"Just tell him."

"Tell what?" Lewis put down his cup.

"I know where my mother is. Only she's not Monica Kramer. She's Monica Weaver."

His first impulse was to laugh. The name made no sense. "Why do you think she's the right Monica?"

"Mr. Wahl, my lawyer, checked that all out carefully. She was married, divorced. No children. Kept her married name. She is a professor, teaches sociology at Oklahoma State."

He did laugh. "Monica? Come on. She hated college. Barely got through. And she certainly never cracked those kinds of books while I was with her."

Miriam shrugged. "So? And I suppose you walked around New York currying horses. She wouldn't be surprised to hear you are a well-known horse breeder?"

He began to bring those separate images of Monica together. Miriam was right, of course. If anything, during those years in New York, bitterly determined to return to Judson only in triumph, he spoke sneeringly, if at all, of farming, animals, almost everything except the woods in themselves which he might hold up as an image with which to belittle the city, her city, when it seemed objectionable. No matter what she did read, she read a lot, had an abstract but intensely emotional way of arguing about social issues — the plight of criminals, races, religious groups. Miriam was staring at him.

"You and Annie have been discussing all this?"

They both nodded.

"He called me three days ago."

"Good of you to let me in on it." Lewis wiped a hand over his brow. "What a dimwit I am."

"True." Annie smiled. "But in what way?"

"So that's what has been bugging you lately?"

She looked away. "Shouldn't it?"

When Miriam said quickly, "I don't think so," Lewis could tell they had been arguing already.

"That's naïve. I tell you I'm glad for your sake, but for Lewis? For me?"

"Annie thinks it's something else I'm doing to you both. Do you?" Miriam leaned at Lewis but he did not have a chance to speak because Annie spoke gently.

"You could leave us out of this part, at least not expect Lew to help you."

"But I don't know if I can do it by myself." Miriam's voice went high and tense. "Why should I have to do it all alone?"

"That makes no difference anyway," Lewis burst at them, both hands flying up. "I don't want to see her."

"That's even more naïve," Annie murmured.

"Why? I'm not going if she finds Monica."

"We'll see," Miriam said quietly.

"What is there to see? What I see is I've already got two women pecking away at my bones. Why make it three?" He held his breath, then let it out slowly, shaking his head. "Jesus, you don't get a moment's peace around here, do you?"

Annie began talking slowly before he had finished his sentence. "I don't know why it is. It's all done and over, but I can still be jealous. If that's the right name for it."

"Can't you listen? I'm not going looking for Monica. *She* is."

"We'll see."

"So help me, if you say that once more, I'm going to treat you like my child, not my grown-up daughter."

She had that maddening, straight-lipped smile, and her eyes did not waver.

It was Annie who started talking. "Sometimes, dear friends, I think of going away. Did you ever think how easy that would be? Just some money, clothes, a bus ticket. There's a whole new life out there." She was not looking at either of them as her arm swept out over the table.

Lewis put both hands to his head. He kneaded his aching temples. "One of you has me taking a trip I'm not going on, the other is going to take a trip she never returns from. Can't we just sit still a minute? Can't we talk about the deer herd or what Buddy did last week?" He sat back. "What time is it?"

Miriam looked at her wrist. "Six-thirty."

Lewis stood. "Excuse me. I'm going out to see my friends for a while."

Annie was staring at him hard. "If you get stinking again don't bother to come here — front door, back door, or windows."

"I'm going up the road to spend time with the only friends I understand. My goddamn horses."

They glared at each other, then she waved. "Oh, go muck out a few stalls."

They were talking heatedly when he came downstairs to put on his coat. Silence was what he wanted, and found as he trudged down the Sunday night road with no rides likely, stepping into the snowbank when the occasional trailer truck exploded past. His head was as jumbled as the turmoil of air behind the trucks. Even as he had spoken standing in the kitchen, he knew those were almost his father's words hurled one night at his mother — *My horses are my only friends* — and there was Annie also talking like his father about wandering off, disappearing. *Well, sleep with them, then,* his mother had said, and Foster did, finishing a fifth of Bourbon in the hayloft as Elmore conjectured the next day, showing the bottle to Lewis, and that had been the morning his father in drunken rage had let the horses out at dawn, flailing them as they passed him, yelling obscenely, screaming that he hated them, hated them. Now Lewis swung his arms against the cold and stretched out his pace. There were no stars and the mountains showed only as low humps. He wished he could walk on and on without getting or going anywhere. He did not want to go back; he did not want to arrive. In his anger he heard himself saying to a merged figure of Miriam and Annie and Monica, *Look. I have no idea who I was then or who the hell I am now, so leave me the fuck alone.*

The first car that passed him was obviously not going to stop for anything until it got where it was going. A Cadillac, it flashed by with only the swish of tires, moving straight as a rocket. From his glimpse of the interior Lewis imagined the tightly closed, plush vision of a snowy world curling off to each side, perhaps a stereo playing. He had traveled once like that, driving a Lincoln to Florida for one of the car dealers in the Flatts. He wondered if dealers still moved their stock that way. He could stand some time on the road.

When the next car approached from town, he could tell by looking at the veer and wobble of its lights that it had to be a local, something irrevocably wrong with its suspension. He stood aside, decided not to thumb since he was almost there. Leo was hunched tensely over the wheel, face lit by the dashboard, cigarette trailing down. He was staring straight ahead as if driving through a thick fog. The car passed and Lewis spat to one side, trudging back into the roadway. He was almost smothered by the cloud of exhaust trailing behind the car like a crop duster's spray. He spat again. But he would do nothing about Leo. After all that time he was not going to chase after a scuttling rat.

He groped in the barn for the main light switch. The long row of hanging lights burst on, making the rafters, the partitions of the stalls leap into sight. Joker neighed. There were four or five new horses, riding nags cared for by Howard and a man Phoebe had hired to come from the Flatts every morning. Lewis still tended his own, and he wished more than ever that he had finished repairing Foley's shed. He did not care for the new hand, had already forgotten his name as if he refused it; he was much too dandy and smug, a retired Army man who lived in the Flatts, had started going to vet school but quit before finishing. Lewis could tell the man had no real sense about horses. He treated them with the precise, disciplined motions of a sergeant directing his troops. Lewis had quietly forbidden him to touch Melissa and Joker, and the man had simply shrugged, said, *Suit yourself*, and to Phoebe suggested they be removed as soon as possible since their presence disturbed the thoroughbreds.

Thoroughbreds, hell. She had been taken by some horse trader. But in a year or so she would probably be passing them on to another sucker. Maybe he did not know much about riding horses, but Lewis knew enough about breed to see that she knew less. And as if to emphasize the flighty quality of the operation, she had bought them all and shipped them up in midwinter from an auction in Arizona. He tried not to think about Phoebe and last night, but what if she came into the barn now? She was wrong, of course. She probably thought every man wanted her. He leaned his shoulder against an empty stall. He had known her since she was a child. But she was a woman now. If that was what she wanted, he would know what to do. He had seen her once when she was a teenager, tangled in the back end of a stall with some visiting cousin, her jeans unbuttoned at the waist and his hand plunged under them, working hard. They had been too busy to see him and he left quickly.

Joker and Melissa stamped and blew impatiently. As he approached, he spoke to them quietly, sidled in by Joker. Even though it was dark and getting late he ought to let them have a run before feeding them. He stroked the long, mild face of the aging horse. He had neglected them lately. That was wrong. His own confusions had nothing to do with them.

He backed Joker out, sensing the nervous anticipation in his bunching neck muscles. At least horses were clear. The work was drudgery at times, but peaceful in some core beyond his own muddles. Only acting had been like that at times. When he had learned the part well, when the other actors in the cast around him were so good that he was lifted above the level of his more meager talent, he would be seized by a voice, a way of moving that was exhilaratingly unlike anyone he had ever been, and then, looking back, he would see himself serenely, at a great distance. Other actors told him that this was only the first stage, that he would be unable to count on that happening, and craft would have to imitate those moments again and again. He took their word for that. He had to, because he never went beyond those few touches. Now they were vague memories, and nothing compared to walking beside the strong, subdued body of his own horse, down the long, well-lit corridor. Behind them Melissa whinnied impatiently. He called back to her and Joker swung his head.

He could depend on these two horses. They were survivors, the last of a breed he could trace back with certainty, other than Cassandra's unborn foal, and Bernie owned that. These horses could become the fixed point of a new way of life for him. He had read *The Draft Horse Journal* regularly for years, had seen the statistics of rising purchases, horses bought not just for show purposes but for labor again on small farms or larger operations where they were used to supplement machinery. He could probably get a loan for his own small operation, and those plans that he had mulled over vaguely for years had begun recently to seem more possible. Now that he knew Joker was still potent, he could buy a brood mare, get a start.

They walked slowly down the packed snow of the ramp, Joker's breath steaming out around his face so that the ground wavered in and out of sight in the slip of light thrown by the barn spotlight. He turned to the closest paddock, swung the gate open, released the bridle. Joker tossed his head, pounded off in his rolling heavy gait in the space where the distant light made the scoured snow gleam dully. Lewis latched the gate and went back for Melissa. He would have to build a barn, would prefer that to renting or buying one elsewhere.

But there were some things about his plans that worried him. Elmore had offered to stake him, but he could not accept that, even though he had never liked putting himself in the hands of banks. He mistrusted them too much, hated the dependence of having to come up with money every month. They had you then, because you came to love the things you were doing, forgetting that you did not own them at all, and then some slips, a wipe-out not anticipated, and everything was taken away. He would have to put up the land and cabin as collateral. But that was making the things he loved vulnerable — Joker, Melissa, his land.

He had named Joker. Born in the middle of the night after

two false starts, the foal had looked unpromising as it lay on its side, small chest heaving irregularly.

I give him two days, Lewis said.

He and Coleman were both stooped at the entrance to the stall. The birth had interrupted a game of poker Lewis had been winning and he was certain he would not get his luck back if they continued.

Name him. Coleman was breaking a long stalk of hay into small pieces. *Let him have that much.*

The mare turned to sniff with her heavy, tired head drooping to the foal, and she began licking as if the gentle motions could pass on some strength.

Joker, Lewis said as if he had been thinking about it for some time, and Coleman laughed once, but laughed genuinely five years later when Joker was sire to most of the Percherons in the area, that weakling foal grown into a massive frame of bone and taut sinew. He would slap a hand on Joker's neck and say to Lewis, *The joke was on us.* But Lewis liked to remind him how he had even been wrong about his luck and the next night had walked away from Coleman and two of his guests with three months' extra wages.

When Melissa whinnied as they neared the doorway, she was answered out of the dark air by Joker, and a horse behind them kicked nervously at its stall.

"Whoa," he had to say as she shied at the figure near the fence. Howard was puffed up in the down of a long parka, his face staring out of a wool hat low over his ears.

"Geesum, Lew, we thought someone was trying to steal the horses or let them loose."

"Sorry to interrupt."

He released Melissa and latched the gate. The horses touched noses, swung, ran tightly side by side around the fence, wheeled in unison, and stopped suddenly again, heads up, before they took another dash.

"Aren't they something?" Howard's voice was truly admiring.

No matter what, they shared that. He put his hand on Howard's bulky shoulder as they leaned on the top rail, watching the horses slow to a walk, beginning to nose each other.

"It's not so cold after all," Howard said, and Lewis thought his voice either tired or tense, he could not tell which. "But anyway, Merry Christmas, Lew."

"Not yet." But it was two days away and he had not bought presents for Annie or Miriam or even for his brother and family.

"We'll be gone by then. Leaving tomorrow afternoon."

"So she's taking you along?"

Howard's face, catching the glare of the spotlight behind Lewis, was a mask; the smile was wide, the eyes glistened but shifted nervously back and forth, and when he laughed, his voice was high and tight.

"We're flying to New York from the Flatts in a little plane a doctor friend of hers owns who came up here to ski this week, and we're getting on a big plane and flying to New Orleans because she says I ought to see that. Then we'll get on another plane and go to Montana or Colorado or someplace where she goes to ski. They take you way up onto the mountain in a helicopter and leave you there and you ski down for miles all day, and she says she wants to go there to be sure to see some people she'd never be able to get hold of otherwise to invite to the party, and that's only about a month or so off, I think, or something like that—"

"Hold on. Slow down or you'll rip your tongue out."

Howard stopped, his mouth open, and his shoulder relaxed a little. "I've missed you. I get scared sometimes."

They both went back to leaning on the fence. Lewis kicked his boots against the post because the cold was beginning to numb his toes.

"Scared of what?"

"First off, she's crazy. Sometimes I worry am I going to get that crazy if I'm around her too. I catch myself doing things now I couldn't have imagined myself doing a few weeks ago because I'd never heard they were possible, and doing even the smallest things as if I'd done them all my life—like shaking up a bunch of Bloody Marys first thing every morning while she cooks us some breakfast that might be this goose liver stuff on crackers rather than eggs—and I think, 'Howard, who the hell are you?' And then the traveling. I mean, I've been to the Flatts, Lew."

He swallowed. At the house a door slammed and he lifted his head.

"She'll drop me soon. I know that. She even says it. She's honest with me. But I don't want to be dropped in New Orleans, or Montana, or wake up someplace and find her totally cracked. Because sometimes I think that's what's going to happen first."

"Why?" Lewis did not want Howard to pause like that because in the silences he veered back into a fixed image of Howard and Phoebe naked, locked together.

His voice lowered. "You ought to hear her at night when she's asleep. She'll be dreaming and talking out loud. It's not what she says, Lew. I can't understand much of that anyway, and when I do, it doesn't make sense. But it's the voice itself. I swear it would cut your gut out to hear it. And she laughs sometimes too. When that happens I have to make a noise or get up and go sit in the living room. It scares the shit out of me."

Lewis shook his head slowly. "Poor old Howard. Things have sure come a long way. You haven't forgotten you can get off anytime you want, have you? You don't have to go with her, you don't have to stay there," and he jabbed his gloved hand at the house. "You're not a prisoner."

Howard looked glum. "I know. I'm just speaking for the part of me that's scared. Jesus, the rest of me's having a hell of a time."

Lewis kept his eyes on the horses, dim but solid forms at the far side of the paddock. "Think about this, then. I've in mind to go into the business, set up a horse-breeding farm. I'd like you to come in with me."

"You mean that?"

"Yes."

Howard held still, finally saying quietly, "I'd like that. But I'm not sure. Sometimes I wonder how anything will ever be the same. I think of the good people in my life like my folks, and Elaine, and I wonder if they'll ever speak to me again."

"Well, Elaine's getting married."

"I know. But I wish you hadn't said that. Look, I gotta be going." He turned, then stopped, his back to Lewis. "I don't know what I'd do without you, Lew."

Before Lewis could say anything the figure was striding toward the house. Lewis whistled the horses over, released the gate, took them both at the same time now that they were exercised and anticipating the filling of their feed boxes, which he began to do as soon as they were safely back in their stalls. For a while he stood and listened as they ate, then he walked down the aisle to the doorway. He paused with his hand on the switch.

The long night behind him, the abuse of his body and exasperation of arguing in areas where he was bumping blindly into unseen objects, left him weary. He would walk to Annie's now. The back door would be open. Maybe Miriam would still be up reading, as she often did, late into the night. He would not stop to do much more than say good night. Then a hot shower. He would slip into bed beside Annie, trying not to wake her. Soon he would talk to her again about his plans for the horses. Would he suddenly feel it was a useless dream? Not if he could really describe it to her. That was always the problem with plans that were still only wishes, they were so hard to put into words that sometimes they slipped away like fog in a cold wind. But he and Annie would at least have something different to talk about. Howard was with him. He might try Buddy. He had even thought about Bernie. No one could drive a harder bargain than Carbonneau when he was buying. It would be good to have him on his side.

He flipped off the light. The clouds had broken and rifts of quicksilver from the moonlight opened across the mountains and fields. When Lewis stood still on the path turning at Annie's house, he began to be unsure which way to go. The house was dark. He could walk up to the cabin. As if edged in ice, the pattern of his own life came to him again — a cabin, a house in town with a woman, and now a daughter, horses, nothing even to indicate where he would sleep in only a few minutes — but why after a few years of finding most of that perfectly easy did it all seem so confusing? The wind cracked the big branches of the maples like whips and rushed on toward the hillsides. A light went on downstairs, and a figure moved across the frosted glass. For a second he yearned only to be in there surrounded by the clear facts of light and warmth. When he was a child returning from the barn after doing the simpler chores required of him, he would stand that way in the yard, getting cold but savoring the moment to come when he would enter the warm kitchen, drift through the smells of dinner almost ready. Would he ever understand what any of this was about, this jagged, unpredictable life? He wished he could talk about the horse farm with his father.

13

"**W**hy should I give a damn what you do with it? It's your property."

Elmore leaned back in the old wooden swivel chair, his hands curled over the ends of the arms, looking out the broad window where his own reversed name was printed. He had not offered Lewis the usual cup of coffee, but Lewis waited stubbornly. Rumors had reached him about his brother and Eleanor. He did not want to ask a direct question.

"That abandoned town road across your field. I'll have to use it."

Elmore's hand waved. "No problem. I won't prevent anything."

"I wouldn't want you to be the last to know."

Elmore shifted his toothpick. "Frankly, I think you're a dreamer. Tractors are here to stay. People won't go backwards no matter what."

Lewis did not care to discuss that again. Their mother had always sided with Elmore.

"I guess I have in mind a combination of horses and machines."

Elmore shrugged. "Might work."

The secretary in the other room answered the phone, her voice fixed in friendliness, and then her typewriter began clacking again.

"Business doing okay?"

"Slow. Inflation doesn't help. Interest rates." Elmore tilted forward to the desk strewn with unsigned letters, catalogs, and boxes. He pushed some things aside and folded his hands on top of the blotter. "I wouldn't want you to be the last to know." He smiled wryly at his desk top. "Eleanor and I are living apart for a while. We need some space."

Lewis had heard the phrase about "space" from others too often, even remembered using it with Annie.

"I can see my news has left you speechless."

"I always thought you and Eleanor would work it out somehow."

"Who says we won't?" His tightly clasped hands were lifting at the wrists and tapping down on the desk top. "Hard for Elaine, too. She'll stay on with me here. Because of school, her job. Not that Eleanor's really going far away. She'll be with Marianne Springer at the Flatts. Oh, I don't know." He surged back in the chair again, breathed out, but even with his hands behind his head, he did not appear relaxed. "She wants to get a job, get out of the house, quit sitting around waiting for me to come up out of my own swamp. I don't blame her. But I'm not happy Marianne's mixed up in it. She's a little loony about women's rights and all that. But it's not another man, anyway."

Elmore's pose congealed, and Lewis searched frantically for some way to keep the conversation going, but everything that came to mind seemed wrong. How could he give advice to his brother when he woke every morning to sense his own life bobbing around him like flotsam?

"Do you think he really started out to do it, or did he make up his mind on the way?" Elmore spoke to the window again.

"Who?"

"The old man. Was there any clear sign he would run away for good?"

"He never told us much."

"No, he wouldn't have waffled like that. If Dad was anything, he was determined."

Lewis looked away, read the window by making a mirror of his mind: *Contractor — Homes Built to Specification — Caretaking.* "I didn't know what to do, Elmore. You were away, I didn't have anyone to talk to. Except Buddy."

Elmore shook his head. He never had approved of Buddy, and when they were younger did not like Lewis to hang around with him.

"I blamed myself for a while, as if I could have talked him into staying, or changed something for him."

"Seems like you didn't have much choice. Anyway, I can imagine going off like that. But I can't see sticking with it forever. He must have wondered about us sometimes."

"Listen to me for a minute, will you?" Lewis stood and walked to the window and when he spoke he kept his back half-turned, one foot on the windowsill. He did not wait for Elmore to answer but plunged, finding whatever words he could, trying to tell his brother about Monica, New York, and the way that Miriam wanted him to come with her now. At one point he heard Elmore stand, close the door to the secretary's room, and come back. In the garage across the street Andy was on his back, rolling himself under a battered pickup. "I can't go, I can't stay, I don't know what Miriam wants from me, I want her to go away, but I can't bear the idea of losing her again." He stopped abruptly. He had said nothing. What was Monica or all that past history of his to Elmore? They had kept their lives secret and apart for so many years that there would be no way he could understand now. "Oh, hell, what's the use."

He turned. Elmore was staring at the top of his desk.

"Lew, did you ever imagine for even a moment that it would be this way?"

"What way?"

"When you were younger. Didn't you think you would know by now, that people our age did know what they were doing?"

Lewis laughed sharply, leaned back on the windowsill. "Sometimes I still think others do."

"But look at Dad. For all his shifting in and out of rage and silence, I never thought he did not know what he was doing."

Lewis pushed away from the window impatiently. All this was not solving anything. The truest sign of his confusion was that he had blurted these things to Elmore at all, and now he had only another useless gesture to live with. Elmore started to say something, Lewis interrupted, "Talking never helps anyway," but the popping of a cap gun made them both turn back to the window.

Elmore swung out of his chair and joined Lewis. A gorilla was jumping up and down at the rear of a car stopped beside Fulton's gas pumps. The driver had leaned out the window and was laughing and firing the gun. The ape pounded its chest, flung up its arms, flopped on its back with legs straight up in the air. When it sat up, removing the head with the fixed grimace of anger, the man's face was much too small for the rest of the suit. His pate was mostly bald, a pale round of flesh in the heap of shaggy fur.

Elmore's mouth wrinkled in disgust. "They've been piling in all day. There was an idiot Batman and Robin this morning in a car with cardboard fins. Looks like every loony in America's been invited to Phoebe's blast."

The ape was leaning on the back of the car, talking with Andy Fulton. They passed a bottle of beer back and forth.

"You going?"

"I'm down, Lew, but not that low. Dressed up like Halloween? Kids' stuff."

Lewis decided he had better check the horses, get their exercising and feeding over before too many drunks were rolling around shooting off cap pistols or firecrackers or whatever other kind of nonsense they might take up. He had no intention of going either, suspected very few people in town would in spite of those invitations, fancy little cards with masked revelers and a twiddly script saying: *Mardi Gras comes to Judson.*

Elmore spoke quietly. "She's good, that daughter of yours. Elaine's been spending time with her, needs someone to talk to. Most of her friends are giving her a hard time because of Elly and me. You know how that is. It's just gossip to them. Then there's some problem with Jonathan. She won't talk to me about it."

Lewis ached to place a hand on his brother's shoulder, his uncharacteristically slumped back, but Elmore turned abruptly and walked to his desk. "Well, I've got to make some calls."

Lewis was starting to open the door when Elmore said, "I was thinking again how next fall maybe you and I could go hunting. Up on Moonstone. Remember that spot you and Dad and I used to go?"

Lewis looked back but Elmore had already lifted the phone, was dialing.

It was evening before he walked the road to the barn. The house was lit up as if it contained a heap of coals, every window throwing rectangles onto the snowy lawn, and the light shimmered and blinked when figures passed back and forth. Already the yard near the barn was filling with cars. Lewis could hear voices, slammed doors, an electric guitar being tuned, so magnified that it twanged down out of the dark sky. He stood aside to let a low, sleek car fishtail by. The driver was tucked in as if tied to a dogsled.

But in the barn the noises from the house were deadened by thick beams and heavy air. He took the horses out the back way to the small paddock so that the barn would be between them and the cars arriving. Joker and Melissa were nervous, pausing in their runs to stand still, ears pricked. The air that afternoon had turned balmy as a strong wind from the south blew up, then died. What stayed was that faint odor of someone else's spring beginning, a deceptive promise since late February was far too early for anyone in this land to even think of spring. For Lewis it always roused an odd longing and memories of passing through the Gulf States on one of his journeys. He had sat on a bench in Biloxi with a long wait between buses, shocked to discover that in his own native country there were places where spring came in February, flowers already casting odors, trees unfurling and blooming, and the air promising a long, sweet slide into summer. He had sat there, eyes closed, breathing deeply, wondering why anyone would live where he had chosen to stay, where spring was a flood of old waters let go for a week or two before summer arrived, and whatever bloomed exploded with all the fierceness of a brook thrashing its ice against rocks and shattered tree trunks.

He leaned on the top bar of the fence. If he were a horse he would pause like that also, striking the still-hardened ground as if to remind himself that only the air had given way for a moment. There would be at least two more snowstorms, and then that long, gray period when the ground, even more bleak than November before the first snow, clung to its bauchy patches of discolored ice. He clucked and Melissa trudged over to him, her head in slow bobbings as she came. He had brought an apple for each of them, and when Joker heard her chomping and blowing, he came too. They stood side by side, chewing, patient faces staring at Lewis. He put a hand on each of their foreheads and they did not toss or sidle.

Sometimes the shape and texture of horses appealed to him so intensely that he was certain what it would be like to inhabit their bodies. The hard bones of their foreheads spread the skin taut, and the hairs were fine and thickly matted. He was always held close by their wide, deepening eyes, and the long, smooth stretch of their full sides. The slight cleft along the back and the rounded croup and quarter would fill him with the same passionate towing as a woman's body, naked as she lay on her side, the first light edging the curve and dip from shoulder to hipbone and descending thigh.

Someone fired a rocket. A long hiss ascended, then with a boom the sky filled with an umbrella of cascading pinks and blues that faded back. The horses wheeled, Joker whinnied, they raced to the near fence and veered just in time. Voices were cheering. When the horses returned, Lewis took the bridles firmly and led them back to their stalls. He did not want to have to deal with panicked horses. The riding nags were nervous too.

He had finished putting out their feed when Howard came. What Lewis saw at first was a pair of boots, legs bound in chaps, pants ballooned out slightly at the thighs—a World War I uniform, British or American, or most likely a mixture of both—and it was only after Lewis had looked at the costume carefully that he took in Howard's face, watchful and a little defensive.

"Do you like it?" Howard had not moved, his hands stiffly in his belt, legs slightly apart, like a mannequin.

"Off to the wars, Howard?" Lewis hung the bucket and walked back through the stall to stand with him in the aisle, and then they strolled toward the tack room, leaving Joker and Melissa to their eating.

"She had it made for me. In Chicago. Said I would've made a good soldier."

"I'll bet."

He had seen Howard briefly since he and Phoebe returned from their looping run around the country. Howard had not tried to describe it. That he had survived was enough, although seeing him in this old uniform, his young face too perfectly a replica of some blurred, browned photograph of that war long ago, Lewis could not help thinking of him as a veteran of some sort, gassed or wounded or missing in action.

He looked very weary when he said, "It's going to be noisy up there tonight."

Since the heaters were not on, the tack room was hardly warmer than the barn. But the smaller space, the light filling all its corners, made conversation seem more possible.

"I think this might be my last party, Lew. I can't take much more."

The wince on Howard's face was enough to keep Lewis from laughing, and the boy's hand was up to silence him anyway.

"It's not what you think. There are times now when we lie in bed together and she sleeps all curled close to me or I hold her face and watch it going to sleep, and I know I'll miss her."

"Then what's wrong?"

"It's all inside out. When it's dark and we're lying together, or when we sleep and dream close to each other, or in the morning when we first wake and everything is so clear and quiet, I can live with her. Does that sound crazy? I mean, I've come to think we all have this whole life at night we don't think of as being alive, but when we're with someone all night like that, and touching, and our lives are going on even though we don't know most of it in the morning, that's living too."

Lewis nodded.

Howard looked at the chair as if he might sit, but they both could hear another car churn by, then voices high and ebullient in the barnyard. "In the daytime she's a different person. She's mean and turns and twists and bites at everything. She's going crazy and I don't want to be around anymore to watch it."

"Don't, then."

But he was continuing, shaking his head. "I used to think I could do something about it."

"She was always nuts, Howard."

"But I don't mean just that kind of crazy. I mean crazy crazy." He took off his hat, folded it, and thrust it through an epaulette as neatly as if he had been living in the suit for years, and then, with a shock, Lewis realized he must have been wearing it often. Howard was nodding as if he read Lewis's mind.

"When she bought the uniform in Chicago and said it was for the party, and then asked me to wear it all the time, and she started dressing like some kind of flapper and all, well, that's nothing new. That's what everyone who knows her calls 'eccentric.' 'Oh, Phoebe — she's so eccentric,' they always say. I'm talking about something else, like what happened in Panama."

"Panama?"

Howard gave the briefest grin at Lewis's discomfort.

"We were on our way to Idaho. The plane put down in St. Louis and she made us get off, buy tickets. She'd seen a picture of the canal in the airplane magazine. She wanted to see it. We went there. I thought that was fine. I never expected us to go straight somewhere. Hell, if she says she's going to Judson, she's just as likely to drive through and end up in New York City. But we went to a hotel that she picked out of the phone book — a place I wouldn't use for raising chickens. The second day there, she started getting really bounced up, talking all the time. Said she could speak in any language and then she'd do that, speaking French for an hour, and German for the afternoon, and all nonstop. I wouldn't know the difference, but one man in the lobby, if that's what the pigsty was, when she spoke Spanish said it was gibberish and laughed because he said it sounded Spanish but made no sense at all. She did that for forty-eight straight hours, no sleeping. She'd sit up in bed rattling along, her voice so hoarse she could hardly talk. Toward the end she started making up other people and talking for them in her 'conversations' because she said no one would talk to her."

Howard paused, wiped his face with his sleeve. He was sweating.

"Then she went stone quiet. It was like her lips were sewed together. Wouldn't eat, or drink. Lay naked on the bed, got up to pee, laid down again. Damn hotel was hot as a steam iron, had cockroaches the size of frogs, and I had to spend my time brushing them off her, she cared that little."

He stopped again, his own lips tight, as if imitating her face.

"What brought her back?"

"God knows. One afternoon she flicked out her hand to swipe at a cockroach and sat up and looked at me and in a perfectly normal voice, a little tired, she said, 'Let's get the hell out of here, Howard.' We packed up and went to the airport. She passed out twice in the waiting room, lack of food, I figured, but we were all right once we got to San Diego. She acted, still does, like we'd never been to Panama at all."

Another rocket went off, scattered pops ending in a large boom. They both stared at each other for a moment.

"Lew, I gotta ask you a favor. It's why I came."

"Shoot, Howard."

For the first time the face went shy and boyish again. "Can I come stay up to your place soon? Would you mind? My folks still won't touch me with a cattle prod, and when I leave here, I don't want to be alone. I don't know if I'll believe any of it when it's over." He looked sideways toward the door as if trying with his eyes to urge his reluctant body into motion. "And I'll be lonely as hell."

Lewis hesitated. Miriam. Now Howard. He threw up both hands. "Why not? You're welcome to."

Howard breathed deeply. "Thanks. I'll tell you one more thing. I knew I had to get out when we went skiing finally. Just like she said it would be. They dropped us off from a helicopter way the hell up on a mountain in Idaho. It was miles back. She and a few other people with us went down zip. I'm not so hot on skis, took my time. Fell once and got up, and they were out of sight. Only me and the snow and miles and miles of mountains." He swallowed. "Peace. I couldn't even hear them. I want to be alone or with people where I can find the same quiet. I was as happy as I've ever been in my life. Thank God I'm not crazy, like she's crazy."

They walked together to the barn door and stood side by side.

"I wish I could say it was all experience, you know? Someone, an Australian tennis player I had to share her with in Los Angeles, said someday I'd look back on it all and talk like it was the most exciting time of my life. 'Experience,' he kept saying over and over to me, Lew. 'It's all experience.'"

He said it in such a way that Lewis could not mistake how he felt about it, and then he was walking away down the ramp, his back perfectly straight as he adjusted the hat he had slipped from his shoulder. Seeing the figure silhouetted against the burning house, Lewis thought they must be swept back in time to another moment; surely this must have happened in Grandfather White's days, just such a young man in uniform walking casually back to the old house, a soldier on leave. Then, so suddenly that his throat choked and he had to swallow, he thought of Coleman, his face as clear as the latch by his hand, and as if he were truly experiencing it for the first time, the knowledge that he would never see the man again was absolute.

On the road with the wind at his back, Lewis considered again the possibility of traveling. It had always been so comforting. He could trudge up to the cabin, pack that battered brown suitcase he used now for storing his old suits, maybe drop by Annie's to tell her in the morning that he would be away for a week or so. She would be annoyed, but he would not go for long. A chance to think things over before he committed himself to the farm. Maybe if he left Miriam to herself, things would straighten out or she might go to Monica without him. Certainly, by staying, he was not helping anyone. He had never been able to describe clearly enough to Annie the exhilaration of driving alone all night, voices of towns and cities filling the privacy of his quiet, dimly lit chamber, those truck stops where he did not have to talk if he did not want, could sit over coffee and doughnuts in the murmur of small talk, and then go back out to a road where the landscape always shifted and dawn might reveal shapes of trees or shoreless oceans of prairies that could not have been imagined. He never should have sold his car.

He had wandered mostly in the years before Jim died, sometimes in restless bursts of frustration, wondering two hundred miles away why he stayed in Judson at all when everything spread out new forever. But he never broke free entirely. Not only because of Annie either. At some point, in the shadow of a mesa, or sitting in a bar with the salt breeze of the Pacific blowing the map he had unfolded, that long, slow undertow would reclaim him — the faces of people he had cursed only a week ago, the familiarly cracked wall still holding in the bank by the grocery store, Moonstone shaped like no mountain he had seen elsewhere. He never remembered the names and faces of the women, and they were rarely as intensely experienced as the landscape. Only one he had never forgotten, a woman named Cal in Wyoming. She worked days in a shoe store, evenings as a waitress at a Mexican restaurant. He had not thought much of her when he picked her up at the local bar. She was a little overweight, nothing delicate about her features, a white scar across her lower lip, from a bad car accident, she said. But that night she sang to him in her darkened room, sitting naked with him on her bed, a guitar she lugged out of a battered case propped under her sloping breasts. For the next three nights he could not have enough of her. When she talked he heard the voice she sang with held back and waiting, and for the first time in all those years of sudden wanderings he forgot Judson, Annie, drifted into Cal's singing as if he had no past at all. As he drove back to Judson, after he had come uninvited one night to the door of her room and found it locked and heard her singing inside to someone else, he had wondered if his father had found and kept a woman like that. Maybe it was possible to forget.

Nothing was happening at the Bear, and Lewis did not want to go in anyway, so he passed slowly, looking in the window at the dim bar, the slumped figure of Jake picking his teeth. An aureole of fog surrounded each streetlight, and the dampness was heavy to breathe. Annie was dozing on the couch, a book slipped sideways from her lax hand. She opened her eyes slowly.

"Miriam not here?" In the past weeks she had returned to her restless pattern of trips to Philadelphia, even more erratic than before, and now that she was just as likely to stay with Annie as with him, Lewis was even more uncertain of where she would be.

She shook her head, sat up blinking, hands flat on each side of her as if she might tilt. "She went up to the cabin. Said she wanted to be alone."

He left his boots by the door. They were caked with the grit and muck of melted snowdrifts. "Now what's wrong with her?"

Annie looked at him with sleepy puzzlement. "I have to tell you that?"

"You mean Monica."

"Do you think that's all easy for her?"

"No. But I wish she'd make up her mind."

"Sometimes, Lewis Beede, I wonder if you have any idea what life is like for other people. She's trying to decide whether to go see a mother she has never seen before, who she has thought she wanted to know all her life, and now, suddenly, with a damn lot more confusion than anything she went through with you, she's not sure if she wants to."

"I know."

"Then what do you mean, 'What's wrong?'"

He stood near the fireplace, gave the smoking logs a kick, and flames began to flap up between them. "What can I do about it?"

"Hell" — but her eyes were mild when she glanced at him — "you're part of the problem anyway, so she can't expect much from you."

She came over to the fireplace, leaned one hand on the mantel, gave her own prod to the logs, and then her arm was around his waist and they were both looking into the fire.

"What she finds is Lewis Beede, and an odd woman he lives with when he wants, and some horses he loves, and a town probably no one would choose to live in, although some of us have. All of it could never have been imagined, and if it's even hard for us to accept at times, how could it be anything else for her? Look at her, Lew." She leaned her head on his shoulder and her voice hummed on him, her breath close to his neck. "She's doing everything backwards. At her age, she should be the child who has finally broken away from home completely, has her own life, is just beginning to bend back a little, treat her parents as if they needed attention from time to time. But what is she doing? She's come back to be a child, and a woman, and an adolescent, and everything all at once — with strangers."

He tried to listen, but something else was bothering him now. He interrupted her.

"Are you saying she might not go?"

"She's already told you that."

He frowned, shook his head. "But I guess I never believed. It wouldn't exactly be fair."

"What?"

"If she didn't go. If Monica didn't have to live through all this too."

Annie did not answer, and he did not want to talk about that anymore but could not help imagining Miriam confronting her mother, a dim figure at the far end of a bare and unfamiliar room. *I am your daughter.* Monica deserved as much as he did to bear the shock of contact with a frayed past she had tried to avoid forever.

"I hope to hell she goes," he said flatly.

They stared into the fire, which had risen to consume the last of the logs, throwing a heat against his legs that made the damp cuffs steam. Drowsily he watched the shapes of the flames. Often as a child he would lie on the kitchen floor on his back near the stove when all the lamps were out, naming the patterns the flicker of light made on the ceiling: weasels, the eyes of wizards, horses with wings of fire. She yawned and stretched.

"Elaine came by looking for Miriam. We had a talk. I don't think there'll be a wedding. She's finding Jonathan dull."

"She's right."

"But Howard isn't dull. She says awful things about him because of Phoebe and the way his folks feel, but I think she's still stuck on him."

When the fire blazed up, the light washed over her face and he saw her as she had been, so young and stubborn that nothing could change her mind, and he reached out with the back of his hand to stroke her cheek once. She turned her face to him and looked puzzled, not from the gesture of his hand, but from some expression on his face.

"Sometimes you don't marry the person you're stuck on," he said quietly.

She did not answer but took his hand, and they went upstairs to bed. He wondered why it could not be like this all the time, Annie and himself talking quietly, or touching as they both slipped into the certainty of sleep.

He woke with his heart pounding, and before the next heavy

thump, he had no idea where he was or who he was, but he was certain that a meteor had fallen and struck the room.

With the next pounding on the door, a voice was calling his name. He tried to place it as he swung out of the bed, heard Annie say, "What the hell is it?" was halfway down the stairs when he knew it was Howard, his voice strained and breathless. He flipped the hall light as he passed, wrenched open the door, and the soldier staggered in with hand raised to knock again, his head hatless and hair awry.

"Quick. It's the horses. They let them loose."

From that moment Lewis clenched like stone. He did not ask any questions. Annie in her bathrobe on the landing stared while he passed and found his clothes and came down again. Howard had been jabbering, but he only half listened, something about how they'd all been drunk and some of them wanted to go riding and he told them that the riding horses were in the front stalls, he'd warned them about that, and when Lewis had his coat on, before he pushed Howard out the door toward the car that hunched with its engine running, he slapped him dispassionately but sharply across the mouth to shut him up. He looked back once as he was closing the door to see her sitting on the stairs, chin propped on her knees, and that was the only moment until late into the next morning that he thought he would break, would open his mouth and tear his voice apart with one wordless howl.

Which he finally did somewhere in the woods on a ridge of Moonstone when the sun was disappearing behind the monotonous gauze of clouds that had to be snow, would be snow by noon, that fine, soundless mist of flakes that could fall and fall for days, and it did that also, piling up against the houses, weighing the roofs, rising to meet the pine boughs it bent down from above, smothering everything in absolute white. He heard his own voice begin that yell, his body was lifted and shaken and shattered as it grew, cutting at his throat and lungs. When that was done he walked on, as he had already for hours, wandering the mountainside as if he were looking for a way out of a landscape too familiar to have a secret exit.

Howard drove hunched down over the wheel of the sports car he had borrowed, driving in whatever gear he could shift to, and Lewis sat straight, staring at the road that seemed to slip under them so slowly, his head nudging the low roof when they skidded into a curb or slewed out onto the shoulder. Howard kept muttering from time to time, "Jesus, Jesus," but the only thing Lewis said after they left the town streets was, "Turn on the lights."

When they took the last curve they could see far down the straightaway to the cluster of lights, the purple winking of the State Police car and red flash of a wrecker. The closer they came, the more the jumble came apart into cars with their lights on, spotlights shining on both police car and wrecker, the shapes of men moving, and then Lewis could see the huge wall of a trailer truck jackknifed across the road, its van tilting off at an angle from the scene as if drawing away from it. Finally as he swung out of the door even before they had stopped, his boots dragging in the road, eyes fixed on the scene ahead of him, he could see the horses. He ran. Everyone stood back.

Joker was lying on his side, long neck stretched forward, lips working convulsively over his teeth. The great cavity of his chest heaved up from the reddened macadam like the body of a beached whale, but below it, the gut and hindquarters were a twisted, mangled shape unrecognizable except for the skewed legs, the massive hooves. Melissa lay by the side of the van, her legs under her as if she had folded them preparing to roll in the dust, but her head was turned awkwardly, half her face ripped back and jawbone exposed.

Lewis did not pause. He refused to feel anything. He walked over to Simpson, who was staring at him.

"Give it to me."

The trooper did not understand. Lewis pointed.

"Give it to me, damn it, or do I have to take it."

Simpson unstrapped the pistol and put it in Lewis's hand. He did not wait to hear what the trooper was saying. He went to Joker first and stooped quickly, placing the barrel behind the animal's ear, sensed the eyes rolling at him, would not look directly. The first time he pulled, nothing happened because the catch was on, so he released it, now hearing Simpson's words that he had spoken a few seconds ago and his own voice inside him was saying calmly, *So that's what the bugger was telling me,* but he could not avoid

215

the eye, stared into it, knew the animal saw him clearly, the flared nostrils smelled his flesh, and he fired. The shot was clean. The long swift shudder told him that another would not be needed. He rose quickly and went to Melissa. But she was already dead. What had seemed like a sitting position was merely a propped collapse against the undercarriage of the van.

He turned. The gun dragged heavily at his arm. Simpson was beside him. Only now did he realize how bright the lights were, painfully exploding in his head when he turned to them, making dim the shapes of people standing around with the dark behind them, and for a moment he had a wild hope that he might be in a dream or mad because, although they had arms and legs and the dimensions of human creatures, they were dressed in the hides and furs of animals — pigs with great bare, pink bellies and grinning snouts; a rooster with wattles that swung down close to the road; even a unicorn with a mild human face, its one horn flashing silver as the head turned. Then he saw Phoebe by the truck. She clutched her arms to herself, a bulky raccoon coat thrown over her shoulders, and her pale, round face stared and stared without blinking at the body of the horse between them.

"Take it." He almost threw the gun at Simpson. "Take it, take it."

He heard Simpson explaining — had panicked, no one able to get hold of them, actually ran out this way because some fool started chasing them, all that slush and ice and the rig full-weighted couldn't stop — but Lewis did not wait to hear him out. He looked hard for Howard, did not see him. The passenger door to the wrecker swung open and a short, very round-faced man with a cut on his forehead and a handkerchief he kept dabbing it with stepped down and came toward Lewis and even before he was there he was saying, "Mister, I'm sorry as hell, but honest to God, I didn't see them, they come up out of nowhere and I tried to miss them. Christ, you can see what it done to my rig."

"Howard," he yelled.

He was beside him.

"Come on."

He did not have to tell him where or how, but together they walked quickly to the car. A harlequin was standing there and when they started to get in, Lewis at the driver's side this time, he grabbed Lewis's arm and said, "Hey, wait a minute, not again, that's my car," but Lewis only had to give him one hard shove to be free, and he started the car, found reverse, swung in a slithering half circle, and drove away while Howard was still slamming his door. At the Bear, Howard started getting out, but Lewis said, "Don't. Take this back to the guy. Do what you want with it," and when Howard tried to say something, Lewis yelled, "Get the fuck out of here before I break your neck."

14

Lewis downed the first few shots quickly, then slowed the pace. He kept a rope stretched tight inside. He watched it very carefully. If too taut, one end might tear loose. But no sagging was permitted. Many hours could pass by quickly if he kept that image constantly in mind. A companion for one long week of drinking in Savannah after Annie's wedding had said he was going to invent an IV system for nights like this. Just the right amount per minute dripping in.

He was grateful to the people around him for not disturbing his concentration. Jake kept his shot glass full. Good old Jake. Knew when a man really needed top treatment. Trusted Lewis too, would soon simply put the bottle there but understood how, at first, carefully measuring by the shot was best. When the body dulled, not responding as quickly or finely to delicate tuning, a bottle was the thing. Much as you wanted at one time. Panic sometimes. Had to resort to the bottle itself, direct. Mouth to mouth. Jenny sat beside him for a while, did not speak loudly or say things he needed to answer. Kept it simple. *Too bad* was all she said about that. Then a full weather report. Big storm blowing down slowly from Canada. Feet and feet of snow. The road would be covered over. Would there always be a stain there?

The usual noise prevented silence. Singers, stabs of electric guitars. Clack-clack of pool balls like crows whetting their beaks. Buddy pulled up to the bar. No problems with Buddy. He floated along with Lewis for a while. They'd all done this for each other at some time. Lucille had almost died once. Some kind of food poisoning. Words were no help anyway. Lewis concentrated on the idea of words for a while. He was standing on the summit of Moonstone on a windy fall day. He had a bushel basket full of shredded paper, picked out fistfuls of it, and threw them up into the wind. They fluttered off in a ragged cloud, over the edge of the rock slides, into the valley. Words. They dropped randomly. Caught in the trees. Some in the brook. One or two by high soaring cleared the ridge to Judson. Coming down with the last leaves. Never mind. Buddy was all right, knew how to sit, his shoulder just touching. The sense of another body, making motions only when he lifted his glass, was a way to help keep the rope taut.

Bernie might have broken it, but he did not. Maybe because Lewis decided quickly, letting go of the old hesitations once and for all, that Bernie was as close to him as anyone in his life. Foolish to act otherwise. All their lives touching, even in the fights. The man's hand came down on his shoulder. Buddy and Jake went silent. They'd all seen what that could do to a man when he was tightened up. A trap going off. Don't jiggle it. Sometimes the person would start swinging for no reason at all, wildly.

But Lewis let the shock of that touch pass down and through and out. Bernie clearly was his brother. The man's voice was saying he was sorry. Saying if he were Lewis, he'd kill the sons of bitches. Saying he was going to help Lewis in any way he could and Lewis would please remember because Bernie Carbonneau stuck by his word. Lewis was pleased. This was a relief, deciding once and for all that Bernie was a good guy. So he also decided he could afford a word or two.

"Thanks, Bernie. Have a drink and I'm sorry I don't feel like talking."

To which Bernie replied that he understood perfectly, and

he moved away, taking his hand with him, but Lewis had to compensate quickly, no time even to pour from the bottle.

Hazy for a long time after that. They did not kick him out. When he went to the bathroom he tried not to think of Phoebe crouched there in the dark, her denims binding her skinny ankles. It wasn't quite dawn when he was on the street, a pint stashed in each pocket. He was imagining dogsleds by then and the possibility of stepping out of a bar like this, wrapping up tightly into one, commanding the dogs (did one yell or were there reins? He tried hard to see pictures, old movies — whips? — a long uncoiling over the heads of the huskies, a crack, sounds of barking). Instead the main street of Judson spread black in front of him. No storm yet. Cancel the dogsled. He stood under the rearing bear, put out his hand to touch the belly. Its dead fur was stiff and matted. Turning slightly, he saw Jenny standing in the doorway in her bathrobe, arms clutching herself against the cold.

"Lewis?" she said quietly.

He let that voice fall down in him slowly, all the way to the place where the rope was. He had not noticed before how remarkably gentle her voice was. What if one could learn to hear nothing but the tones, taking measurements of people by that, not the words. Deep voices, shallow voices, medium-range voices. He would have to try his own now, forcing his numb lips to move. "I love your voice."

Later, in the woods with the sun already fading into an opaque sky of gathering clouds, he could not remember if she really ran out onto the sidewalk in her slippers to hug him, or if she had done that many years ago, or if that sense of her body wrapped tightly to him, warm to his touch in spite of all the night air around them, was a wish made somewhere between dawn and whatever time this was — a time when he found himself walking under the lower cliffs of Moonstone's east ridge on Buddy Harlow's snowshoes. He and Jenny had been friends for years but she had never done that. The snowshoes needed some explaining, too.

He was nearly through the first pint by then. The image of concentration had changed. Not a rope after all. Now it was a small disk, not much larger then his two feet, that he had to stand on perfectly balanced because the small circle itself was balanced on a long, high pole. Of course, he could not really see the pole because it was directly under him, but he knew it was there anyway. Very dangerous. The underside of the disk was highly polished. One wobble and it would slip off the pole. Curious how the feet he walked on in the woods were not the same ones he used for keeping balance in his mind.

They were Buddy's snowshoes because he had walked up the street and known for certain that he could bear the sound of only one such voice as Jenny's over a considerable period of time. He would need Annie's later. Buddy was not asleep. He was sitting in his own living room watching the signal pattern on his new color TV. Lewis stood still in the woods. Some things should be carefully noted for future reference. Where was Lucille? Buddy did not look happy. Did he steal Buddy's snowshoes? That was precisely so. They were leaning against the porch railing. He had spied on his friend Buddy, and had stolen the man's snowshoes.

He jettisoned the empty bottle, floating it over the edge of a cliff. He closed his eyes, and considered joining the bottle. He would switch easily into orbit. His capsule wobbled dangerously off course for a while before the small rockets were fired automatically from Mission Control to put him back on course.

Manual pilot was obviously not working well. Weightlessness was affecting his mind. He had to report sadly to Earth that he had forgotten his mission. His destination surely was not another galaxy. Systems not devised for that. Time too immense. Light-years away. Black holes in between. Not enough light to see through the portholes anymore. He wrung the neck of the next bottle. Slowly now. This far out there were no more supplies. At that point all things must run out together. Oxygen, food, fuel, mental control, physical coordination, descent into cellular breakdown, whirling out beyond all.

Lewis looked hard at the sharp ascent. Had he ever been here before? There was a definite tactical confusion. Was he out of his space capsule, or was this it — trees, half-bare rocks and gray earth, gray sky? Could a man walk in snowshoes up the side of a capsule? He had seen Easter eggs once when he was a child constructed so that if he picked them up and looked inside through the frilled peephole at the end he could see a landscape so real his body entered in behind the eye and walked there among the rabbits and fields and gay fences. He began to climb the ridge. His eyes were pulling him along, up the steepening slope. He needed trees to hold on to. Saplings whipped at him. He beat them back. His snowshoes caught. Breath tugged out of him. The sky was cracking open beyond the pines. The tumble of his craft was inordinate. His hands could not reach the controls, but the emergency ax was floating free of its glass case and dizzily the handle swung away from his reach. He grabbed, raised it high. The trees fell back. The sun was a pale disk slipping off its pole. His own arms drove the blade down toward the rope with all his strength.

As the strands snapped and parted he saw two horses being dragged behind a wrecker, their legs bound by ropes, the ropes tied to the truck's chains, the bodies dragging along the harsh ruts, bone and flesh wearing down against the earth. His voice was torn from him.

The snow began falling densely, and the day descended with it. He could choose to stop somewhere, stretch out and sleep, or he could continue walking at any pace he wanted. For a while he limited himself to those two choices. The landscape began to change, reshaped by the snow. He would think himself lost and then some tree, some angle of rock and slope, would become familiar and he would know his way again. But he wanted to be lost. He let his feet step aimlessly. Sometimes he crouched over his snowshoes and shut his eyes for a few moments, and when he stood again, the snow would fall from his shoulders. He decided that getting lost was almost impossible if you had lived somewhere for too long. Wasn't there anyplace on the broad spread of Moonstone that he had never seen?

Finally he was certain he was lost. The light had almost faded. A stand of giant hemlocks was to his left and directly in front of him an old maple almost entirely dead and stripped of its bark was trying to keep a cleared space under its wide, rotted boughs. The snow was deep now. The hemlocks were somewhat familiar, but he had never seen a grove like this on Moonstone. He was tiring now. There was still a small amount of whiskey in the last bottle, but he did not want it. He had become sober some time ago, was now dazed and numb with fatigue. He had stooped once to drink from a cold stream, but did not feel hungry.

When something moved on the slope he held still. Although it, too, was covered with snow, its dark fur showed in patches and now Lewis could see the long nose and furtive eyes. The coydog was moving haltingly, pausing to sniff the air or the ground. But as he watched, the animal moved in a slow circle, and when he stared hard in the dim light, Lewis could see a mound in the center of its movements. Finally the coydog dug there with its paws, uncovering the dark fur of another animal. It sat back on its haunches, staring into the woods beyond, and slowly lifted its head as if sniffing some current just past its muzzle.

When Lewis moved forward, the animal growled and ran in quick bounds into the border of hemlocks. He could see the vague form waiting under the lowered boughs. He stooped to the carcass. It was another coydog, stiff, frozen with its legs tucked up as if in mid-leap, and Lewis could see the wound in its brindled fur where the bullet had entered.

He turned back at the far end of the clearing to see the animal circling in warily. It would do this for a few nights, howling over the body of its mate. That was one of the ways farmers knew their shots had been accurate enough. He walked on. In the dark he sensed the falling snow only by the cold flicking on his face. He had to move slowly not only because he could not see well, although the fresh snow almost glowed at times, but also because, in his weariness, his legs would buckle and he would find himself leaning against a tree trunk, having to use the lower branches to pull himself up. He was glad to be lost. If he chose to let himself sleep, which increasingly seemed a good thing to do, he might never be found. He began to look for a place. Ahead the sky opened away from the trees. Perhaps a clearing. When he thought of people he had known, he could see their faces, but often could not recall their names.

He stopped at the edge. Gradually the shapes became much too familiar. He took a few steps forward, looked hard at the dark square ahead of him, then saw the black rectangles of glass, the slope of a roof. It was his own cabin. He was not on Moonstone. Somehow in his wandering he had crossed over to the other side of the valley. In the drifting snow he must have missed the roads that would have cut his way. Or had his mind completely turned off at some time as he walked? He almost wept with anger.

He stumbled on, paused at the door. He heard nothing so he unstrapped his snowshoes, stepped in. He could tell she had been there recently. The room was still warm, coals glowing in the stove. The coydog gave two high yips and began to howl. He went to the bunk and dropped onto it and slept.

He woke like a startled animal, sat up in the dim light of day. It was still snowing. He had not dreamed or moved and his body ached. But he could hear the dim clicking, went quickly to the window. Miriam was coming slowly from the edge of the woods. He opened the door, grabbed his snowshoes, and plunged off through the deep snow, keeping the cabin between himself and her. From behind the spruce trees he watched her reach the cabin, look at the tracks, push open the door. He did not wait to see her come out again but slipped into the bindings and moved off quickly, pausing from time to time to listen.

He spent that day circling slowly down into the valley, skirting houses. Sometime toward evening he crossed the frozen river, kneeled at the field's edge, and watched the highway. There was almost no traffic, and the snow was drifting high everywhere in the wind that had started gusting from the north. He crossed the field and road, made for the dark shape of the barn. There was only one light on in the house.

He did not stay long in the barn. Somewhere in the dark interior a horse stamped, and the noise made him feel nauseated. He found the can of kerosene and rags and groped for a while until he had the box of matches on the shelf. A crate fell off the table as he passed, nails, some screws, small tools cascading out with bright metallic janglings. In the silence that followed he held still. Not even the horses moved.

As he walked carefully around the field to approach the house from the rear, he thought how pleasing it was to be in a state of mind where one both knew and did not know what one was going to do. The function of the items he was carrying was unmistakable. If applied to the house that was now close enough for him to touch, even to enter the small back stoop where the trash barrels were kept, the consequences would be certain. But between those objects, the rags he piled against the weathered wall of the house, the kerosene poured over them, its sweet odor reminding him of lamps and sheds and old stores, even the match he fumbled out of its box, there was a gap that prevented him from sensing any clear connection between them and someone choosing to do those things. Someone else controlled the hand that had the match turned correctly while the other hand felt for the striking surface. With a scratch the flame blazed.

But he did not lower it to the rags. He recognized his own hand and stared at it. The fingers were steady, although his wrist bent as if the match were a great weight he had been holding for a long time. The flame consumed the stick, burned into his fingers, and he turned quickly to drop it behind him. He leaned on the screen door matted with snow, then pushed it open and walked out, scooping his burned fingers into a drift.

But he could not walk away. What he heard was a voice, yet it had no words, only the tone of speaking like a wind rising and falling around fixed objects in a wide space. He closed his eyes and even at the same time that he allowed himself to think the house had found a voice to tell him to return, he assured himself that it could not be true — not because he did not believe at that moment that houses could speak, but because this house had never spoken to him before.

He walked slowly back through the screen door, pushing it with his numbed hand. The back door was not locked, gave to his touch as if someone inside were lifting the latch off the hook at the same time. He closed the door behind him and stood in the dark kitchen waiting for his eyes to adjust. The room was only a little warmer than the air outside. His ears hummed from the absence of wind or hissing snow.

Gradually he began to distinguish the lumped tables and stoves, and all surfaces were heaped with ragged shapes. Now he could smell the grease of food beginning to rot, the spilled beer, and the vinegar of empty wine bottles. He edged forward with one hand out toward the hanging light, touched its bell, and pulled the cord. As the glare burst on, a pile of dishes toppled in the sink and a rat scrabbled out of sight behind the cupboard door. He blinked against the pain of light, pulled the cord, and waited again for the dark to assume its shapes.

His footsteps were muffled in the corridor by the thick rug and he kept one hand out, but he knew the plan of the house almost as well as Annie's. In the living room, faint coals still glinted in the fireplace and a pale white shone in each window as if the snow were phosphorescent. He stood still at the bottom of the stairs. All he could hear was emptiness sifting down. The whole house had been detached from its foundations, was sinking slowly into an ocean of snow. They were sliding past the white that pressed against the windows. He breathed slowly. There was only as much air as the house contained.

He knew that could not be Coleman standing in the hallway by the door, but the hunched figure breathed in and out with him and whatever the voice was that he kept hearing lifted and fell also. *What?* he wanted to yell. *What do you want?* But he could not speak. He became very uncertain whether this was Coleman's house or the farmhouse of his childhood, whether it was winter or almost dawn on a chill spring day of heavy fog. He might be half-asleep, risen to do the early chores, standing alone to listen and discover whether Foster would rise too. Was his mother alive or dead? She was smothering in some room upstairs, her heart clenched into stone. Then he was sure he was in neither house, that this huge diving bell with stairs to farther and farther floors was the vacant shell slowly built around him year by year. He could walk up and up but never come to an end of stairways, snow-filled windows, empty rooms. He turned away from the figure in the hallway, put a hand on the banister. But it was wrapped in fur, and he lifted a pelt, distinguished the flattened face of some creature with holes where eyes should be, the long arms drooping toward the slowly swinging weight of paws. He dropped it, took one step up, and stood still again. The hollow hoofbeats of a horse stuttered above him. He could tell the horse was bunched tightly, on the verge of panic. Each echoing stamp pressed heavily on his chest and his own shoulders clenched as if someone he could not see were coiling a rope more and more tightly around him from the neck down and soon his arms would be pinned against him.

He took the stairs two at a time, did not see the turn, slammed into the wall, and scrambled up the last flight. The long hallway was a tunnel ending in the distant window and he groped along the wall for the first door, his hands flopping against its panels. It swung open and he lurched in, flicked on the lights. The disheveled bed was empty, the floor strewn with cartons and beer bottles. He left on the light, crossed the hall to the next room, and flung it open too. A broken window had been stuffed with its own curtain. There was no horse, but he whirled on down the hallway, the lights behind him spilling out in harsh rectangles. Then he stopped because the voice had words.

Muffled by the closed door on the other side of the corridor, Phoebe said, "Howard? Is that you? Did you come back?" and at the same time he heard the animal stamping now either in that same room or in the attic above it. He slammed the door back against the wall. In the silence that followed its report the broken plaster sifted down.

She was sitting up in the bed holding the covers to her naked body, her small, pale face clenched. When she spoke at first he could not hear her because of the clatter of hooves, exactly the sound the horse would make if being forced into a van, and he put his hands to his ears, yelled, "Stop it, stop," and when he took away his hands there was absolute silence.

Her clothes were strewn on a chair. In one corner a space heater's coils glared red, filling the air with a dry musk. When he looked at her again he could not take his eyes from her face and he moved forward slowly to the foot of the bed. Her wide eyes hardly blinked, her mouth moved, and fisted hands still held the covers at her chin like a small child hiding.

"I thought you were Howard. But I don't expect I'll see him again, do you?" Even though her eyes were on his she seemed to be looking past his face. She shivered. "Not talking tonight? You look worse than I must, Lewis. Wrecks. Two derelicts in a derelict house. I do wish you'd given me time to dress, though. Couldn't you step outside for a moment?"

"No." He had not spoken for so long that his own voice was unfamiliar, and it must have sounded strange to her, too, because her expression was puzzled.

"What in God's name have you been up to?" But now her eyes were shifting over his face nervously. "They're all gone, Lewis. Party's over. Went away. You were invited. Really should have come." Her hands held the covers so tightly that her knuckles had turned white. Her voice went very quiet. "I'm sorry, sorry about the horses."

His arm swung out involuntarily as if he were catching something thrown, and when his hand struck hard against the bedpost he held on to it. She flinched. He spat quickly onto her bed. She looked at the stain, then up to his face, and her eyes narrowed as if her hair were being drawn back tightly.

"You're going to hurt me, aren't you?"

The words cut him off from whatever the tensed muscles of his arms and shoulders wanted. Her voice was so unexpressive that she could have been commanding.

"I could kill you."

Her face was pale, but she had stopped shivering. She shook her head.

"You don't think so?"

"Really, Lewis Beede. Such melodrama at your age? Tawdry small-town murders? Man strangles heiress in lonely country manor. 'A whore for a horse,' he maintains to county prosecutor."

Her mouth became the focus of his attention, those tightly drawn lips, small delicate teeth showing as she bit out clear syllables.

"Shut up." He leaned over the bed rail at her.

She laughed quickly, but even with her head back, the eyes did not leave him. "My God. I haven't heard someone say that since I was in grade school."

What followed was a silence in which Lewis was uncertain whether either of them was breathing. A wind clattered the panes as if a hand had shaken the house. Her voice was quiet again.

"Look. I could goad you to all sorts of violence and still have the last say. Don't be a fool, Lewis. Get out of here. We've hurt each other enough. You won't see me again. I sold the place. That's partly what the bash was for, anyway. Prospective buyers. Poor drunks, they outbid each other. Clever Phoebe? Got her money's worth."

He reached out, her hands jerked back, but he was stronger and pulled the covers to him, tumbling them on the floor by his feet. She kept her hands where they had been. Her long, bare legs pointed at him like two stiff bones and shivered. Her pale belly, scarred above the dark mound of hair, moved in jerks as she breathed.

"Give them back to me."

He stared at her, letting his eyes move slowly over her body.

"Stop it. Stop staring at me."

He walked to the side of the bed, gripped her hair, and bent back her face. Her bare flesh was cold white, and her voice was so muted that he could not make out the words. He put his face close to hers; she went silent, her mouth open. He could see the skin stretched over the blue veins of her temple.

"Fuck you, fuck you," he said slowly, and he kept saying the words monotonously as she stared at him, his face coming so close now that all he saw were her own eyes wide, unblinking, the greenish irises flecked with pale gray, the dark pinpoint of the center that seemed to pull at him, in and in. He jerked away, flinging the head by its rope of hair. She twisted onto the floor, her arms and legs flailing for holds.

As he backed away he bumped into the corner of a bureau, turned over a chair that held a tray, and the glasses shattered against each other on the floor. She was crouched on the rug, a small, cold animal trying to cover its nakedness.

"Get out, get out," she was shrieking, then she began crawling toward the heap of bedclothes.

He covered his ears and backed into the bright hall, then he was running past the strewn and quiet rooms. He stumbled on the landing but whirled on to get away from that voice, out through the kitchen again. The screen door smashed against the porch wall and did not spring back. He clutched the snowshoes, plunging through the front yard and down the half-filled ruts of the driveway. He did not look back.

Nearing town, he stopped by the side of the road, knelt to push cold handfuls of snow against his face. His body was suddenly so exhausted that he could barely stand. He would go to Annie's. He only wanted to sleep now.

Annie and Miriam were sitting in the living room when he walked into the house. "Do I really look that bad?" he said to their startled faces, and began to laugh, but his lips cracked painfully when he spread them, so he walked up the stairs and stretched out on the bed and did not object when Annie pulled off his boots and put a hand on his wrist to test his pulse before she spread the blankets over him. In the middle of the night he half waked, or maybe only dreamed he was waking. He had been sitting up in the room, dark except for the bright slant of light from a streetlamp.

No one was beside him on the bed. But a figure was crouched in the far corner of the room, naked, clutching its knees as if very cold, a face staring forward unblinking. From the open mouth came a moan but as if the body were only an opening the sound used to express itself, rising and falling like a distant wind.

When he woke he was tired and so hungry that sitting up in bed, affronted by the stench of his own neglected body, he breathed in gasps and the room dimmed and narrowed to a single point of light. He made himself breathe deeply, went to the bathroom, where he stood for a long time in a hot shower and then borrowed Annie's razor to shave off the grizzle of days. Only the sound of the heat going off and on came up from below. Although he recalled no dreams or thoughts, he sensed that his mind had not been still. As if they were a shucked skin, he could not bear to touch his soiled clothes, and he put on some old pants and a shirt he kept in her closet. Halfway downstairs he paused with his hand on the banister to steady his wobbly legs. He looked out the window on the landing at the snow piled high against the houses, obliterating path and street, still descending and again undriven by wind. He pressed the blistered tips of his fingers.

He was glad no one was there. Once he had started cooking, he became unbearably hungry, could not wait until the eggs were hard but took them out of the boiling water and broke them into a bowl and began eating so fast that he could barely swallow between mouthfuls, and then he slabbed two thick pieces of bread with butter and ate them, choking down hot mouthfuls of coffee, not caring how his throat was scorched. He was ashamed of his trembling haste, but he tasted it all as if he had been numbed for years, and even the smell of the coffee rising in its steam made him fill the cup again and burn his lips in haste to drink it.

When he was through he sat at the table and leaned his face in his hands. His body tensed against the food, held it like a single large stone. Then he relaxed, breathing deeply. It would be all right, all right. When he looked up, Annie was standing in the doorway in her hat and coat, snow melting off onto the floor. She did not say anything but walked over and her hand was cold on his face, the water dripped on him as she stooped and kissed him, and he leaned his head against her while she held him for a moment.

"Where's Miriam?"

"She's up at the cabin, getting some things."

"What day is it?"

She told him and took off her hat and coat and sat at the table. She described the storm, and how they had worried about him, how Howard and Buddy and some others had tried to find him, had come across tracks, but had given up because the snow came down too fast. When Miriam discovered he had slept at the cabin, they had begun to worry less, but quietly she admitted what was in the back of their minds, what Elmore had finally said for them — that the storm and the woods would not get Lewis unless he wanted them to. He listened, but still she was not telling him what he wanted to know, even when she quickly, as factually as possible, told him that the police had issued citations to some of the partygoers for destruction of property, that the driver of the truck had been absolved.

"Miriam's going, isn't she?"

"Yes."

He did not want to talk anymore. "I'm falling asleep again."

He stood and limped up the stairs, stretched out on the bed. He slept in broken waves. Whenever he woke he would listen to hear whether they were talking downstairs, and once he dreamed that he had overslept and Miriam had left without him. After that, he did not sleep again and tried to lie quietly on his back telling himself that he would be foolish to join her. There was nothing he could do by being there, and why should he help anyway? Later he heard someone moving in the kitchen again and went downstairs, but it was only Annie.

Lewis sat at the table and she poured him some coffee. The snowplow ground and scraped up to the end of the street, probably Buddy. When he was on duty he made certain his own street was as clear as the highway.

"Are you going with her?" She sat opposite him. Her hair straggled loosely around her face and she looked very tired.

"I'm inclined to."

"Want to tell me why?"

"I have to go somewhere. For a while."

She shook her head. "You already did. What happened is awful, but not a good enough reason."

He tried to keep his voice steady, telling her about the rags, the kerosene. But he did not tell her the rest, partly because he was uncertain himself what had been real. His burned fingers were real enough, but what of the voices, the horse, the naked body of Phoebe? He could not bear the thought of seeing her, of having to know by her expression that it had happened.

Annie thought for a moment, then said, "I'm not surprised. But you didn't do it. That's over."

"She wants me to go. She's my daughter."

"Oh, Lewis. Everything you're saying is like an excuse to do what you really have wanted to do all along, but might not have let yourself."

"You can't stop me if I want to."

"Have I ever?"

He thought he was going to be angry at her, but instead his voice started, broke, began again. "Damn it, Annie. I just want to know. Know something sure, for once. Maybe if Monica and I could talk things over a little, with Miriam there, it wouldn't all be so muddled. I want to get out of all this, get things straightened out again."

She stood abruptly, and he thought she would leave the room. She had never walked out on him before. Instead she leaned on the sink, her back to him.

"Listen to me, Lewis. Please. I think you've made up your mind, even if you don't know it. But what if I were saying you have a choice, that if you go, I might not be here when you got back?"

"Where would you go? There's no point in that."

"Maybe I'm tired of sitting and waiting."

"What for?"

"God knows."

"I could come looking for you."

"I might be hard to find."

Again his voice rose. "Why are you doing this? It only makes things more complicated. Don't you understand? There just isn't anything left for me here right now. I have to get away for a while. And she is my daughter. She needs me."

"She's an adult. Not your child anymore. We have our lives, she has hers."

"So you think she's being selfish?"

She turned, arms folded. "Not entirely. She's just very intent

232

on getting the truth, no matter what. That's why she asks us so many questions."

"So what's the harm if I go? I'll be back."

She shook her head. "Haven't we been here again and again? It isn't choosing her or me I'm worried about. Or even Monica. But who are you going to live with for the rest of your life, Lewis?"

He heard those questions dimly and her voice, quiet now, going on. But he was trying hard to find the words that could express the blank space he had entered. Was it simply that he was never able to think things through clearly when they were happening? How often he would know that he was saying the wrong words, that what he really wanted to know would come to him only later, too late for him to do anything about it. Even Monica had always seen things so clearly, but he could never respond as he wanted, driving her to silence. The present was always slipping by and he could not get a hold on it.

Her voice had stopped.

"I'm sorry. What were you saying?"

The bus pulled into the driveway, and then Miriam was coming across the porch, kicking her boots as she cleaned them on the mat.

"Good-bye, Lewis."

"I'll be back."

Miriam's voice from the hallway closed over his. "Annie, are you there?"

15

Miriam was wearing curved dark glasses against the glare of bright snow. She drove faster than he had expected, but smoothly and as if she had often traveled for long distances. They were silent as a truck rushed past, the huge wheels churning a cloud of loose snow at them.

She had been very subdued since they climbed into the car together, almost shy. He wondered if she was as puzzled as he. Now that they had begun the journey, he did not want to be in Oklahoma yet, but certainly did not want to go back. Even more than when they were in the cabin, Lewis felt intimately alone with someone he hardly knew but should know as well as himself. Sometimes as he lay back, eyes half-closed, he would see her turn her face to him quickly again and again, as if she, too, were confused.

"I wish we had time to go to my old home. I'd like to show it to you. All the time I was a child I thought of having you or my mother appear. I would take you by the hand and lead you around to all the people I knew. 'This is my father,' I'd say, and you would shake hands and they would tell nice things about me and you would say how proud you were." She laughed. "Of course I knew perfectly well even then that they would be different. They'd probably shake their heads and say, 'You really must do something about the way she does her homework' or 'Can't you suggest she play with the girls for a change?' "

He nodded and closed his eyes. Why did those descriptions always pain him? He saw her alone, too young to understand what was hurting her, and he experienced those moments as if they came up out of his own childhood.

"I used to watch at the front window of our house. There was a couch beneath it. When I was a child I'd get up into it and kneel with my elbows on the back and stare out over the tops of the bushes. The glass made everything wavery, so I could see the path and the street, but so unclearly that I could imagine whatever I wanted. I'd make a man walk down the street and pause like he'd forgotten something, and then he'd look at the window, I'd wave, and he would walk up the path. I wouldn't be able to see his face clearly but he would be smiling and he'd wave too. He was you. Except he was always the mailman, or Arnie coming home, or shadows from a cloud."

One of their suitcases was rattling against the side of the bus. They had sleeping bags back there and air mattresses. Cheaper, they both had agreed. That was why she had bought the bus in the first place, she and Dan. Who was he? She had waved loosely. A friend.

With his eyes still closed he said, "Let me know when I can spell you." She did not answer.

When he woke there were no more mountains, only hills or long flat escarpments in the distance. The storm had not come this far south and the ground was bare again, a patchwork of grays and browns. He sat up, watched as the road crested a long, gentle lift and then he could see far across the fields and small roads. He had driven this highway often when he was younger, and much of what he saw now was still vaguely familiar, even that collapsed inn to his right, half its name fallen off, the word *Manor* still hanging askew. The late-afternoon sun was broken into wide shafts of light by the slow, high clouds splotching the broad landscape. For a moment he was elated as if he were much younger, and everything were new and waiting to be discovered.

Her hand was on his arm, the car slowing as they angled off into a rest stop.

"I'm getting drowsy."

He walked around to her side and she slid over. At first, sitting there with his hands on the wheel, then pressing the clutch in and testing all the positions of the gearshift, he wondered if he would be able to do it. She had curled her legs up on the seat, her body turned toward him. The first motions he made to engage the gears stalled the engine. The clutch seemed to catch too quickly at the last moment. He tried again, jerked a little, but kept going, the passage into second was easy, and, moving the wheel tentatively to see how much play it had, he slanted them out onto the road.

He drove with one hand, folding the other over hers where it lay on the seat until her fingers relaxed and she was asleep. He glanced at her. His eyes blurred, hand shook, and struggling to get a hold on himself, he concentrated on the road. There were moments he could not fight back when he was certain that he had nothing left but their fragile lives in an old car barreling down a highway. His horses were dead, and his plans seemed faded — in spite of what he might hope at times. He did not know what to think about Annie, who had grown quiet and watchful in those hours when he prepared to leave, or even of Judson, of his cabin and woods, of the landscape and people he had known since childhood. There were no clear and simple connections anymore. Somewhere dimly situated at the end of all this was a woman named Monica whom he did not know anymore. What if her life were as broken as his? Like some piece of junk in space, he might simply pass through another field of fragments, keep falling, burn out. What if these moments were the ones he recalled years afterward as he wandered on? This would be nothing like the dream of wandering he had chased after so often when he was younger. This would be the real thing, tumbling and detached. He had seen old bums when he was younger and traveling. They had made him so uneasy that he often chose not to believe in them, although he was forced to look hard at their faces, still hoping that someday he would recognize his father. It was a fine thing to be twenty-five or even thirty with a wide and unknown land in front of you, the secret knowledge that it was really never too late either to turn back or to stop and make something new and whole. But this was different.

Later she stretched and yawned. "Hello, New Jersey."

Because he could not bear any more silence he said, "I wonder if Elmore will ever forgive me."

He thought she had not heard, when she said, "I'm not sure he should be forgiving anything."

"I feel like I'm traveling with my brother's curse laid on me."

"You're convenient to curse. Elaine says her father is the kind of person who always has to have a reason for everything. He'll get over it. He has to. Maybe he and Eleanor will never find a way back together. But parents and children are different."

"How?"

She paused. "More tenacious."

The sun was bright scarlet and struck at them from under a dark lid of sky, sinking so fast that he could see it move. He always had to remind himself that it was not moving, he was, the speed of earth visible for that last moment of day.

"But it's my cabin. I think Elmore associates me with almost every unhappy fact in the last year."

The sky still glinted with pale reds and now the towns were beginning to crowd in toward the road: houses, gas stations, towers pushing back against the darkening air with bright lights.

"Nobody should be surprised at what happened," she continued. "Elaine and Howard were close for some time before he had his little adventure."

"But poor Jonathan, ditched so quickly."

"Not as quickly as you think. She talked with me about him often. Oh, it was partly her parents. After they broke up she liked to say she believed marriage stinks. But before that she was worried, telling me she didn't think she really loved Jonathan, was not excited about the wedding."

"What did you tell her?"

"Nothing she didn't want to hear."

"We're both in it, aren't we? There are Elaine and Howard living in my cabin together, Jonathan out in the cold, Elmore and Elaine not talking to each other, and Elmore certain we led her into it all. No wonder he told me he was glad to see us leave town."

She leaned her head back again. "He'll come around. And after a month or two of consoling each other and enjoying their desert island, don't be surprised if Howard and Elaine get married."

"I wish something *could* surprise me anymore."

Her sleepy voice said, "We'll see," and they laughed.

When they stopped and ate, the sound of the tires still hummed in his ears and he was not hungry. Back in the dark bus, taking his seat on the passenger side, he watched her fumble the key into the ignition, the engine coughed and started, her hunched figure appeared in the dashboard lights, and for a moment he saw her again as he had in those first glimpses in Judson, a young woman with sharp features, plain but beautiful, especially in her eyes.

Streets passed over them, the lights of intersections blinked red and green and the windows of high buildings blazed. When he woke again they were on a larger highway and he could see the flames of refineries thrust into the dark air that smelled of oil burning into the night. Diesel fumes blurring the lights like a fog made him feel he was in a different land. He had forgotten how years ago he had decided to avoid all this for the rest of his life. One hot summer day on this road, traveling from New York to Philadelphia to try out for a part in a play, his borrowed car had broken down. It was Paul's car, and even though he could not remember Paul's last name, he saw that beaten old Pontiac with clarity. He had sat beside it in the muggy afternoon, waiting to be rescued. The temperature was almost one hundred degrees, the humidity so thick that he felt he was breathing and moving in warm, sticky beer. All the fumes of refineries, car exhaust, baked tar, and the mud flats that had been spread with layers of wastes made him slump on the running board of the dead car, holding his head, certain he would be sick. The hood was up, the engine hulked there, hissing and ticking, absolutely unresponsive to the twist of the key. He had stood finally and walked away to the side of the road to stare out over the flats. His clothes clung to his skin. He stood on the bank, looking out toward the gray-green plain or back up the long, shimmering road littered with all the fallen lumps and fragments of vehicles. He could not deal with what he saw. He had turned, taken his chance with the hurtling cars, and crossed to the other side, where he hitched a ride back to New York. No wonder he could not recall Paul's last name. He had refused to go back and the man had never spoken to him again. Monica had been angry, too. *You can't just walk away like that.* But he had said, *I damn well can when it's someone else's mess.*

When he woke again his neck was stiff from the awkward position of his head, and for a moment his arm was completely numb. The bus was slowing, she was slanting them off onto an exit ramp.

"Where are we?"

"I don't know. But we'd better find a place to stop."

The road was narrow, winding by bare trees and scraggly humps of vines. They drove through an area of motels and large buildings with lit-up fronts, and then they were in the country again. He opened the window, and although the air was still sharp, it was much less cold. She slowed, turned onto a rutted dirt track. The bus hunched and tilted and then they were on a small plateau of browned grass, a clump of trees within the rim of their lights. She turned them off, then the engine. Silence flooded around them for the first time since they had left Judson. He opened the door and stepped out. The air was still, cold, and tinged with woodsmoke from distant fires. He breathed deeply, stretched, walked out over the knobbly, half-frozen ground toward the woods. Overhead the stars were so clearly bright that they seemed within reach, and far off on one horizon a reddish, constant glow showed where some city was. Near the trees he watched the interrupted twistings of headlights on the distant road.

She was not there when he returned, but the sleeping bags were neatly spread side by side in the back, and taking off most of his clothes, he slipped down into one of them and lay there, his body already relaxing. She returned, flipped off the dim light, and in the dark interior she moved in silhouette against the star-pocked windows, slid down also, and lay still.

"I always liked camping out," she said drowsily. "I used to be sent to Girl Scout camp. I liked the nights best. I wasn't much of a Girl Scout, didn't care for most of the girls. They were public school kids and knew each other, and I went to a private school near home. Girl Scouts was Myra's idea of educating me, helping me know how to get along with all sorts of people."

"That sounds more like something Monica would have done. Did it work?"

"I got along all right. They weren't mean."

The lights of a car swept over them, but when Lewis sat up he could see they had merely flashed from the curve in the road some distance below.

"I loved to lie like this at night, keeping myself awake, glad to be alone and listening to the crickets, looking at the sky, and you could always smell hay, wet grass. I would stay up almost all night to be awake enough to feel that way — cozy, I guess."

When her hand grasped his, he was startled.

"Thank you for coming."

He could think of nothing to say, so he closed his fingers tightly over hers.

It was late into the night before he realized he must not be sleeping very well. His limbs had stiffened, unused to the constrained position of the tight cocoon of his sleeping bag, not adjusting easily to the odd shapes and ridges of the bus floor that humped up through the thin mattresses under them. He sat up, thought the sky had clouded since all the windows were totally black, but when he rubbed the moisture away, the stars reappeared. He heard Miriam's steady, high wisp of breathing.

He sat waiting to become sleepy again. When he was younger, he would have been alone and probably sleeping even more uncomfortably in the backseat of some car. But that was long ago. How fixed his habits had become. That seemed very odd because he had thought for all these years he had been living randomly, sleeping in a cabin that was certainly no weighty structure of stone or brick, staying now one night with Annie, another alone, maybe sometimes on Buddy's couch if he was too drunk, or even Coleman's chaise lounge on the porch.

He lay back again. In fact, his movements in the last years had become fixed and patterned, and he imagined a little crisscross of paths like the kind a deer herd makes, worn by his motions in the valley and along the slopes of Judson. Miriam stirred. If she woke, he would tell her what he was thinking. She lay still and he could not help realizing it was not Miriam he wanted to turn to in the dark and talk with sleepily but Annie.

When he woke at dawn, the moisture on the windows had frosted and all that came through was the rosy tint of the first sunlight where it splashed here and there on the landscape. He dressed quietly, wriggled his stiff body into the front seat, and eased open the door. He did not bother to shut it tightly for fear the noise would wake her.

The air he breathed was sharp and clean. He would not have been able to guess the topography of the land from last night's view. There was the road they had moved along in reaching the turnoff, but the view itself of the fields fanning toward the broken horizon, interrupted by sworls of wooded hillocks, occasional roads and houses, was more sweeping than he had expected. Fog filled the deeper hollows, the bare trees were finely etched in gray and black against a ground with every shade of brown and russet and in patches a green so dark that it was almost black. The sunlight at its sharp angle lit each layer of receding countryside as if from beneath, and he was sure he was looking at a structure the land held beyond all change.

He buttoned his jacket tightly and began walking. The ground was hardened by frost, but not into that compact and granitic depth that he would sense if he was walking on bare ground at home. The top surface was only a brittle crust, and even the air he buttoned himself against was more gentle. He breathed deeply, began to stride along the ridge with the crest above him. Why had he let himself become so dulled in these last years? There were so many places to go, to see, to swing through like this with every sense alive. He stood on the top of the low ridge, turning again to look out directly into the sun. His eyes strained to be wide enough in focus to take in everything at once. But they could not.

She was awake when he returned, and she started the engine as he climbed in.

"Look." Her hand was pointing down over the field toward four horses being ridden slowly into a gully with a wooden bridge, a pack of hounds loosely surrounding them.

"Picturesque," he said. "Where to now?"

"Breakfast?" She backed out with a thump onto the road.

The bus was warm and, like some animal lair, still smelled slightly of their bodies sleeping through the long night. They passed close by the horses and he could not help thinking of Joker stretching high to bite down an apple from the old tree in the corner of the paddock.

As always, the spread of the country to the west was much larger than he remembered. On the map of his mind the known geography of his immediate landscape in Judson had swollen out, compressing the rest of the country between the fixed boundaries of ocean. But Pennsylvania extended forever through hills, mountains, quickly viewed streams, and then the states they slanted through insisted on a breadth of their own between borders as arbitrary as the wandering banks of a river or the faults of a sharp valley. They drove purposefully now, taking turns at the wheel or at dozing in the back, and Lewis tried to accustom himself to sleeping independent of the rise or fall of the sun. The quirks of surface under his bag were made even more evident by the jolt and sway of their speed. If they were both awake they might try to talk, exchanging the constant hum in their ears for the sound of voices, but mostly they were silent, until when he did speak, Lewis heard his own voice as an explosion in a pressure chamber. When they stopped to eat, the floor of the diner or restaurant vibrated under him, and in the washrooms he would douse his face with cold water, letting it drip down his neck and under his shirt, trying to break out of the numbness. She was relentless in her ability to stretch with a yawn when he pulled off the road and without complaint clamber over the back of the seat. The engine would still be running, she would check the gauges, slip the bus into gear, and he would try to sit there awake and talking before giving up and easing himself into the back.

At no other time since he had known Miriam was he so aware of the difference in their ages. Her body could go on like this, but his would balk soon in an agony of stiffness and overloaded nerves. By the time they crossed into Arkansas, the map of the United States had become a blueprint for torture, and he marked their slow progress past cities with a fierce check of his pencil. By the middle of Arkansas he was beginning to be leery of talking because he was not always certain when he was dreaming, when awake. He found Miriam shaking his shoulder once, sat up quickly, hearing his own voice break off in mid-sentence. He had fallen asleep without making it into the back of the bus. It was dawn of a rainy morning, the wipers slapping snakes of water.

"Where were we?" he muttered.

She laughed. "I don't know. I felt left out when you asked me if my feet were cold, and when I was trying to answer, you told me to kick the snow off the bottom of the bed."

Lewis rubbed his eyes. "My turn to drive?"

"Not for a while."

"Then I'll see if I can settle the problem of the cold feet." He wriggled into the back. The ends of every bone in his body had been beaten by small hammers.

He dreamed he was dreaming, he dreamed he was awake and afraid of dreaming, he sat up in the back awake but certain he was dreaming he was awake. He began to find it perfectly logical that Annie was beside him from time to time or even that Doris passed them in her pickup, hunched forward over the wheel, her mouth rounded in a song. A woman named Monica was driving sometimes, but she never turned to him when she was talking, so he only saw the back of her head and her words made no sense.

They were close to the Oklahoma border when he made her pull over at a truck stop and park by the telephone booth. He had been dreaming so insistently of Annie that he knew he had to talk to her and hear her real voice. Miriam looked at him curiously as he groped in his pocket before getting out.

"I think I'll call Annie, see how she's doing."

The weather had cleared again. It was evening, and as he breathed deeply before stepping into the booth, he was certain that they were about to be surrounded by an outburst of spring.

Everything was swelling into buds, and fine tongues of grass bristled the red earth. In the booth he slipped his coins in, dialed, the number coming up clearly out of the rubble of his mind. The line crackled, whooshed, settled into a steady flush of air, and then began to ring. After four rings he realized he was holding the receiver too hard, as if it were a handle on a heavy object he was trying to lift. He let the focus of his gaze wander, past the silver and black box of the phone, past the snub nose of the bus to the high fence on the other side of the road. When he climbed back into the passenger seat stiffly, she said, "You walk like a zombie. Everything all right?"

"I'm glad we're almost there."

"How was Annie?"

"Not there." He looked at his watch. She was almost always home at this time.

She started to say something but stopped, for which he was grateful. Possibly Annie was refusing to answer the phone, trying to prove something to him even over all this distance, and that annoyed him. Or she might have gone away for a while. But the house was there, and she would never leave it for long.

As they crossed into Oklahoma the landscape changed, flattening out, trees disappearing, the soil turning darker red and covered only by a scruffy layer of brown grass. There was a hint of green in some of the bushes and the stunted oaks, and a wide patch of white flowers was so low to the ground that at first Lewis thought it was a gully of old snow. The sky began to extend itself, and slowly he became aware of a steady, low whistling at the cracks and openings in the side of the bus, and the trees and bushes were all slightly bent and stretched in the same direction by wind. The towers of Tulsa began to rise ahead, quickly forming, but never, even when they were very close, tall or impressive under such a wide expanse of sky. They stayed on the bypass, were soon past, and the landscape flattened even more. The rivers were shallow ribbons twisting over red sheets of silt. By noon her touch on the accelerator was so light that they were only going thirty-five.

"What will we do when we get there?"

She looked guiltily at him. "I'm thinking."

"What if she's not here?"

She shook her head. "She's teaching this semester."

He had cracked open his window as they went through Tulsa and now the wind was warm and scented almost like sandalwood.

"Must be those little flowers." But she did not answer. "I guess neither of us have planned what we'll do."

"Not planned, but imagined. In too many ways. That's the trouble."

"Will you do what you did with me?"

She shook her head again. "That took too long. And I've

244

made up my mind this time. I hadn't when I came to Judson. But do I call, or write a note, or just drop by her office or home?"

"Want a suggestion?"

"Try me."

"Do it quickly. Don't give her too much time to think. But do it privately. She was a very private person."

"You'll come with me?"

"I'd rather you told her I'm here."

"But I want you to be there. I want to see you both together, if only for a moment."

He turned to look at her. She was staring straight ahead, and the sun, low now and shining directly at them, exaggerated the stubborn set of her mouth and jaw. She shivered and he shut the window, but suspected she was more nervous than cold, and he understood that for her the end of a long process was about to take place and that she had made it reach this point by sheer will and persistence. He had said he would never come with her, and when he said so, this same dogged look would extinguish all other expression on her face as her mind focused on her own resolve. What he felt now was a kind of awe. If it was almost over, what would it have accomplished? He suspected her imagination had run through a thousand scenes of himself, Monica, and herself in the same room, or on the same lawn, or standing on the same porch, but had never gone beyond that once seemingly impossible moment. He had his reasons now for wanting to see Monica, but some of Miriam's still remained vague to him.

"Maybe," he said slowly, swinging the shade down over the window, "we'd better stop somewhere for the night, a motel — get cleaned up, think things over. We're sort of seedy-looking now."

They passed some small wells, the clumsy arms of the pumps rising and falling bluntly, shapes standing so unattended in the landscape that they seemed doomed to their endless and obsessive motions. When the houses began to be more frequent and as they passed a sign reading *Stillwater*, she touched his wrist and he turned his hand over to take her fingers, squeezing them tightly.

At the motel he asked the woman behind the desk why they had built the place so low to the ground, and she said, "Because this is tornado alley, mister, and I've seen some lower places than

245

this get spread out over a few fields. This time of year, don't go trusting any clouds."

Their room was in the back, and beyond the parking lot was a barbed wire fence, a brown field with a gully where a battered truck reared its front end, hood open in outrage, the back end half-buried as if it were a beast sinking slowly into mire. Nearby some steers were going through the motions of grazing, although Lewis could not imagine that they were finding anything on the scoured earth. The sun hung on the endless horizon, a flat, burnished pan, and then it dropped, leaving a blue-black sky and the first stars as bright as the scattered lights of a disheveled marquee. He turned to see Miriam moving in the yellow glow of their room. For that brief moment of sunset, there had been no wind, but now it began again as steady as if someone had flicked on a fan.

They ate nearby, bought a bottle of Scotch, tried to watch some television on a set that had lapsed into unadjustable orange. Stretched out on his bed, Lewis could not keep the muscles in his legs from jerking, and the room was humming down an endless road. He closed his eyes, hoping the Scotch would begin to numb him, but then he heard the ceaseless wind under the clamor of the TV. So he went and stood in the shower for twenty minutes, adjusting the head so that the water pummeled him. She had turned off the TV when he returned, had left only the one light by his bed, and was lying under the covers, hands behind her head. He did not interrupt her almost unblinking gaze at the ceiling, but carefully put his glass and the bottle on the table between them, turned out the light, dropped his towel, and climbed into bed, leaning against the headboard as he groped to find his glass.

He sat there, sipping, listening to her breathing become so regular that he thought she must be asleep. The hot water, the Scotch, the luxury of clean sheets even though the carpets smelled of stale cigarette smoke and years of ground-in dust, began to relax him. The sense of motion was dying away.

"It never stops, does it," her voice said quietly.

The wind did not gust but raised or lowered slightly in intensity like a flow of water, and the moan of air around the leaky window frames would vary slightly in sustained pitches.

"I suppose you could get used to it."

He was trying to imagine living with such a wind forever when she said, "I won't call. I'll get up early and go to her house, and when I see someone is up, I'll try."

"I'll wait here." He put his glass on the table and slipped down into the covers, bunching the pillow under his head.

She spoke drowsily. "Did you ever think how odd this is, to be lying here about to do something to someone's life, and only a short distance away she has no idea at all, not even a vague premonition that her life might be completely changed."

He thought of his life after Miriam had arrived. It was true. Nothing had been the same since then.

"It's dangerous," she continued. "A lot of power. I guess I can see how you could get hooked on that. Politicians must be. Or assassins. Or God."

"Luckily you are none of the above."

"Or a little of them all."

Before he drifted to sleep, floating on the sound of the currents streaming over their room, he could not help imagining again the moment when Miriam would announce herself to Monica. He wished he could be there, invisibly hovering nearby. Strangely elated, he saw Monica draw back as if struck, her mouth open. But through the door behind them the air rushed from the flatland, and they all tumbled naked in a vast wind, their slowly moving limbs shifting them here and there as they called out in broken voices. *I'll call Annie in the morning,* he was saying to himself over and over as if that were something to grapple onto in a landscape without holds.

She was gone when he woke, her disheveled bed the only sign she had been there. He pulled back the curtain. The sun was fully up and the wind was still flagging the stiff weeds and bushes. He ate across the street, hunched at the counter with truckers and men on their way to work, then tried the pay phone in the parking lot. Again her phone rang and rang, but no one answered, and as it buzzed on, he tried to calculate her time, realized it was later there. He could call Buddy. Something might be wrong. But if Lucille answered, what would he say? As he opened the phone booth doors, that question extended itself. What would he say if Annie answered? And what would he say to Monica? He stood on the sidewalk looking up the street as if he were waiting for a bus. There were questions he had to ask, things he wanted her to tell him, but when he imagined them, they did not seem to be what he really wanted to know.

Instead of going back to the room he turned to walk down the dirt road that went away from the outskirts of town and into the open country. He began to see that the landscape was not quite as flat as he had thought. From time to time there were long, gradual rises, and from the plateaus he could see for miles. But the sky was so large that no house or tower or windmill was capable of breaking into it. The crossroads came regularly at precise right angles.

Gradually he began to see the details of the fields around him, as if his eyes had to seek refuge from the monotony of the sky by holding on to small variations. Birds tossed themselves into the wind and fluttered like chaff from bush to bush. Small flowers nestled into the stalks under the bristling bushes. Some of the trees, scarcely larger than himself, had tough, twisted trunks that showed they were very old. On the last height before he turned to go back, he noticed he was learning to walk with the constant pressure of air against one side, leaning slightly into it, sheering like a kite. He looked back to the crossroads and small scurry of a distant car. Everything he saw between the fixed sky and earth that was part of the human life around him was subject to that wind. What struck him was a fierce loneliness, and all he wanted was to be in Judson again.

She was sitting on the edge of her bed when he returned, the door open and sun warming the threshold. Her hands were clasped between her knees and she shook her head when she looked up.

"She says I have the wrong person. She says she is Monica Weaver and she never had a child. I told her I knew she married Bill Weaver and was divorced and all the other things I know and she was very polite and patient and took the piece of paper I gave her with our number here and said I was wrong."

He leaned in the doorway, his shadow cutting sharply on the carpet. "Maybe she's right."

She shook her head wildly. "No, no, no. I know it's her. She's tough, but I could see something in her eyes at first. I'm sure of it. And I saw her watching at the window when I looked back."

"Maybe it's her choice."

"I can't walk off now."

"What next?"

She looked at him, frowning against the light to see his face clearly. "You go. Please."

16

"It's the fourth house on the left. She was alone, but she lives with a man, someone in the English Department." Miriam looked a little guilty when she said, "I didn't get a chance to tell her you were here."

"Surprise, surprise."

The motor sputtered as it always did while idling now. He held onto the door handle, very reluctant to step out. He could never have imagined it like this — a catalpa tree leaning at them on a quiet street in Stillwater where everything around them seemed to be holding its breath.

"Please. Do it or don't, but, God, don't keep me sitting here like this."

He stepped onto the curb, leaned in. "Where are you going?"

"I'll be at the motel."

"There's Scotch left."

She shook her head. "That's your dodge, not mine."

Her face was so young in its clarity of yearning that he knew he must be seeing her as she looked when she was a child, or as close to that as he would ever know. He slammed the door, it rebounded, and she drove off quickly as if afraid the car coming down her mother's street contained someone who could cancel everything she had won so far. But the driver did not even glance at him. Lewis turned in the path. The concrete ended in the inevitable three steps up, the dark green door with brass knob and knocker, and only then did he allow himself a deep breath, a swallowing back against his dry throat. He lifted the knocker and let it drop.

He did not even hear footsteps. As if the person had always been standing on the other side of the door he heard the knob shift, saw it turn and hold in that tensed position, and in the pause he reached out to put his own hand on the knob, afraid it might turn back again. The door pulled at his arm, he let go, it swung open, and a woman was standing there, her eyes narrowed to the light, saying, "Yes?"

Her expression changed gradually from stubborn defensiveness, to blankness, to a flush that quickly paled, her eyes opening wide as if the light were not nearly enough to let her see. Her face was changing in other ways for him as he tried to find in its added flesh, in folds and wrinkles, the face he had known. He was looking so hard for her that he was startled to hear her voice more like a groan when she closed her eyes and said, "Oh, my God."

She snapped back from that quickly, opened her eyes, her mouth set, a gesture he certainly knew. "I guess there's nothing for it, is there? Is she with you?"

He shook his head. She moved back to let him step into the hallway and closed the door firmly. She was not looking at him as she led him into the living room, as neatly arranged and cleaned as if she had been expecting guests, although he could sense by the way things were placed, by glimpses through arched doors to a dining room and white-walled kitchen, that her house was always in order. She was certainly stockier, her hips broad against the pleated wool skirt. Again, it was the wide-boned cheeks, the sturdiness of frame showing in her collarbones that always made her look taller. When she said, "Sit, please," and signaled him to the easy chair of blue velvet while she sat on the couch with the low, glass-topped coffee table between them, he could tell she was not going to do much to help him get started.

She wriggled her shoes off, pulled her legs up under her, and with one hand lying along the back of the couch, the other playing up and down the beads of her necklace, she stared at him. The gesture of chucking her shoes was characteristic enough to make him smile. She had always said her feet were too irregular for standard sizes, and would take her shoes off whenever she could, even under the table in restaurants.

She turned her head slightly at an angle as if appraising a painting. "I'm not sure I would have recognized you at all if I passed you on the street."

"It has been some time."

"About the age of our daughter."

The coolness of her tone, that determination to be blunt, nettled him. But she had blinked when she said that.

"You do acknowledge her, then."

"I guess I have no choice. Two against one."

"But this morning you didn't."

"I wasn't given much warning."

"That was the way she thought best."

Monica smiled slightly. "I wasn't accusing you. I am having some trouble deciding what you have to do with all this, but I imagine she's here because she wants to be. Of course, I could sue, you know." He could tell by her eyes that she was teasing. "But I guess I won't. Did she find you, or vice versa?"

Her tone did nothing to relax him, and he was surprised how vaguely aggressive her control made him feel, but he began to take in more of the room and her appearance. No opulence was in the furnishings or her clothes, but all was comfortably established, a solid, cool good taste in everything, even the subdued beige of the silk blouse she wore that clung loosely to her body. With a shock he remembered how even the act of lovemaking was something she floated through as if intensely self-involved and he were some final extension of her own body—and he had never minded that at all.

"She found me," he said after a pause so long that her eyes finally swerved toward the window and then back.

"I'm not surprised she did it rather than you. And her lawyer was certainly good."

"You knew about her lawyer?"

She nodded. "I don't suppose you even tried, did you?"

"I thought I'd given up that right when we gave up her."

"When I did, you mean. Or that's the way you used to think of it. Do you want some coffee?" She started to unfold her legs.

"No. How did you know about her lawyer?"

He could not keep back the tone of disappointment. If she knew about the lawyer, she knew too much already. He did not have time now to understand why her knowledge of Miriam made him feel trapped. She sat back, this time with both of her hands in the coils of the long necklace that looped into her lap.

"I've tried to keep up." Her voice was steady but much more quiet. "I did go looking for her, Lewis. You never handled her, held her. Maybe that's the difference. Twice in those first twelve hours of her life I watched her hands fold and unfold, gripping whatever I placed in them with no sense of holding or not holding. Then I gave her up. I let myself think it would be easy, and for a while it was, mostly because of the changes in my life — leaving you, trying to decide what to do, going back to college in Chicago, getting married."

"To Mr. Weaver."

"To Bill." She looked up. "We're doing it, aren't we, beginning to tell over our lives to each other?"

He nodded. Again, it was like her to stop something in mid-action to discuss the action itself.

"I didn't have much time to think about her or the past till that marriage began to go. I refused to have children. He was a fatherly father type. He fathered me, fathered his students, thought he wanted to father some children. I was suspicious of so much paternalizing."

"You seem to have it all worked out."

"My dear Lewis, when you're paying a shrink to listen and you're living on the salary of an associate professor at a branch campus of a state university, you try hard. Anyway, Bill moved to San Jose State in California. He's a director of freshman English. He was very fond of programmed texts. For a long time I loved him as much as I can love anyone, and when he left me I cracked, badly."

"He left you?"

She looked hard at him, her hands still. "We got down to Miriam, my analyst and I. I hired a good investigator long before

253

she did. I found her, found the Sternbergs, found her house. I went to it. I stood across the street and watched her come out one morning to go to school. I followed her to the bus stop. I stood with her and watched her flirt with a middle-aged friend of her father's. She was sixteen and didn't know she was flirting, or what she was really flirting about. She seemed perfectly happy to me, perfectly normal. Everything I could find out about the Sternbergs indicated they were doing a better job than what a nearly demented professor of sociology with a busted marriage and history of neurotic stalemates could do. I watched her get on the bus and then I came home."

In the silence that followed he did not look at her, but beyond into the dining room, at the broad table of dark wood, polished enough to catch the oblong reflections of the windows on its legs. The dark mound beneath it was a sleeping cat, fur almost the same color as the brown rug.

"I think I'm jealous," he said slowly.

"Of what?"

"That you saw her then, as a teenager. And as a baby."

"Maybe the fact you didn't when she was a baby is my fault. I'm not even sure about that. The rest is surely yours, though. You could have done what I did."

He started to get up, wanting to pace, but everything in the room constrained him, so he sat forward.

"What do you mean you're not sure? You hid. You wouldn't let me."

Her laugh was abrupt. "It's my experience that it's almost impossible to stop someone who is very determined. Unless they're equally determined to stop themselves."

He chopped his hand at the air. "I did try to find you."

"After I left?"

"No. I mean when you were in the hospital."

"I know. You told me that. But wait. I'm interested. You never came looking for me after I left you?"

He shook his head.

She smiled slightly, rattling the coils of the necklace. "Oh well. I did hold onto the vague dream that you spent a little time pursuing me. But I should have known."

"You wanted me to?"

She paused for a while, looking past his face in an unfocused manner, then back at him. "To tell the truth, I'm not sure. But it certainly would have told me something about you if you had. I did not make myself impossible to find. But that is long over."

"No, wait a minute." He did stand, his leg nudging the coffee table. The cat raised its head out of sleep with a jerk, looking at him warily. "You're making it all sound like my fault. I don't think what you're saying is fair. You walked out on me, after all. I was the one who came home to an empty apartment." He paused to catch his breath, felt ridiculous standing there, and sat down in the chair again. "Maybe what we did was wrong. But we both did it."

She was looking at him with her head to one side, as if stunned. "Lewis Beede, where have you been all your life? What makes you think I can give enough of a damn about all that past garbage to want to make you feel guilty about it? Has life been so dull for you that all you can care about is the dead and gone?"

"No, no, that's not the point. At least we can forgive each other."

For a moment her eyes filled as if she might weep, but her voice was steady.

"That's one of the saddest things I've ever heard. I'm sorry, Lewis. Sorry you would even think that possible. There's nothing for me to forgive you for. By this time, long ago, you should have forgiven yourself."

That was like her. A twist with the words and everything was turned around on him again. His own words were intended well. He had opened himself up to ask for something and once again she had run away. He wanted to laugh out loud. How remarkable it was that after so many years apart they would see each other and in a matter of minutes revert to the old positions. The silence now had gone on too long, but he could think of nothing to say, so he was glad when she spoke quietly.

"Well, enough of that. I'm interested in where you've been. Did you go back to acting?"

He shook his head. "Back to Judson. I'm sure you're not surprised," and he continued, haltingly at times, trying to limit his description to the arrival of Miriam, his own reactions, but inevitably he found himself telling everything that came to mind around that, even lapsing far back to those days after Monica had disappeared. As he talked, sometimes having to force himself against an unexpected weight of reticence, he could feel her relaxing. Mostly her eyes showed him, the gaze opening out to him, the face losing the masklike hardness she had worn. "You're right, of course. I never held her as a baby. But I held on to a bitterness at you, at everything that made us so stubborn. I had as much right as you."

"Yes."

Neither of them moved, and then she breathed deeply, leaned her head on her hand, arm propped on the back of the couch. "I live with someone now quite wonderful. He's ten years younger than I am, but very different from anyone I lived with before. He was a student of mine."

"Is that why you wouldn't accept her this morning? To protect your new life?"

She laughed. "Who? Steve? Lord, no. He knows about Miriam. Wouldn't mind. He's been telling me for years I'm a fool not to go see her."

"Then why?"

"I was angry. Can you understand? The first time I walked away from Miriam I did something very selfish. The second time I did what I thought was best for her. It was hard to give, but it was a gift from me, totally unlike the first time."

"But why angry?"

"What right did she have to give back my gift this morning?"

He shook his head. "You always were too complicated for me."

"Lewis, when I knew you I was too complicated for myself." She stood. "Shall we go?"

The cat stretched its long body, front claws digging at the carpet. But they were already walking to the door by the time it had jumped onto the couch. Her Saab was parked in the street and she pulled away quickly, not even looking through the rear-view mirror.

"I guess you accomplished your mission."

He laughed. "I don't think I had anything to do. I'm sure you had already made up your mind, as usual."

She did not answer. He was weary, uneasily suspecting he

had said some things he had not wanted to. Well, no matter what Miriam did, he was going to go home as soon as he could. There was no point in this. As she drove through the town, she gestured to some buildings, the entrance to the campus, a historical marker. He asked whether it snowed much in winter, if she had ever been in a tornado.

Two blocks from the motel she stopped at the curb, the motor idling. He could see the landscape again reaching out and out to that forever untouchable sky, and the wind was once more sweeping at them, unobstructed by houses or trees.

"Doesn't it ever stop?" When she did not answer, he turned to her.

She was staring straight ahead, quietly weeping.

17

T he sun had set, leaving a red wash on the horizon, and as far as he could see, the darkening land stretched and stretched, glass or metal or water glinting here and there, lights beginning to show. He was leaning forward against the tug of the seat belt in order to see better from the window, and its circles of thin scratches caught and crazed the last light, webbing earth and sky. The air vent hissed above him, the lights were on, and other passengers were reading or already dozing. It had been so many years since he had flown that he had forgotten the exhilaration in that moment he could never believe when the plane lifted away from the runway as if gravity had lost its hold. At this height the horizon showed the long curve of its edge, the closest he would ever come except in photographs to seeing the planet as a whole.

After spending four hours hitchhiking to Tulsa, he had gone to the airport and spent nearly all the money he had on a plane ticket. He would have to hitchhike again at the other end, but at least by the middle of the night he would be close enough to Judson to arrive during the next day. The long, tiring days and nights of reaching Oklahoma now seemed like some self-imposed punishment. But there was no way quick enough to take him home. Going to Oklahoma, he had been unable to imagine a clear destination. Now he could place himself at his cabin's window. Moonstone's rocks would already show in the first deep thaw of spring and under the spongy snow in the woods he would hear the water sliding, too urgent to flow in the channels of streams and brooks, slithering over all the tilted planes of land, too much of it, the earth saturated. The morning fog would trap close to the ground the stale woodsmoke, the musky decay of last year's fallen leaves and grass. Once again he had called Annie and no one had answered. He tried to tell himself it would be enough if Judson was there — the cabin, the absolute rhythm of seasons, his plans for the farm that he had decided were still possible in spite of the deaths of Joker and Melissa.

He stretched his legs until they pressed the tilted seat ahead of him. The stewardess floated by, her face fixed in a smile that fell indifferently on seats and people and luggage racks. Somewhere over Arkansas he had slapped down his hand on the unfolded table, waking his neighbor out of a doze. Fool, fool, he said to himself, turning away from the man's gaze in embarrassment. He had taken that long trip with Miriam, tricking himself into thinking that it was important for him, too. But once again he had only a bit part to play, to be there with necessary props, a witness to Miriam and Monica's crucial event. There was nothing in it for him.

He would see Miriam again before long, since she promised to return in the summer to help him set up the farm, although she was beginning to make plans for her own land in the Virgin Islands. He had offered her a partnership with him and Howard. She would think about that. With a puzzled expression Monica had watched them over dinner chatting on about the numbers of barns or sheds and horses they would need to get a good start. He had in mind Bernie, and Buddy too. Did she mind? *Bernie?* she had said, smiling mischievously, then laughing long and hard while he flushed because people at the nearby table had turned to watch them. *Besides,* he had said, *Bernie has a foal of Joker's coming, the last of the line,* and Monica had understood that well enough to nod and say, *Your father was always more crafty than he looked.* Now he simply missed Miriam, conjuring her face as it had stared through their watery windshield in a Kentucky rainstorm, or her unconscious and absorbed expression as she stared at her mother across the table, the same look he had often seen turned on him when he was reading in the cabin and glanced up from his book. The whole idea of the farm seemed much more possible if she would be there too. He tried to keep himself from pleading with her, and finally she said, *Let's see what it feels like this summer.*

The sky was black. By putting his face close to the window and shielding his eyes he could see the stars. But the bright and many-colored lights of roads and towns below were always visible as if a molten ball had been thrown down and had splashed out in random but intricate patterns. It was a cold and distant beauty.

In Logan Airport he slept fitfully in a chair among rows of others like it, each one identical in its lack of padding and a molded form that prevented him from varying his posture. But he was certain that was better than shivering by the side of some nearly deserted highway. Even the next day rides were not easy to snag. Most were from salesmen. He talked if spoken to, getting dry-mouthed on clichés about the weather or politics. He wondered if, next to being in the barber's chair, there was anything more dull than counting the small change of conversation with strangers. He walked the last four miles to Judson, the air colder at first than he had expected, but the frozen ruts by the side of the road showing there must have been a considerable thaw. Still white, bristled with dark patches of evergreen, Moonstone was its familiar, remote shape. He had been gone for only a little more than one week, but it seemed enough time for everything to have changed.

As he walked past the hardware store, past Gus's Sunoco station, the dimensions of the town seemed wrong. Even though Pete waved from the window of his store, his mouth forming words to someone behind him, a wave as casual as if Lewis had never been away, even though the chimneys of the houses were smoking and the parking lot in front of the post office had its usual group of cars, the town seemed abandoned, and all these people merely a function of his memory, not living in their own lives at all. He passed the library, the church, stood at the corner with the light blinking over him. He could see to Annie's house at the far end of the street. The icicles forming along the edges of the roofs glistened and a flock of chickadees was dropping and fluttering up around the bole of the maple in Buddy's yard. He was waiting to see something shift in the landscape to match his own changes, but everything clung stubbornly to the old forms. That confused him because, after all, what was different? Only this homecoming was somehow different from all the others, and suddenly he would have given anything to be returning as he had often before to a world full of possibilities—even if it was just to know for certain that some warm evening soon he would be in the barn and hear the sputtering of the old Buick driving by and then Coleman would be standing in the doorway, shading his eyes, calling out, *Lewis? Lew? Are you there?*

The door was not locked. He stepped in. The heat had been turned very low and had been that way for some time. He walked through the living room, back to the kitchen. The dishes were cleaned and stacked in the drainer, one of her usual impossible piles waiting to come crashing down if he moved a glass or a dish. But wherever he went, the house looked too neat, as if prepared for a guest, not left by someone who was living there and had stepped out for a moment. Upstairs the bed was made, the towels and washrags were not on the racks in the bathroom. The floors cracked and gave, unaccustomed to the weight of a passing body.

He sat halfway down the stairs. The icicles were melting faster than they formed now, and through the landing window he could see the wide puddles backing up in the street. It would turn to ice that night. The sudden scrape and thump of snow falling off the front roof startled him. Had he ever really seen this house, that street, the vague outline of Moonstone in a steamy, hazy afternoon? The newel post, dark brown in its aged stain and varnish, was shaped like a huge pinecone resting on its base. How often he had turned the landing, gripped it with his hand as he went up the next flight, but had never really seen it.

There would have been a note in the kitchen if she had left any. She had meant what she said, then. He stared at the worn patch of carpeting at the turn of the stairs. He had been away only a week, but all the years they had spent together or had known each other had been drifting toward this moment of sitting in an empty house with no idea of where to go or how to find her. He felt all this had happened years and years ago and he was trapped in a repetition of absences.

A truck splashed into the neighboring driveway. Lewis walked out slowly, pulling the door tight behind him. Buddy waited with his hands in his back pockets.

"Hello, stranger."

"Where is she? Do you know?"

Buddy shook his head. "No messages. Lucille pumped her when Annie said we should keep an eye on the house, but she wasn't telling us anything. We figured you'd had a good row."

"When was it?"

"Day or so after you left. How'd it go?"

"Fine. Did she pack up, take a bus?"

"Couldn't tell you. All I know is that morning she came by, Sunday it was, and said would we watch out for the house. Next morning the paper boy didn't deliver, there's been no mail, and she was gone. Been kind of eerie having the place sit there like a lump at night. Want some coffee?"

"No thanks."

"You might try Doris. She's probably up to Foley's. Helen died three days ago. Doris does the errands, prays with Foley when he's willing. Funeral was yesterday. I saw Annie talking to Doris just after you left."

Lewis started to walk away. Buddy called out, standing with his braced foot up on the porch step, "Say, you gonna start that farm?" His eyes squinted against the glare. "If you do, I'm good for help. I'm fuckin' tired of driving a goddamn plow. Seems every time you knock over another mailbox you make an enemy for life. Rather get my head kicked in by a horse any day."

"We'll see."

"Besides, the judge says I owe that bugger Chase five hundred bucks in damages." He was grinning sheepishly when he shrugged and turned away.

At the corner, Lewis paused, uncertain where to go next. What if instead of going away forever, she came back soon, having disconnected herself from him, living in Judson for him to see from time to time but distantly, like Buddy—the oldest and best of friends? Doris's truck was at the grocery store and she was climbing into the cab, had started the engine by the time he broke

262

into a run, caught her attention before the irreversible moment when she would jam the engine into gear. Her wool cap was pulled down tight over her brow, accentuating the bright, hard stare of her eyes.

"The prodigal father returns." The back of the truck had two cartons full of groceries, mostly canned goods. "Make it quick, Beede. I'm drugging up some food to old Foley and he won't want his Spam froze."

"Where's Annie, do you know?"

The head shook once. "You think I'm Missing Persons Bureau? By now I expect everyone in town knows she isn't in town. But I bet no one but Annie knows where she is."

"She didn't tell you?"

"I didn't ask. Now, I can tell you where Phoebe is, I can tell you where those sinners Howard and Elaine are. Want to know?" He did not have a chance to answer. "Never could keep a secret. Miss Phoebe's gone off to Switzerland and as far as I'm concerned that's good for us and brings the yodelers one step closer to hell. Howard and Elaine quit your cabin and went to stay in the Flatts, where he's got himself a job pumping gas. I don't care what you say, and you'd say it because you've set him one hell of a bad example all along — they aren't married and even if she's a damned sight better than Phoebe, it's whoring all the same. By now even the dog food's stiff as a rock back there," and she tossed her head at the back of the truck, raced the engine.

"She didn't tell you anything?"

"You're a fool, Lewis Beede. That's what I know, and she didn't have to tell me that."

She was wrestling with the shift. Lewis knew better than to risk standing close to her departure, but this time she held still and beckoned him in again, her face clenched forward at him like a shaken fist.

"I ought to leave it at that. I ought to shut my trap. Well, this one's for your mother. That year we spent in Poughkeepsie while she had her baby and Foster kept coming down and trying to drag her off, I told her nothing good could come of marrying a man like that. Hell. It isn't just that all men are alike, and you're a man and dumb as most of them. Some are better than others. Lewis

Beede, the worst of it is, you're just like your damned father, and you're the one never should've been born."

She had it in gear then and he jumped away. She backed out with a vicious slither into the highway, and Lewis glared at the rear end of the truck, wanting to curse her, but not knowing what to say.

He could return to Annie's house, stay there, wait to see if she would turn up soon. But he could not live with that house large and heavy around him. For the first time since those early days after Jim's death, he would feel himself to be a visitor, not rightfully there without her. Going up to the cabin was really the only thing to do. Jake was backing out of the bar, pulling the door closed behind him.

"Hello there, Lew."

Lewis nodded, started to turn.

"Say, I hear Annie's house is up for sale."

"Says who?"

Jake looked at him curiously over the rims of his dark glasses. "I figured you'd know for sure. Morrison, from Flatts Real Estate. He was in for breakfast this morning. She'll get a good price, seems to me. You guys moving?"

Lewis walked across the street without looking, but there was no traffic.

"What's eating you?" Jake called after him. Lewis did not answer.

He had to walk slowly up the stream, stepping carefully on bare roots, hardened patches, because in softer drifts he would plunge through, up to his knees in soggy snow. But even here he did not feel at home, and the closer he came to the cabin, the more slowly he walked as if dreading the moment when he would come into the clearing, look to the pond, probably only fringed with ice now. He would have to swing back the door into the deeply chilled space, shake the ashes down and start a fire, and then he would turn to the window and look again over the tugging sweep of miles to Moonstone, stretching something in him thinner and thinner as if the air between himself and that mountain were the vacant atmosphere of high space. He would go on about his business, and Miriam would return. He would search out Howard and Bernie, hire Buddy if he meant what he had said, do his best even to make peace with Elmore. A life with horses.

He could tell by the dark stains from the old wounds on the big maple that the sap had started to run. He would put out his buckets, patch up the stone hearth outside that he used for boiling down the few gallons he would make for himself. He had been lazy this year about cutting wood, but there would probably be just enough. He was in the clearing, kept his eyes down the slope, saw he was right about the pond, which shone black against its fluted edge of snow and ice. He could not bear to look at the cabin.

18

"You'll have to go slow. I'm not in the best shape."

Elmore paused at the bend of the trail where the first steep ascent began. He leaned against the weight of his pack, mopping his face in the warm sun of early fall. After Elmore's summer of traveling in Europe with Eleanor, the trip he had announced to Lewis as *our second honeymoon, a chance to start again,* Elmore had returned with a row of new flesh around his waist and an extra chin that blurred his features. *The cannelloni did it.* He had shaken his head ruefully, but Eleanor looked more slim and relaxed. She had not eaten much because she wanted to fit into all the lovely clothes she had bought on their way through Paris.

"You'd better help me muck out stalls for a while."

Elmore waved his handkerchief once before he stuffed it into his back pocket. "You can have all that horseshit, Lew. I get tired enough having Elaine complain about the stink whenever Howard comes home from work. I'm going about this in my own way."

Lewis snorted. "Like switching from cannelloni to lasagne."

"I like to eat," Elmore said softly. "I sure do. But when we go hunting, I'm going to walk off a lot of it."

"Might as well start now," and he did not wait to see if Elmore was following.

They would have to leave the trail at the summit of the ridge and turn down the steep north side to the brook. From there, Lewis was uncertain. He knew where the plateau was. Somewhere near the headwaters of the brook the two ridges widened out under the wall of Moonstone's central peak, forming a bowl of tall maples and beech in glades of ferns. He had hoped that Elmore would forget their pact to go hunting again, but his brother seemed to have settled on this trip as one clear point of reference in his still-uncertain life. *Like old times,* he kept saying, and then he would insist on reminiscing about the trips he and Lewis and Foster had made. Once when Lewis tried to get out of it, Elmore had argued with such intense persistence, almost desperation, that Lewis backed down.

He paused where the rocks began to break through and trees thinned to low poplars, second growth in a high section of the ridge burned over years ago. He could hear Elmore's boots on the scrabble a turn or two back. A small breeze lifted toward the mild blue, but already there had been a pale frost at night and one maple by the new barn had turned violent scarlet, a warning.

"Maybe," Elmore said between short breaths as he leaned a straightened arm on the nearest tree, "I'll stick to fishing instead."

Lewis lifted his hand to point. "They're flying early this year."

The flock was small, ten or twelve geese craking along in a very straggling vee as if they knew there was no hurry and, even if they lost contact with each other, more flocks would pass by.

Elmore twisted slowly to follow them. "I tell you, the weather is all messed up. Even the birds don't know what to expect anymore."

"Somewhere in Canada it must have been cold. It'll get here."

The geese disappeared. Lewis hiked up the last yard to the bare rock along the ridge's spine. They could see down the long slope to the fields in the valley and the glint of the river where it writhed between the hard banks of clay and stone. Lewis had found no time for walking in the woods all that summer as he and Howard, Bernie, Buddy, joined finally by Miriam, had raised the barn, and the sheds, and had trucked in the first horses even as

Buddy was still pounding on the roof, his back bronzed by one of the driest summers in years. Now Lewis looked up the river to the side valley where his own land was, and sure enough, with a lurch that made his heart speed, he could see the bright yellow of fresh boards, a glint of roofing, and looking harder, he was even certain he saw the slowly moving forms of grazing horses. Cassandra had foaled. The birth was difficult, a breech, but both the filly and the mare had survived, mostly because Howard had intervened just in time. Lewis had been tiring from the constant effort of guiding the foal's descent, and he had become inattentive. *Watch it*. Howard had pushed him aside. Lewis was angry until he saw that Howard's hands were deftly releasing the cord that had tangled around the foal's neck. Lewis looked down over Howard's curved back for a while, then left the rest to him.

As if following his brother's gaze, Elmore said quietly, "He would have loved it, Lewis—the old man. He wouldn't have said so, but he would have been proud."

"Yes, and then he would have done his best to ruin it."

Elmore shucked his pack and leaned on the big boulder behind him. "He was that way. But mostly after Mother died. At least with her, he had someone to push against. When she was gone, he had to take it out on everything."

"Including us."

"And himself."

Boots scraped on the trail above, a voice was saying, "No, I'd rather take along cans even if it's heavier. I hate that dried shit," and then there were two hikers coming down the rock, their wool socks rolled over the tops of their ankle-high boots, legs muddy under shorts patched with insignia of various clubs. They were strapped into frames with bright green and red packs, neat rolls of sleeping bags.

"Hi," the one who had been speaking said, and his friend, a sweat-band holding back his straggling blond hair, boomed, "How far down?"

"Mile or so." Lewis hoped they would not stop. The woods all summer long had been overrun by hikers who would sit on the street corner in Judson waiting for the bus or would sing college songs together in the Bear. It had been happening for years, but this summer there were so many that Lewis imagined soon a stream of them like ants on every trail would wear down the ground, then the rock itself. He could not stand the way they always traveled in herds and acted as if they were on difficult voyages.

"How far to Wilton?"

Lewis only looked away, but Elmore laughed. "You've come down the wrong side. You're headed for Judson."

The front one turned quickly, almost unbalanced by his pack. "Christ, Hal, I told you we were going south at that last junction."

The other one shrugged. "You had the map."

"Too late now. Judson, you say?"

"Yes. Lovely little town with a river and friendly local inhabitants," Elmore said.

They stomped off and Lewis could hear them take up their argument when they came to the woods. He was going to ask why, when he met people like that, he became so possessive and yet also felt completely estranged from this land he knew so well. But Elmore was already struggling into his pack. Lewis stood, and they turned their backs on the view.

"I'm not sure that I can find the place again."

"Try, Lew. Try."

Elmore bent under the big wicker basket filled with tools, a tarpaulin, objects they could safely leave until their next trip with guns and food. They had to move more slowly, brushing through patches of hobblebush, avoiding the tangles of fallen trees here and there, old blowdowns where winds had bounced hard before whirling off to other ridges. Once they reached the heavier woods again, they crossed soggy patches of springs, sometimes followed the dry rills of runoffs. Lewis tried to imagine the landscape in his mind as a huge map, but since he knew it more by touch and sight than by abstract design, he could not hover over it. So he let his senses move them in shifting directions while he waited for something familiar to appear. At one point, hearing the brook close below them but not wanting to lose more altitude, he knew he had passed some boundary unmarked by paint or poster, a line he had not let himself cross in the years since he and Foster had last been hunting there. He paused. Elmore held still behind him. A small breeze shook the pale leaves high over them.

"What's up?"

"Just checking. I think this is right."

If there was a right to all of this. As they moved on, his resistance increased. Why was he doing this, moving back into a piece of territory he had not wanted to return to? What crossed his mind shocked him. He could lie to Elmore. A patch of green was ahead, another ferny bog where a spring had formed, much like the place they usually camped by. Elmore never had a good memory for the appearance of things. When they came to the opening, Lewis paused, heard Elmore breathing in short gasps as if they had walked the past yards too quickly.

"Here?"

Lewis closed his eyes and then he stepped into the sunlight, his boots sinking slightly in the damp earth.

"No, not here."

That did not tempt him again. But now he walked as if his feet were strapped into those iron shoes he had worn once to strengthen his knees. The brook was closing on them from the right, its ravine would be opening out, and then the water shone through the trees and they were standing by the flat pools. Beyond, the land spread gently upward, the trees large-boled, ferns shoulder-high in full summer growth.

Lewis slipped out of his pack and stooped. The water was perfectly clear, each pebble on the bottom of the pool etched by light falling through the cold swirl. He put his face into the bright shock of it, held his breath, opened his eyes. The bottom was both close and far away, a confusion of depth as if he were staring at the sky on a cold, clear night. He lifted his head, gasping for air, blinded by the water that stung his eyes. He sat back on his heels, put his face up to the sun, his eyes closed.

Teach me. Try. I might be pretty good. They were leaning on the new rail fence by the paddock when Miriam asked him. The horses, a dappled Percheron and two Shires, had been trucked in four days before and were beginning to settle down. He had been reluctant to let her do much more than admire them from a distance. Something about the way she moved stiffly when they

270

came close to her, the nervous hesitation before they accepted her hand on nose or neck, told him what he did not want to know. As when pushing two reversed magnets toward each other, Lewis could feel a force shying them away from each other. He let her be with him whenever he worked with the horses, but found after a week that he was asking Howard to do most of the training, and finally he was the one who broke the silence, stopping Lewis in the barn, hands in his back pockets, not looking at Lewis when he spoke. *I can't get anything done this way. She just doesn't have it, Lew.* Lewis nodded and they did not discuss it further. That night when he tried to tell Miriam that it was only because the horses were new, hadn't settled in yet, she laughed. *Come on, Dad. I'm no good and I know it. Frankly, we scare the hell out of each other.* He tried to deny it, ended by saying, *Look, that doesn't matter. There are plenty of other things around here for you to do.* They talked about the new well, the defective gate latch, but on the way back to the cabin she put her hand through his arm. *Thank you for trying.* They stopped by the edge of the pond. When he started to make excuses for her, she put a hand over his mouth gently. *I'll have to go. But I'll always be your daughter.* As he tried to sleep that night he had wondered why that did not seem to be enough.

Elmore was drinking from the pool above, stooped on the other side of the water. He sat back against the tree trunk.

"It's hard," Lewis said. "I'm not sure I want to do this." Then, without looking directly at Elmore, he told him everything that had happened on that hunting trip he and Foster had taken so long ago.

Elmore did not speak. His face was set with a stubbornness Lewis knew so well, and not having seen it in him for so long, he recognized his father's mute, unchangeable will. But that was not his father's face, and the expression shifted, his brother's voice said, "I'm sorry for that. You and the old man had your problems, I had mine. That's long gone. I just remember some good times we had here and I haven't seen the place since. Lately it's seemed to me that we might have more good times together, you and me." He paused. "Damn it, Lew, I don't care anymore about places and what did or didn't happen there. I care about the people I love. Now. Before they're gone."

The hand Lewis turned palm up in the sun was light as a leaf, floating strangely in that distance between the ground and his own eyes. Elmore stepped over the pool, reached down to grasp and pull at Lewis's arm. He pushed with his legs and rose, and, lifting their packs, they strode into the ferns together, scattering a cloud of small white butterflies.

He found the thick-boled yellow birch with golden wisps of bark curling back, the flat rock barely visible above the ferns. The ground beyond sloped suddenly to another small level and a patch of spruce that had grown in those intervening years into a grove too thick for its own good, the trees tall and spindly and green only at their tops. Elmore did not have to be told they had reached the old camp. Lewis walked away beyond the grove of spruce to sit in the sun with his back to the slope. He closed his eyes, listened to Elmore unpacking, whistling tunelessly to himself. Weary, he let his mind begin to assemble the tasks that lay ahead when they came down. The main pump had been giving them trouble, would certainly have to be looked at carefully before the cold weather came. Howard was sure that Pearce Grain had given them four fewer bags of feed than he had ordered. Now Miriam was talking frequently about her land in the Virgin Islands, and she would be going back to visit her mother in late fall. Elly had warned him that he was beginning to clutch. *Nothing will make her go sooner.* She was right, of course. But not about everything. Now that Annie's house was sold, all Morrison could say was that the money was going to a bank account in Florida. *Oh, she'll be back,* Elly had said, but without conviction.

For a while he had considered another journey — to search for Annie. But what good would that do? If she had left and had neither written nor called since, she surely did not want to see him, and nothing would hurt more than finding her unwilling to return. Miriam had mentioned her a few times, but he would not respond. The last time he had said, *I don't want to talk with you about that, ever again.* Besides, he was through with wandering. Hadn't she accused him of never coming home? He was here now, to stay. It had taken him too long to learn that, and already he grasped Judson in ways he never had before, as if the illusion that he could always leave had kept everything just beyond his touch. Annie could find him if she wanted, would respect him more for staying at last in one place. So Doris was wrong. He would not be like Foster. He could choose that.

The chink of an ax blade against stone roused him and he opened his eyes to see the shadowed form of his brother beyond the screen of low shrubs and trees, moving slowly as he continued to unload the pack. Drowsily he turned his eyes away, looking almost directly at the sun, broken into sharp faces of glint by the leaves. For a moment, his eyes wide, the sparkling brightness drove out all color and he could have been looking dazedly at sun on the uneven surface of the frozen pond, or the shattered reflection from ice on the walls of a room. His heart heavy in his ears, breath held, he was once again in that bare room where his mother always sat to sew and mend — uncurtained, no rugs on the floor, and a closet hung with half-finished dresses, skirts, the patterns she might try and partway through know were not meant for her. He stood there in the bright winter afternoon, the house silent. Elmore was sitting blankly in the kitchen. He did not know where his father was. Soon a few friends and relatives would be coming. They had nothing to serve them.

His hands hung as if they had held rocks tensely for so long that he could not lift his arms and yet he could not let go of the weights. A jagged triangle of stiff cloth with wide stitching around its edge was pinned down by the sewing machine. In one corner of the room the fragments of light shifted as an icicle released a drop of water.

When he became conscious of a low moaning he was not certain whether he had heard it all the time or whether it had just begun. It pressed in from the walls. He walked to the closet and opened the door.

His father stood in the dim interior, back turned. He held his arms around the clothes, bunching them together on their hangers, head held tightly down and into them. His lean, wide back shook with weeping. *Ellen, Ellen,* he was saying in a voice so choked that even the name sounded strange. Lewis lifted both his heavy arms, but his hands could not reach across the final gap, and he walked out of the room.

"Hey, you going to help?"

Lewis stood so quickly that he was dizzy and had to hold the branch of the nearby spruce.

They finished wrapping things carefully in the tarpaulin, which they tied in one of the trees, and then walked away slowly, not saying much. Lewis was thirsty and Elmore promised a stop at the Bear on the way home. "Don't want to lose weight too fast." Lewis did not take them back up the ridge to the trail, but followed the brook down and out into the flatlands, taking a lumber road back toward the field where they had left the car. Just before the woods ended, Elmore put a hand on his arm and stopped him.

"That wasn't so bad, was it?"

Elmore talked personally all the time now as if the habit he had learned in Eleanor's presence of pouring everything out in the hope that something would be what she wanted had spread to all his relationships. Whether or not that was going to work with Eleanor, Lewis was not certain, but he yearned sometimes for his brother's former taciturnity.

"Mind if Howard joins us hunting?"

"Long as he doesn't take my buck." Elmore looked embarrassed when he paused. "But not Buddy, okay? I mean, he talks a lot about guns, but he's a poor shot."

"Just the three of us."

The truck was parked beside their car, Bernie sitting on its hood and looking off to the trail's entrance.

"I figured you'd be down soon," he said as they came nearer.

"What's up?" For a moment Lewis was worried that something had happened—a fire, the foal had died.

"Nothing much. Just wanted a chance to talk to you. Alone."

Elmore was already walking stiffly toward his car. Lewis yelled to him. "You're coming for dinner?"

"If I can still walk on all these blisters."

Bernie backed out slowly but spun some gravel when he drove up onto the highway. Lewis waited, knowing the man would speak when he wanted to and not before. The elderberries and alders along the highway were browned with fine dust. He could tell by the way Bernie drove, face forward, the smoke of his cigarette curling up into his half-closed eyes, that he was preparing himself, finding words. They drove all the way over the dirt road, through the gate, and up the driveway to the barn ramp. The truck stopped with a jerk and dust blew by them.

"What'll you call her?" Bernie asked.

"Who?"

"The filly."

The late-afternoon sun was full in their faces. A cool breeze was blowing up across the fields and through the open windows.

"Any suggestions?"

Bernie shook his head. "She's yours."

"Yours too."

Far down by the corner of the lowest field, Elaine and Miriam were walking together. They climbed over the fence from the road and strolled slowly up, stopping from time to time as if whatever they were talking about took their full concentration.

"It's this way, Lew. I've decided to drop out. You keep the filly." Bernie looked beyond the fields, his round face squinting.

"Why?"

"This isn't my kind of thing, that's all. Don't get me wrong." He glanced quickly at Lewis, then away. "What you did was good shit, cutting me in. But it's just not right for me."

He raised a hand quickly to stop Lewis from objecting. The two women were walking faster now and their voices carried up in the breeze.

"I work best alone. I don't always do so good, but good enough to make a living. I like that sense of seeing something that can be done quick, a gamble, a deal no one else sees right then. That's been my life ever since I had one. On my own." He smiled that quick lift of his lips, showing the glint of scattered gold. "But don't get casual, old friend, if I come next week to sell you a load of oats. Each man for himself from now on. And I'll keep Cassandra and that first colt. He'll cost you someday."

Lewis put his hand on Bernie's shoulder and stared down the wide sweep to the valley. "Under one condition."

"What?"

"You name the foal."

Bernie laughed. "It's a deal."

"Well?"

Only the first slash of sun was left in the pale blue sky. The women had turned and were sitting on the fence, Miriam's arm around Elaine's waist, the breeze blowing the tall grass at their feet into waves of dark and light. Lewis gripped his hand hard on Bernie's shoulder. Everything he could see was slipping away into the last fiery glint of the sun.

"It'll be something French, you know."

"Hell, Bernie, I can't even speak that."

"You'll learn."